EXPOSURE

Also by Alan Russell

Shame
Multiple Wounds
No Sign of Murder
The Forest Prime Evil
The Hotel Detective
The Fat Innkeeper

ALAN RUSSELL

EXPOSURE

St. Martin's Minotaur ✦ *New York*

www.minotaurbooks.com

Book design by Michael Collica

ISBN 0-312-28924-3

10 9 8 7 6 5 4 3 2

To my beautiful daughter Brooke,
without whose help this novel would have
been finished three years sooner than it was.

Acknowledgments

Any novel is an education in itself. In writing this book, I had to call upon the expertise of a number of individuals, most of whom I did not know. Too often, like Blanche Dubois, I found myself dependent on the kindness of strangers.

J. Christoph Amberger, author of *The Secret History of the Sword,* was incredibly patient about answering all my pestering questions that stretched over the course of two years. Chris has the scars to show his years in a dueling fraternity, and was an invaluable resource about the ways of the *Mensur.* I was lucky to have his assistance, and found his insight and wit every bit as cutting as the swords he knows so well.

Sylvain Margaine was my tour guide of Paris and its catacombs. He was very generous in giving his time, and shedding light on the darkness. I hope the gendarmes never catch you in the underground, Sylvain! If they do, perhaps you can tell them you are helping me with more research.

Scott McKiernan is used to looking through a lens, but consented to me turning the camera and lighting back on him. Scott knows all about the world of celebrity photographers, being a veteran of its ranks for many years. I never imagined I would write about a paparazzo, and Scott helped me flesh out my protagonist and his vocation.

Whenever I need to know about drugs, I always turn to friend and legal drug dispenser (pharmacist) Dr. Craig Steinberg. Alice (of Wonderland fame) should have consulted with Craig before taking her pills.

Whatever I might have gotten wrong in the writing of this book shouldn't reflect on the above-named individuals, but what I got right should. Sometimes explanations get lost in the translation.

Innumerable others helped with this novel, including family and friends. Kelley Ragland was very helpful in honing the final product, and Cynthia Manson deserves massive kudos for her involvement from start to finish.

My heartfelt thanks to all.

EXPOSURE

One

The hit had proved to be anything but easy.

Her security was as tight as any he had encountered. She had eight bodyguards, and on those rare occasions when she did go out, they formed a protective phalanx around her. Behind their large bodies, you couldn't even see her.

She was staying at the Copacabana Palace, a landmark neoclassical building styled after the great hotels of Europe. The Palace had opened in 1923, and was still considered the place to stay when going to Rio de Janeiro. Marlene Dietrich and Orson Welles and Madonna had been guests there, as had De Gaulle and Eva Peron, and Queen Elizabeth and Princess Di, but neither celebrities nor politicians nor royalty had ever claimed an entire floor as their own as she had done. Her tab was a hundred grand a night, but for her that was chump change. There was no getting to her by elevator or stairway; her men had those covered. And there was no chance of his posing as staff. Her people had made the upper floors off-limits to hotel personnel. She had even commandeered the private pool on the sixth floor.

Graham Wells strolled along Copacabana Beach. Behind sunglasses, he monitored the hotel. As far as he could tell she hadn't made an appearance on the balcony for the three days she had been in Rio. If she was taking in the view of Copacabana and Leme's famous horseshoe-shaped beach, she was doing it from inside her room, making a point of staying away from the windows.

His prey was wary.

With rolled-up trousers, Graham walked along the white sand in his bare feet. The camera around his neck advertised his being a tourist, which made him a mark for the vendors working the beach. He hoped he wasn't a mark for others. Graham kept one hand on the camera strap, discouraging would-be thieves from attempting a snatch and run. His cash was tucked away in a money belt. The State Department had recently issued a tourist advisory warning on conditions in Rio, but Graham thought its caution was excessive. Rio's poverty was extreme, but he had visited spots that were much, much worse.

He looked once more to the sixth floor. A few years back one of Graham's targets had holed up in a twenty-third-floor New York City apartment. To get to him, Graham had borrowed a window washer's rig. The lift was self-contained with an up/down button controlling the pulley system. As insurance, he stationed an accomplice above him just in case the rig jammed or failed to operate. He started from the thirtieth floor, and slowly made his way the seven floors down. All the while he descended, Graham kept telling himself it was just like being in an elevator. But this elevator had no walls, no reassuring and insulating cocoon. Even wearing a safety harness, he had found it hard to breathe. He kept asking himself what the hell he was doing in a position like that, and like always, he made the same promise: this would be the last time. He would leave the game for good. Graham remembered how it felt being so high. His mortality had revealed itself in so many ways; his pounding heart, his trembling flesh, the bile in his throat. When he made it down to the twenty-third floor he was shaking so hard he could barely hold the squeegee in his hands. The clean windows had made it easier to see in, though.

There was always a way to get the shot. You just had to find it.

The roof wouldn't work this time. She had one of her bodyguards stationed up there. If he was going to get to her, it would have to be away from the hotel. The problem Graham faced was time. She would be leaving soon, going back to her Bel Air estate. On her home turf, his big game hunting would be even tougher.

Thus far Rochelle hadn't gone stir crazy. Rochelle—the world knew the pop star by the one name—had been on top of the music world for five years. For the recording business, that was almost an eternity. Everyone had thought Rochelle's Rio de Janeiro visit would be one long party. For the beautiful people, Copacabana is a high-octane twenty-four-hour experience. But Rochelle hadn't gone out to shake it in the many nightclubs along

Avenue Atlantica. The old Rochelle would have been painting the town red, shopping along Rua Santa Clara, taking in the view and being viewed in the Forte de Copacabana, being risqué in the naughty nightlife strip called the Go-Go Copa, and going lip to lip at sunrise with a just caught fish at Fishermen's Corner. Those were the kind of shots the world had come to expect from Rochelle. But then again, with Rochelle you had to expect the unexpected. Rochelle had a habit of reinventing herself. She was a pop diva, not a flavor of the month. It wasn't only that Rochelle had great pipes—which she did—but her voice was complemented by the package and charisma that went with it.

Carnival was a month away, but Rochelle usually created her own Carnival wherever she went. This time though she seemed to be all business. Her long-awaited album was due out in two months, and she was finishing a last video for one of the sound tracks, a hot love song with lots of Latin flavor. The Rio beat was being showcased in the video. The Ipanema drag queens had come to a set and strutted their stuff to the pounding beat of samba drums, Rochelle dancing with them. And two months earlier Rochelle had sent her film team to shoot footage of Rio's famous New Year's celebration along Copacabana's Atlantic shore. Times Square had nothing on Copacabana. Every New Year's more than two million people crowded together on Copacabana's beach to watch the huge fireworks display. Most of the spectators dressed in white, a local tradition for good luck. The midnight hour was built up to with the pounding of drums. Many of the celebrants indulged in *pinga*, Brazil's version of moonshine. Others came for spiritual counsel. Holy women, dressed in white cotton turbans, set up shop on the beach, offering an ear and guidance to the many who waited in their long lines. At midnight, the crowds rushed to the water's edge, throwing in flowers and other offerings for Lemanja, a sea goddess worshiped by the Brazilian African religion of Umbana. For one night at least, Lemanja had many followers. Rochelle's video was supposed to be a combination of Lemanja and Venus and Rochelle. She would emerge from the sea with a suit of long wet hair, perhaps a little imaginative seaweed, and nothing else.

Graham looked at his watch. It was quarter to twelve. He had a meeting with his local talent at noon at a nearby food kiosk on the Lido. Graham wasn't sure which his confederate preferred more—the food or the view. Carlos Ribiera—called by friends and enemies Carlos the Jackal—knew whom to bribe and what questions to ask. Those were necessary talents for Graham's line of work.

• • •

Carlos was twenty minutes late, but didn't seem to be in any rush to make up for lost time. In Brazil, clock watching is not a popular pastime. He was wearing dark sunglasses that complemented a white linen suit almost as oversized as one of David Byrne's. Carlos wasn't wearing a Panama hat, probably because he was vain about his wavy black hair. He walked along as if he was hearing a samba beat. Maybe he did. Music always seemed to be playing somewhere.

Carlos ordered for them. Graham liked listening to the back and forth of Brazilian Portuguese. It wasn't the same tongue as spoken in Portugal. It was samba Portuguese. On paper plates, Carlos brought over a Brazilian stew of black beans, pork, kale, and rice that he identified as *feijoada*. The two men did their chewing, and drinking of beer, and talking, sitting on wooden boxes and looking out to the beach. There were plenty of dental floss bikinis to keep Carlos happy. He pointed out one sunbather who seemed to have on less fabric than the Emperor's New Clothes, offering up his jackal's smile with his words.

"A few years back one of your kind, and a girl like that, got our president in trouble."

"That's my job," Graham said, "and that's the job of girls like that."

"It was during Carnival," said Carlos. "President Itamar Franco was in a fancy box reviewing the parade. This model came straight from her float, where she had been doing a lot of shaking and dancing for the crowd. Anyway, after performing, she took off her costume, which wasn't very much to begin with, and put on her change of clothes, which was a T-shirt. Being a very pretty thing, she was invited to the president's box. And once there, she and our president got along famously. She stayed at President Franco's side, and the two of them waved to all the passing floats. And people waved back. Oh, yes, they waved back. Because whenever she raised her arms, her shirt lifted, very clearly revealing her absence of panties. A photographer snapped some shots of the president and his companion, and that caused quite the scandal. You can imagine all the jokes and stories. In his defense, our president could only say, 'How am I supposed to know if people are wearing underwear?' "

"The naked truth," said Graham.

Carlos laughed. "Your job is to reveal that, yes?"

"Sometimes." Graham tried to direct the conversation away from scantily clad women. "What did you learn?"

Carlos shook his head, even lost a little bit of his smile. "Bad news," he said. "She won't be doing her beach scene here. She's made alternate arrangements on some island."

Graham opened his mouth to question him, but was stopped by Carlos's raised hand.

"I don't know where. No one knows. All I learned is that she'll be flying out of here tomorrow morning at eleven. Her pilot hasn't even been given a flight plan. Where they're going is a big secret for everyone. After they land, they'll be getting on a boat. I know that because she had one of her assistants go out and stock up on Dramamine."

Rochelle wasn't usually so reclusive, especially with a new album about to be released. She had never been shy about showing her body before, but in doing the production for this last video, she was staying out of the public's eye. All that was left to shoot was what insiders referred to as her "spawning" number. Rochelle was supposedly going to be writhing on the beach with some boy toy eye candy, doing a risqué *From Here to Eternity* number in the sand and surf.

"What did King Momo tell you?" Graham asked.

This year's King Momo weighed in at almost five hundred pounds. Every year during Carnival Brazilians selected their King Momo based on the size of his belly. They wanted a real jelly—or Jell-O—roll to the samba beat. King Momo's job was to shake his stuff during the Carnival celebration. Rochelle had hired him to do some shaking for her.

"He couldn't be sure," said Carlos. "Most of the time he was told to look straight at the camera. While he was shaking his belly, she danced around him. Most of the time she was shaking her—what do you call it?—booty. The camera was on her booty and his belly. That must have been quite a sight."

That sounded like Rochelle. Provocative posing went hand in hand with her CD releases.

"But," added Carlos, "King Momo did say she didn't look like any expectant mother he had ever seen."

If Graham's information was right, in a few months Rochelle's belly was going to be as big as the King's. Small bits of information were adding up to a pregnancy. This video was being treated like a top-secret production, with the filming angles tightly controlled. Rochelle wasn't going out nights, or even mornings, and she was doing everything possible to avoid being photographed. Her usual skintight clothes had been supplanted by a more conservative wardrobe, and two days before Graham had photographed one of her assistants buying two boxes of saltine crackers. He suspected Rochelle was suffering from morning sickness.

A month earlier one of his informants had told him that a disguised Rochelle had gone on a spending spree in an exclusive baby boutique in Beverly Hills. She paid cash, of course. Perhaps afraid that she'd been recognized, Rochelle told the clerk she was buying the items for "a friend." Her deliberations had seemed anything but impersonal, though. She had consulted a few times with a "buff" tagalong male. Her friend had been described as a "surfer type with muscles." It sounded like Jack Wilkinson, a sometimes model, sometimes fitness instructor, sometimes Rochelle lover. The same Wilkinson had accompanied Rochelle on this trip.

Graham wanted a picture of the two of them together. He wanted a shot of a rounded Rochelle, in the first bloom of motherhood. Better yet, he was hoping for a maternal pose.

There were good reasons for Rochelle to not want the same thing—maybe millions of them. Rochelle marketed herself as a sex symbol. While her music audience crossed the ages, more than half her sales went to the twenty-five and under market, a fact Rochelle was intimately acquainted with. With her album due out in less than two months, Rochelle knew her vampy videos would play a lot better if her pregnancy was kept secret. Women might look beautiful when they're pregnant—that's what their men have been telling them since time immemorial—but even Demi Moore's very pregnant, very nude *Vanity Fair* cover didn't work well for her as a Hollywood marketing tool. The entertainment capital of the world was still the same place where a producer had strongly advised pregnant actress Hunter Tylo to "lose it, or lose your job." Rochelle wanted the cash registers to sing along with her siren songs. That was reason enough to not want to prematurely trade in her tight spandex outfits for maternity clothes, or navel rings for prenatal vitamins. Maybe her next album would be a rendition of her favorite children's lullabies; this one was about steam, and eroticism, and sex.

"We'll need to shoot her on the way to the airport," Graham said.

Mountains and hills, in particular the Sierra da Carioca range, divide Rio into the generally impoverished North Side, the Zona Norte, and the more upscale South Side, the Zona Sul. There are many bends and turns to the roads as they follow the path of the terrain. Because of the mountain range, tunnels are common in and out of the downtown area of Rio.

"The tunnels are a natural speed reducer," Graham said. "Even in this country, cars usually slow down as they approach a tunnel."

Carlos offered a smile and wave of his hand as explanation. "For Cariocas," he said, "driving is a passion."

Cariocas—what residents of Rio and the surrounding area call themselves—love to speed. The national speed limit is eighty kilometers per hour. Even in parking lots, Cariocas seem to exceed that limit.

"I'll need you to arrange a roadblock as her car approaches a tunnel," said Graham. "Something that will make her driver stop."

"A barrel on fire? A stalled car?"

Graham shook his head. "Nothing like that. I want a shot of a maternal Rochelle, so it needs to be done with children on the scene. The more innocent the kids look, the better. Have them kicking a ball, or put a few bikes in the street, or tie a dog to a leash and make it look like the kids are trying to get him back. I want some real little ones, the kind with big eyes that look so adorable you can't help but say 'Ahhh.' That will be the honey that I hope draws Rochelle out of her car."

For years ambition had ruled Rochelle. You didn't get to the top of her field without wanting to succeed more than anything else. But now he was betting she was pregnant and that something even stronger was calling her shots: maternal instinct.

"We can assume they'll do their usual caravan to the airport," said Graham. "The Land Rover sandwich with the Mercedes filling."

On their few outings from the hotel, they had used three cars. Between the scout vehicle and the shotgun car was Rochelle's Mercedes.

"The first Land Rover usually keeps about a thirty-second lead on the Mercedes," said Graham. "That's our window of opportunity. As soon as the lead car passes, we have to act."

"It will help that we make the stop just before the opening to a tunnel," said Carlos. "The lead car won't be able to turn around."

"They'll still be in radio contact though," said Graham. "We don't want to spook Rochelle's car. I want the driver to come to a stop not because he feels threatened, but out of necessity. At the same time, we want to pique Rochelle's interest enough for her to get out of the vehicle."

The Jackal showed all of his white teeth. "Don't worry about that, boss. I'll bait the hook and throw the line. All you got to do is tell me where we're going to do our fishing."

"Cars go too fast along the Airport Expressway," said Graham, "so the Rebouças Tunnel is out. Ditto the Two Brothers Tunnel. Unless you can think of something better, I'd say our best bet is the Novo Tunnel."

Carlos nodded. "That's where I'd do it," he said. "They finally finished widening the Princesa to four lanes. They even put granite walls on both sides of the center aisle, and expensive streetlights. The papers said a lot of developers got rich on the project. It's time we made some money too."

He rubbed his thumb along his fingers. It sounded almost like the rubbing of sandpaper.

Graham pulled out a map of Rio de Janeiro. The Novo Tunnel was located on Princesa Isabel Avenue, a street that ran down to Avenue Atlantica and was the border between Copacabana Beach and Leme Beach.

"There's lots of foliage right over the entrance to the tunnel," said Graham. "I've already been up there. It's a perfect blind. I'll be up about twenty feet high shooting down. Assuming she leaves when you say, the sun's going to be over my right shoulder as I'm looking down."

He pointed to an area on the map.

"The closer you can make her car stop in relation to the tunnel, say two hundred yards and in, would be best for me. But if you have a problem with that, I can nail her from farther away."

"No problem," said Carlos. It was a favorite phrase of his.

Graham handed Carlos what appeared to be three palm-sized radios. "Family Radio Services," he said. "FRS devices. Have you used them?"

Carlos shook his head.

"They're like walkie-talkies," Graham said, "but you can lock into your own private channel, and you don't have to worry about electronic disturbances. Their only drawback is that they're only good over a relatively small area, but I did a test run already. I was at the tunnel and had a bellman transmit to me from the Copacabana Palace. The reception was perfect."

Graham pointed to a button. "To transmit, all you do is press here. I've already programmed the code. That will allow our team to listen in on everything that's occurring. You're going to need to bring aboard two reliable lookouts, one at the hotel, and another right about here."

He jabbed at the map, pointing out the corner of Viveiros de Castro and Princesa Isabel.

"Lookout one will transmit to us when they leave. And lookout two will give you a one-block heads-up. That should give both of us time to have everything ready."

"No problem," a smiling Carlos said.

The more he heard those words, Graham thought, the more nervous he felt.

• • •

Graham had attached one of his three cameras to a small tripod. He used it much like a spotting scope, swiveling it around to take in the lay of the land. There was a doubler on the 800mm telescopic lens. He zoomed in on Carlos and his group. His party, and that seemed to be the right word for it, were camped along the bicycle lane that paralleled the street. Carlos didn't look too worried over preparations. He and a group of children were busy playing hacky-sack. Carlos was a big hit with the laughing kids. Half of them seemed to be hanging on to him.

Carlos and the children were behind a concrete embankment that ran along the street. He had told Graham the children were locals, kids he had picked up in a van from one of the nearby *favelas*—shantytowns. They were all related to one another, Carlos had said, with most of the children coming from just one family. The ringleader was the oldest, a boy who looked to be eight or nine. Carlos had explained what he wanted from him, and the boy seemed anxious to please.

The children, especially the little ones, were as precious as Graham could have hoped. The two smallest girls were picture perfect, with huge brown eyes, heads of hair with rich dark curls, and colorful dresses. They were wonderful little peas of the same pod, the older one perhaps three, and her younger sister no more than two. The girls were barefoot. Carlos had brought the children to his waiting area almost two hours earlier. In all that time the girls had held each other's hand, never letting go.

Graham snapped a few pictures of the girls just for something to do. Rochelle and her party were long overdue. He picked up his FRS and hit the transmit button. Carlos had brought in one of his friends, a fellow named Sergio, to monitor the hotel. Sergio seemed competent, but Graham was still nervous.

"They still haven't left yet?" he asked.

"Not yet," said Sergio. "But they loaded the luggage in the cars. Hotel security has roped off the entryway, and no one is getting by who's not a registered hotel guest. Her guards are keeping everyone well away from the cars. Most of the photographers have given up. They're making it impossible for them to get a shot."

Graham didn't mind Rochelle's being so zealous about her privacy. It would ultimately make his product that much more valuable.

He didn't have to say it, but he did anyway: "Call the moment it looks like they're leaving."

It was big game hunting. Waiting around the watering hole hadn't worked, so Graham was making his own watering hole. In his work, he was the carnivore. Like any hunting animal, if he didn't get the kill he starved.

Graham turned his camera on Carlos and saw him lower the FRS from his ear. By the looks of it, he wasn't suffering from Graham's case of nerves. He had brought a boom box along, and some of the children were dancing to its music. There was also food and drink, making it look like a roadside picnic.

It was hot and humid. Biting insects had found Graham amid the green jungle above the bridge. There was no footpath to the top of the bridge; Graham had bushwhacked through the brush to his concealed spot. Though the greenery mostly shielded him from the sun, Graham could feel its hot presence on his head and back of the neck. As morning had stretched into the afternoon, the sun had grown ever hotter. Graham leaned over and looked through the viewer of his state-of-the-art Canon EOS. The camera automatically read the glare, and compensated accordingly. Most of the time all Graham had to do was shoot straight.

"There's movement!" Sergio's excited voice emerged from the FRS. "You hear what I'm saying? There's movement!"

"I copy," said Graham. "If you can, confirm that it's Rochelle getting into the Mercedes."

He doubted she would be using a decoy, but stars wanting to avoid the press often used look-alikes, rushing them into cars. The dogs were usually only too ready to chase after the lure rabbit.

Graham swung his camera down and focused on Carlos. He wasn't playing hacky-sack anymore. He was listening to Sergio.

"They're pulling out," said Sergio. "The car and her bodyguards blocked my line of sight. I couldn't see her face."

"I copy," said Graham. What was there about these devices that made him sound like a cop? "Does she have a police escort?"

"No. Just the two Land Rovers."

That had been their only concern. You don't fool around with the Brazilian police. They would have called off their operation if she had utilized them as an escort.

"Are you in position, Leonardo?"

His shouted reply made Graham hold his FRS out at arm's length. "I don't see nothing yet!"

Leonardo was another one of Carlos's cronies. His English wasn't as good as Sergio's, but it was still understandable. He was positioned on the corner of Viveiros de Castro and Princesa Isabel, about two hundred meters from where Carlos was waiting. Timing was all important.

"You ready, Carlos?"

"No problem."

His famous reassurance. Graham felt another pang of anxiety. He'd left many of the details of this operation up to Carlos, knowing greed was a great motivator. Carlos knew the score. It would be feast or famine for him. If Graham succeeded, he would get a major payday. Failure would mean he wouldn't get more than the per diem he and Graham had worked out.

"The first car!" screamed Leonardo. "She passes."

Graham lowered himself to his viewing camera. He swung the arm of the tripod down, raised the tilting head, and started scanning. From his vantage point he could look far down Princesa Isabel. He sighted the lead Land Rover, then searched for the Mercedes. It was a full block back. Graham tracked the black and shiny vehicle. He wasn't the only one seeing it.

"Now the second car!" shouted Leonardo. "Her car comes! She comes! She be in the right lane! I tell you, the right lane!"

He was shouting so loudly that he might not have even needed the walkie-talkie. Graham swiveled the pan handle down and over. With a press of a button he autofocused on Carlos. He could see him gesturing and pointing, his little general at his side. The troops were breaching the bicycle path, spilling out on the shoulder of Princesa Isabel.

It almost looked like a Chinese fire drill. Children were running both up, and across, the street. Graham wondered what the hell Carlos was up to.

Everyone seemed to know their positions. Those in the front looked back to Carlos and signaled. The glare had intensified. The children were using their hands as visors to deflect the harsh rays of the sun so that they could better see Carlos. As the Range Rover passed by the first group, they started gesticulating wildly.

Two of the boys who'd navigated across the street had their backs to the center aisle and were looking down Princesa Isabel. Graham saw them suddenly gesturing and shouting to Carlos.

Now what? he wondered. He tried to read what was going on, and a sudden thought made his stomach lurch. Carlos couldn't be considering that. It was unthinkable. But he had sent all of his troops out into the field, save for the boy general and the two smallest of them all.

Their brother the field leader was shouting directions at the two little girls. Hand in hand the small sisters took tentative steps forward. Their tiny steps took them out to the busy street.

"No!" Graham jumped up out of his blind and continued to scream, "No! No! No!"

The girls couldn't hear him, of course.

"Carlos!" Graham screamed into his radio. "Carlos!"

The momentary respite in traffic had passed. A car was charging down the right lane. It was about one-hundred meters from the girls when the flag waving began. The children danced into the right lane, snapping their bright red towels. They had the agility and nerve of rodeo clowns, putting their limbs and lives in jeopardy, trying to not only get the attention of the driver, but forcing him into a sudden detour. The driver pressed on his horn and brakes at the same time, working both vigorously, before swerving into the next lane. The miniature bullfighters successfully averted disaster.

Graham was screaming so loudly into his radio set it looked like he was chewing it. "Stop this the fuck right now! You hear me, Carlos? Get those kids the fuck out of the street!"

The little girls were now in the middle of the far right lane. Carlos and his young-old boy were motioning for them to stand there. The youngest girl was crying.

Another car zoomed toward the tunnel, this one in the middle lane. Its windshield reflected the glare of the sun. Graham could see the driver fighting to see. He was only one lane over as he sped by the little girls. It appeared the driver never even saw them.

"Carlos! You fucking answer me! Carlos!"

Graham wasn't sure whether he was being ignored, or whether Carlos was so intent on what he was doing that his voice wasn't registering with him. He swung his camera around, and watched the children hand-signaling each other.

Another car was powering down the right lane, but this time the young matadors moved back. They didn't wave their red flags. The Mercedes was where they wanted it. They weren't even trying to slow it down, for God's sake.

Graham's throat felt as if it were caught in a squeezing vise. "Carlos," he croaked.

They were trusting that Rochelle's driver would be able to see the girls. Never mind how small the children were, and how easily they could be overlooked, even with optimal visibility. And it was anything but that now. The sun's glare over the bridge was hellish.

The Mercedes kept coming.

Graham was waving his arms. He was praying that the driver was wearing the ultimate in UV sunglasses, the kind potent enough to casually view the sun during a solar eclipse. For an instant, Graham considered leaping off the bridge. Maybe that would get the driver's attention. But he also knew it would get him two broken legs minimum.

The Mercedes didn't seem to be slowing.

Graham forced a scream out of his constricted throat: "Get those girls out of the street!"

Maybe Carlos heard. Maybe not. He had been hunched behind the concrete barricade, but now he was up and standing, waving his arms too. The window of the Mercedes looked like a ball of fire. In a desperate attempt to reach the driver, Graham swung a camera in each hand, hoping they might reflect against the sun and be seen.

A terrible realization hit Graham. It was too late, he thought. Even if the driver slammed on his brakes, he wouldn't be able to stop in time.

At that moment, as far away as he was, Graham heard the shriek of brakes. The driver had to be putting his foot almost through the floorboard. The car was shrieking and trumpeting like an elephant being brought down. The ABS brakes kept the car on a mostly straight line, though it was shaking and bucking from bumper to bumper. Smoke from all four wheels obscured the Mercedes in a black, moving cloud.

Graham dropped down and looked through his camera's viewfinder. The smoke made it hard to see. He didn't want to look, but he couldn't turn away. Despite the best intentions of the driver, the Mercedes was still bearing down on the girls. They were looking with wide eyes as death charged them, their bare feet frozen into immobility.

The girls were holding on to each other very tightly.

"God," Graham said over and over. "God, God, God."

And then, in despair: "Goddammit."

The car hit the girls, knocking them down.

Too late, the Mercedes came to a shuddering stop. The terrible damage was already done. The girls were down.

Down, he realized. But not run over. They hadn't been thrown into the air. The Mercedes had all but come to a stop before hitting them. Through his camera, Graham watched Carlos bending over the sisters. Even after being struck, they were somehow still hugging each other. Then he saw something else. Movement. A tiny foot was twitching. Then Graham heard something that normally would have alarmed him, but now was music to his ears. As far away as he was, he could hear the girls screaming and crying.

They were alive.

Almost ten minutes had passed since the near-accident, but Graham was still trembling. Climbing down from the bridge, his legs had twice buckled under him. It wasn't the treacherous footing, but his being so shaken. Even now, he found it hard to walk in a straight line down Princesa Isabel.

Carlos saw him approaching from the distance and waved. The party was on again. His boom box was blaring and the children were dancing. The little girls were being feted as heroes.

"Hey!" said Carlos, flashing a big smile. "A bloody mouth and some scrapes, that's all. We cut it a little close, but—"

Graham's fist caught him on the side of his face. He followed up with a second blow to his stomach, and then a hard smash to his nose. Carlos covered up while Graham continued to pummel him. Graham didn't mind the pain shooting up his hands and arms. It ridded him of his trembling.

Carlos's head was tucked inside of his protective arms. He kept shouting, but Graham wasn't in any mood to listen. Only when Graham's arms grew tired from striking him, and he was doing more heavy breathing than hitting, did he hear what he was saying.

"What the hell's wrong with you, man?" Carlos shouted. "Are you fucking crazy?"

"Yeah," said Graham. "I'm the one who's fucking crazy. You all but send two babies to their deaths, but I'm the one who's crazy."

Carlos hazarded raising an eye to look up. Graham's fists were still clenched, but his hands were at his sides. The Brazilian unwrapped himself, coming out of his shell. Blood was coming out of his nose, and he had a cut on his lip. He rubbed some of the blood away from his mouth.

Graham turned away from him to the girls. Their eyes were wide, frightened. Graham got down on his knees and examined them. They shied away from him, retreating into each other. The older girl had a bump on her forehead, while the younger one's lip was puffy.

"I'm sorry," Graham said.

He knew they didn't understand his language, but he felt compelled to apologize anyway.

One of the other children turned off the music, and their street festival grew quiet. Carlos broke the silence by saying, "The car barely bumped them. They got their scrapes from the street."

Graham knew kids came from the playground looking far worse.

"So," said Carlos, "did you get your shots?"

It sounded as much an accusation as a question.

Rochelle had come running out of the car and scooped up both little girls, her boyfriend Jack hovering behind her. Rochelle kissed the two girls, drying their tears and hers. She hugged them for at least a minute, holding them close to her body—the same body he focused on. His camera zoomed in on the suspicious bulge in her abdomen, that much more noticeable because of her slender and lissome body. Before leaving, Rochelle pressed money into the hands of the girls and made sure of their safety.

Graham had caught it all. Everything he wanted, from pregnant Rochelle to maternal Rochelle, was put on display for him. She stayed around long enough for him to go through seven rolls of film.

"Of course you got the shots," said Carlos, answering his own question. "I'll bet you were clicking away even while death was charging down on those little ones."

Raised fists wouldn't have made him step back. Carlos's words did. "You should have found another way—" started Graham.

"Your concern for the children is so touching. I'm surprised you haven't been to one of our *favelas* documenting the plight of our poor. That's about half our country, you know."

Graham didn't say anything.

"Plenty of pregnant women for you to shoot there. But your precious magazines and entertainment shows wouldn't be interested in those pictures, would they?"

"You didn't have to endanger the lives of those children—"

"They already were in danger," said Carlos, interrupting. "You know what happens to street children? They used to be target practice for the police. Nowadays the police are more discreet about their hunting, but it's no less dangerous for the children. And there are plenty of other threats all around them. Is that a pictorial you were planning on doing? If so, we won't have to pose the action shots. Where these children live, crime, and drug dealing, and violence are very much in the open."

Carlos reached for his nose, and put some pressure on it to stop the flow of blood. His shirt already sported droplets of blood all over.

"You should have told me what you were planning," said Graham.

"Why? I gave you just what you wanted. And if everything had gone terribly wrong, you still would have had your all-important exclusive shots.

They probably would have been even more dramatic if things had ended badly. You would have kept shooting—I know you—and then afterward you could have blamed me."

"The girls' parents—"

"Knew what they were doing. I told them there was risk. When I took the children, I gave them enough money to buy food for a year. They knew only too well that there were—how do you say it?—strings attached."

"Strings are one thing. A hangman's rope another."

Carlos shook his head, then laughed, but it wasn't his usual boisterous laugh. "If it makes you feel better, then you can pretend you didn't know."

"I didn't."

Carlos met his eyes for a long moment, and finally shrugged. "Then you should have."

There it was. Graham knew he was right. He had left all the arrangements, all the staging, to Carlos. That wasn't how he usually operated. He was always the one who was hands-on, the one who was in control. But he had deferred to the other man's expertise, had even distanced himself from the setup. A part of him must have known that the orchestration would turn dirty. He had turned a blind eye, but not a blind camera.

"Did you see Rochelle pushing all that money in their hands?" Carlos asked. "Did you get that picture?"

Graham nodded. His moral outrage hadn't interfered with his shutter finger. He had gotten everything.

"Big payday for us, right?" Carlos's smile was back.

"Yes."

"We're not the only ones who benefitted," said Carlos. "Rochelle pushed hundreds of dollars into those girls' hands. This is the best thing that ever happened to them."

Graham walked away, but not out of disgust. He left because what Carlos was saying was beginning to sound only too reasonable to him. Behind him, Graham heard the music start up again, but he didn't turn around and look.

He feared that if he did, he might turn into a pillar of salt.

Two

Moving had been a way of life for Graham's entire youth. Every other year his father assumed a new posting. When people asked Graham where he was from, he never knew quite what to say. There was no one place he could call home. By the time he went off to college, he had lived in ten countries. His taking a hiatus from L.A. should have come as no surprise; wanderlust was in the family bones. When friends asked him why he was leaving, Graham said, "It's a GALA urge: Get Away from L.A."

After Rio, he had been away from L.A. more than a year. The change of address had helped for a time. Now he was thinking of running away again, his way of keeping a step ahead of doubts. The modern Paladin, have camera will travel. Graham was that rarest of American exports, a paparazzo overseas. Usually it was the Fleet Street snappers that were the émigrés, settling in L.A. or New York. His home was London, though he was on the road more often than not. When he awoke in the morning, the first thing he did was figure out where he was.

Tomorrow morning it would be café and a baguette. He would find a quiet spot for his eardrums to compensate for the workout they were getting tonight.

The loud music permeated the room. There was no escape from the noise, and besides, he had to be near enough to the dance floor to have a good vantage point. Graham was trying to make out faces through the pulsating light. He was looking for one in particular.

He felt a tap on his shoulder and turned around. "*Voudriez-vous danser?*"

Graham was used to being mistaken for a local. Throughout Europe, he blended in. When in Rome, do as the Romans do. But he wasn't in Rome. He was in a gay nightclub on the French Riviera, and that was why his would-be dance partner assumed Graham was gay. The costumed Frenchman was wearing a fleece wig. The ringlets appeared to have been newly taken from a sheered sheep. The same soft curls covered his hands. On his backside was a sheep's tail. It was a club where every night was Halloween optional, and many patrons liked to dress up. That's why Graham was there. Supposedly one of the Monaco royals was dolling himself up in drag and dancing his nights away in Nice.

Instead of answering in French, Graham said, "I don't dance." Being an American, he hoped, would be deterrent enough. For many Frenchmen, it would have been. Unfortunately, it only seemed to encourage this Frenchman.

He was smiling now, and Graham noticed there was something different about his teeth. His canines were overlarge and sharp. They were the kind of vampire fangs Goths enjoyed flashing. "Then perhaps you would like to join me for a drink?"

"Another time perhaps," Graham said. "I'm going to be leaving soon."

The rebuff didn't seem to sit well with the Frenchman. His eyes narrowed, and he eyed Graham suspiciously. He had used a lot of dark makeup to accentuate his eyes and make them look feral.

Graham tried to think of something nice to say. "Your outfit's very clever," he said. "What are you? Goldilocks?"

"Goldilocks?" The man spat out the word as if it were something distasteful. "I am a wolf, of course."

The teeth. The wool. It made sense, of course. A wolf in sheep's clothing.

"The question is," said the Frenchman, shouting over the loud music, "what are you? You are here as what? A spectator at the zoo? You have come to look at the animals?"

People were taking notice of them, just what Graham didn't want. His stock in trade was blending into the woodwork to get anonymous shots. Stealth shooter, he thought of himself, escaping the radar. But apparently not the gaydar.

"So sorry," Graham said, trying to step by the wolf in sheep's clothing. It was time to cut his losses. The prince who would be Cinderella looked like a no-show for that night's royal ball anyway. By way of explanation Graham added, "I guess both of us were trying to pull the wool over people's eyes."

The Frenchman either found the pun, or Graham, or both, unforgivable. A string of curses followed Graham as he made his way out of the club.

The pension where he was staying was six blocks from the beach. From experience, Graham knew that every block closer to the water cost an extra fifty dollars per night. It was a Spartan room, with a thin cotlike mattress that made sleep elusive. Graham wondered though if he would have slept any better on a luxurious king-sized bed.

Another night wasted. He wasn't sure if he would have felt any better though, getting pix of the wayward royal. The late-night whispers were in full throat lately. Getting away from L.A. hadn't changed that. There was a time when Graham had gotten a charge out of his work. Few people did what he did. Plenty of photographers carried cameras and used them, but most of those just covered events. They snapped pictures of stars at film premieres, and of performers at gala affairs. On the whole, those kinds of gatherings didn't interest Graham. The real money was for exclusive photos, one-of-a-kind shots that no one else had.

Like crown princes in dresses. It was a living, dammit.

He tossed and turned. It was probably the sheep he was trying to count. They all had fangs.

The next morning he was awakened by the ringing of his GSM phone. The mobile phone was his constant companion. It was about the size and thickness of a sticky pad, and enabled callers to reach him wherever he traveled. Graham didn't even have a hard telephone line in his London apartment. Home was where his phone was. Whenever he picked up, callers never had any idea where he was.

"Graham, my friend."

Abdul didn't need to identify himself. He was an information broker who often called Graham with tips. Abdul had been good friends with the Shah of Iran and had fled when Khomeini came to power. Old habits died hard. Abdul was still a toady to royalty, though he sold them out all the time.

"I'm not ready for another wild bull chase, Abdul."

A few weeks earlier Abdul had told him that Antonio Banderas was taking bullfighting lessons from a private instructor in preparation for an upcoming movie. The lead had proved to be bullshit.

"Of course not, my friend."

"Madrid was not a pleasant place to be in the middle of July—"

"And I still feel terrible about that, dear boy, which is why I'm giving you this exclusive."

"What do you have?"

"Gold, my friend. Absolute gold."

Gold that was meant to circulate. If the pictures ultimately panned out, Abdul expected to be handsomely compensated.

Abdul asked, "Where are you?"

"Nice."

"Perfect. What I have for you is springtime in Paris."

"It's August, Abdul. Paris is a sauna."

"But there's still not a more romantic city. The Lady Godwin is already on her way to the City of Lights. She will be meeting with her lover."

"Good for Lady Godiva."

Lady Anne Godwin—now known to the world as Lady Godiva—had made herself a household name by posing in the nude for *Playboy* earlier in the year. Lady Godiva had taken a page—a centerfold actually—from the "Women's Institute Pinups"—the eleven middle-aged housewives from the Yorkshire Dales who had taken off their clothes for a charity calendar benefitting leukemia research. Lady Godwin wasn't middle-aged though. She was a stunning twenty-three-year-old woman with one of the most aristocratic pedigrees in England. Just as Lady Godiva had shed her clothes for good reason in 1057, so had Lady Godwin some 950 years later. Lady Godiva rode naked to reduce the taxes on the people of Coventry; Lady Godwin took her paycheck from *Playboy* and turned it over to a soup kitchen that she operated through her foundation. The infusion of funds saved the kitchen from having to be closed down. The resulting publicity had brought millions more in charitable contributions to her foundation, and worldwide attention to Godiva and her good causes. There was even a movie in the works. Graham knew the Hollywood mind-set. He imagined the picture would be short on Mother Teresa and long on cheesecake.

"What kind of shots am I going to get of Lady Godiva that the world hasn't already seen?" Graham asked.

"You haven't asked me about her lover," said Abdul.

"I'm listening."

"He is famous, someone very recognizable. That's why she has to meet him in secret. I think he's married."

"Think?"

"The Lady Godwin bared some, but not all, of her soul to the countess of Wickham. She is a discreet woman."

"Real discreet. What she didn't bare to the countess, she did to the world."

"She did that so as to feed the unfortunate."

"Please."

"She is called the Naked Saint for good reason. Before she bared all, she went through her own personal fortune trying to make the world a better place."

"Yeah, I know. She gave the shirt off her back."

Like many immigrants to England, Abdul's accent was more English than the English. In a highbrow tone he said, "What she gave away was her own personal fortune, reputed to have been several million pounds. Her pater, Lord Geoffrey, wasn't pleased at her largesse."

"Can you think of a better way to kick off a PR campaign? Ever since the pictorial, she's been turning up everywhere, TV, movies, magazines. I would say it was money well spent."

"You are a cynic, dear boy."

In his best Sinatra, Graham sang:

> *"She'd never bother, with people she'd hate,*
> *That's why the lady is a tramp."*

"Bravo!" said Abdul. "But would that your reasoning was as good as your singing. Lady Godwin is no tramp."

"I don't understand you, Abdul. You keep singing this woman's praises, and yet you're setting her up for me to wave her panties on a flagpole."

"Lady Godwin is a rose, but every rose has a thorn. That's what makes roses so interesting. Many have tried to woo this English rose, but she was not to be plucked. I am interested in the man that succeeded."

"So who is the lucky fellow?"

"Isn't that your business, dear boy? To ferret out those kinds of things? I know where she will be staying, and that you had better move chop-chop if you want to get this story."

"Maybe it's Antonio Banderas."

"This one is big, my friend. I feel it. You know that I seldom *steer* you wrong."

There was no better chop-chop transportation than France's TGV bullet train, the *train à grande vitesse*. Graham left from the Ville Station in Nice carrying his usual two bags. One held his clothes, the other his bag of tricks.

The ride on the TGV belies the speed in which the train travels. While looking out to the passing blurred landscape, Graham made a call to Emile Rousseau. Even though it was ten in the morning, he woke him up. Catting around again, no doubt. Rousseau seemed to think women were his real job, but the young man had a good pair of eyes and a fast set of wheels.

"I need you for a job," Graham said. "Can you start right away?"

Rousseau offered a noncommittal grunt, clearly unexcited about having to get out of bed.

"Lady Godiva's flying into town this morning."

"Oui?" Suddenly Rousseau sounded ready to work.

"She'll be staying at the Victoria Palace Hotel. I need you to be my eyes and ears. I won't be arriving for a few hours still."

"I am on it."

Graham considered making reservations at her hotel. It would probably make the shoot easier, but the expense wouldn't be inconsiderable. This was a freelance job, and he didn't have the dole of one of the tabloids. If Abdul's tip looked on the up and up he might try and book a room for the night, but in the meantime he flipped through his notepad and found the notation he was looking for. Father had given him a "just in case" address to an empty apartment in Paris. Like any self-respecting Parisians, father's old friends Pierre and Odile Thierry fled their hometown for most of August, a month when tourists took over the city. Staying at the Thierrys' apartment would save Graham from having to scramble for lodging in prime-time tourist season, not to mention having to get a rent-a-car. The Thierrys had left a car behind for their guests to borrow.

From the train station, Graham took a cab to the apartment. The concierge provided him with a key, and as promised, the car keys were hanging in the front hallway. It was an older Citroën CX. Graham navigated the vehicle along the Left Bank, and found the Victoria Palace on a quiet street just off the rue de Rennes. He parked a block away from the hotel, went in search of Rousseau, and found him slumped down in the driver's seat of his Renault scouting out the hotel. He looked despondent.

"She cut her hair," he said. "All those beautiful locks—poof—gone."

"She's already arrived then?"

"Almost two hours ago. I wouldn't have recognized her if I hadn't known what to look for. She was wearing a very unflattering business suit. No makeup. Hat and glasses. She was hiding her beautiful body."

He made it sound as if she were guilty of a serious crime.

"What kind of car is she driving?"

"A tan Peugeot 607. She already went out for a drive."

"Where did she go?

"Nowhere. She seemed to be consulting a sheet of directions, but she never stopped the car. She drove almost to the Seine, and then drove back."

Graham thought about that. "No sightseeing?"

Rousseau shook his head.

"Do you think she made your tail?"

Rousseau looked offended: "No."

"No stops?"

"Only one. She pulled over to the side of the road, checked the street sign to make sure of where she was, but she never got out of the car. After that she came back to the hotel."

It sounded more like a trial run than a pleasure drive, thought Graham. It was possible she had been scouting out the area.

"Where did she stop?"

"On a residential street a few blocks north of St. Germain and rue St.-André-des-Arts."

Saints everywhere, thought Graham. Driving the Paris streets, you needed them.

"It's a narrow one-way street," said Rousseau. "Now what is its name?" He thought for a few moments, then came up with it. "La rue de Savoie!" he said triumphantly. "Yes, that is where she stopped."

"And then she turned around and came back to the hotel?"

"*Oui*. Since then her car has been parked in the garage, and she's been parked in her room."

Graham looked at the hotel. The building was U-shaped. Some of the front facing rooms had balconies overlooking rue Blaise Desgoffe, a relatively quiet street, at least by Paris standards. Rousseau's car was parked across the street from the hotel. It was far enough in the shadows to offer them the obscurity they wanted, but had a vantage point to the hotel's entrance and garage that they needed.

"Can you see her room from here?" Graham asked.

Rousseau shook her head. "She's in their Grand Suite. Its balcony overlooks the courtyard."

"In that case," said Graham, "I'm going to go play the tourist for a few minutes. Call me on my phone if anything comes up."

It was a boutique hotel, intimate and expensive. A bored clerk told Graham they were sold out, but gave him a tariff sheet with a property layout for future reference. Self-tours, Graham knew, were usually best for his purposes. He turned right at the reception desk, went through a large breakfast room and out into a private courtyard.

With the hotel diagram in hand, Graham figured out which room was hers. Any questions he might have had about which suite she occupied was answered by a pair of very blue eyes looking down at him from her balcony. Each took in the other before Graham looked away. He wondered if his methodical tracking of her room had given him away. His dark clothing looked acceptably expensive, and he had a talent of being a chameleon and fitting in. Maybe Lady Godiva thought he was just another rich tourist taking in the view. Graham could feel her eyes still on him. He walked around the grass courtyard, paused over some colorful flower beds, and tried to look like someone out for a little stroll. Without looking up at her, he retreated back inside the hotel, then took an elevator down to the garage. There was no attendant there, allowing him easy access to her Peugeot 607. He reached inside his pocket, pulled out some reflective stickers, and affixed them to the front and rear bumpers of her car. The stickers, what Graham referred to as "cat eyes," were a poor man's tracking device. They glowed at night, making it easy to tail a car from a distance.

Graham rejoined Rousseau at his car. Rousseau was about ten years younger than Graham's thirty-five years. The last time they had worked together Rousseau had whiled away his time by combing his hair and talking about his many girlfriends. He was already working his comb through his long Gallic locks.

"I am hoping Lady Godiva changes her clothes," Rousseau said. "Maybe she puts on something sexy for us, yes? It is hot enough that she doesn't need to wear much."

Graham wiped his brow. His shirt was already wet from his short walk through the hotel.

"Did you see her pictures in *Playboy*?" asked Rousseau.

Graham shook his head.

"It was very sexy. She was on a horse in some of them. Her long hair covered her bosom."

"I did see that one," Graham said. "It ran in *Stern* and *People*. She was posed to look like one of those John Collier paintings of Lady Godiva."

"Yes. Some of those pictures look like a painting. But others were more—"

His English seemed to fail him, but not his hands. Rousseau gestured and groped.

"Graphic?" asked Graham.

"Yes." He draped his index and middle finger over his hand. "There was one where she was riding this way on her horse."

"Sidesaddle?"

Rousseau nodded with satisfaction. "The camera was shooting from inside a glass, and she was looking back."

"They framed the shot from inside a window?"

"Exactly. She was leaning back on the horse. This time her hair no interfere with the pictures. Her legs were apart and her hand, it dig into her thigh. She have these long nails, very red. Her breasts were lifting to the sky, her perfect nipples pointed like arrows. I remember the picture so well because it felt like I was spying on her while she was having this sexy daydream. I feel naughty, yes? Like I was seeing something risqúe. Like I was a voyeur."

"A Peeping Tom," Graham said.

"That's right."

"They set up the shot to make you feel that way," said Graham. "When Lady Godiva took her famous ride, the townspeople of Coventry all agreed they wouldn't watch as she passed by. But supposedly there was one fellow, a tailor named Tom, who violated their agreement by peeping at her through an open shutter. Peeping Tom paid for his lecherous ways."

"What happened to him?"

"One version of the story is that he was struck blind; the other is that he died."

"Maybe I close my eyes if I see her without clothes," Rousseau said.

"I doubt it."

Rousseau laughed. "You are right. Any man with blood in his veins would look at her. I do not blame that Tom. If his Lady Godiva was like this one, how could he not look?"

For some reason, Graham found himself annoyed. "She didn't take her ride because she was some kind of exhibitionist. Lady Godiva accepted the challenge to get some tax relief for the people of Coventry. The townsfolk showed their respect for what she was doing by turning their backs on the exhibition. All except Tom, that is."

Rousseau answered Graham's story of the past with an all too present inquiry: "So now you are trying to be like this Peeping Tom, yes?"

Maybe that's what was bothering him. He was Peeping Tom, but worse. At least Tom had a prurient interest. He was just out for the almighty dollar. There was this feeling that he, like Tom, was targeting something that should have been left alone. In way of answer, Graham shrugged.

"I hope you are not blinded," said Rousseau. "What is it the English say? Tom paid the piper."

Graham shook his head. "No. He paid the peeper."

The hours passed slowly. Every hour Graham did a surreptitious check of her room, then returned to Rousseau's car. He came back from his latest surveillance, paused at the open driver's window, and shook his head. The men had grown increasingly silent around each other. Rousseau was even tired of talking about women.

"It is past eleven," Rousseau said. "She is not coming out tonight."

"Possibly."

"Were there lights on in her room?"

"No."

"We are wasting our time."

"We'll see."

Rousseau tapped his watch, his finger spanking the crystal. "She is in her bed. She is asleep."

"Maybe she's taking a nap."

"I have to go."

"I want you here until at least one o'clock. You know how things are. One moment everything's quiet, and the next it's crazy."

"There is a woman—"

Graham interrupted. "What's a few more hours?"

"It is silly to wait. I am hungry for more than a candy bar. And it will be nice to pee in the toilet instead of a soda can."

He reached for Graham's pack and extended it out through the open window. "Call me if you need me. I can be back in fifteen minutes."

Graham didn't take his bag. "Screw that. You took this job—"

"And I worked all morning and evening, and I will be ready to work again when you need me, but now I am leaving."

Rousseau shook Graham's pack. His cameras were in there, dammit. Reluctantly, Graham snatched the bag. The Renault's engine turned over. "*Au revoir,*" Rousseau said.

Graham pointedly spat on the ground. He would have preferred to offer a salty editorial, but didn't want to draw attention to himself. It wasn't the first time someone had bailed on him. People didn't realize how tough stakeouts were. It was hard, mind-numbing work that defined monotony. Graham could almost sympathize with the Frenchman. Almost. It would be all too easy to call it a night like he had, but Graham often succeeded where others failed because he steeled himself to be patient. Still, it wasn't easy watching doors that never opened, and windows that remained dark.

Graham threw his pack over his shoulder, then set off at a quick jog up the street. He was a naturally fast runner, his speed more a result of genetics than any workout regimen. Over the years he had managed to get shots his colleagues missed just because of his speed. His car was parked a block away. Rousseau's surveillance spot of the hotel was too good to give up, and Graham needed to reclaim it while he could. Even that late at night, parking spots didn't last in Paris. He jumped into the Citroën, and was able to park in the same spot again.

He adjusted the driver's seat, trying to find a comfortable reclining spot. Killing time, Graham thought. He understood prisoners when they said there was nothing more difficult than killing time. The foot traffic around the hotel was slow. He liked it when guests showed themselves; it gave him something to do. Graham studied the faces of all the guests coming and going from the hotel. He used his small Zeiss binoculars, scouting for a familiar face. Mostly what he saw were chatting couples. Nothing seemed out of the ordinary.

Almost all of the garage traffic was incoming, cars returning from an evening out, but at a quarter of midnight he saw lights emerging from the gloom of the garage. He also saw that the car had a glowing bumper.

Graham's pulse started racing. The hunt was on. Maybe the Lady was just going out for a drink or an ice cream, but it was possible she was going to rendezvous with the mystery man. He started the Citroën, but didn't turn on its headlights. He stayed slouched down into the seat, waiting for her to drive by. As she passed, he snuck a look to confirm she was the driver. Lady Godiva, he saw, was out for a ride.

After pulling out of the space, he made no effort to close the gap between them. The reflective stickers allowed him to stay well back. He debated about calling Rousseau. Graham was quite familiar with Paris, so navigating the city wouldn't be the problem, but he could use a second set of eyes and wheels. He pulled his phone out from his pocket, hesitated a moment, then put it back, deciding to wait and see what developed.

She drove along rue de Rennes, turning on rue de Vaugirard and traveling along the perimeter of Luxembourg Gardens. Someone had told Graham that in Hemingway's destitute days he used to catch pigeons in those gardens and make a meal out of them. The Lady headed south on rue de Medicis, then turned on boulevard St.-Michel. The more she drove, the more it appeared she was lost.

Then, without even the warning of brake lights, she turned on rue Michelet. As he approached, Graham watched her make a U-turn, ending up with a view to all cars continuing down St.-Michel.

Graham cursed, unsure of what to do. He didn't look at her as he passed, even averted his head slightly. Turning on rue Michelet would have put him directly in her sight. And he couldn't duplicate her U-turn without all but announcing that he was following her.

There really was no choice. He continued down St.-Michel, keeping his attention on the rearview mirror. He saw Lady Godiva reversing her route. Graham turned on rue du Val de Nicole, then sped up Henri Barbeuse. It was clear now that Lady Godiva had been cautious, not lost. Her route had been designed to lose any potential tails. Graham wondered if she had picked up on his car. That's why you always needed at least two vehicles working a tail operation. Fuck Rousseau, he thought.

In Graham's gut, he knew she was meeting with her mystery man. There was no other reason for her to be so cautious. Graham's adrenaline was pumping. He wanted to push hard on the accelerator, but a car barreling up on her bumper would only bring him to her attention. His only chance was to get ahead of her.

He took a chance on where she was going, pushing the Citroën through the Paris streets. It responded ably, if not spectacularly. His hand-eye-foot coordination was pressed into service as he navigated through Left Bank pedestrian and car traffic.

Earlier in the day she had driven to a residential street, but for no apparent purpose. It was somewhere north of boulevard St.-Germain. What was the name of the street? Graham worked his mind as feverishly as he did the accelerator. Rousseau had struggled to come up with the name. It was a side street off rue St.-André-des-Arts. Graham's mind was working in two languages. A red light slowed him for an instant, but didn't stop him. He pushed through.

The car's clock wasn't digital. It was an older model. In the dim light Graham made out that it was five minutes until midnight. Her rendezvous would be at midnight, he was sure of it. That would be when his Citroën would turn into a pumpkin unless he remembered the name of that goddamn street.

Rousseau. Of course. That bastard knew. As Graham pulled his mobile phone out of his pocket he hit a pothole about as big as the Grand Canyon. The jolt sent him upward; his head bounced into the ceiling. As he grabbed at the steering wheel his phone flew down between his feet.

The jostling served one good purpose: it cleared his head. La rue de Savoie, he remembered.

He barreled down the tree-lined Boulevard Saint Germain, hoping Lady Godiva was somewhere behind him. Then he followed rue St.-André-des-Arts. His laptop was equipped with a GPS program, but he hadn't thought to map out her earlier location, and now he didn't have time. He debated on where to turn, driving from instinct. Rousseau had said it was north of rue St.-André. Graham made some turns and lucked on Savoie.

It was a short, one-way street. He traveled it from one end to the other, and saw no sign of her Peugeot. But one car did catch his attention. Someone was sitting in the driver's seat of a rather conspicuous Porsche 911 GT2.

Graham turned the corner and parked on rue Seguier. He grabbed his camera, and tried to sneak up on the Porsche, using parked cars and building stoops as cover. A car door opened just as Graham hunkered behind a bumper four car lengths away from the Porsche. He heard footsteps, and tensed. Graham lowered his head, looking between the tires for approaching feet. The footfalls continued, but not in his direction. This wasn't someone used to waiting. The driver of the Porsche had grown impatient, and was out pacing.

Graham snuck a look. Just his luck. The Porsche was parked as far away from the streetlight as possible. Graham was afforded little more than a moving silhouette. Male, he could see. Medium height. An athlete, Graham immediately decided.

Like birds of a feather, celebrities and jocks often hung out together. They had their youth, fame, and riches in common. Graham had seen enough professional athletes to know them at a glance. They all had a certain walk. It wasn't a swagger exactly, but more of a coordinated strut. It was the cock of the walk way a rooster strolls around a barnyard, or the way the king of beasts regally pads across a savannah. Only professional athletes carry themselves with that absolute confidence. Even though the man was only pacing, Graham was sure of what he was in the signature way he carried himself.

Car lights approached. The man turned his face, looking out from an angle. It was a good technique of obscuring his features. That's what people with very identifiable faces did. He needn't have worried. It was her Peugeot.

There wasn't a space open for her to park. She edged into half a space, leaving the back half of her car jutting out into the street. He walked across to her. Graham raised his camera, then lowered it, knowing the shots wouldn't come out. At best he'd have a back in shadow. He would have to bide his time.

The man leaned his head into the car. It appeared they had a long and tender kiss. Then they started talking, keeping their voices low. Graham could only make out every third word or so. The man's accent was French.

". . . worried . . . late," he said.

Her garbled reply, ". . . might . . . following."

"Haven't seen . . ."

"Probably . . . jumpy."

They stopped talking. Graham didn't think they were kissing, but he couldn't be sure. He wished he were carrying a parabolic listening device.

"Sure . . . shock . . ." she said.

". . . unexpected."

"That's . . . face-to-face . . . not . . . worry."

". . . not fair . . . responsibility."

Both of them, Graham decided, were sounding too virtuous. Hearing only snippets was frustrating. It was like listening to a foreign language, and only being able to make out a word here and there.

". . . your sake, as . . . foundation," she said. ". . . appearance . . . tainted money."

"Not . . . fair . . . you."

"Not me . . . want . . . normal life . . . chance."

A nearby door opened. Their talk stopped. The clicking of nails, followed by footsteps, announced a nocturnal dog walk. They only resumed their conversation when the dog walker was out of earshot, but now their conversation was more of a whisper than anything else. For Graham, their buzzing was like having to listen to mosquitoes humming around his ears. Without making a sound, he moved closer to them.

Graham raised his head, looking through the back window of the car to his targets. His light and vantage point were much improved. He turned off his camera's flash and autofocus. To even hope for a visible shot, he would have to get creative with the aperture, maxing out the available light. But shooting through the car windows would only blur the already obscured. Graham decided to shoot over the hood. He raised his head, then followed with the camera, pressing the shutter several times. The response between clicks was so slow it almost sounded like time-lapse photography. And even if the pictures came out, he still had little more than the back of the man's neck.

Who was he? Graham tried to think of French and Belgian athletes. He had lived away from the United States long enough to know the sporting world didn't begin and end with baseball, football, and basketball. The French athletes made their mark in such sports as skiing, tennis, bicycling, and automobile racing. There were household sporting names known throughout Europe that few Americans were familiar with.

Of course Graham could be wrong about the man's being a professional athlete. He was assuming a lot based on the way he walked.

Another set of headlights approached. The lighting could help him get a shot. But as the car neared the man made sure his head was ducked out of sight.

"Afraid . . . followed," the Lady said.

"Didn't . . . suspicious," he said.

A light came on in an apartment behind Graham. He turned and saw an older man looking down to the street. Graham wasn't sure if he was the object of his scrutiny or the couple. He drew closer to the side of the car, hoping he was indistinguishable from its shadow.

"Thought . . . private," he said.

"Men . . . hotel," said the Lady. "Can't go there."

Dammit, thought Graham, she had made them.

"Know . . . perfect . . . adventure?"

"Great!"

". . . caves . . . like . . . need . . . light . . . very dark."

The man ran back to the Porsche, opened the driver's side door, and retrieved something. As he hurried back to her car Graham raised his camera and focused on him. When he opened the passenger door he was illuminated for a moment. Graham hoped for the best, snapping two pictures. If he was lucky, the lens caught the same thing his naked eye saw, the man's flashing a smile at Lady Godiva just as the light cut out.

His teeth were the giveaway. Could it be?

Graham was already up and walking. When they noticed him, he hoped they would assume he had just emerged from one of the buildings. He was glad they were taking her car. There was no hope the Citroën could keep up with his Porsche, but with the cat eyes he might be able to keep the Peugeot in sight. He wanted to run to his car, but that would be too obvious. Graham covered the ground with long, purposeful strides. Behind him he could hear her car approaching. The camera was tucked inside a pack. At least he wasn't carrying a neon sign advertising his profession.

From what he could observe, they didn't pay him any mind. When they turned the corner, he started to sprint. There was reason to run. He couldn't be sure any of the pictures had turned out, and big game shots like this didn't come around often.

It was no wonder the man was so shy of being seen. Georges "Le Croc" LeMoine was a national icon and an international football star. His teeth carried more wattage than Tom Cruise's choppers. They, and the way he chewed up the opposition, had earned him his nickname. In most of the world soccer is king, and Le Croc was king of that world. He certainly had more endorsements than any other athlete. His face was omnipresent, featured on commercials, billboards, and posters. There was a "Le Croc" clothing and athletic shoe line. He was that rarefied sports icon like Michael Jordan or Tiger Woods, making more off the field than on.

Le Croc was the toast of France, and Paris in particular. He was a hometown boy, his legend beginning in the City of Lights. France was pinning its World Cup hopes on him.

Graham reached his car, jumped inside, and floored it. The Peugeot was already out of sight. He hoped they hadn't turned on to some other street already. Where the hell were they going? The two of them had talked about finding privacy, and he had said something about an adventure. The Lady had seemed to like that idea. She might be a do-gooder, but that didn't mean she spent her time going to teas and knitting doilies. Rock climbing and spelunking, Graham remembered, were favorite hobbies of hers.

Without slowing the car, he feverishly swiveled his head at every cross street, looking for any sign of them. He was pushing the Citroën hard, had it up to 130 kilometers. Shit. He couldn't let them get away now. Catching the two of them in a picture together would be gold. From their conversation, it sounded as if Lady Godiva was taking the high road in their relationship, doing everything possible to keep it private. She obviously knew about Le Croc's engagement to supermodel Tatiana. Everyone in the world did. They had very publicly set their wedding date, which promised to be the social engagement of the year, for after next year's World Cup. Le Croc had wanted to be able to focus on the Cup without any distractions.

You play, thought Graham, and you pay. Lady Godiva would be a front page distraction if Graham could get the shot of them together.

He sped through an intersection and suddenly braked. There, off to the right. Was that the telltale glow of his cat eyes? Graham couldn't be sure. He was already well past the turn. To backtrack would take too long.

He punched the Citroën into reverse, raising smoke. Traffic was light, but not that light. Headlights were coming up behind him. He floored it backward in a race against the speed of light. Horns were blaring in his ear as he made the turn. Now he had to find that elusive glow. He hoped he wasn't following a will-o'-the-wisp.

Le Croc would know his Paris, but where the hell was he going? He had said something about a light, and gone to his car. Why would he need a light? And where was this private place?

Where could two celebrities disappear? Graham drove along streets that were more residential than commercial. Maybe Le Croc was going to a trusted friend's home. Graham's head was in constant motion searching for the car. He was already second-guessing himself, afraid his eyes had played tricks on him. It was possible he had seen some other reflection. The neighborhood didn't look promising. It was as unassuming as Paris could be, not touristy by any means.

There was no sign of the car. Graham kept pushing the Citroën. He was lost now; every street he passed was another that the Peugeot could have turned on. He followed la place de Rungis, and felt defeated by the maze. Then in the distance, he saw the glint and as he neared the cat eyes were like a nugget of gold shining out from a covering of mud.

The unoccupied Peugeot was parked on the side of the road. Graham slowed down and looked around. The area wasn't well lit. The darkness could be hiding them anywhere; in one of the houses; behind a fence; nestled in the grassy lot. Just as Graham was thinking how easy it would be for them to stay hidden from him, their path became apparent.

Their flashlight stood out in the darkness. He could see it bobbing maybe a hundred yards off. Instead of running after them, Graham took a moment to think. It was possible they could miss him, or find a way to elude him. If that happened, he needed to slow them down.

Graham went to his knees, felt around, and came up with some sticks and stones. He ran over to the Peugeot, hunched over the left front tire, jammed a stick in the air valve, and wedged it with a pebble. To be safe, he did the same thing to the back tire. As he hurried off, he could hear the hissing behind him. It sounded as if he had stirred up a den of serpents.

He left the road behind him and followed a path that took him by several old storage buildings. The only light was from a shop with a white neon light blinking VTT CENTER. Aside from that, everything appeared abandoned. As Graham went forward it grew increasingly dark. Where were they? He continued in the direction they'd been heading, and crossed some railroad tracks that looked long unused. *La petite ceinture*, Graham thought. It was an ancient railway that surrounded Paris and was no longer in operation.

Graham caught sight of their light, or more of a glow really. It was only there for a second or two, reminding him of a scuba diver's light fading into the depths. The reason for that soon became clear. They had entered into a tunnel. Graham hesitated outside its entrance, momentarily put off by the darkness. The tunnel was long abandoned and signs warned of dangers, as well as threatened prosecution of trespassers. Walking in blind wasn't a heartening prospect. There could be open pits and broken glass and countless other hazards. Graham decided his best bet was shuffling forward along the rusty, though intact, metal rails.

One step, and then another. He couldn't let them get too far ahead, but hurrying was out of the question. The darkness slowed him down, as did the slippery way. The old stones were weeping overhead and the water kept dripping on Graham's head. It was hard to tell how far he went—time seemed to slow in the dark tunnel—but he was glad to see a light at the end of it.

The tunnel opened to a residential area, with high, unattractive apartment buildings visible on both sides. It wasn't the kind of spot you would find on any Paris postcard. Graham looked around for the telltale flashlight, but didn't see it. There was no easy exit from the old railroad tracks, so he assumed his prey had continued forward. Ahead he could see another tunnel, and quickly crossed the open space to it.

The second tunnel was shorter; he could easily see to the other side. Graham traveled around fifty yards, and came to another opening. Greenery and trees hung over and around the tunnel, encroaching on the rails and blocking much of the sky. From appearances, he looked to have surfaced in the middle of an urban park.

The light he was looking for was far enough away that it appeared to be little more than a flickering match. He hurried forward to the third tunnel and didn't even hesitate before entering. Perhaps he should have. It was far longer than its two predecessors. The light in the opening behind him quickly dimmed, leaving him to trudge forward in blackness. The only illumination was the far-off flashlight. At least they weren't near enough that he needed to worry about them hearing his pursuit. There were spots in the third tunnel where it almost felt as if it were raining, the water insistently dripping. The *drip, drip, drip* echoing sounds made him edgy; it was easy to see how water torture worked. There was the smell of mushrooms, decay, and abandonment.

He counted off steps in his mind. It was better than whistling in the dark, and gave him a reference for how far the tunnel went. He had traveled 423 steps, and closed the distance on the flashlight, when he noticed the light's advance slowing. The beam started alternating between the rails and the left wall of the tunnel. It appeared as if Le Croc was looking for something. His search lasted for a minute or two, long enough for Graham to draw close enough to hear them. The two of them had left the rails, and were standing on the left side of the tunnel.

"You first," Le Croc said, shining his light down.

She followed the direction of the light and seemed to disappear. Then it was Le Croc's turn to do the disappearing act. In their wake was a short-lived glow, almost like the bioluminescence of a firefly.

Shit, thought Graham. What now? He wanted to follow them down their hole, but he didn't dare. Graham wished he hadn't given up smoking. With a lighter, he would have dared to go after them. Then a thought came to him. He had a light. Of course he had a light.

Graham grabbed his day pack, and pulled out a camera. He was so used to the equipment that operating it blind wasn't a problem. Graham set off the flash, used the light to walk over to where the couple had been standing, then set off the flash again.

They had pushed aside a heavy metal grating and descended downward through a hole. Graham leaned over the opening in the ground and set off the flash. The hole was narrow but appeared manageable, with stone rungs leading down. Still, it would be a tight squeeze. It was one thing following them through the tunnels, but another to go down some hole. He pressed the flash again and was glad to see there was no sign announcing, *Abandon all hope, ye who enter here.*

He could go back and wait for them near their car, do a photographic ambush. If they were wary though, they could cover up. He still didn't have his money shot, the picture of the two of them together. And beyond that, there was the secret between them. He had heard it in their voices. There was a story here beyond their stealth romance.

Graham took a deep breath, as if he were breaching the water instead of the ground, then descended into the darkness of the underground. He crawled along to his right, then listened carefully. He thought he could make out footsteps, but the acoustics of the underground made it impossible to determine on which side of him the noises were coming from. Graham set off the flash in one direction, and then the other, seeing narrow corridors in both directions.

The grip of claustrophobia tightened around Graham's throat. His feet didn't want to move. Something felt wrong. It was like being entombed. That was it. This wasn't any storm drain, he realized. The structure was old, very old. The obvious struck him: he was in the catacombs. The real Paris underground.

Graham knew something of the history of the catacombs. Centuries back extensive mining had taken place underneath Paris, with hundreds of miles of tunnels quarried for their stone, gypsum, and clay. The underground started to be referred to as the catacombs after millions of skeletons were transferred out of Paris cemeteries and moved by night into the quarries. Between six and seven million skeletons were given new resting spots in the tunnels.

The hundreds of miles of corridors still existed. Tourists could avail themselves of an "official" tour of a sanctioned portion of the catacombs. A friend of Graham's had told of descending down a long spiral staircase, then walking through a tunnel whose walls were lined with bones and skulls. He had said that "souvenirs" were discouraged, and that packs and purses were checked by guards to make sure no bones were purloined.

It wasn't the usual place, Graham thought, to bring a date. But then again, it was easy enough to go incognito among the dead.

Why would Le Croc take her down here? They could have more easily talked just by parking at some deserted spot. But this place was apparently familiar to Le Croc from his days as a Parisian youth. He was showing his old haunt to her. Adventure, he had said. She had probably told him about her cave explorations. Graham guessed it was their shared derring-do that had brought them together in the first place.

Pick a way, Graham thought. He started walking. The narrow passageway forced Graham to hunch over. His shirt was already wet with sweat. He breathed mostly through his mouth, not liking the stuffy smell of the tunnel. Every ten steps Graham set off the flash. The bursts of light illuminated cornerstones with street names and dates, some dating back more than a century.

The light kept showing him sights, but not his quarry in the quarry. There was no shortage of graffiti on the walls. The writings were time capsules of sorts, going back many years and inked in many tongues. Graham was surprised at how many paintings were on the walls. But then again, this was Paris. Some appeared to be true works of art.

Graham came to a stop, thinking he heard sounds ahead. Not voices, not exactly, but something. It would have been easy to believe it was the moaning of ghosts. He felt along the walls and suddenly encountered nothing. Graham brought the flash up, popped it, and saw that he had come to a side tunnel. Which way had they gone? He stood at the crossroads listening, then continued forward.

His calves and shoulders already ached from having to amble along like a gorilla, and some hard encounters with the ceiling had him fearing for his scalp. He felt all turned around, like Alice down the rabbit hole. He set off another flash, and saw some official-looking German writing on the walls that dated back to World War II. The Nazis had evidently been down there before him. Graham knew they hadn't been alone in the underworld. His father had told him the French Resistance made good use of the catacombs, operating out of sight of their occupiers.

Graham continued forward. The cross draft on his face coincided with his groping hands encountering open space on both sides of him. It was hard to tell if he was standing at the crossroads of another tunnel or just a side gallery. Graham pressed the flash, stood listening and staring, then flashed again. The noises were still coming from ahead. He pressed forward, wondering at what he was hearing. It sounded like music. Could Le Croc have brought a radio? The tunnels twisted sounds, swallowing some, echoing others.

The darkness was breached for a moment by a flash of light. His targets had to be near. Graham tried to move forward silently. He resisted using the flash. Better a few more scrapes on his body than alerting them. As he closed in, the music became clearer. It was a techno beat, the same kind of music that had plagued him the night before. For a moment, it looked as if a lantern flashed on, but then the light disappeared.

Graham sniffed the air. There was an acrid, familiar smell, the heavy smoke of marijuana. Had they gone down below to smoke grass?

He turned the corner. Off to the side was another gallery. At first glance, Graham thought that glowing eyes were staring at him, then he realized he was seeing the light of candles—candles angled through the eye sockets of skulls. Someone was inhaling on a joint, and Graham watched the cigarette flare red.

There was a second, larger flame bobbing in the air. Not a cigarette, but a small torch. Suddenly the torch seemed to explode. Flame shot out, and the cavern lit up. A fire breather was spotlighted spewing flame, a black man in shorts and tank top. For a long moment, the entire gallery was illuminated.

His display was greeted with a scattering of applause. The fire breather offered an encore. This time he exhaled his fiery breath in Graham's direction. His throwing of flames outlined Graham's figure.

Voices rose in alarm. A miner's lantern was turned on, lighting the cavern and blinding Graham. In French, he heard voices demanding to know who he was, and what he was doing there.

"I'm looking for friends," Graham said in English, raising a hand to shield his eyes from the light.

His foreign tongue seemed to reassure those there. Graham guessed they were worried about the tunnel police busting them. The fire-eater had an audience of four, three males and a female. They were young, all in their twenties.

"A man and a woman came down here," Graham said. "Did you see them pass by?"

"We have only seen you," said the man holding the joint. Then he tilted one of the skulls. "And the dead."

It wasn't the kind of company Graham wanted to keep.

The woman raised a bottle of wine. "Have a drink," she said in accented English. "Stay for the show."

"No thanks," said Graham, but he paused before leaving and turned to the fire breather. He raised his camera in a questioning gesture.

The fire-eater nodded and smiled, his white teeth dispersing some of the gloom. He raised a bottle to his lips, tilted it, then brought the torch close to his mouth. In the red light, Graham could see beads of sweat on the man's forehead. He tilted his head back, brought the torch almost to his lips, then spat out the liquid. It looked as if he were spewing flames. Graham snapped the photo. It would be his proof that he hadn't been hallucinating.

Graham hurried back the way he'd come. It was possible the couple had gone in the opposite direction or veered off into one of the side tunnels. Or, if they suspected pursuit, they could have tucked themselves into a gallery and waited for him to pass them by. Graham set off flashes faster now, forgoing stealth for speed. He paid a price for hurrying. Twice he fell, each time scraping flesh and tearing fabric. Grime covered his hands and face.

In the darkness, he almost walked by his exit, but felt the draft from above. The flash confirmed the opening. Though by the clock he hadn't spent much time in the catacombs, it didn't feel that way. He crawled up and it felt as if he were escaping out of a tomb.

After being in the catacombs, the third tunnel felt positively spacious. Graham knew the way, and hurried. He was afraid his prey had already surfaced and were ahead of him again. Le Croc might even have taken them out of another exit. No doubt there were many secret entrances and exits to the underground.

His eyes had adjusted to the dark, and the tunnels seemed more gray now than black. Graham continued to set off flashes, but more for comfort than need. He followed the rail lines back, putting the tunnels behind him. The neighborhood, and old buildings, didn't look so rundown now. His ascent out of the catacombs put a luster on everything. He was just short of la place de Rungis when the sound of voices and laughter put him on alert.

Graham crept forward. The Peugeot's front windows were half-opened, probably for ventilation. Still, all the car windows were fogged up. Graham wondered if that was a result of their exertions in the catacombs or the car. He checked on the two tires and saw they were still flattened. The car wasn't absolutely disabled, but it would probably handle like one of those clown cars with different-sized tires.

The Citroën was parked down the street, out of sight of her rental. It was angled for a quick getaway. Graham made it to the car, started its engine, but kept the headlights off. As an extra precaution, he left its front door ajar. There would be no fiddling for a door handle.

At last satisfied, he cautiously backtracked and turned his attention on the couple. He crept up on the Peugeot, but his caution seemed unnecessary. The two of them were still talking away.

"If you need money," Le Croc said.

"I won't want your money."

"But what about all the expenses?"

"I am sure I'll manage."

"I can set up a fund—"

"No," she said, interrupting.

In the face of her firm denial, he said, "I wish things could be different."

Whether she did or not wasn't clear. By the sounds of it, some mutual comforting was going on. It also sounded as if each was done with their say, and that they would depart soon. He needed to act before that. Graham studied the car, trying to figure out the best shot. He ruled out shooting through the windshield. He considered not using the flash and shooting from the open driver's side window. They might be preoccupied enough not to notice him. But the shot would be clearer with the flash. Graham decided to use it, and do a shoot and run.

He went down on his haunches, approached closer, and sneaked another look at them. They weren't making out. His arm was draped around her, and her cheek was nestled into his shoulder.

Graham's blood was racing; it was show time. Camera ready, he moved in, mentally readied himself, then popped up. He snapped off half the roll before they even knew what had hit them. Then they were ducking their heads and raising their hands, but it was too late. His motor drive finished the entire roll of film in less than two seconds.

In his line of work, you didn't tarry. Graham was halfway to his car before a car door opened behind him. He prided himself on his speed, but Le Croc's footwork was legendary. As fast as Graham was moving, Le Croc's footsteps sounded ever closer. Graham looked over his shoulder for an instant. Le Croc's face was a terrible thing to behold. Their race was going to be closer than Graham could have imagined or wanted.

He lunged toward his car as if it were the finish line, throwing himself on the seat. Instead of trying to close the door behind him, he engaged the gear and kicked at the gas pedal. Fingers closed on his shirt as he punched on the accelerator. Graham grabbed hard on the steering wheel so as not to be pulled out. As the car patched out his shirt ripped, and Le Croc was left holding a fistful of fabric.

Graham drove without lights. If Le Croc was watching, he didn't want to identify where he was going. Not that Graham was exactly sure where he was. The best plan was just to put distance between them. He passed several potential turns while maintaining stealth mode. Without lights, he sacrificed speed, but still managed to stay on the road. He made a left. If he was being pursued, it was more likely that Le Croc would make a right. After a minute, Graham turned on his headlights. He doubted whether Le Croc had gotten a good look at the car anyway. And the two flat tires would certainly discourage pursuit. Graham slowed down to the speed limit and kept his eyes open. It was hard to travel very many blocks in Paris without hitting a main boulevard. The lights ahead told him he was coming to a major street.

The lights behind told him he wasn't alone.

They were coming up fast. At night, you can always tell a speeding car by the way its lights bob up and down. What he saw was more extreme than that. The car almost looked like it was hopping. Its suspension and struts were being pushed hard, the uneven air in the tires making the car buck up and down. For all that, it still wasn't slowing up.

Graham remembered the look he'd seen on Le Croc's face, and floored the accelerator. A world-class athlete doesn't accept defeat. He was trying to find a way to win even when there didn't seem to be one. Amazingly, the car race was going like their foot race. Even with two disabled tires, the Peugeot was closing on him.

Neither car yielded to the red light. Graham half hoped the police were waiting on the corner. No one could outrun a siren. But that might be the worst thing for him. The police would certainly fall all over Le Croc. They would do his bidding and confiscate Graham's cameras. Maybe that was Le Croc's plan. Get noticed, get both of them pulled over, and get the film from Graham.

Graham decided to get off the straightaway. The way the Peugeot was listing, he could better hold it off through a slalom course. He swerved off rue de Sèvres, made three fast turns, and found himself barreling down rue de la Convention. Through the hard turns Le Croc managed to hold his car on the road, even though he seemed to be hanging on by two wheels.

The Paris sights were going by in a blur of lights. It felt odd being in the lead. Graham was used to being the chase car, not being chased. He made a series of turns, gaining some ground. For a moment he thought he had lost his pursuers, but then the telltale lights came into sight again. Graham was almost annoyed at how persistent they were. So what that their love affair had been uncovered? Didn't they know the world loved nothing more than dragging its heroes through a little mud? Screw both of them. They wanted the adoration without the scrutiny. That wasn't how it worked.

The road dropped, and the turns became tricky. Good, thought Graham. With the condition of the Peugeot's tires, their teeth ought to really be rattling now. He pushed on the accelerator through a series of curves. When he looked back, they had disappeared from his rearview mirror. Maybe one of the axles had finally given out. Graham saw an entrance to the boulevard Peripherique. If he hurried, they might not guess his route. He crossed over and merged onto the main road.

Graham checked his rearview mirror, then checked again. Finally, he was clear of them. But just as he was exhaling in relief he turned his head and saw a car being driven ridiculously fast on a city street that paralleled the Peripherique.

The Peugeot. "Am I fucking Captain Hook?" Graham yelled. He couldn't seem to rid himself of the crocodile. Did the bastard think he was going to intimidate him into stopping? Graham shot a look at his gas tank. It was full. He would outlast him if necessary. Graham pushed the accelerator to the floor. The older car groaned loudly as the speedometer ticked upward.

At this time of night, the Peripherique was almost like a highway. The wide road was one of the main arteries circling around Paris. There need be no guessing as to where you were. The traffic signs were well designed and prominent, showing what was coming up in not only distance, but approximate time.

He'd have to get off, but where? The Bois de Boulogne would be a good spot, Graham decided. It was Paris's answer to Central Park, located on the city's western edge. There were thousands of acres of woods there. If necessary, he could park the car and get lost among them.

Graham was studying the road signs instead of watching in back of him. A jolt from behind sent his head into the wheel. He grabbed the wheel, pulled out of a swerve, and centered himself in his lane. Somehow Le Croc had crossed over onto the Peripherique and blindsided him, bumping into him from behind. Graham looked in his rearview mirror. The Peugeot was right on his tail. Le Croc was furiously signaling for him to pull over. Lady Godiva's hand was over her mouth. She looked terrified.

To hell with him. As unbalanced as it was, the Peugeot wouldn't be able to chase him for long. Le Croc was almost driving on two axles. Graham held tight to the wheel and kept driving. Though he was expecting another bump from behind, when it happened, the jolt still shook him up.

"Son of a bitch!" he screamed. Graham's eyes lifted to the rearview mirror. The asshole was still right on his tail. He was pointing over to the side of the road as if he were a traffic cop.

"Bastard!" He wasn't the only one making noise. Cars around them were flashing their brights and honking their horns. But that didn't slow either of them.

Le Croc played bumper tag once more. Then he pulled up alongside of Graham, again motioning for him to pull over. Graham was tired of his orders. He reached into his camera bag, pulled out a loaded camera, and autofocused with one finger. Shooting, steering, and screaming, he sprayed the flash like he would an automatic pistol. Le Croc recoiled; his car swerving into the next lane.

Graham grabbed his opportunity, pulling hard right on the wheel and angling toward the exit. Too late, Le Croc saw what he was doing. On wobbly wheels, he tried to stay with him. The two cars aimed for the opening of the Lac Superieur Tunnel.

Just before the tunnel's entrance, the Peugeot smashed the Citroën's left tail light, shattering glass. Then the two cars were side by side in a sea of sparks. Graham jockeyed for control, fighting to free himself from the other car's deadly embrace. Le Croc struggled just as desperately, evading metal on one side and concrete on the other. He shot ahead of the Citroën, and appeared to make it through the gap just as the blowout occurred.

To Graham, the Peugeot looked like a plane shot out of the sky. It was spewing smoke and violently rolling over and over. The car's corkscrewing ended at a concrete pillar. The collision was so violent that in the enclosed space of the tunnel it sounded like a bomb going off. With no time to think, Graham reacted. He pulled hard at his wheel and barely averted smashing into the wreck, mere inches separating him from the accident.

One hurried look of the mangled car was all that Graham got. Behind him he could hear the wail of the Peugeot's horn. It screamed at him like a fatally wounded animal. As fast as he was driving, he still couldn't outrun its sound. The wailing followed him throughout the tunnel and far beyond.

Three

They called him "Ivan the Terrible," but never to his face. Even behind his back, most were careful to whisper the nickname, afraid that he might somehow overhear. Ivan Proferov was a crime boss who claimed he came from Cossack stock. His forebears, he said, used to ride their horses along the Russian steppes, their blades running with blood. History seemed to be repeating itself. Proferov had risen in the Mafia ranks the old-fashioned way—by strong-arming his way up.

Signs of his trade could be seen in his custom wood-sided fish house. The two whores had passed out on ermine furs. One of them, the dyed redhead, was still clutching a bottle of Cristal champagne. Drugs were scattered along the folding table that also held imported cheeses, Danish sugar cookies, and Beluga caviar.

His father, whose idea of luxury had been to bring along a stool when he went ice fishing, wouldn't have approved of fishing this way. He had liked to brave the elements, his only concession to the cold an occasional sip of vodka. Ivan's father would have thought his fish house decadent, even without the whores. Outside it was freezing, but inside a thermostatic heating system was keeping the opulent American fish house warm. There was indoor carpeting, customized paneling, bench seating, a bathroom, and even running water. Ivan had stayed in dachas with fewer amenities.

The fish house had been driven right onto the ice, and lowered down with a hydraulic lift. Ivan had stayed in his Mercedes while one of the bodyguards had cut through the ice with a chainsaw.

No, his father wouldn't have approved at all, not of the way Ivan fished, nor the way he lived. His father had remained a loyal Communist even without the benefits of being a member of the party. His father had died a poor fool.

Ivan leaned over and looked into the dark water. So far he had only caught one fish, a scrawny little grayling. He had hoped for a string of big fish.

Maybe in the future he would go on a real fishing vacation to Lake Baikal. There were big fish there. But now wasn't a good time to stray from Moscow. Ever since Russia's Mafia godfather, Vyacheslav Ivankov, better known as Yaponchik, had been sentenced to ten years in an American prison, power struggles had been going on in the Solntsevskaya crime organization.

Big fish eating little fish. But that's how it had always been.

"Bite, you sons of bitches."

The blond whore mumbled something. Her hand reached up on its own, fumbled for cocaine, and dropped when it didn't find any. The redhead kept snoring.

He should probably bait the hooks again. Ivan had brought live minnows. No fake lures for him. His father used to always say that there were no shortage of stupid fish or stupid men ready to be lured by trinkets. Stupid fish, he lectured, never got to be big fish. And big fish, said his father, knew the difference between real food and fake food.

Maybe, thought Ivan, I should throw some of the caviar into the water. The big fish might awaken for that. His father had always done his ice fishing along the Moskva River. Ivan had decided to try his luck on the Ivankosky Reservoir, which was fed by the Volga River. Big fish lurked in the reservoir, huge pike, but none had paid him a visit yet.

"Bite, you sons of bitches."

Russians were serious about their ice fishing. The year before a floe of ice suddenly broke away from the shore, stranding a group of ice fishermen. The iceberg raft floated out to the open sea, and was soon lost to sight. A helicopter was dispatched for a rescue operation of the fishermen, but as it turned out no one was very keen on getting saved. The fish were finally biting and the fishermen were loath to leave their iceberg. Fistfights broke out over who could have the privilege of being rescued last. It didn't seem to matter to the men that their next stop was the Arctic Circle. The fish were biting, and that was what mattered.

It was a fish story, thought Ivan, but a true fish story.

Ivan could hear one of the bodyguards stomping his feet outside. There were a dozen men patrolling the area, all with Kalishnikovs. And not the old AK-47s, but the newer AKMs. Ivan paid his mercenaries top dollar. His back needed watching. There were men like Sergei Khramtsov with ambitions that couldn't be satisfied. Nothing was enough for Khramtsov. In that, they were alike.

"Bite, you sons of—"

Ivan cut short his oath. There was a pull on his line. A major pull. Oh, this was a fish. It was a monster, something that had come up from the depths to satisfy its hunger.

He began to slowly bring the line in. This wasn't a fish that was going to get away. He let the line play out a little, applying the brakes every few seconds. His prey would tire soon. Ivan didn't want to chance losing the hook.

There. He could feel it weakening. Ivan reeled on the line. The fish was getting closer. Soon he would be able to see it. He reeled some more and leaned over the hole. Ivan thought he saw a flash of silver. The fish was almost his.

The silver came closer, but the line suddenly went slack.

"Shit!"

Ivan pulled hard. He was sure he had lost the fish, but then something broke through the water's surface, something silver. His head was only two feet from the hole when the silenced pistol clicked.

The spray of blood woke up the redheaded whore. Bleary-eyed, she looked around. The assassin leveled his pistol at her, and then she dropped back onto the furs, a hole in her head. Even in death, she managed to hold on to the bottle of Cristal, never spilling a drop.

Not my brand, thought Jaeger. He made a point of only drinking Veuve Cliquot.

Jaeger removed his diving mask and looked around. The blood was soaking into the ice, but it would take some time before the red flow spread outside the fish house. Ivan's underlings wouldn't act until then. They would be afraid to interrupt their boss, especially when he was entertaining. Jaeger would be long gone by the time they found him, even though his car was more than two kilometers off. Proferov's goons had cleared the other ice fishermen from anywhere near their spot on the reservoir. Ivan had been careful, but not careful enough.

The second woman was still snoring. Jaeger couldn't chance her waking up in the next few minutes, so he raised his gun and fired. Something between a snore and a sigh escaped her lips, then she died.

The hole in the ice was too small for Jaeger to surface. There was barely room enough for his head. But he had come prepared. There was a small grappling hook in his pack threaded with heavy fishing line. Jaeger swung the hook and tossed it beyond Ivan the no-longer Terrible. He snagged Ivan and brought him forward to the hole. With a fishing knife, Jaeger removed the mobster's pants, cut off his dick, and stuck it in Ivan's mouth. The mob liked to leave calling cards like that. They would figure a larger shark had come calling, even if they didn't know which one.

Jaeger always practiced misdirection with his hits. No two kills were alike. Staying anonymous had extended his career, as did having the right contacts. His employer had told him that he "wasn't even a blip on any of the intelligence radar screens." His employer, Jaeger was sure, should know.

He took a last look at Proferov. Jaeger had served as a middleman between his employer and the Russian. The relationship had been very profitable, but then the Russian had started bragging about his "silent partner."

The silent partner had decided on the best course to stay silent.

The assassin opened up a special fold in his dry suit, and slipped his gun inside. He spat into his mask, rubbed the spittle around, and then rinsed it with water. He had to get going. His employer had another job for him, one he had labeled "most important."

A moment later, Jaeger disappeared under the ice.

Four

Graham stared down at the waters of the Bay of Biscay. The sea was turbulent below. The water's visibility was poor, boiling and roiling as the water pounded the rocks. There was no beach, no access to the water by any path. The rocks were too sharp and the drop too steep.

It was a good place for something—or someone—to disappear without a trace.

There were only a few radio stations Graham could pick up, a combination of the Citroën's substandard radio and his being in an out-of-the-way area. But no matter what voice came over the radio, or what language, there was only one story: the deaths of Le Croc and the Lady. Not since Princess Di's death a year before had there been such worldwide mourning. People were already talking about the similarities in the accidents. Paris tunnels had claimed them both. And there were the mysterious "other cars."

Witnesses to the accident described what looked like an escalating case of road rage. The gendarmes were already looking for a driver of a "white car" that was suspected of having had a run-in with the rented Peugeot. It would just be a matter of time before tests determined the make and model of car they were looking for.

The net was closing in.

And as if that wasn't enough, Graham had fled the scene of the accident. The scene of his crime. Even if he was judged innocent of everything else, he was guilty of leaving the accident without helping. In France that was a crime. On their books, everyone in France was required to be a "good

Samaritan." Authorities were using the accident to remind their citizens of their responsibility to offer assistance to the hurt or injured if at all possible. If convicted, he could be sentenced to up to five years in prison.

Five years, Graham thought. Even if he was sentenced to only a year or two, he probably wouldn't live out the time. The French prisoners wouldn't forgive the death of Le Croc. Around the world, there was a universal outpouring of grief for the deaths of Lady Godwin and Georges LeMoine. He would be a marked man in prison.

I could ask for solitary confinement, Graham thought. I could do my time that way.

But if he lived, there would be the prison sentence when he got out. He'd be a marked man, the notorious paparazzo who had helped kill two beloved figures. There would be no peace. He would be hounded—hounded by people like him. He would be on the other side of the camera. "Stalkerazzis," they were called. Or "Stalkernazis." People regarded them as parasites, not realizing that the stars and the star-catchers had a symbiotic relationship. Neither could exist without the other. It was the photographers flashing cameras that made the light that made the stars, but the stars forgot that once they were established in the firmament.

Maybe he would be lucky. It was possible no one could place him in the car. Rousseau had never seen it, and the Thierrys hadn't even known he was in town. He needed to destroy the evidence, and hope for the best.

Graham got back in the Citroën. He drove off the dirt road and steered it up a rocky pedestrian path, pushing at the accelerator until the Citroën's wheels were toeing the edge of the precipice.

He sat in the car longer than necessary, then finally put the car in neutral, pulled the hand brake, and got out. Graham placed some large stones under the tires. He wished the Citroën were an automatic. He could have put it in drive and let it commit suicide on its own. The stick meant he had to push it over the edge.

Graham released the hand brake, then put his shoulder into the vehicle. He only needed to push it maybe four feet, but it was an inch by inch turf war. Twice he pulled the brake and rested. Once, his foot almost gave. He caught himself, but just in time. He stopped and laughed over that one. Part of himself seemed to be observing this crazy man laughing. The car that killed the Lady and Le Croc had almost killed him as well. For some reason it seemed funny.

Gravity finally took over, and the Citroën plunged into the sea. Graham lay down in the dirt, his head resting over the cliff's edge. The car didn't sink right away. It listed for a few seconds before stubbornly giving up the battle and dropping from sight. For several minutes Graham stared into the angry water. The spot seemed well chosen. The sea would be his coconspirator. It would hide his secret.

Finally, Graham got up. He had a long walk back to the main road. Once there, Graham would use his thumb. He didn't care what direction his ride was going. His only plan was to go somewhere and get drunk. He needed to get shit-faced and forget everything that had happened.

Five

The copy of the *International Herald Tribune* was only a week old. News didn't reach Graham easily these days, and for the longest time he had been grateful of that. He had chosen isolation as his way of coping. Getting out of the news habit had been like kicking a drug addiction. It was different though, being a part of the story. It was as if he had been eaten by the beast. If that was the case, he was now only its remains, its scat.

For the longest time Graham had expected to be arrested. But now, if he could believe the story in his hands, he no longer needed to be afraid.

MYSTERY CAR INVESTIGATION ENDS

FEBRUARY 10, 1999, PARIS—Police investigating the deaths of French international football star Georges LeMoine and English philanthropist Lady Anne Godwin have decided to terminate their search for the so-called mystery car that is believed to have played a role in the crash that killed them.

Eyewitnesses to the August 28, 1998, crash reported seeing two cars engaged in a reckless race along the boulevard Peripherique, a throughway circling Paris. The fatal accident occurred just inside the entrance to the Lac Superieur Tunnel.

Police lab technicians analyzing paint traces found on the Peugeot LeMoine was driving determined the scrapings came from a Citroën CX manufactured in the "late eighties." Other car debris found at or near the accident scene was also linked to a Citroën CX.

Since the accident, Paris authorities have done physical inspections of thousands of Citroëns. Records indicate that in the Paris area alone there are well over one hundred thousand Citroëns that qualify for what one police official described as "the years in question."

This is the second "mystery car" that has eluded French authorities in the past two years. A Fiat Uno that was believed to have been involved in an accident just prior to the crash that killed Princess Diana was also never found.

Critics of the police investigations have questioned how such high-profile cars could just disappear. The police have defended their efforts, describing them as "exhaustive." Authorities say they have been hindered in their work by incomplete and misleading car registration records.

The driver of the Citroën is described as a white male with brown hair between the ages of 25 to 45.

Intense speculation has surrounded the deaths of LeMoine and Godwin. The two were believed to have been carrying on a secret short-term romance. Speculation was further fueled when Godwin's autopsy revealed she was in the early stages of pregnancy.

Police say that though they will not be conducting any more physical inspections of Citroëns, their investigation continues.

Graham read the article again. It didn't bring him the relief he thought it would. Now he had to get on with his life, a prospect he found more tiresome than exciting. His mind was made up though. It was time to leave.

Months before, Graham had received permission from the Abbot to stay at the Poblet Monastery in Spain. Now he was attempting to take his leave on a light note.

"So one celebrity photographer is talking to another," Graham said. "He says, 'I have this moral question for you.

" 'Mel Gibson is doing this scene in a raging river. Instead of using a stunt man, he's decided to be macho and do it himself. Well, things go wrong. His safety line snaps and he is holding on to this tree limb for dear life. You can see he's weakening. If he lets go, he is facing certain death because the whitewater is raging straight toward this killer waterfall.

" 'So,' this photographer says, 'you can either drop your camera and save Mel, or you can take this million-dollar picture of him losing his grip and being swept away to his death.

" 'Now your moral dilemma is, what kind of lens do you use?' "

The Abbot laughed. Mirth became him, but if Graham thought he was going to let him leave without a final session of soul searching, he was wrong.

"So tomorrow your pilgrimage comes to an end?" The Abbot's question came with a smile.

"It never was a pilgrimage," Graham said.

"What would you call it then?"

Prison? Penance? A hideaway? Graham rejected the easy answers. "A walk that resulted from a case of mistaken identity."

"Maybe that old woman knew what she was doing."

Graham shook his head. "She needed glasses."

"There are times when eyes can get in the way of truly seeing."

"She was blind as a bat. And I was as drunk as an Irishman at a wake."

"Sober, were you?"

The Abbot was Irish. In his time at the monastery Graham had gradually told the Abbot about the accident. The story had been related in bits and pieces. Now he was at its beginning—and its end.

"After ditching the Citroën, I hitched a ride and ended up in Roncesvalle. I don't think the place has changed too much since Roland and his horn put in on the map.

"I started drinking as soon as I arrived in town. *In vino veritas*. That was part of my problem, Irish. The more I tried to escape their deaths, the more they seemed to follow me. Even in Roncesvalle they were in mourning. They were burning candles for them. Stores were draped in black."

"And how did that make you feel?" the Abbot asked.

"Angry. Guilty."

He looked around the Abbot's study, did his best to avoid his eyes. The room was old. Much of the Poblet Monastery had been built in the Middle Ages. The cloister and chapel of St. Stephen, and the infirmary, dated back to the twelfth century. The abbey had stood the test of time. Behind the Abbot's desk was an old wooden bookshelf. Its bookstands were ancient as well; seven elaborately carved figurines depicting the Deadly Sins, or what the Abbot called the "Cardinal Sins." Staring out from the books were the embodiment of pride, lust, envy, anger, covetousness, gluttony, and sloth.

Reminders of the real world, thought Graham.

The Abbot said nothing, waiting on Graham to continue. "Even in that sleepy Spanish town I found reminders of them everywhere. I decided I wasn't drunk enough, and I went in search of my cantina, but it seemed to have moved. I didn't know what I was doing or where I was going.

"Earlier I had picked up a backpack, a hat, and some clothes. That's what I was wearing when the old woman stopped me. You've heard my Spanish when I'm sober. I can halfway carry on a conversation. But I was drunk, and shell-shocked, and it was all I could do to stand up straight.

"The old woman was very serious. She kept talking about her son Hernando. I dutifully repeated his name several times, and did a lot of nodding as if I understood what she was saying, the drunk pretending to be on top of his game. Only at the end did I realize that I was agreeing to pray for her sick son at the Santiago de Compostela.

"I was thinking too slowly to clarify the situation. I let the old woman believe I was something that I wasn't. She kissed my hand a few times and gave me these penitent bows as she shuffled backward. Me."

The Abbot nodded. "You were the pilgrim she chose."

"I was the drunk she got, Irish. How was I to know that Roncesvalle was the kickoff point for the Camino?"

El Camino de Santiago—the way of Saint James—is a five-hundred-mile path that pilgrims have walked for more than a thousand years. It begins in Roncesvalle and continues west almost to the Spanish coast.

"The old woman needed someone to carry her prayer, and there you were."

"And I needed an excuse to drop out of the world. What better way to do it than a five-hundred-mile walk?"

"You could have dropped out by vacationing on some tropical island."

"But I was in Roncesvalle. I figured a long walk would clear my head, but not even forty days of walking could do that. Someone on the Camino mentioned this place, so I ended up here."

"We made an exception by taking you in. We don't usually accommodate outsiders."

"Why did you?"

"I had this sense that your pilgrimage wasn't finished. And I could see your heart was still troubled."

"You must have X-ray vision then."

"What do you mean?"

"People who know me would tell you I have a heart of stone."

"You mislead them."

"If I have misled anyone, it's you. I stare at those seven sins on your bookshelf, and they wink at me, and tell me it's time to get back to my work. I've had enough of sackcloth and ashes, Irish."

"Are you sure that's a raiment you ever wore?"

Graham shook his head. "No. I'm not sure of anything. I wish I could say that this experience somehow changed me for the better, but I'd be lying if I did.

"My walk, and my playing at monkdom, were just ways of killing time."

"And now you'll leave and act as if nothing ever happened?"

"If I'm lucky. The French police are still on the case, but it looks like I fell through the cracks."

"So it's back to work?"

"That's the plan."

The Abbot didn't hide his skepticism: "I wish you luck with your plan."

"People do get on with their lives, you know."

"So I have heard."

"What's my alternative? Would I be better off in a French prison?"

They had always skirted that subject. Graham had been afraid of hearing the Abbot's answer.

"Maybe you should be asking yourself *how* you should spend your time," the Abbot said, "instead of asking *where* you should spend it."

He paused for a long moment before continuing. "But I think you can better pay off your debt outside of prison than inside it."

"What debt?"

"Your actions contributed to lives being lost. You need to acknowledge that."

"It was his driving that killed them."

"Then why do you sound so angry?"

Graham confronted the face of anger among the bookshelf figures. His eyes were popping out, his cheeks red, his mouth pursed. The contorted face seethed hatred. I'm looking at my face, Graham thought.

It was too late to explain to the Abbot about Rio. Graham couldn't shake this feeling that Rio had been a warning. Intellectually he knew that was a lot of superstitious bunk, but there it was. Death had tapped him on the shoulder and he had ignored it.

"Because now I'm the one with the dirty secret."

"Is that what they had? A dirty secret?"

"I suspected the romance, but not that she was pregnant. Usually I have all the angles figured out. When I think back, it should have been obvious. I even heard them talking about the baby, though I didn't make the connection at the time. It was difficult hearing what they were saying, and I didn't fill in the blanks until later."

"She was there to make a courtesy call, is that it?"

Graham nodded. "She evidently wanted a face-to-face with him before her condition became known, or obvious. Maybe it was the last time she ever planned to see him, and she wanted to get things straight between them. I know she was already thinking about her unborn child, and was trying to be careful to not complicate an already difficult situation."

LeMoine was engaged, and she had her foundation to operate. They first met when he had handed her a well-publicized check of one million pounds for her charity. A short-lived relationship ensued, one they kept secret, but with one huge ramification.

"She was afraid of saddling her child with the famous name of the father," said Graham. "I think she wanted as normal a life as possible for her baby. She was also afraid that LeMoine's contributions would look tainted if their relationship was known. The Lady had already been condemned by many for taking off her clothes for charity. She probably knew there were those who would have categorized a romance with such a generous donor as prostitution. But it was anything but that. I know. I saw."

Graham heard it in their voices, and saw it in their regard for one another. Their dying together and the subsequent revelation of her pregnancy had resulted in all sorts of tawdry speculation.

"Do you think you have an obligation to set the record straight?" asked the Abbot.

"Not at my expense. They were public figures. If you embrace the upside of fame, you have to accept the lumps of the downside."

"They received more than lumps."

"He was the one who was driving like a madman. He just wouldn't quit."

"That's what made him what he was."

"And that's what makes me what I am. You think anyone ever says, 'Oh, the poor paparazzo'? No one hands me my shots. I have to scratch and dig and hustle for them. Was I just supposed to roll over?"

The Abbot's calm voice contrasted with Graham's vehemence. "You tell me."

"No. Hell no."

"Don't you think people are entitled to some privacy?"

"People. Not public figures. That's the key word: public."

"There's no sanctity in anything? Would you monitor a confessional booth?"

"Don't give me any ideas."

"It seems to me you find it easier to be angry than to face your sadness."

"In my trade, a conscience is a hindrance. I don't need that dead weight. I don't want it."

"Then find a way to remove it. That will allow you to forgive yourself."

Graham shook his head. That wasn't him. This was all too silly. A paparazzo needs his thick skin. Self-help lectures weren't for the likes of him. The heat was off now. He was free and clear, and it was time to get back to work. But he wasn't ready for Hollywood yet. He needed a war instead. A civil war, that was the ticket.

Graham consulted the faces of the figurines and settled on Pride. There was a sneer on Pride's face, almost a disdain. Pride had seen it all. Graham took note of his resemblance to the figurine. Asking him to change his face was like asking a leopard to change his spots.

The Abbot reached into his desk and brought out two glasses. He poured a few fingers of brandy into each glass, and passed one over to Graham. The two men raised their glasses to one another, clicked them lightly.

"Happy trails," said the Abbot. He was a fan of westerns, and had told Graham on several occasions that it was a shame that Hollywood didn't make those kinds of pictures anymore. The Abbot had once confessed to Graham how upset he was when John Wayne had died, and how he still remembered exactly what he had been doing, and where he was, when he heard the bad news.

The thought came to Graham, unbidden and unwanted, that many people remembered the precise moment when they heard Le Croc and the Lady died.

Damn their intrusion into his life.

The men drank in silence for a few minutes, each of them contemplating sunsets. The Abbot finished his glass, put it down with a sigh. He always limited himself to the one. There was something on his mind, something nagging at him.

He asked, "Did you ask for a blessing for that old woman's son when you reached the cathedral?"

Graham picked up his drink, sipped, shrugged, then sipped again. He didn't answer directly. The last ritual of the Camino was to touch the figure of Santiago. To get to it, you climbed a narrow staircase that went behind the altar. Santiago's cloak is silver. In one hand he carries a walking staff, in the other a scallop shell.

"I touched his walking stick for luck, and as I did I said one word: 'Hernando.' I probably should have said more."

But saying that one word, Graham remembered, was hard enough. He was a skeptic and a cynic, not a pilgrim. At journey's end, Graham neglected to have his last *credentiale* validated at the pilgrims office. The Church would never recognize his journey. He even skipped the free meal the Hotel de los Reyes offered to any that walked the Camino.

"You didn't pause to offer any other prayers? Not even one for yourself?"

Graham shook his head.

The Abbot smiled. "When I offer up prayers to Santiago de Compostela—Saint James of the Starry Field—I will remember you as well."

"Thank you."

"You will be in good company. Santiago de Compostela is the patron saint of Spain."

"Who's the patron saint of lost causes?"

"Saint Jude."

"I'd feel more at home being remembered with him."

The Abbot nodded as if taking Graham's comment seriously. He raised his glass. "*Vayo con Dios*."

Six

Graham struggled to awaken. At some level of consciousness he knew something was wrong. He was usually instantly awake and alert, but this time just thinking straight was a struggle.

At first he thought he was back in Kosovo, where he had gone after Spain. Graham had almost felt at home there. He didn't have to look hard for horror stories. Rape, murder, pillage, and ethnic cleansing—they had it all. There were no shortage of subjects for his camera. In the face of such atrocities, Graham could almost feel good about himself.

But everything had a way of twisting itself back to Paris. When he was led to a mass grave, he thought of the Paris catacombs, and when he heard about such terrible Serb atrocities as killing babies, he didn't feel so superior.

Still, he felt as comfortable in Kosovo as he could have anywhere. There was plenty of guilt for all to share. The Serbs killed the ethnic Albanians, then the Albanians killed the Serbs. The area had a long and bloody history that no one could feel good about. Graham shot the ravages of war, and the plight of the victims and the dispossessed, until there came a time when no one cared about Kosovo anymore. The market for pictures dried up. He considered finding another war zone. The hazards were many, and the stringer pay low, but misery loves company.

His head was clearing. No, he wasn't in Kosovo. He had decided to come home. The sounds of crashing waves filtered through his hazy mind, and he knew that wasn't right either. His apartment wasn't anywhere near the ocean. He opened his eyes and found he wasn't lying on his bed, but on a metal decking. And he still heard waves.

Graham sat up and looked around. He was atop some kind of tower. A floating tower. There was water on all sides. He started to get to his feet when a voice came out of the darkness:

"I wouldn't wander too far. You might be dizzy, and it's a long drop."

The speaker materialized. He was taller than average, and carried himself with the confidence of someone used to giving orders. He had a long, gray face that would have suited a cadaver. It was made even more ghoulish by his smile. If the smile was supposed to make Graham feel better, it didn't.

Graham tried to hide his shaking. It was cold, but not that cold. He was wearing a coat that wasn't his.

"I was drugged."

The man nodded. There was no thought, or even hint, of apology.

"Who are you?"

"Call me Mr. Smith."

"John Smith, I suppose."

"Or Adam."

Graham's head was clearing, and his eyes were getting used to the darkness. They were on an oil rig and in the far distance he could see lights on the shore. He guessed at their location: "Is that Santa Barbara?"

A nod. Somehow he had been taken from his apartment and transported to an oil rig off the Santa Barbara coast. The drive alone was close to a hundred miles, not to mention the logistics of getting him from shore to the oil rig.

"Why am I here?"

"I wanted to meet with you."

"Hell of a place for a meeting."

"I thought it would suit our needs."

"What's wrong with a Hilton?"

"It was necessary to ensure our privacy."

"You're a spook." Graham wasn't asking a question so much as speaking aloud. There had been men like this on the periphery of all the armed conflicts Graham had covered.

"I'm in intelligence, yes."

"Which acronym?"

"Does it matter?"

"I suppose not. You'll have to pardon my curiosity for wanting to know who shanghaied me."

Graham eased his way over to the edge of the platform, cleared his throat, and spat out toward the dark sea.

"It was difficult tracking you down," Smith said. "One day you were a successful paparazzo, and the next you just vanished."

"I'd had enough of the trade and needed a break."

"There was speculation you had a drug and alcohol problem. You were doing some serious binging. The word was that you were drying out."

"I was."

"At a monastery in Poblet, Spain? I understand you even led the life of a lay brother."

"I tried to earn my daily bread."

"You weren't raised a Catholic."

"I wasn't raised much of anything."

"Despite that, you spent six months at a Cistercian community being your basic Benedictine monk. You chose to live behind medieval rock walls and live the life of an ascetic."

"My liver needed that."

"Your liver or your soul?"

Graham didn't answer.

"You've never spoken of your monk days with anyone, and no one knows you were there."

"Then how do you know?"

The man who called himself Smith continued on as if Graham hadn't spoken. "I'm surprised you lasted a day in the monastery. You've always had a problem with authority. At Poblet you had to rise before dawn. There were no comforts of modern life. You had to follow rules, something you've had a notable problem of doing throughout your history."

"Their rules made sense to me."

"That's a first. In the dozen years you've been a mercenary with a camera, no one has ever doubted your skill with a lens, or your photographic instincts, but your detractors always thought you too aggressive, and not a team player. That's why you never managed to last with any newspaper or magazine. You've always disregarded any rules or guidelines that got in your way. During the Gulf War you defied military orders and refused to stay behind with the other journalists. You somehow procured a Jeep and drove it into Iraqi territory. You were arrested by Iraqi armed forces, and detained in their custody for over a month."

Smith offered a condescending smile. "Your colleagues said that probably ended the war sooner than anything else."

"The government was setting up Kodak picture moments," said Graham. "I wanted something more than that."

"After the war, because you were perceived as a loose cannon, you had trouble finding work."

"I was blackballed."

"So even though you've always fancied yourself a photojournalist, you went back to being a paparazzo, something you've been doing off and on since the late eighties."

Graham wondered where this was all going.

"You took a leave of absence though. You abruptly quit for a time. Something happened on August 28, 1998, that made you stop."

There it was. He knew. *They* knew. Graham didn't look up. He turned and stared out at the water. He was almost too numb to think. His stomach felt as if someone had taken a bat to it, and his throat was too tight to even swallow.

"You were in the Citroën that was sideswiped moments before the accident in the tunnel that killed Lady Godwin and Georges LeMoine."

Graham said nothing. Smith was doing more than exposing his Achilles' heel. His every word was wrenching out what Graham had thought was his terrible secret. His—not the world's. Graham pictured the crash, just as he had remembered it thousands of times before.

"I assume you were playing a little photo tag."

Still not looking at him, Graham worked up enough spit to answer, but his words were spoken as much to himself as to Smith. "He was trying to run me off the road."

"I'm sure he was. But the big question is: would he have lost control if it weren't for you?"

Graham had played that "what if" game too many times by himself. He didn't answer.

"It's rather amazing," said Smith, "that you got away with it. You kept expecting the other shoe to drop. And you knew that when that information came out, you'd be the most reviled man on earth."

Graham finally turned and looked at his interrogator. He wondered where all of this was leading.

"How did you get rid of the car?"

"I dumped it in the Bay of Biscay."

Smith nodded. "What did you do with your pictures of them?"

Graham said nothing.

"You wouldn't have been involved in a high-speed chase if you didn't have film of them. What happened to it?"

"I destroyed it."

Smith shook his head in disbelief. "How could you have done that? That film was worth a fortune."

"It could have convicted me."

"I know a certain collector who doesn't suffer from moral or ethical qualms. He'd pay a considerable amount for those pictures."

"I wish I had them to sell, but I don't."

"Are you quite certain? I am confident I could get you six figures."

"Why are you so interested?"

"As the broker, I would benefit as well."

Graham shook his head. "I can't sell what I don't have."

Smith shook his head. "That's a shame. Enough others cashed in on their deaths. You and your kind helped make them icons. They'll always be young and beautiful and immortal."

"Small consolation."

"What surprises me is that it got to you, Wells. No paparazzo has ever been mistaken for a social worker. Most of your ilk would trample your grandmother to get a good picture. Word is, that goes double for you. Hard as nails is how people describe you. Thick-skinned and uncaring. Yet you ended up hiding away in a monastery for six months before slipping out of your robes to play photojournalist in the killing fields of Kosovo. Tell me, were you hoping for redemption, or did you just want to get killed?"

"I don't know."

"Finally, the prodigal son has returned home. Now you're back in Hollywood, just like old times."

Graham thought about all that he had heard and been told. Smith's being there still didn't make sense. As a photographer, he wondered where he was in the picture. Smith finally answered that.

"We need your services, Mr. Wells."

"Who is *we*?"

"You will be serving the interests of the United States government."

"You sure you have the right guy?"

"Very sure."

"What services are you talking about?"

"Your assisting us through your paparazzo work."

Graham started laughing. It was either that or cry. "You want me to gather intelligence in Hollywood? That's an oxymoron."

"From time to time we'll need you to study certain individuals who could potentially be working to undermine our government."

Graham shook his head. "Why me? You guys are the cloak-and-dagger experts. All I do is say 'cheesecake.' "

"Hollywood is not our bailiwick. Our agents would stand out. In your case, you don't have to worry about being low profile." Smith offered his supercilious smile again. "Like us, your job deals in gathering information."

"I'm a sneak, not a spy."

"Of course, you are free to refuse. It would be a shame though, if certain information fell into the hands of the French government."

Smith had a vise on his balls. Graham knew there was no choice. The thought of prison was daunting enough, but even worse would be his having to face up to what had happened in Paris.

"What would I have to do?"

"Your job, and nothing else. But on very rare occasions, we might narrow your focus to a certain target or event."

"How many people know about the accident?"

"Only a handful. If you cooperate, your secret will always be safe."

"And I'll just be on your string forever."

"A few years at most, and a few assignments."

"And that's it?"

"That's it."

Graham offered a small nod. It was enough for Smith.

"When we need you, the caller will identify you by your code name of—"

Smith paused, and offered that smile again.

"Pilgrim."

Seven

Pilgrim."

The one word brought everything back. It had been a month since Graham had encountered Smith on the oil platform, and even then the mystery man had stayed in the shadows, never allowing himself to be fully seen. Smith made him relive the shame of Paris, and when the spook finished talking and offered his gloating smile, Graham felt as if he had been physically beaten. It hadn't taken much to break him, Graham thought, but then he had already laid much of that groundwork himself.

Graham remembered Smith directing his glance to a spot somewhere above and behind him, and then had noticed his almost imperceptible nod. A moment later Graham felt a sharp pain. He tried to reach behind him and probe where it hurt, but his coordination was suddenly shaky. He fell to one knee, and when he tried to get up, his other leg gave out on him. Several times he attempted to rise, though a part of his mind knew he was doing little more than rocking from side to side.

When Graham awakened the next morning in his own bed, his back was very sore, and there was a bandage that hadn't been there before. He assumed a tranquilizer dart had been used on him, though his memory of the night was shaky enough that he could almost think of it as a dream.

Until now.

"Pilgrim."

Not a dream, thought Graham. Just a lingering nightmare.

"I'm listening," Graham said.

"In the future," Smith said, "do not try and record our conversations."

Knowing that Smith would eventually have to come to him, Graham had installed a voice-activated telephone recording unit. They knew about him, and about *it*. He felt the need to know about them.

"I don't know what—"

"Don't lie or waste my time."

Smith probably had one of those phones that alerted him to recording devices. That was the problem with gizmos, Graham thought. If you relied on them, eventually you encountered someone with more gizmos.

"When you play back your tape," Smith said, "you won't find my voice on it. I am calling from a secure line with a bypass setup that makes it untraceable, and a baffle that makes it impossible for any recording device to pick up my voice. Nonetheless, be warned that any future attempt to record our conversations will result in your losing that beach-boy tan you currently possess."

Smith's threat revealed to Graham that he was being monitored: Graham's skin was bronzed from a recent outdoors assignment. It was possible Smith had him in his sights that very moment. Graham moved away from the windows into the shadows.

"Your target is Joseph Cannon," Smith said.

In the industry, Cannon was a well-known director, with two nominations for Academy Awards. Still, his name wasn't a household word.

"Why Cannon? Celebrity photographers ignore directors unless their last names are Spielberg, Lucas, Scorsese, or Tarantino."

Smith didn't answer, save to say, "Give him your full attention for a week, starting tomorrow."

"Is there anything in particular I'm supposed to be looking for?"

"Your usual."

Smith hung up before Graham could ask him any other questions.

His usual, thought Graham. Smith, in his supercilious tones, had made that sound like something rather unsavory.

Graham played back the tape, and listened to a one-way conversation with himself. Like all good spooks, Smith had vanished without a trace.

Joseph Cannon liked young men.

That was hardly a sin in Hollywood, but having sex with a minor was. Graham caught Cannon and actor Mitch McCoy cavorting with four attractive and youthful men in an exclusive clothing-optional Palm Springs retreat. Cannon should have checked the birth certificate of one of the young men. From what Graham saw, the minor acted like anything but an innocent, but what mattered was that he was sixteen.

It wasn't a new story. Cannon could have learned from any of a number of headlines that preceded his. Director Roman Polanski's sexual relationship with a thirteen-year-old girl resulted in his fleeing the United States never to return. And Charlie Chaplin and Errol Flynn drew the wrath of a nation for consorting with young girls.

When Graham's pictures ran in the tabloids, Cannon got dropped from a big film he was supposed to direct, McCoy stopped being considered a leading man for anything, and the minor got his fifteen minutes of fame.

As for Graham, he wondered what the hell his assignment had to do with national security. Something about the work made Graham feel as if he were a hooker decoy doing john patrol. He wondered if he was just being tested, or whether there really was some good reason for Cannon being targeted.

Months had passed between Graham's last conversation with Smith when the phone rang in the middle of the night. In Graham's profession, that wasn't uncommon. Late-night clubs attracted many of the younger actors, and Hollywood soirees often ran late. But Graham knew intuitively that Smith was on the other line. His heart was racing when he picked up the phone.

"Pilgrim."

Graham tried to stop the pounding of his heart. The middle of the night was when goon squads always did their best work. That was when the Gestapo had liked to descend on the innocent, when Stalin's thugs wreaked havoc. Nixon's dirty tricks boys used to make calls after midnight on "behalf" of George McGovern and the Democratic National Committee while pretending to be African-Americans. There was no better time to intimidate than when waking someone from a deep sleep.

"Why don't you try calling during banking hours?"

Smith didn't acknowledge his protest. "We need Haley Robinson put under your lens."

"Half the photographers in L.A. are already covering her."

Robinson was coming off a breakthrough movie and was being offered most of the plum roles in town. She was blond and had a huge smile, with teeth bright enough to attract moths.

"Miss Robinson has a problem," Smith told Graham. "She's a kleptomaniac. Somehow this has escaped the attention of the world. You are to immediately remedy that."

"And what is there about her petty thievery that interests the government?"

"Perhaps you're right. Maybe there are other matters that should concern us more, such as an accident in Paris."

Smith let the words hang in the air for long enough for Graham to feel like a bug with a foot overhead.

"Do your job, Pilgrim," he finally said, then hung up.

Blackmail is a great motivator. Graham studied Haley's haunts and her routines and found ways to photograph her surreptitiously. Graham colluded with one waiter to set up a hidden camera above her secluded table at her favorite restaurant. It was a pinhole photography job, the camera placed in the ceiling with a time-lapse shot every three seconds. The film was special order—a thousand shots to a single roll—and cost an arm and a leg. While positioning the camera, Graham kept thinking about exercise-room pictures once taken of Princess Diana. She had been working out in a London gym, and a hole had been cut in a ceiling panel where the gym's owner had installed a hidden camera. The *Sunday Mirror* paid a quarter of a million dollars for photos that showed Diana in spandex cycling shorts with her legs spread apart. Diana couldn't even sweat in private. The pictures were splashed across the tabloids.

Just like Haley's "KLEPTO!" pictures. At the restaurant she was caught on film taking a ramekin, a section of the centerpiece, and a steak knife. Graham also got pictures of her stealing a stapler at a charity function and slipping two softballs into her oversized purse at a celebrity softball game.

Haley's sticky fingers gained national attention, and her thievery became fodder for every would-be comedian. She "stole" scenes. The ten million she received for her last picture "evidently just wasn't enough for her to make ends meet." Surprise, surprise: Haley was having another "really big" garage sale.

The publicity caused Haley to drop out of a picture just before the shoot was to begin. Her publicist announced she would be undergoing "therapy" for her problem. That started a new wave of jokes: the therapist wondering aloud what had happened to the pen he was using to take notes, the shrink's office looking more sparsely furnished each week.

The Haley jokes would soon pass, Graham knew. He only hoped she knew it. Not a month went by without some actor having to work his way through an embarrassing situation. Rob Lowe was still making pictures long after his infamous three-way video surfaced; Hugh Grant's boyish screen charm survived his tawdry arrest for backseat oral sex with a hooker; Paul (Pee Wee Herman) Reuben's career outlasted his arrest in an adult theater and all the ensuing jokes.

The world loved a good Hollywood scandal, then forgot about it. Hollywood's memory was almost as selective. Tinseltown could forgive anything but a flop. It wasn't judgmental. And Graham couldn't afford to be.

Eight

Jaeger was out big game hunting. His chosen watering hole was a Hollywood tittie bar called Jugs and Mugs. He was searching for a very large man, one over six feet three, and weighing at least 350 pounds.

The sign in front of the strip bar described it as a *Gentleman's Club*. Emily Post might have had qualms with that description. Judging by the parking lot, most of the club's clientele were bikers. Hogs and trucks with lots of chrome dominated the area. Jaeger parked his paneled van on the street.

The club's sound system was loud enough to rival the comings and goings of the Harleys. Heavy rock. Appropriate, Jaeger thought, for what he needed.

A bouncer silently collected money from Jaeger. The man was big, but not big enough for his purposes. He was over three hundred pounds, but only stood about five-nine. Jaeger needed to work with more area than that.

He stepped inside the club, stood a few moments to let his eyes adjust to the darkness and his ears to the noise. A woman wearing a low-cut tropical sarong materialized in front of him with a drink tray and pad.

"Can I get you a cocktail?"

Jaeger asked what kind of beer they had. He eliminated the American piss-water and settled on an Amstel. While waiting for his drink, he looked for the best observation post. A long rectangular stage took up most of the club's space. Off to the side was a game room. The stage had poles on both ends. At the moment, one of the dancers was swinging on the south pole.

If Jaeger went ringside, he'd have a good view of the dancers, but little else. The tables above the stage offered a better vantage point, but they were reserved for parties of three or more.

Jaeger's eyes settled on the bar. It was purposely small, only five stools, designed as a walk-up bar for the servers to collect their drinks, but it would afford him a central location. He collected his beer, tipped generously enough to have some ridiculously long eyelashes batted at him, then claimed one of the two empty seats at the bar. Jaeger slowly swiveled around on his bar stool. He had a good view of the entrance and the stage, and could see anyone entering or exiting the game room, which consisted of the usual pool tables and video games.

As the loud music concluded, the club DJ worked on the crowd. "All right," she said with her whiskey voice, "get your hands out of your pants and use them for something useful. Put them together and give Amber a big hand."

As Amber slowly gathered her clothes, and her tips, Jaeger's eyes passed over her, more interested in the audience than Amber, looking for his fat man.

"Hey," the DJ said, "I was a Girl Scout once, but I got kicked out of my troop. They caught me eating Brownies."

Jaeger searched for double chins, red faces, and biker vests stretched far too tight. There was no shortage of those things.

"And now we have Tiffany coming on stage," said the DJ. "Let me hear how much you want her."

The lukewarm response prompted the DJ to say, "Geez, you guys need Viagra." Her challenge was met with more applause.

"That's a little better. Tiffany comes to us from Canada. And she knows how to warm up her Mounties on a cold night."

The music blared over the speakers. Subtle it wasn't, but neither was Tiffany. Jaeger signaled the bartender for another beer, and then went back to looking for his fat man. With the men seated, and the room dark, it was difficult to determine if anyone out there met his criteria. A few of them had potential, Jaeger decided, but he wasn't sure if any had quite the mass he needed. For appearance's sake, Jaeger did his looking while he eyeballed the dancers. They performed to three songs, progressively losing all their clothing.

The dancers blended together. All of them looked alike, sporting the same dyed blond hair, overdone raccoon eyeliner, and oversized boobs. As far as Jaeger could determine, every stripper there had undergone cosmetic surgery. The result was performers whose chests didn't jiggle, didn't bounce. They just took up space, lots of it.

Jaeger smiled to himself. Stuffed human flesh. Oh, yes, he'd come to the right place. Before the night was over he hoped to be performing some plastic surgery himself.

He was at the bar for almost an hour before the first real possibility walked into the club. The man was big—probably six feet five—with a long, round torso. His hair was long, dark, and slicked back, and he had a full Fu Manchu mustache that extended almost to his chin.

Fifteen minutes later another huge man entered the club. The man mountain found two open chairs on the opposite side of the stage from where Fu was sitting. He needed the vacancies—he was on the north side of four hundred pounds, both heavier and wider than Fu. The hair on top of his head was thinning, the only visible part of his hirsute body short of wiry reddish hair. Erik the Red, thought Jaeger. The man looked like a Viking.

Jaeger divided his attention between Fu and Red. To appearances, he was suddenly much more interested in what was occurring onstage. It seemed appropriate that Fu had the south pole and Red the north. Both men commanded their own space. If they were any larger, they might have had their own moons.

When Fu was joined by friends, Jaeger started focusing more on Red. The man's salami-sized fingers were rarely still, thumping out the beat of the music on the stage. He liked to stroke his beard, rub his nose, and scratch at his pelt. It wasn't only testosterone. Jaeger suspected Red of being a pill popper, probably wired on crank. He wasn't thin like most speed freaks, but the way he drank beer could account for that. Red was downing a full pitcher every half hour.

He was probably a dealer too, judging by the way the performers singled him out for their gyrations. Or maybe it was just that Red tipped well. When the women danced in front of him he studied them with the scrutiny of a gynecologist before peeling a five-dollar bill from a large roll and dropping it on the counter.

It was just before midnight when Red raised himself for the second time in half an hour and made his way over to the rest room. Jaeger suspected he wasn't only getting rid of the beer. As had happened with his earlier visit to the john, Red returned more boisterous, and bright-eyed, and amped.

Jaeger had seen enough. Red would probably close down the bar, but that was fine with him. Better that Jaeger be seen leaving well before the big man.

He waited out in his van, and as he suspected, it wasn't until 2:00 A.M. that Red left the bar. Jaeger was pleased to see that he was alone.

Red started his bike. It was overly loud, even by Harley standards. The hog was fixed up in a Nazi motif, its mirror shaped in the form of an Iron Cross, and silver SS lightning bolts airbrushed on both sides of its black fuel tank. Red's helmet was Third Reich with a Darth Vader glossy finish.

The motorcycle patched out of the parking lot, and Jaeger kept far back, letting the bike fade in and out of visual range. He wasn't worried about losing it. The motorcycle was so loud he could have followed it blind.

Red avoided the freeways, traveling east on mostly deserted roads. He might have been mindful of the highway patrol, or maybe he thought he could make better time on the back streets. Jaeger considered ramming the van into the bike, but that would mean accident evidence to worry about, paint and metal that police techs would try and match up. Still, that wasn't the determining factor. Honor wouldn't be served that way. There were good ways to make a kill, and bad ways. Given a choice, Jaeger always chose the good way.

Up well ahead, Red made a left. Jaeger accelerated, closing the distance between them. The bike's brake lights flashed red before making a right turn into the parking lot of a large apartment complex. Jaeger followed behind, driving by a security gate that looked as if it had been broken for years.

Red pulled his bike under an overhang. Despite the late hour, and the proximity of other apartments, he seemed in no hurry to cut his engine. Jaeger slowly drove forward along the asphalt, scanning the setting. No one was around, and Red was out of sight of the apartment windows that overlooked the parking lot. The area appeared to be clear of any people. The plan was still a go. Jaeger was glad of that; the alternative was to stake out a greasy spoon off of Interstate 5 and wait for an oversized trucker. He much preferred to act now.

Jaeger pulled in next to the still thundering motorcycle. He walked over to Red, reached out with his hand, and the hog was suddenly silenced.

"They call that the kill button, don't they?" said Jaeger.

Red looked at him in disbelief. No one touched his bike.

"I know all about kill buttons," Jaeger said.

"What the fuck do you want?"

"I have need of your body."

"You fucking faggot."

Red stepped off his bike. He was wearing thick black Doc Martens shit-kicking boots with metal toes. They clicked sparks on the asphalt, a bull charging. Red reached his slab of a hand out to grab Jaeger, but only caught air.

"Human flesh stretches. Think of all those breasts you were looking at tonight stuffed with silicone and saline."

"Fucking faggot followed me home."

Red swung at Jaeger, but missed. As the smaller man backed away, he kept talking: "I need to stuff you like a Strasbourg goose. That's not only an expression. The goose is force-fed, stuffed so full of food and water that its liver distends. Have you ever had paté? Such a wonderful taste for such a cruel act."

The big man lashed out with his oversized right boot, trying to knock Jaeger's feet from under him, but again didn't connect. For someone so large he was agile, but still all too predictable.

Jaeger pulled out two stilettos, but instead of brandishing their points he extended their handles. "Your choice of weapons," he said.

Red shook his head. He didn't really smile, but he showed his teeth. "Don't need to choose," he said. "I've got my own."

He pulled up his T-shirt. A scabbard hung from the inside of his dirty jeans. He yanked at the hasp and pulled out an enormous bowie knife.

Red ran a mocking finger down his face. "It's time to give you another fucking scar on that face of yours."

Jaeger's scar was prominent, stretching down from his cheek almost to his mouth, a long, white line that marred his otherwise handsome features.

"I learned from that mistake," Jaeger said. He flipped both stilettos in the air, and caught them by their handles. He pocketed one, then held the other out almost casually. He waited for the other man to make his move, his knees and shoulders slightly bent.

It was a truly enormous man against one little more than average-sized. In comparison to the thin little stiletto, the bowie knife looked monstrous.

The contest was hardly fair. Red, with his long reach, lunged. Jaeger slipped inside and let Red's thrust do most of his work for him. Red looked at his own chest in disbelief. He couldn't see any rip in his shirt, and reached down and felt where the blade had entered. There was just a little blood, yet something was very wrong. Red had once taken two bullets, but it was the shooter who ended up going to the ICU, not him.

The fight wasn't over, Red thought. It couldn't be. They hadn't really even started yet. Red took a step toward Jaeger, and then another. He staggered, then dropped to one knee. His body had never failed him. He tried to rise, almost succeeded, but then fell over.

Jaeger used a fireman's hold to drag Red over to his van. He opened its back doors, pulled down a hydraulic lift, then rolled Red's body atop it. Jaeger pushed up and down, grunting like a power lifter, and Red rose. When he was level with the opened van doors, Jaeger pushed him into the back. Red didn't seem to want to roll, so Jaeger made a few adjustments not found in any chiropractor's handbook, and then shut the back doors.

The easy part of the job was done. The goose still needed to be stuffed. Jaeger would have to be careful there. First he'd have to hollow out that enormous chest, taking out the heart, lungs, and liver, and much of the subcutaneous fat. And then he would replace the innards with Semtex.

Plastic surgery, thought Jaeger. Plastic explosive surgery. And after all that, he'd still have to go out and kill someone else.

But then tomorrow was another day.

Nine

The body was found in a parking lot just outside of L.A.'s Elysian Park. It was situated little more than a mile away from the L.A. Police Academy, almost as if to taunt the future officers. The first person to see the body was a homeless man who was out collecting cans. He didn't know if the man was dead or not, and didn't get close enough to find out. Even in death, the very size of the man was intimidating. The homeless man knew this wasn't someone he wanted to encounter dead *or* alive. He pushed hard at his shopping cart to get away as quickly as possible.

The second person to witness the body sighted him from the safety of his car. He drove close enough to get a good look, but at the same time made sure all his doors were locked. Then he called 9-1-1 from his car phone and said, "Either I'm looking at a tattooed beached whale or an incredibly large body." As the Pacific Ocean was about fifteen miles from where he was calling, the dispatcher assumed he was reporting on something human.

The first cop on the scene amplified on the caller's remarks. After securing the scene for the homicide detectives, he contacted the coroner's office: "Better bring an industrial-strength gurney. You're going to be bringing in Shamu."

The homicide detectives spent some time examining the victim. They found not only the small wound to his heart, but two larger wounds, one a deep cut into his navel and the surrounding stomach area, and the other a "necktie" gash along the throat. The victim's license identified him as Frank

Kurtz. He was the same Frank Kurtz with half a dozen arrests ranging from assault to trafficking controlled substances. Truth be told, the detectives couldn't care less that another scumbag had died, but they still were damn curious about the wounds on his body.

With gloves on, Detective Ken Connelly studied the cuts. Kibitzing over his shoulder was Detective Mike Kuhlken. "Major overkill," said Connelly. He pointed to the victim's upper chest. "I'd bet this one was the only stab wound." His hand pointed to the throat and then the navel. "These other cuts look almost surgical."

"Postmortem? Ritualistic?"

"I don't know. Maybe they just wanted to make sure he was dead. Guy this big, you can't take chances."

"Probably drug-related. Frankie's no stranger to dealing. Maybe he was skimming from his biker buddies. I'd bet four or five were in on it."

"Based on what?"

"Hell, it'd take at least that many just to get his carcass into a car."

"Whoa!" Connelly brought his head down next to the body.

"What?"

"Stitches. Someone sewed this guy back up!"

The L.A. coroner's investigator examined the body even more thoroughly than the detectives. Ross Brockman had been working his job for a dozen years, and while he'd seen corpses even larger, he had never seen a body that presented itself like this one. The victim's wounds had been sewed up with a virtually transparent nylon thread. The stitches were tightly spaced and showed an almost surgical precision.

As an investigator, he was supposed to examine the decedent, but only superficially. The in-depth work would have to wait for the laboratory. Brockman documented the scene with photos and sketches, did a fruitless walk around in search of witnesses, then scratched his head alongside of the homicide detectives.

"Lab boys are going to like this one," Brockman said.

"Glad somebody is," said Kuhlken.

"You done with the body?" Brockman asked.

With an exaggerated magnanimous gesture, Connelly said, "He's all yours."

Brockman signaled the body detail, a moment the man and woman team had been dreading.

Adnan Fayed shook his head. "I got a bad back," he said. His dark Semitic face was already winced in pain.

"I don't," Emerita Suarez said. She was oversized herself, but nowhere near the biker's league. "But I got a feeling that's about to change."

They collapsed the gurney. Compressed, it folded down to no more than eight inches off the ground, but the distance still seemed daunting.

The homicide detectives came over to offer advice, if not assistance. Kuhlken said, "You guys gotta do the clean and jerk, you know, like those weight lifters."

The woman offered a less than respectful look at the dead. "No, we gonna have to jerk the jerk."

"Leverage," said the other detective. "That's the key."

"In this case," said Brockman, "the key is having a bulldozer."

"Mohammad went to the mountain," Fayed said. It was hard to tell by his words if he was offering a prayer, or a curse, or signifying his own approach to the mountain.

"I'll help," said Brockman.

Dead weight isn't merely an expression. The three of them worked on the dead weight, putting their all into moving Kurtz. He was as stubborn dead as he had been alive. Working as a unit, they managed to roll him forward. For a moment the corpse threatened a Sisyphean ending, almost dropping off the gurney, but with shaky arms they were able to steady their load. "Allah be praised," said Fayed.

Detectives Kuhlken and Connelly offered polite applause.

Jaeger knew when the body was rolling. Inside its flesh he had planted a transmitter/receiver. The timing, as he had hoped, looked perfect.

The second—and more important—body had already been collected. That's where his attention had been directed. Now there would be a confluence of the dead.

The L.A. coroner's office on Mission Street was a busy place. Every half hour of every day the investigators handled a new case, and on any given day twenty autopsies took place. With over nine million people living in the L.A. metropolis, and two hundred people dying daily within its borders, the numbers weren't altogether surprising.

From the first, Jaeger had faced the stumbling block of the coroner's office. The pathologists and medical technicians were very good at their jobs. Given a chance, it was likely they would have questions about the *other* victim. They couldn't have that. It was upon that death, Monroe had told him, that everything else was being built.

Getting into the coroner's office would have been problematic, if not impossible. The guards could have been bypassed, but not the video cameras. And all attention would have focused on that one victim. The evidence needed to disappear, but he couldn't snatch the body. That would be too obvious, and raise too much attention.

That was the last thing they wanted.

Jaeger had given considerable thought to the problem, looking for a back door. Invariably, there was a back door. And then it became obvious: the living weren't welcome at the L.A. coroner's office, but the dead were.

All Jaeger needed was the right Trojan horse.

Jaeger had done a detailed study of the 55,000-square-foot four-story building. He learned its routines and how incoming bodies were handled. The dead were taken to a staging room, the coroner's Forensic Science Center, where they were fingerprinted and weighed. After personal effects were inventoried, the police signed off on the belongings. Then photographers took pictures of the body, both clothed and unclothed. After that the decedent was stored in a huge walk-in refrigerator, one of three so-called cold storage rooms, along with the rest of the dead.

It was possible they would want to process his Trojan horse more quickly than most bodies. His biker might not have to wait the day or two that most homicides did. They would probably earmark his autopsy—or toe mark it—for Room B, the so-called VIP room. But in the meantime they would still take him to one of the cold storage rooms.

Jaeger was counting on protocol. It would be unlikely for them to fluoroscopy the victim until just before the autopsy was to take place.

He drove toward the coroner's office in East Los Angeles. Jaeger was in no hurry. It would take about two hours for the body to be processed. After that it would be housed above the subbasement on the Security and Service floor. There was no vantage point into that floor, but there were some good inconspicuous spots that afforded him a view of the off-white coroner's building. If at any point it appeared that the bee hive was agitated, that his Trojan horse had been discovered, he would abort the mission and walk away.

Blackwell had been adamant about that. He always was. Anonymity was the first rule. The second rule was compartmentalizing all tasks. Jaeger knew what he had to do, even if he didn't always know how it fit in Blackwell's scheme.

It hadn't been easy stuffing the biker full of Semtex. First he'd had to do some draining and clearing out of the body, and that was only the beginning. After placing more than thirty pounds of the Czech plastic explosive inside the biker's stomach cavity, he'd carefully wired the Semtex to the detonator.

The Semtex was more misdirection. It was mostly associated with the Irish Republican Army. C-4 would have been easier to use and procure, but the Semtex would be adequate for the job.

Jaeger got off the Interstate and drove along Mission. With time to kill, he stopped at a McDonald's and had a leisurely lunch before continuing on to the coroner's office. He found a space on the street near enough to see the building, but far enough away from any potential surveillance cameras. The transmitter/receiver was working perfectly. It told him what he needed to know: the biker's body was inside the building.

So was the other body.

Fifteen more minutes, Jaeger decided. He drove a dozen blocks, passing by Juvenile Hall and Lincoln Park, before reversing direction. Fourteen minutes later he parked on the street again and appeared to be consulting a map. The coroner's office, what some referred to as the "Monument of Death," was as quiet as could be expected. Jaeger couldn't discern any unusual activity. For someone who didn't know any better, the coroner's office could have passed for a small hospital.

Jaeger got back on the road again. He was two blocks away when he activated the signal. His windows were down, and in the distance he heard a rumbling. From where he was, it sounded like thunder. Clear skies belied that possibility.

The building wouldn't be totaled, but the cold storage rooms would now be history. All the bodies housed within would be vaporized. The pieces of human remains would be microscopic. The wreckage would rival that of a crashed airliner.

Their victim was the new Humpty Dumpty. Even if they somehow identified him, they wouldn't be able to put him back together, or at least not in such a way as to jeopardize Blackwell's plan. The history of his death would forever remain a mystery.

There was only one thing more to do: Jaeger needed to make a call claiming responsibility for the bombing. More misdirection.

In the distance, sirens started wailing. Several dogs joined in the chorus, their howls loud and lachrymose. It was, thought Jaeger, a chorus for the dead—the now very, very dead.

Ten

Is this Graham Wells? The photographer?"

He was used to being called worse: "Speaking."

"This is Tina Wiggins. You probably don't remember me, but we talked a few months ago at the Tri-Star reception."

Graham had no idea who she was, but pretended he did. While making with friendly patter, he typed Tina's name on his notepad computer. Collecting names was his business, and Graham's database was extensive. Stars and power brokers were few, but their underlings were many, and everywhere. They were the eyes and ears Graham counted upon.

He got a bingo. Tina's name was in his database. She was one of Lanie Byrne's assistants. In Hollywood parlance, the title of "assistant" could mean anything from secretary, to maid, to au pair, to personal trainer, to sex slave. The title that really mattered was Lanie Byrne. She was gold, at the top of the "A" list. Lanie was more than the actress du jour. She was that rarity, a commercial and artistic success. Her star had risen to the point where she was a one-namer—Lanie—and even that was being abbreviated. Now many were calling her "Miss L." They could have pronounced it "missile" the way her career was rocketing.

Graham hoped Tina was still working for Lanie. Current contacts were best, though he was more than willing to settle for a "someone done me wrong song."

"The last time we talked," Graham said, "you were working for Lanie."

Her answer was soft, tentative: "I still am."

Graham needed to get Tina talking without scaring her. He had to warm her cold feet.

"I hear she can be difficult."

A laugh. "No comment."

"I hope when she gets her next Oscar she remembers you in her acceptance speech."

"Fat chance."

The resentment was there on the tip of Tina's tongue. It just needed a little push to come spilling out.

"Well, at least you get the big bucks."

"I wish."

Most stars have their employees sign nondisclosure contracts. This means their employees aren't supposed to say word one about their employer during, or after, their term of employment. Graham had yet to see the contract that kept an employee from talking.

"In fact, that's sort of what I was calling you about," Tina said. "The last time we talked you gave me your card."

Some people chase ambulances for a living. Graham chased stars. He didn't think there was much difference between the two trades, though ambulance chasers would probably take umbrage at the comparison. Graham passed out a lot of cards.

"And," continued Tina, "you said that I could make some extra income by providing you with certain information."

"Cash sent to the address of your choice."

"What kind of money are we talking about?"

"It all depends on the payoff. I need to get something I can sell, preferably an exclusive. If it's good, your finder's fee can be quite substantial. You're like a film agent. You get your ten percent."

"Ten percent of how much?"

"I know photographers who have gotten more than a million dollars for a single roll of film."

And he had photographed people who had won the lottery. Sometimes the one in a million shot happened, but it was the rare picture or pictures that commanded more than five figures, let alone six or seven. That wasn't something Graham wanted to emphasize.

"See," he explained, "I submit my work to my film agency, and they peddle the product worldwide. Money comes from the initial sale. And then there's always reprints. Some shots have legs. They bring in money for years to come, and sometimes that lets me play Santa Claus for a long time."

"But you only pay me if something pans out?"

"That's right."

She thought about it. Graham didn't want her to think very long. He sensed that Tina had something good. There was a pearl awaiting just a little shell prying.

"Anything you tell me gets locked in the vault," Graham said. "I never reveal a confidential source."

"I live out at the Grove," Tina said. "That's Lanie's house in Malibu."

She stopped talking again.

"Nice digs," Graham said. "I've seen pictures of the place. It looks more like Xanadu than the Grove."

"It used to be this big orange grove."

"And now there's probably not an orange tree left."

"There are a couple, but they're on the outskirts of the property. Sometimes the gardeners bring us fresh oranges."

The prod: "Life sounds idyllic."

"It's a beautiful place, and a gorgeous setting."

"You make it sound like a museum."

"With limited visiting hours."

He could hear the rub: "What do you mean?"

"It's supposed to be home. But lately we've been discommoded."

"Discommoded?"

"That's Vera's word. She also lives at the Grove. Vera is Lanie's aromatherapist. She also takes care of her animals."

"What's this about being—discommoded?"

"Last weekend Lanie gave her live-ins—there are three of us—the weekend off. She also told us to stay away from the Grove for the entire weekend. Vera and Tim didn't mind. Vera's got a boyfriend. And so does Tim.

"I decided to make a little vacation of it. I drove down to San Diego and stayed at a motel in Shelter Island. Well, this weekend Lanie has decided she wants the house to herself again. So either I'm going to have to pay for a motel again or impose on some friend."

"How often does she give you these weekend walking papers?"

"Last weekend was the first time it happened, and I've lived at the Grove for over a year. Lanie's got one wing of the house that's off-limits to everyone and has its own private entrance and exits. And believe me, the Grove's big enough for Lanie to have her own space. It's not like we have to be 'discommoded.' "

That word again.

"The non-live-in staff has also been given the weekend off, and there are a lot more of them than us. Lanie's got her little army, you know, security, the gardeners, her dietician, her personal trainer, people like that. But they get paid, so they don't care. For them, it really is a paid holiday."

"Why do you think Lanie doesn't want anyone around?"

This time the pause was just for effect: "It's got to be a new boyfriend. She's trying to keep him under wraps."

"Any guesses as to who the boyfriend is?"

"Tim thinks it's Leonardo DiCaprio, but I think that's wishful thinking on Tim's part. Tim's the one with the crush on Leo."

"Has Lanie entertained other men at the Grove before?"

"When I first moved in, Kurt Taylor used to stay over. Kurt was nice. But since their break-up, I don't think there has been anyone since."

Taylor was a producer.

"I thought Lanie was going out with Matt Damon," Graham said.

"He's her sometimes escort, not her boyfriend."

"Unless he's the mysterious Mr. X."

If he was, Graham guessed that their liaisons would be short-lived. Relationships between thespians rarely lasted very long. There were never enough mirrors to go around. Graham had to assume he was working under time pressure. There was no greater perishable commodity than a Hollywood romance. Pictures of Lanie and her new boyfriend would be very profitable, especially if that boyfriend was a name actor.

"What I'll need from you," Graham said, "is a layout of the Grove and its surrounding grounds."

Eleven

For as many years as Graham had worked L.A., it still wasn't an easy beat. Most of the problem was geographical: the world's entertainment capital was spread out from the beaches to the valleys. Celebrity photographers working New York, London, or Paris had a much easier time navigating their city. Graham had covered wars and military inventions. He liked to say that shooting a war was always easier than shooting Hollywood.

His West L.A. apartment was convenient to Interstates 405 and 10. In his time away from the United States, what Grant called his "European tour," L.A. hadn't improved, or maybe the baggage he brought back just made it seem that way. He thought the freeways were that much more clogged, the bullshit piled up that much higher, and the lunatics that much more in control of the asylum. Absence hadn't made Graham's heart grow fonder.

The extended leave of one celebrity photographer hadn't been noticed by many. To those who commented, Graham merely explained he had been "in rehab." It was a frequently heard story in the Southland, and besides, if forced to elaborate, Graham knew the rehab turf well. Over the years he had spent time hanging around such clinics as the Betty Ford Center. He had once suggested to one of the tabloids that they have a weekly feature called Gentleman Junkie. Some star was always drying out, and that made for a good photo or two.

Graham took Interstate 10 over to Santa Monica, and then headed north on the PCH—Pacific Coast Highway. He drove a Ford Windstar van, the sort of vehicle a soccer mom would be driving, but behind the tinted glass he wasn't carrying three kids and the family dog. His van was set up to be a surveillance vehicle, the custom glass allowing him to photograph without being seen. Tricks of his trade filled up several bags. Graham had never been a Boy Scout, but he tried to live up to their motto: Be prepared.

Along with his Canon EOS, he had an entire case of lenses, including a night-vision monocular and an IR light source. Hidden away was his parabolic microphone and recorder, complete with a laser to better pinpoint the area he wanted to eavesdrop on. He had his Palm Pilot and computer laptop with him, as well as his cell phone and pager. His usual easy listening was a police scanner. Under his seat was a voice changer. With a flick of the switch he could disguise his voice, change his gender.

The Friday traffic along PCH was heavy, the affluent escaping the L.A. area for their parcels of paradise. The road began to clear after Pacific Palisades. Without bumpers on every side of him, the sights opened up to something more than painted metal. The Pacific Ocean looked blue and inviting. Surfers populated pockets known for their waves, and were corking atop their surfboards while waiting for their rides. On the ocean side, a gentle breeze made the palm fronds wave; across the road the chaparral was green and lush, the recipient of recent rains. A picture-postcard day, Graham thought, but he knew only too well how everything could appear differently with but a tweak of the lens. Beaches in the L.A. area periodically had to be closed because of pollution; surfers regularly had turf wars while they fought for waves, rats nested in most of the palm trees, and heavy rains brought mud slides to the canyons. For the natives, winter officially arrived when stretches of PCH were closed due to mud.

The sun set as he passed Topanga Beach, a red fireball that lit up the horizon all the way to Malibu. From past experience, Graham knew Malibu wasn't an easy place to take pictures. A number of streets were blocked off to the public, barred by gates and guards. Though there are no private beaches in California, there are private roads. People were welcome to walk along the tideline unimpeded, but getting to certain spots sometimes took miles of trekking.

The light of day didn't linger. Graham had checked; there would be no moon that night. He exited from PCH on Malibu Canyon Road. Lanie wasn't part of the Malibu Colony beach crowd. Her home was up in the hills.

He passed by Pepperdine University and wound his way up the hill. For much of the way the road paralleled the meandering Malibu Creek. Graham approached a tunnel that some locals still referred to as the Naked Pink Lady Tunnel. For years, that artwork had adorned it, until some bureaucrat decided it offended the public's sensibilities and had it painted over.

Graham turned on Pluma Road, then wended his way farther into the hills. Lanie didn't live on a private road, but it was close enough. There were only three residences on Vista de la Ballena—View of the Whale—but it was the rare kind of street where all the houses had their own names. At the top of the road was the High Ground Ranch; the Whitman Estate had the middle ground; the Grove anchored the bottom stretch of asphalt. Each of the properties sat on twenty acres or more. In California, major developments had been built on less land. The homes were all situated on the west side of the street, their windows facing the blue ocean off in the distance.

Graham didn't park on Ballena, opting instead to pull off the road onto a bluff. Though Lanie's personal security had the night off, Tina had told him there were several security services that periodically did a drive-by of the area. Graham threw on a black turtleneck, tossed a backpack over his shoulder, and grabbed a bag he had prepared earlier. He wished he could have packed lighter. The Grove was more than half a mile away.

He kept to the unoccupied side of Ballena. The road looked to have been paved out of a natural canyon, and the overhang allowed Graham to make his way forward in the shadows. Shrubbery offered abundant hiding places, but Graham didn't have to hunker behind a bush. Night traffic was as nonexistent on the street as Tina had said it would be. He passed by the considerable manors of the High Ground Ranch and Whitman Estate. The Grove was farther removed from the street than the other properties. Its design seemed to be a combination of country living and armed camp. A high gate fronted Lanie's property and extended along the property line. Threatening signs warned away trespassers, and prominently mounted security cameras and lights offered no hint of a welcome mat. All that was missing was a tower and gun turret. The exterior of the property was meant to intimidate. Even without security present in the guard gate, it did.

Graham worked his way forward along the south side of the property. The open land next to the fence was undeveloped and rugged and sloped downward. Plenty of cactus and prickly plants were there to dissuade any casual stroller. Graham kept within sight of the fence. He didn't want to trespass on Lanie's property if at all possible. The moment he stepped foot on it, he would be opening himself up to a lawsuit. There were certain invasions of privacy even the tabloids didn't condone. Some photo editors were skittish about publishing any photos that were too invasive, but Graham knew they would have no qualms about buying pictures of Miss L and her new boyfriend. Magazines never minded facing up to an invasion of privacy lawsuit if the pictures were exclusive enough.

Scarcity dictated price. Even so-called legitimate periodicals shucked their journalistic ethics whenever a major photo opportunity presented itself. When Madonna first gave birth, every major magazine and newspaper was out for that exclusive photo of baby Lourdes. Investigative reporters were set on the trail like bloodhounds. Names were run through databases, and friends and relatives of Madonna were staked out. Bribes were offered, kin encouraged to betray for considerably more than thirty pieces.

Graham managed to avoid the beaver-tail and cholla cactus while making his way through the chaparral. He walked for several minutes before stopping to get his bearings. He pulled out a penlight, stuck it in his mouth, and studied Tina's diagram of the house. Lanie's wing was on the southwest side of the house, and had its own spa and deck. It was time for him to cut over. Tina had told him her quarters were about as far from the street as they were from the fence. A telescopic lens would be a must. Unfortunately, the distance didn't tell the whole story. From ground level the house was obscured, hidden behind the fence, foliage, and blinding lights. Because of the slope, Graham found himself looking up. It wasn't unusual for him to snap photos from upward of a quarter mile away, but in most cases he was shooting down on a subject. He wished he had a periscope that could plumb upward, but he hadn't come totally unprepared. In his pack was a high-tech metal alloy tripod whose legs opened up like tent supports, and extended somewhat higher than your average NBA center.

The spotlights needed to be disabled first. The lights weren't mounted on the fence, but on stanchions in back of the fence. They were too high, and too far removed, to reach by hand, but security lights and motion detectors were obstacles Graham had encountered before. Extendable lightbulb changers were wonderful things. He let the pole out, positioned it, then worked the grip to the bulb, chanting "righty-tightie, lefty-loosie" while turning it counterclockwise. Graham proceeded slowly, quietly, letting several minutes pass between disabling each spotlight. It was possible Lanie was out on her deck, and he didn't want her to take notice of the sudden patch of darkness. By all accounts, Lanie was a fresh-air junkie. Even when the mercury dipped, she kept her windows open. Graham was counting on that for his shoot.

Disabling four spotlights gave Graham the darkness he needed. He set up the tripod, adjusting its legs to compensate for the sloping ground, as well as the lens heavy camera and night-vision monocular.

Graham moved in close to her property line. If security had been around, they would have moved in on him, perhaps tried to arrest him for trespassing. Or stalking. That's what Barbra Streisand and James Brolin had done to a photographer following them around Malibu. But it was worth taking the chance. Needing a vantage point into the property, Graham decided to climb up the black wrought-iron fence. There was no razor-sharp concertina wire at the top, but the grating, spaced about six inches apart, raised upward to spearlike projections. He laid his backpack atop the points, and felt like a fakir resting on a bed of nails. His perch was damned uncomfortable, but at least he could see into the estate.

Placing his night-vision binoculars up to his eyes, Graham scanned the area. The house was dark, and he didn't see any movement inside. One of the sliding-glass doors was open. He examined the patio area carefully, but there was no sign of Lanie out on her private deck. It might have just been a publicist's story, but Lanie was supposedly an astronomy buff who enjoyed unwinding by studying the night sky. Graham looked up. Too early for stars, he thought, or at least her kind of stars. Maybe his kind would emerge first.

Graham lined up the camera for a shot of the opened patio door. It was a likely spot for a couple to stand together. People generally paused at the doorway, one person waiting for the other. That momentary pause had afforded Graham hundreds of shots over the years. He checked the viewfinder several times. He had put a doubler, an optical attachment, on his 800mm lens. That gave him a 1600mm lens. But he wasn't worried so much about the distance as the darkness. The problem with doing a night shoot was that it was like looking into a sea of green. Even with the night-vision monocular and special film, Graham knew the pictures were going to be on the grainy side. That wasn't necessarily a bad thing. More often than not photo editors picked out shots that looked rough and unfinished. Unstaged photos often needed that patina of verisimilitude. The less finished the picture, the truer it looked. Graham had a six-foot cable linked in to the shutter. That gave him the latitude of not having to hover over the camera. A single click and he could get ten frames in a second.

It could be a long night, so he set about rigging himself a better perch. Using carabiners, rope, and the remains of a leather coat, he made a swinglike contraption that he could both sit and stand upon. Graham's makeshift seat was at least a bit better than sitting on a spike. The minutes passed slowly. Graham had forgotten how difficult it was just to wait. Despite the image that most people have of paparazzi, it is rare for celebrity photographers to do stake-outs. There is usually too much time invested for too little payoff, not to mention the boredom and discomfort involved. It was generally a lot easier, and more profitable, to hang out at clubs and snap photos of actors from popular television series, or get pictures of hot recording artists. That was easy money.

What Graham was doing was rolling the dice. The downside was obvious—loss of time and money. Celebrity hunts were expensive, especially when no one was staking you. The potential upside explained why he was straddling a pointed fence.

Since returning from Europe, Graham had done few stakeouts. He told himself it was the long hours. Detectives know the toughest way to spend a shift is on a stakeout. There is nothing to do but watch and wait and think.

The thinking part was the hardest. On busy days Graham could almost forget what had happened in Paris. The accident, in a roundabout way, had brought him home.

Though the Lady and Le Croc had been dead for years, the media was still perpetuating their myth. Somehow they still appeared on magazine covers. The world wasn't yet ready to let them rest in peace. There seemed to be an industry out there devoted to perpetuating them as icons. In death, their romance was played up to fairy-tale proportions.

They would always be a once-upon-a-time story.

Yeah, and I'm a regular Hans Christian Andersen, Graham thought.

Graham raised the binoculars, but again saw nothing. It was possible Lanie wasn't even home. Time would tell. He rubbed his hands together. It always felt colder when you were just sitting. He tried to dredge up the thrill of the hunt to keep him warm. In the past, nothing had energized Graham more than nailing a rumor down. But Rio had opened his eyes, and then Paris had killed that feeling. The moment of truth had changed for him.

A flickering light coming from a room captured his attention. Someone had turned on a television set in the darkness. For almost an hour, that was the only sign of life, then a light went on in a room off the kitchen.

In an instant, Graham put the lingering memories aside. He forgot about his cramps, and how many places his body was hurting. Night-vision binoculars in hand, all his attention was focused on the illuminated figure. It was Lanie.

Graham was already shifting positions, reaching for the arm of the tripod. He swiveled the camera over, and caught her reaching for something in the cabinet. She didn't stand still long enough for the camera's autofocus to kick in, exiting the room with a bottle in hand.

Holding his breath, he waited for her to reappear. He was exhaling when a light went on over a table in the living room. Lanie poured from what looked like a bottle of Courvoisier into a glass. In a little over a second he went through half a roll of film. Even if nothing else panned out, what he already had would make the shoot worthwhile. Editorial could get very creative even with seemingly innocent pictures. But there was nothing innocent about Lanie's pour. She was filling her glass, and it was a tall glass.

Her shoulders were hunched over, her head down. Graham zoomed in on her face. He liked to take shots of stars when they thought they were unobserved. Those were the true pictures, the unguarded ones. Lanie's face was drawn and pensive. There was a stillness to it that even the distance and night couldn't hide. Graham pushed the trigger, finished the roll, popped the case, and then reloaded.

He fiddled with the lens, trying to compensate for the black sweater and even blacker pants she was wearing. Her light hair was pulled back and she was wearing a double strand of pearls. Her makeup had been carefully applied. He wondered if she had come from the set that way, or had just put it on.

Graham trained the camera on her eyes. They were the most talked about peepers this side of Liz Taylor's. No one could agree on their color, only on their beauty. Like fine gems, the color seemed to change in the light, and had been described as cerulean blue, aquamarine, even lavender. But at the moment, Graham would offer a different description: they were tired eyes.

Lanie reached for the glass. She swallowed the liquor as if it were medicine, then swallowed again. Graham clicked away. In less than a minute she had finished the sizable glass. She took no pleasure in her drinking, just went about getting drunk in as expeditious a manner as possible.

Graham reloaded the film. He had a bad feeling about what he was seeing, but that didn't stop him from shooting away.

For several minutes Lanie just sat there, then, as if awakened, she bowed her head, brought her hands together, and began to pray. It looked as if tears were falling down her cheeks. Graham doubted whether her tears would come out on film, but he did his best to frame her face.

Lanie moved though, dropping from her chair to take up her prayers on her knees. The table and angle obscured Graham's view. He raised the tripod over his head and shot blind, depressing the cable and hoping the shots would come out.

She prayed long enough for him to go through three more rolls. Then it was back in the chair, and back to the booze. She poured herself another glass, but apparently decided she wanted a mixer.

Some pills.

Graham kept shooting. Maybe she's just taking vitamins, he thought. It was possible Lanie's self-destruction only went so far, and that she was replenishing the vitamins lost to the drink. Hollywood was that strange place where narcissism and self-destruction often went hand in hand.

But she was taking an awful lot of vitamins. One after another.

He wondered if it could be some kind of medication. Lots of people who were HIV positive had to take a whole battery of pills every day. But none of them took it with alcohol. Graham thought of Marilyn Monroe.

He thought of his own mother.

Lanie had cleared the house. She had dressed in black. She had offered up her final prayers.

She was killing herself.

Graham flashed back onto a dream that often plagued him. He was back in the tunnel, but this time he stopped the Citroën instead of fleeing. But he didn't go and try and help the couple. He took pictures of them, oblivious to everything but getting the shot.

Lanie was raising a plastic bag up to her head. She wasn't taking any chances. Death by asphyxiation was a sure thing.

Graham patted his body for his cell phone, and came up empty. Dammit, he'd left the phone in the car. He didn't hesitate then, just pushed himself off the fence and landed on Lanie's property. Somewhere there had to be a path up to the deck, but he didn't see it. With a long lens, you forget how far away your target is. As he ran, he realized the house was at least a hundred yards off. Foliage barred the way. He clawed at the greenery, fighting through trees and plants. The ground was slippery, and made more so by an abundance of snails. With his every step, gastropods were popping like small firecrackers. Twice he lost his footing in the ice plant, but he was up immediately. Seconds counted, and he knew it. Everyone had always commented on how fast he could run, but his speed seemed to have vanished. He felt slow, slothlike, entered in a race he couldn't win.

Graham finally stumbled upon some steps and followed them forward. The winding path led up to the deck. The screen door wasn't locked and he threw it open. Lanie's head was slumped on a dining table. The bag was still wrapped around it.

He grabbed the plastic and yanked upward, pulling out some of Lanie's hair. She was still breathing, still responding to pain. Her hand reached up and waved as if she were shooing away a mosquito, then dropped back to the table. She opened her eyes, blinked a few times, and tried to focus. Her mouth opened and closed, as if on a trial run of sizing out the words, before she whispered, "Who are you?"

"A friend." Graham couldn't see a phone. "What kind of pills did you take, Lanie?"

She mumbled incoherently, and started to close her eyes. Graham grabbed the pill bottle. He scanned the prescription and found she had downed a bottle of Valium.

Lanie was slumped over again. "It's not bedtime, Lanie," Graham said, shaking her until her eyes opened. "Where's your phone?"

Her eyes were closing again. "Kitchen."

"Walk with me." Graham tried pulling Lanie to her feet. Her legs were limp. Dead weight. He pulled her along. "Help me, Lanie. We've got to get you an ambulance."

The words had an unexpected effect. Lanie started struggling in his arms. "No ambulance," she said. "No hospital! No hospital! Not like this. Not like this."

Lanie started weeping. Her hands were shaking. Miss L apparently preferred death to indignity. Her legs found some reserve of strength, and her heels dug into the carpeting.

"Call doctor."

"There's no time for a house call, Lanie."

"Dr. Burke."

That was the doctor's name on the pill prescription.

"Please."

Graham paused for a moment. This was one of the movie's power players. She wasn't the kind of person to say "please." Lanie needed immediate attention. She should have thought about her star image before trying to commit suicide.

"Please."

It was time for his deaf act. The louder the cries, the harder his hearing. But instead Graham asked, "What's his first name?"

"Arnold."

"Here's the deal: if I see you falling asleep I swear I'll call for an ambulance. And the only thing that's going to beat that ambulance to the hospital is a bunch of photographers. If you promise not to sleep, I'll call Dr. Burke."

"Promise."

"Keep your eyes open, Lanie. That's it."

Graham grabbed the portable phone. He punched in information and got Dr. Arnold Burke's number. His service answered on the fourth ring.

"This is an emergency," Graham said. "I'm calling on behalf of Lanie Byrne. She needs to talk to Dr. Burke immediately."

"What's your number, sir?"

"What's your telephone number, Lanie?"

It took another prod, and several seconds, before Lanie answered. The numbers were uttered in painfully slow fashion. Graham translated them, then added, "This is an emergency."

He hung up and waited. "You're not going to sleep, are you, Lanie?"

Sluggishly: "No."

"Because I'll call that ambulance."

The threat got her more alert and vocal: "No."

The phone rang. It had been less than a minute since Graham had hung up on the service, but Dr. Burke was already calling back. Star treatment.

"I'm with Lanie, Doctor. She's swallowed a thirty-day supply of Valium, and chased them with cognac. She doesn't want me to call an ambulance, and she doesn't want to go to a hospital."

It was the doctor's turn to agonize over the decision. "When did she take the pills?"

"Within the last ten minutes."

"What are her vital signs? Is she conscious? Is she talking and making sense?"

"She's still conscious, Doc, but she's already acting like a zombie."

"Don't let her sleep. Keep her talking. If she starts vomiting, make sure her mouth and nasal passages are kept clear. Do you know CPR?"

"Yeah. Some. It's been years, though—"

"My office is on Stuart Ranch Road. That's off Civic Center Way. Do you know where that is?"

"Yes, but—"

"I'll meet you there."

The doctor offered one final word of medical advice: "Hurry."

Twelve

Where are your car keys, Lanie?"

A small, bothered shake of the head. "Not sure."

"Where do you think they might be?"

"Ignition?"

Graham gathered her up, got Lanie to her feet. Mostly supporting her with his arm, they did their version of the three-legged race up two flights of stairs and into a cavernous five-car garage. Four of the spaces were occupied. Graham lowered Lanie to the ground, propping her against the garage door. She was beginning to lose muscle control. He ran from vehicle to vehicle, starting with the PT Cruiser, then moving on to the Infiniti, the Toyota Prius, then the Range Rover. No keys. His last chance was the XJR Jaguar.

Keys dangled from the ignition.

Graham ran back and collected Lanie, then hit the garage door opener. He lifted her in his arms, then tossed her into the backseat. She barely noticed.

The driver's seat was uncomfortably close to the wheel. Graham patted with his hand, searching for the electronic controls to the seat. He found the switch, and punched both his seat and the car into reverse at the same time. Smoke rose from the wheels. He accelerated up the long driveway and was already going sixty when the gate loomed in his headlights. He slowed, expecting it to open automatically, then had to slam on the brakes. Even with its antilock brakes, the Jaguar fishtailed before coming to a stop just before the gate. Graham gave a quick look to the backseat. Though she had been tossed around, Lanie was all but oblivious.

Graham patted around the Jag, looking for a control to the gate. He knew there were typically three ways to open such a gate: by transmitter, by swiping a keycard, or by punching in a keypad number. He came up empty on the transmitter or keycard. The only thing in the glove compartment was a copy of a rental agreement from Celestial Motors.

"Shit." Graham looked around for the keypad, and found it on a post in the driveway leading up to the gate.

"Lanie." He raised his voice: "Lanie!"

Her eyes remained closed, and her answer sounded tentative. "Yes?"

"I need to know the code for the gate."

"Gate?"

"The driveway gate."

"Control's on the visor."

Graham checked. It wasn't there. "Not here, Lanie," he yelled, but she wasn't listening. Her head had dropped to her shoulder. Graham reached back and started patting her on the cheek. The pats escalated to slaps before she became aware enough to try and push his hand away.

"Stop it."

"What's the gate code?"

She strained to remember, shook her head.

"Think!" Graham commanded.

"X," she said.

"X-what?"

"X." She motioned with her hand from upper left down to right. "One, then nine, then . . ." She gave up with words, but not gestures, this time going from upper right down to left. "Then three and—and—that bottom X."

Graham looked at the keypad, and understood. Or he thought he did. He hit one and nine, then three and seven.

The gate began to open.

Graham charged through the gap, leaving no more than a quarter inch to spare between the car and the gate. He rocketed up the hill, opening the windows. The cold air swirled through the car.

Lanie didn't like the draft. Her nose and mouth wrinkled up, and she raised a hand to ward off the wind from her face. "Cold," she complained.

"It's your wake-up call, Lanie. You can't go to sleep. You promised me, remember?"

"Who are you?"

"Your guardian angel."

Since returning to Los Angeles, Graham had driven quite conservatively—at least compared to his former habits. Paris had had that much of a residual effect on him. But now he was flooring it, pushing the Jaguar down a grade at almost eighty miles per hour where the speed limit was posted at thirty-five. It was the premium model Jaguar, the supercharged sedan. Its headlights were on high beams, and with the darkness of the canyon around him, it almost felt as if he were outrunning his lights.

Suddenly there were glowing eyes in his beams. Graham braked and swerved at the same time.

"Shit!" he said, fighting the wheel.

The thump was immediately followed by the bump of the front right tire, then back right tire. Graham had control by then, and eased up on the brakes. Stupid, he thought. He had almost gotten them killed. First he'd taken out a Lady, and now he had almost done away the Queen of the Screen. And all for the sake of a—

"What was that?"

He glanced back in the rearview mirror. Lanie was sitting up and looking surprisingly alert. The cold air had her trembling and hugging herself.

"A possum. I tried to miss it, but I didn't."

Lanie started shivering all the more. Graham raised the front windows some. He checked his rearview mirror again. Though Lanie's eyes were open, they were unblinking, and she wasn't moving. He was afraid she had fallen asleep with her eyes open.

"How are you doing back there?"

There was an annoyed blink to show she had heard. He apparently had interrupted her catatonic state.

"I'll probably need your help to find the doctor's office, so you're going to have to stay alert."

No response.

"You want to show me some sign that you're still alive?"

Her pride momentarily reasserted itself. She weakly raised her right hand just high enough for him to see, and flipped him off. For once, he was glad to be on the receiving end of the bird.

He barreled down Malibu Canyon Road, passing two cars on the narrow two-lane road. Horns blared behind him. Ahead, Graham could see the Pink Naked Lady Tunnel. It wasn't a long tunnel, but Graham's palms still began to sweat. Tunnels had brought him nothing but bad luck. He found himself holding his breath as he entered into the darkness. He was afraid his fear was all too noticeable, and snuck a look at Lanie. She wasn't paying any attention to him, or anything. Her eyes were closed. No, more than closed. They were shut tight as if she too was afraid. He wondered if she was claustrophobic.

Graham mentally counted their way through to the end of the tunnel. Only eight seconds. Once past it, Graham heaved a sigh of relief, but the relief was only momentary. He had to grab hard at the wheel when the ride suddenly got bumpy.

"What was that?" Lanie's eyes were open again.

"Cobblestones. Probably from the recent rain."

Lanie started shaking again. It wasn't that cold, Graham thought.

Graham continued down the hill. When he saw Pepperdine University's cross in the distance, he knew they were getting close to their turn.

"We're almost there," he announced to Lanie, but she said nothing. He glanced back and saw that she was slumped on the seat.

"Lanie!" he shouted. "Lanie!"

She didn't stir.

Graham kept his left hand on the wheel and reached back with his right. He grabbed her arm and pulled her toward him. Her face, one of the most recognizable faces in the world, was cold. He reached up along her chin and felt for a pulse. Nothing.

He didn't know whether to pull to the side of the road and try to remember CPR, or drive like hell the last mile to the doctor's office. His right foot responded for him, pushing the accelerator to the floor.

And then he felt something under her chin, a flutter that repeated itself. She still had a pulse.

"Remember your promise to me, Lanie. You were supposed to be my company during this ride. You were supposed to talk to me. Are you listening? You can't die. Hold on, Lanie. Just hold on."

Thirteen

Graham had this sinking feeling in his stomach. It felt like Paris all over again. If Lanie died this whole affair would blow up in his face. Hollywood would want a scapegoat, and he fit the bill to a T. His having tried to help wouldn't matter. The star machine would crucify him.

This is payback, he thought. This is karma doing its boomerang act.

He shot along Civic Center Way, then turned on Stuart Ranch, looking right and left for the doctor's office. He took a look back at Lanie, and what he saw made him drive faster.

From a distance, he saw a man waiting at the curb with a wheelchair. Dr. Burke, he presumed. Graham screeched up to the curb. His hopes that the doctor would grab Lanie and forget about him didn't pan out. Burke impatiently motioned for Graham to come and help get Lanie into the wheelchair.

The doctor didn't waste any of his bedside manner on Graham. He was tall and thin, and had white, wavy hair that was set off by his black, bushy eyebrows. His face was a map of wrinkles and frown lines, the kind of face that advertised concern. Looking at Lanie, the frown lines got that much deeper.

He checked Lanie's eyes with a penlight. "Did she vomit?"

"No."

"Any seizures?"

"No—"

Dr. Burke waved off any more words and felt for a pulse. "When did she last speak?"

"Two, maybe three minutes ago—"

"You wheel, I'll lead the way."

The doctor had to be pushing seventy, but there was plenty of spring in his step. As the two men ran along, Dr. Burke continued to ask questions of Lanie's condition. Graham got a feel for how paramedics were pumped for information as they delivered their charges to the ER.

The office was unlocked, and they lifted her atop an examining bed. Everything had been set up in readiness to receive Lanie. There were monitors, and the counter was laid out with tubes, syringes, and oxygen.

"Alcohol in combination with valium causes respiratory depression," Dr. Burke said. "She's essentially switched off her respiratory muscles. I am going to have to switch them back on." He lifted up a syringe. "A shot of Romazicon is usually efficacious."

"Good luck," Graham said.

"Wait in the next room," Dr. Burke said. "Stay handy in case I need you."

As Graham walked out the door, the doctor added, "Don't think about leaving."

The doctor was apparently a mind reader.

Graham paced in the waiting room. Despite what he had been told, he thought about taking off anyway, but he couldn't quite bring himself to leave. It was possible the doctor might really have some need of him.

The minutes dragged. At one point he heard some kind of alarm sounding in the next room. He wondered if Lanie's heart had shut down. It was easy to imagine the worst, especially since he was involved. The alarm eventually went off. Graham held his breath and waited for the emergence of Dr. Burke, and the telling sad shake of his head. When the doctor didn't appear, Graham crept over to the room and looked in. Dr. Burke was still working on Lanie. There was a tube in her mouth, and IV drips going into her arms. She was still alive, but she looked like hell.

Graham framed the picture in his mind. The tabloids would have loved that photo for a cover shot—assuming Lanie lived. How the mighty had fallen was one of their favorite photographic themes. Weight gain photos were always well received, as were any pictures that intimated death, disaster, or duress.

He backed away from the door. Part of him was glad he didn't have a camera. It saved him from the inner debate of whether he should snap pictures or not. But the absence of a camera made him feel naked. He never went anywhere without his cameras. Since leaving them behind, he had felt unbalanced. The only thing he had from the night's shoot were a few rolls of film in his pocket—film that could ultimately be worth a fortune, or could land him in jail.

Graham finally took a seat. He needed to make some calls, but decided to wait until the verdict came in on Lanie. There was still a story that needed to accompany the photos.

It wasn't every day that stars tried to kill themselves. Most of them worked too hard to get to the top, and invested too much of their egos, to want to end their lives. Graham went through his mental checklist of actors that had committed suicide. The subject was personal to him, one he had morbidly researched even before becoming a paparazzo.

Marilyn Monroe headed the list, though some contended she just popped one pill too many. The same could be said for Judy Garland. Freddie Prinze killed himself, as did Gig Young. Prinze was depressed, and Young shot himself after murdering his wife of three weeks. Graham could never watch *The Wizard of Oz* without thinking that Clara Bandick, who played Auntie Em, committed suicide, but then she had been eighty-one years old and suffering from a severe case of arthritis. Like Lanie, Clara had used sleeping pills, and tied a plastic bag over her head. Actress Lupe Velez had purposely overdosed on sleeping pills, but she had been four months pregnant at the time and distraught at her condition and a failed romance. Milton Sills ended his life in his limousine on Dead Man's Curve on Sunset Boulevard, and Carole Landis celebrated the Fourth of July by going out with a bang. Gwili Andre went out with the vanity of the bonfire, using her press clippings as her own funeral pyre. Her creativity was only surpassed by Albert Dekker, who in 1968 dressed himself in women's lingerie and used red lipstick to excerpt from his final reviews, writing the words on his outfit. The notices, all unfavorable, were his final words. Dekker hung himself.

Naked, John Bowers went into the Malibu surf with the intention of drowning himself. He did.

Patricia "Patty" Porter died in a similar manner. Her body washed in along Santa Monica's beach. But Patty Porter's death never even got a mention in any of the Hollywood exposés. She was considered a bit actress at best. Her film résumé was scant: three credits, two of them as a stand-in. She was mostly an extra, a face in the crowd. For all her dreams, her one speaking role amounted to a dozen words in a very forgettable film called *Lace Wings*.

Patty Porter was her stage name. Her married name had been Mary Wells. She was Graham's mother. He had been three days shy of his tenth birthday when she killed herself.

Ancient history, Graham told himself. Mom had been desperate like the others. None of the actors had gone out like Centurions proclaiming, "It's a good day to die." The closest thing to that was George Saunders, whose suicide note said, "I'm bored." There had been reasons behind what they had done, just as something had driven Lanie to her act of desperation.

The plastic bag around her head showed how serious Lanie was. There had been no suicide note that Graham had seen, nothing to explain her act. She had chosen an efficient, if anonymous, manner to die. No grand exit à la actress Lillian Millicent "Peg" Entwhistle, who committed suicide by jumping from the famous HOLLYWOOD sign.

I'm ready for my close-up, Mr. DeMille, thought Graham.

It was a tough town. There was no shortage of directors and former studio heads that had also killed themselves. But most of the suicides were second-tier actors, not like Lanie Byrne. She breathed the rarified air of a genuine superstar. It didn't make sense for Lanie to want to leave the stage at the top of her game. Graham couldn't think of anyone else in her position who had ever done that.

Maybe Lanie was sick. She might have a terminal illness and not want to deal with the pain and suffering. That was something he would have to check.

Or it could be that her heart was sick. Stars weren't immune to love affairs gone wrong, but usually they loved themselves more than anyone else. Still, it was possible Lanie had pursued a drastic cure for a broken heart.

Depression was something else he would have to look into. Some people found it impossible to crawl out of that black hole. It was hard to imagine why she would be depressed, though. In terms of her career, Lanie's last two films had been both commercial and artistic hits. As for her most recent project, filming was wrapping up on *The Blue Waltz* and insiders were saying Lanie should be practicing for her Oscar speech. Still, Graham knew that when it came to clinical depression, accomplishments didn't matter. He wondered if Lanie had been put on antidepressants. Maybe Dr. Burke had prescribed Lanie Valium because he misdiagnosed her condition, or maybe she had misrepresented it.

Graham needed to try and get the story behind that prescription. The doctor didn't strike him as a pill-pusher. There were plenty of those around town, doctor feelgoods happy to practice their license to pill.

Approaching footsteps from the other room prompted Graham to stand up. Dr. Burke looked like he wasn't too far from needing emergency care himself. His shirt was sweat-soaked, and his face pale.

"I wouldn't have done this for anyone but Lanie," he said.

"Is she okay?"

"She's breathing by herself now, and resting as comfortably as could be expected."

"Did you have any idea she was suicidal?"

"Lanie says it was an accidental overdose."

"She chug-a-lugged two glasses of cognac along with the bottle of pills. When I found her, she had a plastic bag over her head."

"God. I never would have imagined she would do anything like that."

"Why the Valium prescription? Did something happen to her recently?"

Burke ignored Graham's questions. "Excuse me. I have to see to Lanie."

He was probably going to make sure there were no sharp objects or pills in Lanie's reach. Graham wished he had gotten an answer or two out of the doctor. Soon enough, the only people who would be available to answer his questions would be spin doctors.

The doctor's pager went off before he could exit the room. Annoyed, he looked at the number on the readout and grunted.

"It's my service," he said. "You'll need to sit with Lanie while I call in."

Her eyes were shut as Graham tiptoed inside the room. Lanie's face had regained some color and she looked a little more like the Lanie Byrne you saw on posters and marquees. A thin medical blanket partially covered her. Lanie had fared better than her ensemble. Her makeup was smeared, her skirt wrinkled, and the top three buttons of her blouse were either missing or opened. Graham rearranged the blanket to better cover her up.

She opened her eyes, and the faintest smile came to her face. The reassurance, Graham felt, was just for him. Still, he sensed that a second chance at life hadn't brought her any joy. He stood frozen, expecting her eyes to close, but she didn't release him from her sight.

"My guardian angel," she rasped.

Her whisper made him wince. He could feel the rawness of her throat, but she ignored it, as if it was an insignificant part of her pain.

"I get in trouble when people think I'm something that I am not," he said.

Her inquiring eyes made him continue. "A few years ago a woman thought I was a pilgrim. I should have disabused her of that notion right away. I won't make that mistake with you. I'm no guardian angel."

Lanie motioned for him to sit. He found a chair and pulled it up near her. "You talk," she whispered. "Tell me your pilgrim story."

It occurred to Graham that he had never told anyone about his walk on the Camino. He knew where not to start his story, but not where to begin.

"I was in this little town in Spain. I sort of stumbled upon it, and didn't know for the last thousand years or so it was the traditional starting place for pilgrimages across the north of Spain."

At first the words didn't come easily. There were too many blanks in the story, too many gaps that he couldn't explain, or didn't want to, but his listener didn't interrupt, and gradually Graham found his rhythm. He described the history of the Camino, and where it started and ended, and remembered some of his tales from the road.

"What I liked most was that no two days were alike. The scenery kept changing, and so did the accommodations. Pilgrims get to stay in the *refugios*—refuges for those walking the Camino—that are spaced about a day's walk from one another."

Graham noticed Dr. Burke enter the room, but he didn't stop talking. Lanie seemed to be enjoying what he had to say. "The Camino is a mix of every type of road. One day you trek along a dirt path, and the next you're walking along a highway. Mostly, it's a rural route. You pass by farms and country roads. Some days I would have long stretches of solitude, and on others I would have the company of other travelers, or locals who would always begin the conversation by asking me if I was going to Santiago."

Lanie's breathing was more regular, and her eyes were beginning to close.

"Not a day went by where I didn't wonder what I was doing on the Camino, but a part of me wanted the road to never stop. I had this purpose of walking toward a goal every day. But roads always end."

For a moment, Graham tensed. He was getting too close to the other story, to his secret. But Lanie had fallen asleep and Dr. Burke didn't seem to have noticed. The doctor motioned for Graham to quietly leave the room. Outside it, they spoke in whispers.

"I guess what Lanie needed as much as anything was a friend."

To the doctor, Graham's storytelling must have made him appear as if he was a good friend. Graham didn't do anything to dispel that notion.

"It's already started," said Dr. Burke.

"What has?"

"That page. The caller misrepresented himself to my service by claiming he was a patient and saying it was an emergency. But it was only some reporter."

"Reporter?"

A nod: "He kept asking, in a rude and offensive manner, 'Is Lanie alive?' "

"How could he have known?"

"The vultures always hover over Lanie and never give her any peace. The only reason I agreed to treat her here, especially under these conditions, is that I know how much she values her privacy. If Lanie had gone to the hospital she would have been harassed beyond belief."

"What did you tell that caller that paged you?"

"I hung up on him without saying anything."

"It's just the start."

"I know. For Lanie's sake, I intend to release a statement that she's suffering from exhaustion and what appears to be the flu."

The flu. That was the favorite excuse of publicists. It was good for everything from a hangover to a bad hair day. But this was the blue, blue flu.

Dr. Burke continued, "We need to get Lanie out of here before the paparazzi start camping on the doorstep. I've called for a medical van to pick her up and take her back to her house."

"What's going to stop her from trying to kill herself again?"

"I'll be putting Lanie under the care of an exceptional psychiatrist I know, as well as assigning her round-the-clock staff. They'll be under my instructions not to leave her alone for a moment."

"Will they know it's a suicide watch?"

"They'll know to be vigilant."

Fourteen

Graham wasn't worried so much about other photographers arriving any minute as by the expected arrival of the police. If they showed up and started asking questions, Graham stood to be exposed, and the film he was holding could potentially be confiscated. Around town the police and County Sheriffs had the reputation as acting like private security for the stars.

He considered putting the film in the car, but wasn't sure if he would be driving the Jaguar back to the Grove. Besides, the police might extend their search there. Graham knew he was probably being paranoid, but he didn't want to chance giving up possession of the film. He knew of another paparazzo who had been forced to surrender his film to the L.A. County Sheriffs after a celebrity had falsely complained that the photographer had been stalking her. When he got his film back, every frame was exposed.

If possession wasn't nine-tenths of the law, it was close enough. Graham once snapped several rolls of film of Demi Moore skiing with her children. When Demi's bodyguard noticed him clicking away, he gave chase. Graham escaped capture, but didn't take into account that he was in a resort town with limited outlets for developing pictures. The bodyguard found where Graham was having the film processed and promptly claimed the pictures for his own. What the hired muscle did was illegal, but short of suing, there was nothing Graham could do. Now he always erred on the side of caution.

Graham remembered seeing a bank of mailboxes in front of the medical building. After a short search, he found some FedEx mailers in the bottom drawer of the receptionist's desk. Graham sealed the film inside a manila envelope, which he put into the FedEx mailer. He scrawled out his address and billing information, checked the one-day priority, then ran outside and tossed the mailer into the box. The first pickup would be at eight in the morning.

Depending on how the night turned out, Graham thought, it was possible the film might even beat him home.

As the evening wore on, Graham regretted his precautions in mailing the film. The police never showed up, and even more surprising, neither did the expected photographers and news crews. For once, news hadn't traveled fast. Dr. Burke's caller apparently hadn't made like the town crier, and from what Graham could see, he inexplicably never showed up himself. For as many people as were gathering at the medical building, all part of Lanie's support system, it was a miracle the jig wasn't up.

It was almost midnight when the assembled help finally set out for the Grove. The return trip was much slower than his ride into town, and for that Graham was grateful. Estelle Steinberg, Lanie's publicist, was waiting at the gates of the Grove. At Lanie's request, Dr. Burke had called and asked her to be there. Estelle was a veteran at damage control, and greeted the arriving caravan of doctors and nurses like a strict camp counselor taking in new charges. While everyone else was tending to Lanie, Graham parked the Jaguar and slipped out the front gate.

For the second time that night Graham made his way along the fence line of Lanie's property. He wanted to grab his equipment and get out before security showed up, or someone thought to start asking him questions. The disabled lights made it easy for him to pick out his surveillance area. As he approached the patch of darkness, he came to a sudden stop. His cameras should have been hanging from the fence, and the rest of his equipment lying nearby. Graham turned around in a circle, taking inventory of the area. He was in the right spot, but everything he had left behind was gone.

"Shit!"

The equipment he could replace, albeit for a few thousand dollars. But the film was potentially irreplaceable. You never knew which picture would turn out. The thief could now be holding the only viable shot.

From what Graham knew, the Grove had remained deserted except for Estelle, and it was unlikely she would have scouted the grounds and found the cameras. Someone had, though. Maybe the same someone who had paged Dr. Burke and asked about Lanie's condition. Graham might not have been the only one monitoring Lanie. That would have meant his actions were also being watched. Graham looked around. No one was in sight, but he knew only too well that meant nothing.

Graham didn't linger. He couldn't exactly go knocking at Lanie's door and ask if anyone had seen his equipment. Without the weight of his bags encumbering him, Graham ran up the hill. Several times he glanced back to make sure he wasn't being followed.

When he reached his van, Graham found that his luck was still running bad. Someone had broken into his vehicle. Whoever it was hadn't needed to resort to a smashed window or jimmied lock. The neat break-in didn't extend to the inside of the van. There, his visitor had left more signs of entry than Goldilocks. Bags and boxes had been opened, and everything examined. Tidiness hadn't been a priority. All the papers in the glove compartment were scattered.

Not your usual smash and grab, thought Graham. The CD player and other electronics were still there. His car had been methodically rifled.

It was a little after one when Graham pulled into his apartment's parking garage. The traffic had been light on his drive home, giving him a chance to concentrate on the events of the evening. He suspected someone else had been watching Lanie while she downed her pills. If that was the case, her observer had done nothing to try and prevent her suicide. That might not be defined as murder, but it sure qualified as cold-blooded.

Graham wondered if it was another photographer. His was a cutthroat business. If the son of a bitch had his cameras and film, he might try to pass off Graham's work as his own. In celebrity photography, the race was to the swift. You got the money and the credit if you beat everybody else. Not for the first time, Graham kicked himself for mailing the remaining rolls of film back to himself. The other bastard could be developing his film at that very moment. First thing in the morning Graham would make some calls. There were only so many outlets for those kinds of shots.

But if there was a second photographer, why hadn't he just sabotaged Graham's film? That would have been easy. And Lanie's rescue would have made for the most compelling shots anyway. All he had to do was keep clicking away, and he stood to have the true exclusive.

Graham stepped out of his van, reexamining the puzzle in his mind. He was too preoccupied to notice the two men in the shadows.

They came at him without a sound. One applied a choker hold, yanking him up so that his feet dangled just off the ground. With his breath cut off,

Graham flailed with his hands and feet, but his struggles didn't help. He was close to blacking out when his assailant eased off the pressure, allowing Graham to breathe again. While he was gasping, the second man used duct tape to tie his hands and feet. Graham coughed, fought off nausea, then tried to suck in enough breath to shout. The choker hold was tightened, and this time he fell limp, not quite unconscious but completely immobilized. A strip of duct tape was applied over his mouth, forcing him to breathe in and out through his nose.

The entire struggle, if you could call it that, lasted no more than ten seconds.

One of the men lifted him into his van and threw him in the back while the other stood lookout. Graham's nose was making teakettle sounds. It was the only noise he could make. Graham felt himself being patted down. His car keys, wallet, and cell phone were taken. He didn't resist as his legs were tied to the seat frame.

"No film," announced the man who had frisked him.

Graham had been hoping this was just an everyday mugging. Now he knew better.

His second assailant stuck his head inside the van's sliding door. The two men looked too alike not to be related. They had to be brothers. Both had dark, curly hair, olive skin, overdeveloped chests, and aviator glasses. They were wearing white button-down shirts along with a tie and dark pants, but Graham had the feeling that they weren't on a Mormon mission.

The two studied him behind their aviator glasses. Mugged by the fucking Wright Brothers, Graham thought.

Orville, the one who frisked him, was the tacit leader. "If you cooperate," he said, "I will remove your gag. That will allow you to breathe more easily. If you scream or shout, you will be severely punished. Do you want me to remove your gag?"

By the sounds of it, English was Orville's second tongue. At Graham's nod, he pulled off the duct tape. Orville waited while Graham took some deep breaths.

"Our interest in you is very simple," Orville said. "We need to know what you did with the film."

Though Graham had a good ear for accents, he couldn't place Orville's country of origin.

"Care to tell me what this is all about?" Graham asked.

Neither man answered.

"I have maybe forty bucks in my wallet," he said. "You are welcome to the credit cards as well, though I am afraid they're mostly maxed out."

Orville removed his aviator glasses. "Where's the film?" he asked again.

"I don't know what you are talking about," Graham said. "I'm missing some film as well. And some cameras. I lost them earlier tonight. If you know anything about them, I'm willing to pay a substantial reward, no questions asked."

"Where's the film?" Each time he asked, Orville sounded more menacing.

"The film was in the cameras. If you've got those cameras, I'm not kidding, we need to talk."

Wilbur lifted up his left hand. In it, he cradled half a dozen empty film containers. "Explain these."

Graham shrugged. "Empties. So what?"

The probing eyes waited for a better answer.

"Film canisters are like hangers," said Graham. "They just seem to multiply on their own. My bags are always littered with those things."

Orville and Wilbur seemed to come to some understanding. The gag was back on Graham's mouth before he could even protest.

Wilbur drove without speaking. Graham wondered what happened to Orville. His answer came when the van stopped in a deserted parking lot. Orville had apparently driven ahead and was there to open one of the sliding doors.

"Would you like me to remove your gag?" Orville asked.

Graham nodded.

"Then I need you to do as I say. With your cooperation, you'll come out of this night with little more than a hangover."

He raised a brown bag, and pulled out a liter of vodka. "Truth serum," Orville said, unscrewing the top of a liter of vodka.

Wilbur removed Graham's gag while Orville filled most of a cup with vodka.

"Why are you doing this?" Graham asked.

"Because I don't have sodium pentothal," said Orville, "so getting you good and drunk is the next best alternative. That, or torture."

Orville seemed to be considering that as he pressed the cup to Graham's lips. He swallowed it in several large gulps. The liquor burned his throat as it went down, then his chest felt warm.

Wilbur leaned over with the gag. "Open your mouth," he said.

"No gag," said Graham. "I'm having trouble breathing. I have this deviated septum."

The duct tape went back over his mouth.

• • •

In his job, Graham's van served him well. No one could look in and see him. But now it worked against him. He couldn't signal anyone, and he couldn't move.

They drove for almost a quarter of an hour before the van pulled over at what must have been a prearranged rendezvous spot. Orville was once again waiting. The Brothers didn't need to confer. One played bartender, the other bouncer.

"No sounds. Is that understood?"

Graham nodded, and the duct tape was removed from his mouth.

"Tilt your head," Orville told Graham, then raised a cup to his lips.

"If this vodka is supposed to be truth serum, why haven't you asked me any questions?"

"You'll be more receptive after a few more drinks."

"Is that your dating technique or interviewing technique?"

Orville pressed the cup to Graham's lips and he reluctantly drank. When Graham finished the glass, Wilbur leaned over to put on his gag.

"I have to go to the bathroom," Graham said.

"You can wait," said Orville.

"I don't think so."

As Wilbur gagged him, he said, "Then piss quietly in your pants."

They took to the road again. Graham could see they were traveling north. They drove along Sunset, then got on Laurel Canyon. Traffic was light, but not nonexistent, but there was nothing he could do to make himself seen.

He didn't spot Orville's blue Camry on the road. Since they were meeting at prearranged spots, it appeared they were driving out of sight of one another. Any chance at escape, Graham realized, would be improved if he had to contend with just one of them. They exited off Laurel Canyon and started traveling along more residential roads. Graham didn't hear Wilbur's phone ring, but did hear him talking. The conversation was brief. The van made several turns, then pulled into the parking lot of what looked like a deserted park or soccer field. Orville was already there waiting with the vodka.

This time Graham decided not to go along quietly. When his gag came off, he said, "I'm not drinking anything until you tell me what's going on."

The Brothers didn't choose to have a dialogue with him. Without warning, Wilbur held Graham down while Orville forced a plastic funnel into his mouth, then filled it with vodka. Graham tried not to swallow, but Orville pinched his nose. When he gasped for air, he took in some of the vodka down his windpipe, coughed, then swallowed and gasped, and swallowed and gasped some more. They made him drink two full funnels of vodka before gagging him again.

Graham tried to think through the alcohol, his anger battling the fogginess overtaking his brain. He hadn't been so drunk since Roncesvalle. Booze hadn't brought him the amnesia he wanted back then, and now it just brought back memories of that night. Truth serum. His captors were right. Since the accident, Graham had learned not to drink too much, because whenever he did he thought of Paris.

A tear ran down his cheek. That angered Graham. The booze was breaking him down. Self-pity wouldn't help. He had to act. So far they had dictated everything. He had to somehow loosen their control.

Graham tried to focus on his surroundings. He had to act before they force-fed him more booze and he became even more debilitated. Feigning loud retching noises, he doubled over. His acting sick didn't go unnoticed.

"Hold off," Wilbur said. "I'll pull over."

As he parked, Wilbur picked up his phone, autodialed, and had a hurried conversation with his brother.

They were on a residential street. Graham knew he might not have a better opportunity to escape or get noticed. In a quiet neighborhood, screams traveled far.

He was still doubled over when Wilbur came up to him. When his gag was removed, Graham said, "Let me out. I'm going to throw up."

"Breathe in and out. I'll let you out in a minute."

In a minute his brother would be on the scene. Graham knew he had to act now. He retched, and Wilbur grabbed for the top of a box.

"Do it on this," he said.

Graham leaned over toward it, then jerked his head up and tried to ram Wilbur's head with his own. His abductor seemed to be expecting something like that. He easily eluded the blow.

There was a house not fifty yards from the street. Graham started screaming. His shouts were abruptly silenced. Wilbur's hand lashed out, striking him in the temple. Then the gag was over his mouth again.

The sliding door opened, and Orville appeared. The two men spoke quickly in another language. Romanian, thought Graham, or perhaps Bulgarian. Orville loomed over Graham, looking down on him. He didn't take his eyes off of him, just reached into his pocket, pulled out something, then flicked his wrist. The blade of the knife was finely honed. For a moment it hung in the air, just above Graham's throat. Then Orville plunged it downward. The blade easily passed through the duct tape, making a hole in it. The sharp blade tickled Graham's throat, but drew no blood. Orville pulled it out, then inserted the funnel into the hole.

This time he filled the funnel full of vodka three times.

Once again, Graham teetered on the edge of consciousness. He tried to will himself to be alert, to be ready to act, but his body refused to respond. He had already blacked out two or three times. A part of Graham's mind recognized that he was close to succumbing to alcohol poisoning. If they wanted him dead, all they needed to do was force another glass or two of vodka down his throat.

If they wanted him dead . . .

Drunk as he was, Graham realized they *did* want him dead. But they weren't planning on having him drink himself to death. They had other ideas.

Wilbur turned his head and looked back, and Graham stayed sufficiently still for him to think he had passed out again.

Eyes closed, Graham struggled to hold a thought or two in his head. Though he knew his life might depend on it, the images kept slipping through his mind. It was like holding on to mercury. He had struggled too long. Slipping away became ever more attractive. But there was a part of him that wouldn't give up.

Sounds filled the van. It was a long time before Graham realized they were his own groans coming through the hole in his gag. His pathetic little whistling moans were about all that he could do.

"It's all right, Pilgrim," said Wilbur. "We're almost there."

At first what he said escaped Graham's attention. Everything was so hazy that he almost overlooked it, but the echoes replayed the word over and over in his head.

Pilgrim, Pilgrim, Pilgrim.

His abductors were with Smith.

Wilbur's attention was diverted by his phone. The conversation was brief, and apparently to Wilbur's satisfaction.

Graham tried to focus. It was as much as he could do to raise his eyes open. But he had to do more than that. As addled as he was, Graham knew his death would be made to look like an accident. Odds were that no one would investigate much beyond his blood alcohol level.

His stomach told him they were on a windy road, but he couldn't afford to get sick, not with the gag in his mouth. As drunk as he was, Graham realized they were driving on Mulholland Drive. It was a windy road, full of blind turns and dips and swerves. Graham closed his eyes and tried not to feel dizzy. He concentrated on centering himself, but the world refused to stop spinning.

It was long seconds, maybe even a minute, before his conscious but stupefied mind registered that the van had stopped. Someone else seemed to be staring out from his own eyes. He watched as Wilbur poured vodka on the driver and passenger seats, saturating the area.

The knife appeared in his sight again. The blade moved in and out, sawing through the bindings, and Graham was suddenly free to move and speak.

"Sick," said Graham.

"You need fresh air."

Graham was helped out of the van. His legs were unsteady; without a guiding arm he would have fallen. Wilbur assisted him into the driver's seat.

His synapses were trying to spark, but they were alcohol-logged. Graham knew his life was on the line, but he felt helpless, pulled down by weights he couldn't throw off. The surface seemed incredibly far away.

Think.

Something cool dripped down his face. The vodka. It ran down his shirt and pooled in his pants. Hands other than his own buckled him in. His wallet was returned to his pants, and his cell phone was tossed on the passenger seat.

"You need a quick drink," said a voice in his ear.

"Sick," Graham said. He tried to open his eyes, but even that was a struggle.

"Just one more drink."

His eyes opened a crack. In Wilbur's right hand was the drink, but there was something palmed in his left hand.

The knife, was Graham's first thought.

But he knew that wasn't it. He was almost insensible, but he still recognized what Wilbur was holding. His head was spinning, but he refused to let his sudden insight tumble out of his skull. Graham had to hold on to the thought.

From the other side of the van, Orville said, "Hurry up."

In a leap of befuddled thinking, something in Graham's mind kicked in. He remembered another man who had been playing with fire.

"Drink up, now."

The glass was pressed against Graham's mouth. "Can't," he protested. He held his hand up to his mouth, as if fighting off nausea. "Sick."

"Last glass, I promise."

Graham opened his mouth, and drained the vodka. He raised his hand to his mouth, as if to fight off his retching. Wilbur tossed the glass to Orville, then he reached inside the van and turned over the key. With the engine running, he closed the driver's door. All the while, Graham was hunched forward, apparently fighting his nausea.

Wilbur tossed the vodka bottle on the passenger seat, then tumbled his thumb. Flame shot out of his lighter.

Graham had one hand on his mouth, the other near his eyes. His sickness wasn't an act. Only an act of will was keeping him from vomiting, that and the solitary plan he had managed to frame in his head.

Wilbur reached over with his lighter. The vodka-soaked upholstery would torch quickly.

Graham raised his head and spat the vodka he had never swallowed at Wilbur. The man cursed. His first thought was that Graham had thrown up on him. He realized too late that he was on the wrong end of a flamthrower. The alcohol became a line of blue flame igniting his shirt. Wilbur slapped at the fire with his hands, but couldn't put it out.

Graham couldn't run. He could barely think. He fought to get free of his safety belt, but couldn't even manage that.

Orville screamed to his brother in their native tongue, and suddenly Wilbur was rolling on the ground.

Graham knew he only had moments. But he couldn't react. They would catch him if he tried to run. He had to try and drive away. Graham reached for the key, then realized the van's engine was already running. He turned around, prepared to reverse the van, but parked directly behind him, blocking his way, was the sedan.

His head movement alerted Orville. He stepped forward and reached for the passenger door.

With exaggerated precision, Graham put the van into drive. But he needed to see where he was going. He found the lights just as Orville's hand ripped the door open.

Graham saw ahead of him, but wished he hadn't. He accelerated over the cliff.

Fifteen

Blackwell wasn't sure if there was a term for someone like him. He wasn't a spy, at least not exactly. A spy sells secrets to another country, and that's not what Blackwell did. And he wasn't a double agent, because that would have meant he was working for another power. Blackwell worked for intelligence, but most of all he worked for himself. The information he gained during his day job often benefitted him personally.

A spy who was an entrepreneur.

When he was a Princeton undergraduate, the best piece of advice Blackwell received didn't come from one of his Ivy League professors, but from a senior vice president of a manufacturing company whom he was interning under. The company was in the throes of a major reorganization, and even top management was running scared. All except for Higgins, the veep who was mentoring him.

"I'm safe," Higgins had told him with absolute confidence. "You're always safe when you know where all the bodies are buried."

At the time, Blackwell had assumed that Higgins was speaking rhetorically. But there had been something about the cruel, certain manner in which he made his pronouncement that caused Blackwell to wonder over the years if there was more than a little truth to his boast. Whatever the case, Higgins proved untouchable. Though the reorganization ax chopped off many of the top heads all around his mentor, Higgins ended up getting a promotion.

Blackwell decided that in his career he would make a point of knowing where the bodies were buried—whether figuratively or literally. And for that, there was one occupation that would suit him best. His classmates had assumed Blackwell would go into business; his career choice surprised them. Blackwell gained entre into the secret society of intelligence.

He didn't bring some master plan with him, didn't know that governmental secrets might eventually benefit him personally, but Blackwell was attracted to the hidden in much the same way a miser covets gold. He always had this *desire* to know things the world didn't.

After a time, many years of toil and bootlicking and a much too slow rise up the Agency's ladder, Blackwell began to act, but he did so very carefully. He studied those who had fallen, and tried to learn from their mistakes. It was easy to see where the fallen angels had gone wrong. Blackwell had his pick of the hen houses, but he worked them very methodically, very cautiously. He knew not to merely sell information. That had done in CIA alums Aldrich Ames, Harold James Nicholson, and Douglas Fred Groat, FBI agents Robert Philip Hanssen, Richard W. Miller, and Earl Edwin Pitts, Colonel George Trofimoff of U.S. Military Intelligence, Naval Intelligence cryptographer John Walker, NSA employee Robert Lipka, and a number of others. Selling information was a double-edged sword. You sold yourself along with whatever intelligence you were brokering. Too often the end result was that when the winds changed, and they always did, you found yourself hanged out to dry—or just hanged.

Ames, a counterintelligence officer of the CIA, was paid more than two million dollars over a ten-year period by the Russians. It was blood money. At least a dozen spies were executed because of the information Ames supplied. He sold the name of every Western agent, as well as all the Soviet double agents. But Ames himself was sold down the road by the Russians and arrested in 1994.

Nicholson, a CIA station chief and training instructor, didn't profit as much. It was believed he only received $180,000 from the Russians. He was just as willing to betray, though. Nicholson sold the names of U.S. agents in Russia, including many he himself trained, before he was arrested in 1996.

John Walker passed on more than a million secret documents. He even made it a family affair, recruiting his son, brother, and best friend. And Jonathan Pollard claimed he was spying out of love for Israel, though he was more than willing to pocket some cash in the process.

Convictions continued in the new millennium when Robert Philip Hanssen, a twenty-seven-year FBI veteran who spent most of his career as a counterspy, was arrested for spying for the Russians. Hanssen was said to have collected 1.4 million dollars in cash and diamonds during his fifteen years of spying.

Blackwell knew there was no shortage of reasons for individuals to betray their country. Greed, sex, ideology, anger, and self-interest drove them to act, and provided some a rationale for doing so. But the amazing thing, thought Blackwell, was how little money most of the double agents actually received. By doing what they did, they put their lives on the line, subjecting themselves to the worst possible vilification, or even death.

On the whole, Blackwell thought them not only stupid, but lazy. Their risk/reward ratio was laughable. Assembling raw data was like picking fruit. Anybody could do it.

Blackwell believed in using information in creative, profitable ways. But the money wasn't his only reward. He reveled in the power of it all. And he never grew tired of not only knowing things that very few other people on the planet did, but using these secrets to his own advantage.

It seemed that in the spy business cupidity bred stupidity. Ames and his ilk were so blatant in their actions they had all but attached "catch me" balloons to their person. Blackwell wondered if there were others like him out there. He assumed there must be some offshore bank accounts like his, money parlayed through the efforts of U.S. intelligence.

The problem in intelligence is that one hand often doesn't know what the other is doing. Even within the same organization, agents usually work on a need to know basis. For Blackwell's purposes, he had a need to know everything.

When Blackwell had gone into business for himself, he had remembered Benjamin Franklin's words: *Three may keep a secret if two are dead.* Blackwell kept up a firewall between himself and those he employed. That was the best way to operate a sub-rosa organization. Only Monroe and Jaeger, his money man and his muscle, knew of his existence. And Monroe and Jaeger in turn limited their own exposure. That's how it continued down the line. Blackwell, of course, knew everything.

He thought his position was much like a baseball manager's. Instead of calling in a relief pitcher, he called in relief teams. He had the designated hit, instead of the designated hitter. And sometimes the game called for a sacrifice.

Like now.

It was ironic, really. Eventually the paparazzo's time would have arrived, but his work had accelerated his demise. The synchronicity of his being on the scene for Lanie's attempted suicide was rather remarkable—and rather regrettable, at least for him. The photographer had worked, albeit unwittingly, to help create Blackwell's Hollywood web, but had himself got stuck on the strands.

At least the paparazzo had served his purpose before dying.

Blackwell looked at his watch and saw that it was six-thirty eastern time. Any moment now he should be getting the confirmation that Pilgrim was dead.

It was a shame that the actress hadn't succeeded in killing herself, thought Blackwell. That would have been one more bargaining chip. It could have even been doctored to have that much more of an impact.

What had Stalin said? "Once you pull a man by his balls, his heart will follow."

But Lanie's attempted suicide couldn't be overlooked. He was surprised she had taken everything so—personally. But her action earmarked her as a potential liability. It was time to consider how they might best help her along to end her life.

After all, she had set the precedent.

Sixteen

From atop the road the two men watched the van crash down the hill. In the darkness they heard, more than saw, its descent. When the noises stopped there was no grand explosion, but flames began to fill the vehicle.

Orville could see no sign of movement, but the brush was thick and his view limited. He wanted to continue watching, but couldn't chance lingering. The flames would draw attention. In minutes the whole canyon might be on fire, and that would bring all sorts of emergency vehicles.

"Get in the car," Orville said to his brother, snapping off his flashlight.

"He has to be dead," said Wilbur. His shirt was still smoldering, and his hands, chest, and part of his face were red and burned. The lower half of his right eyebrow was singed, giving him a surprised expression.

Orville said nothing, but his silence spoke of worry. His brother's lapse allowed for the possibility, albeit small, that the photographer was still alive. Before reporting in, they would need to confirm his death.

The van was really starting to burn now, and the flames were spreading to the brush. His brother was right, though. The crashing vehicle had probably killed him. The vodka would certainly have immobilized him. And if that wasn't enough, it was unlikely he could get out of the van, let alone outrun the spreading fire. But things hadn't gone exactly as planned, and the German wouldn't like that.

As dawn broke, the Brothers waited in a deserted parking lot. They had made one stop at an all-night convenience store for some Neosporin and aspirin. Wilbur's face was pumpkin color, but he didn't have the jack-o'-lantern grin to go with it. His hands were blistered; the gloves he had been wearing for the job had burned into his hands. Slumped in the backseat, out of sight of probing eyes, he did his best not to groan so as to not interfere with his brother's listening to the police scanner.

Americans were so accommodating, thought Orville. They even published a National Law Enforcement Frequency Book that listed all the broadcasting channels for federal, state, and local law enforcement agencies. They almost encouraged the kind of eavesdropping he was doing. By monitoring the emergency calls, he had tracked the fire, and the personnel called in to combat it. From miles away, safe from scrutiny, he had followed all that was going on. The canyon fire hadn't been easy to rein in, but now it was under control. There had been no word of survivors.

Pilgrim had to be dead. All that was missing was the announcement and the body bag.

"Shit!"

Wilbur straightened at his brother's curse. He hadn't been listening very closely to the scanner. Its constant static and squelching had given him a headache. There wasn't a part of his body that didn't hurt.

"What?"

Orville had already started the engine. "They are taking someone out of the canyon. He's burned, but he's alive.

"For the moment."

Rather than walk into a potential trap, Orville made a series of calls posing as a *Los Angeles Times* reporter. He contacted police, fire, emergency services, and hospital personnel.

Most didn't want to comment to a reporter, referring the calls to PR people, but Orville didn't let them hang up on him that quickly. He gathered his bits and pieces of information, all "off the record."

The burns were described as "substantial." No one had given him the name of the victim, but he learned that he was being rushed to Cedars-Sinai.

Orville waited for several minutes, then made the call to the hospital and asked to be connected to the Burn Unit. Someone who identified herself as Sylvia answered the phone.

"Yes, Sylvia," he said, trying to do his best American accent. "My name is Jim Wells. The police just called and told me my brother Graham's van was involved in an accident on Mulholland Drive. I understand he was brought over to your place."

There was a long pause on the other line. Orville wondered if they were trying to trace the call. If so, they wouldn't have any luck. All of his calls were routed through a relay system that appeared to come out of England. But her delay wasn't for technical reasons. She was confused.

"What did you say your name was?"

"Jim Wells."

"I think someone's given you some erroneous information, Mr. Wells."

"How is that?"

"Perhaps I should transfer you—"

"The police identified my brother's van by the license plate and VIN number. There's no mistake about that."

"Your brother isn't here, Mr. Wells."

"They told me a burn victim was taken from the fire."

"That's true. A Mexican national was brought in."

With considerable effort, he stifled a curse.

"The translator tells us that he was camping in the canyon when suddenly he awoke to flames all around him."

He knew that the German wasn't going to like this, wasn't going to like it at all.

"Mr. Wells?"

"Thank you."

He hung up the phone, then reached over and turned up the police scanner. The paparazzo had to be dead. They would find him among the burned brush. He had probably been thrown clear of the van when it crashed.

He was dead. He had to be.

Seventeen

When the somersaulting van finally came to a stop, the words of the Abbot came unbidden into Graham's head: "God apparently has a soft spot in his heart for fools, drunks, and Americans."

He was alive—for the moment at least. By hitting the trifecta, he had somehow been spared. His seat belt had saved his life, but wearing it hadn't stopped him from being thrown around violently. It hurt to move, but he had no choice. The fire was spreading throughout the van.

Graham fought to free himself from his seat belt, won, then pushed on his door, but it wouldn't budge. He used his hand to try to pat down the flames reaching for him, then grabbed at the handle to the passenger door. It swung open. With the fire licking at him, he fell heavily out of the van.

The race was to the slow. Graham couldn't take more than a handful of steps without falling. The ground was uneven and his equilibrium was shot. Try as he might, staying upright was impossible. With each fall the fire seemed that much closer, but luck was again with him. The wind fanned the fire away.

Still, Graham knew that the wind could change. He walked mostly blind, fighting his way through the chaparral, making a path through the stands of sage, greasewood, and lemonade berry. With every fall, it was that much harder for him to get up. He passed out once, and had no idea how long the blackout lasted. He awakened to the sounds of sirens, and answered them like a punch-drunk fighter responding to the bell, fighting his way to his feet. His only plan was to move away from the fire and steer clear of the main road. The men who wanted him dead might still be there.

He stopped to get his breath, and saw all the activity atop the hill. The firefighters were backlit by the lights and the fire. Graham was tempted to call to them, but instead he moved farther into the shadows. Drunk as he was, Graham instinctively didn't fear the fire so much as the men who had caused it. He was aware enough to know that he wasn't yet ready to answer the questions the firefighters would have for him. In a few hours he might be able to tell what happened without looking like a drunk with a wild story.

Graham staggered along. Every step was agony. He felt as if a couple of heavyweights had used him as a punching bag. His ribs ached, his head ached, and his own arms and legs were fighting him as if they had a mind of their own. He fell hard, pushed his way up, then fell a second time and didn't get up.

He awakened to a ringing and realized the sounds weren't only in his head. Reaching down to his pocket he found his cell phone. Graham looked at the phone for a long moment, trying to remember how it had gotten there. He had the vaguest memory of falling out of the van, grabbing for the phone as if it were some kind of lifeline, and stuffing it into his pocket. Graham turned off the ringer. He wasn't ready to talk to a friend, let alone a stranger. Or worse, maybe his insurance agent.

Not far away Graham heard the sounds of cars driving along a road, a reminder that he wasn't very far removed from rush-hour Los Angeles. He sat up and immediately felt dizzy. Graham raised his hand to block out the morning sun. The rays were weak, but he still felt like one of the undead having to face up to daylight. With an effort he rose, took a step, then stumbled. This many hours later, Graham thought, and I still can't walk a straight line.

His head pounded with migraine proportions. It was the worst hangover Graham ever remembered having. He took another step, then was overcome by nausea. Bending over, he threw up. His brain didn't seem to clue in to his painfully emptied stomach. Helplessly he retched, then retched again, his stomach muscles convulsing with the effort.

I'm not dead, he thought, but I wish I were.

When Graham was able to straighten, he felt a little, but not a lot, better. He tried to think between the throbbing in his head. He was dehydrated, and not in any condition to walk very far. He considered calling the police, but something in him resisted. I need to shower first, he thought, and I need to make sense of what happened.

Two men had tried to kill him, men who appeared to be associated with the government.

I'll call a cab, Graham thought, but then reconsidered. If his assailants were still out there, they would be on the alert for a cab. And besides, where would he ask the cab to take him? His home was probably being watched. They might be waiting for him there.

It was easy to be paranoid, especially when it came to potential spies. They might be monitoring *everything*.

Graham made for the sounds of passing cars. He cut over onto a dog-walking path, but didn't continue onto the street, choosing to only go far enough to see the road's name before retreating back into the brush.

He had to make a call. No, *the call*, the one where your life has gone to shit and you need someone to pull you from the toilet. *The call* you're supposed to reserve for an emergency, a desperate situation. Graham tried to think about whom to call. Normally he would have called his sometimes partner Ran, but Graham knew he was out of town on assignment and wouldn't be back until late that afternoon. There was no family member to turn to. He was an only child whose mother had committed suicide when he was ten, and whose father was overseas. Graham thought about, and then rejected, various friends. They were fair-weather sorts, and in this instance there were definite storm clouds around.

One name, one face, kept surfacing. In some ways Graham was lucky the alcohol hadn't burned off. Sober, he might not have been able to call her.

Even after four years he hadn't forgotten the number to her direct line. He punched it in, and Paige Harris answered on the second ring. She still didn't have a secretary screening her calls. At least that hadn't changed. Early in her career Paige had read about a Wall Street mover and shaker who made a point of answering his own phone. He said he didn't want his position to buffer him from the world he was dependent upon. Paige adopted that philosophy as her own.

"Can you talk?" Graham asked.

The line was silent for several seconds. Graham thought she had hung up when she finally said, "Yes."

It had been years since Graham had asked her that question. Even when they had been going out, he had always prefaced their phone conversations with those words. It was the kind of question you needed to ask a married woman.

Graham knew she wouldn't say his name aloud. Old habits died hard, and he was glad of that. If the cellular phone conversations in the area were being monitored, his might not stand out.

Doing his best not to slur any words, Graham said, "I know you probably have appointments lined up all day, but I really need to see you."

Again, she was slow to answer. "When?"

"Now. And to add insult to injury, you'll need to drive. My car's in the shop."

He knew that Paige would be able to pick up that he was only telling part of the story. It helped that in the past their phone conversations had always been cryptic.

"I can't get away—"

Her rejection wasn't unexpected, but it surprised him how much it still hurt. It was an indictment of his life. He didn't have anyone on the other end for *the call.*

"—for at least an hour."

The unexpected reprieve felt like a call from the governor.

"I'm at my mother's house," he said. Paige knew his mother was long dead. "You probably remember that it's on Briarcrest Lane. That's one word."

He didn't want to mention Mulholland Drive, wanted to offer as few giveaways as possible to anyone who might be monitoring their conversation.

"Briarcrest."

"Just park on the street. I'll be looking for you."

"I understand."

"Thank you."

While Graham waited, he thought about Paige Harris. Their affair had lasted a year. He had originally sought Paige out as a contact. *People* magazine had profiled her in an article, headlining Paige as "The Money Manager to the Stars." Her clientele was a virtual *Who's Who* of the silver screen. Graham made a point of getting to know her.

She wasn't what he expected, and maybe he wasn't what she expected. Graham had represented himself as a freelance photographer, and said that his agency represented him to a number of magazines and newspapers. While that was true enough, his purported pictorial—"Where the Street Meets the Surf"—was complete fiction. His lunch with Paige was subterfuge for getting an inside track on some of the stars she represented. At the time, Paige was in her early thirties. When Graham first met her, he expected the personality of a bean counter. He knew she had looks; that's what the *People* spread had shown. But he hadn't expected Paige to appeal to him on so many other levels.

Graham took special pains to do a good job on her shoot, and then sent her the best pictures along with a thank-you note. She called him, and one thing had led to another.

At the time, Paige had been at a crossroads in her life. She said she loved her husband Dave, but wasn't in love with him. Dave was everything Graham wasn't. He had a high-powered job as CFO for a high-tech company. Dave was steady and reliable, and had a long-range vision for their future. He was a workaholic, but had the money and desire to spoil his wife with material goods.

On paper it was no contest. Graham couldn't stack up to her husband. Paige was thinking about a family. She was used to the comforts of a wealthy lifestyle. She and Dave had met at Stanford University's graduate school of business, and had much in common.

And yet it was Graham she wanted to spend the rest of her life with.

In the time they saw one another, neither Graham nor Paige ever felt so alive. And neither ever endured so much pain. Paige was willing to give everything up for Graham—marriage, perks, seemingly her sanity. She knew that he used her to get his pictures, knew that their relationship had begun under false pretenses, but she was still willing to forgive him virtually everything.

For a year they lived double lives, until she asked Graham to commit.

He wanted to. He never wanted anything so much in his life. Yet he knew it was wrong. In the bedroom they were perfectly suited for one another. With her, he lost himself. Their hunger was raw and primal and each time they were together it surprised them anew. But Paige made no bones of wanting a family, of expecting him to be there like some kind of proper tin soldier.

Her husband knew that Paige was seeing someone else, but he loved her enough to tell her that he was there for her no matter what. Graham knew he could never be that unselfish. He was too used to being independent, too used to loving himself above all others. Paige needed a stand-up man like Dave, not someone like himself. He decided to bow out of the picture. Graham wanted to think his decision was noble, but maybe he just lacked the guts to commit. Paige had offered him the gift of herself, and he let her slip through his fingers.

Six months after they stopped seeing one another, Paige became pregnant. The commitment of a child seemed to bring her closer to her husband.

Between losing Paige and getting the scare of his life in Rio, Graham had decided he hated L.A., and took his camera overseas. In the years since they hadn't talked, but Graham had kept up with Paige's life. She was his "what if" game. He knew it was a game he would play until he died.

From Graham's vantage point, he watched Briarcrest. He camped under a laurel sumac off the trail, and hoped that no dogs would pick up his scent. As the morning passed, the day grew hotter. The smoke from the fire hung in the air, and Graham felt as if he were slowly being barbecued. His mouth was caked and filmy, but he didn't have saliva enough to spit. He felt like roadkill, and knew he smelled like it.

What better present could he give Paige, he thought, than showing her so vividly that she had made the right choice staying with Dave?

A car slowly circled along Briarcrest, a Lexus SUV, then came to a stop and parked. Its windows were tinted, making it difficult for him to see inside, but he could still make out a woman behind the wheel.

Graham moved down the trail. Before emerging on the street he looked around and made sure no one was watching the Lexus. Already he was having second thoughts about having involved Paige. They had kept their affair quiet, but Graham knew how secrets could be unraveled. That was his business. If someone looked hard enough, they would find her.

He kept low to the ground, approaching the rear of her SUV. He sidled up to the back door, and tapped on the window.

Paige started. She took a long look at him before unlocking her car. Graham had seen his reflection in the window and understood her delay. In the best of circumstances, he probably would have disappointed her. The last few years had aged him; the last few hours had made him even more unrecognizable.

Graham hunched down on her backseat. Instead of turning, Paige looked at him through the rearview mirror. Perhaps it was easier for her to view him that way. In the enclosed space Graham's odor dominated. He reached for the car window control, and lowered the back window nearest him.

"A few hours ago I was in a car accident," Graham said. "I know I smell like a brewery that's burned down, and that I look like shit. I'll tell you that my current condition isn't my fault, but I don't want to tell you any more than that, because it's best that you don't know. Not that I really know myself."

Paige shook her head. "I've imagined this moment for a long time. I always wondered what we would say to one another. I thought of all the different scenarios. None of them resembled this."

Graham had a lump in his throat. He was glad he was too dehydrated for tears.

"One more thing," he whispered. "I am so parched, I'm ready to pass out. If I do, don't be surprised."

"I have some water," she said. She reached down to her sports bag and pulled out a bottle of Evian.

That's why we weren't meant for one another, thought Graham. I'm a tap water kind of guy. But thank God she wasn't. She handed him her water bottle. With shaky hands he took it, pulled off the top, then upturned it.

He drained the water, then fell back, his head resting on a child's car seat. Paige started up the car and began to drive.

"If you want to stretch out, you can put the car seat in the back."

"I'm fine," Graham said. "I hope Dorothy doesn't mind my using her seat as a pillow. What is she? Two?"

"Twenty months."

"And how's Sam?"

"He's a treasure."

Paige smiled at the thought of her children. She was pleased that Graham had kept up with her life. "I wasn't even sure that you knew I'd had children."

"Each time I wanted to send flowers. But I thought the best thing to do was just stay the hell out of your life."

"I've watched for your photo credits," she said. "A couple years back your name kept cropping up on overseas pictures."

"I was out of the country for a while."

"Then I didn't see your pictures for some time, until they started appearing again on the Hollywood shots."

"Sewer rat returns to sewer," Graham said, but his brief smile was genuine. They had stepped out of each other's lives—that was how it had to be—but both had still been watching for the other.

"Where do you want me to take you?"

Graham put a hand up to his temple, and tried to think through the lingering headache and booze. "To an ATM, and then a convenience store. But they can't be close to one another. Can the government monitor ATM transactions? I'm sure they can."

"Government?"

Graham realized he had been thinking aloud. "Forget what I said."

"What kind of trouble are you in?"

He didn't want to involve her, didn't want to have his affairs somehow boomerang back to her. "It's nothing. I upset somebody's apple cart."

Paige bypassed the mirror, turned her head, and in a glance took in the measure of his lie. Neither said anything for a few minutes. Graham finally broke their silence when she pulled into the parking lot of a bank.

"Don't park where any security cameras might pick up your car."

She did as he said.

"Thank you," said Graham. "Thank you for everything."

"I was glad to finally hear from you."

They chose a convenience store several miles from the bank. Because of how he looked, Paige shopped for him. When she returned to the car, the first thing Graham did was drink the better part of a gallon of water. He dumped cologne on his face and body, chewed breath mints, and devoured some candy bars and chips.

"They only had T-shirts fit for the sub-teen crowd," Paige said. "I thought I'd stop at a clothing store and get you an outfit."

"Bless you."

"Thirty-three waist," she said, "thirty-two inseam. Collar fifteen and a half, length thirty-four."

"If you say so. I don't even know."

"You've kept your same trim figure."

"So have you."

She laughed. "You always were a wonderful liar, Graham. No woman goes through childbirth twice and retains her same figure. It's one of Newton's laws. Fig Newtons."

"You're beautiful."

"You're deluded." But she didn't sound displeased.

While she shopped for him, Graham cleaned himself with Dorothy's baby wipes. He almost looked human by the time Paige returned with his clothes. She had bought him some khaki pants, a light blue polo shirt, tan socks, and soft moose-leather loafers. Old habits apparently died hard; Paige had always been trying to upgrade his wardrobe in the time they were together.

"There was no such thing as a generic baseball cap," she said. "They all came with logos, or words, or team names. The closest thing I could find was a Dodgers cap."

She handed it to him. Graham didn't tell her that he hated the Dodgers. Even though they had lived overseas, his father had kept up with his Giants through the *International Herald Tribune*. Graham had accepted his father's team, and the rivalry that went with it, as his own. Still, the cap with the blue L.A. letters suited his purposes. And he could always look forward to burning it in the future.

"Perfect," Graham said.

"Oh, and I got you some underwear."

Graham took off the wrapping. Mickey Mouse smiled from the boxers.

"I couldn't decide between Mickey or Goofy."

"Yeah, it's always tough to choose between a *small* rodent or a dumb dog."

"A *cute* rodent. You don't approve?"

"My first choice wouldn't be to have a mouse covering my privates."

"My mistake." She tried to keep a straight face, but failed.

"Payback," Graham said, "for that time I took you to Disneyland."

"You made me go on all the rides alone."

"I was working."

"You were waiting for Godot."

"Michael Jackson."

"Same thing."

It was general knowledge that Disneyland management regularly helped the disguised Jackson slip into the park through a private gate. Graham had gotten a tip from an employee that Jocko would be making one of his visits to the park. Knowing Jackson was going to be there was only half the battle. Graham had to pick him out, and Jackson wasn't one of those stars who settled for dark glasses and a scarf. Professional makeup artists always gave him a different look. On that day, Graham missed getting the shot of the incognito Jackson. Later, he heard that Jackson had been disguised as a groundskeeper.

He took off his shirt, glad to be rid of it. "I know you have to get back to work," he said. "Would it be too much of an imposition to ask for a lift out to West L.A.?"

"Got an address?" she asked.

He gave her the name of a major intersection near where he lived. Paige started the engine, looked back in the mirrors, and noticed his bare chest. She whistled softly, and then started driving.

Twenty minutes later Graham had her pull over at a spot about a half mile from his apartment. That was as close as he wanted her to get to what was going on in his life.

"I think you are safe," Graham said, "but if anyone comes and asks you about getting a call from me, just tell them the truth: an old friend asked for help, and you gave it."

"What's this all about?"

"That's something I have to find out myself."

He paused before leaving her car. His dirty clothes were tucked in a bag under one arm. He saw his reflection in her rearview mirror. He had dark circles, a few bruises, and a one-day beard, but he looked presentable enough save for the Dodgers cap.

"I wanted to call you a million times before," Graham said. "I wanted to hear your voice. I wanted to see you. I didn't want you to think I had forgotten. I've never forgotten."

"I'll always love you too, Graham."

That's what he had meant to say. She just said it better.

"Thanks for being there. Thanks for being you."

From the backseat he reached for her hand, and squeezed her fingers. Then he opened the door, tapped the child's safety seat, and stepped outside.

"I'll look for you in pictures," Paige said.

Eighteen

Blackwell used his mouse to click off his "safe-deposit box." Communicating electronically sure beat the days of mail drops, and the electronic bank was much better than talking through a so-called secure line. The National Security Agency was the biggest eavesdropper in the world. Most people were oblivious to the world's largest intelligence organization—what insiders called the "No Such Agency"—unaware that NSA supercomputers worked day and night monitoring domestic and international telephone calls coming in and out of the United States.

Most of NSA's operations were conducted in their thousand-acre complex in Fort Meade, Maryland. But their really interesting stuff was buried underground where they kept over twenty-seven acres of computers. The machines were listening, always listening, taking in information from satellites and microwave towers. And their techs and cryptoanalysts liked nothing more than decoding digital signals sent over "secure" phone lines.

As an insider, Blackwell knew how difficult it was to beat the system. That's what made the challenge—and his David versus Goliath game—so appealing. Where a giant would be noticed, a mouse was not. You just had to know where and how to creep. There were plenty of pickings to be had, but Blackwell desired more than to graze off the crumbs. He wanted a seat at the main table.

The news wasn't what Blackwell had hoped. Pilgrim was apparently still alive. Monroe had tried contacting the paparazzo, but without success. Pilgrim was probably running scared, was likely holed up somewhere. It was possible that he had gone to the police already. But even if that was true, the authorities wouldn't know what to do with his wild story. They would probably view his tale as an attempt to escape culpability for the fire his vehicle had caused.

No, there was no immediate threat, but Pilgrim's continued existence posed problems. Jaeger would have to recall his two operatives, or at least have them disappear for a time. They were Pilgrim's only link to what had occurred. Jaeger would have to clean up any loose ends they left behind.

You had to expect glitches like this. Thus far everything had gone unbelievably well. Blackwell's plan had been a pipe dream at first. He had proceeded carefully, slowly. It could have been derailed countless number of ways. What Blackwell had liked from the first was the simplicity of the plan. The expenses hadn't been inconsiderable, but he had profited enough from other ventures to look at them as necessary research and development. As Thoreau had said, you need to break some eggs to make an omelette.

He was willing to break eggs—or legs—whatever it took. He was close now, so close.

Blackwell tapped out his message over the computer. It was cryptic, but not coded. Jaeger would understand.

Nineteen

Graham was used to staking out homes, but not his own. He studied all the likely spots where someone could be watching for him, and then he looked at the unlikely spots. He was used to working with good surveillance equipment, and tried to analyze the area using his own experience, but he knew the Feds had gear that put his to shame. They could be using satellites for all he knew, but if that was the case they still needed people on the ground to intercept him, and Graham didn't spot any likely agents.

He still couldn't make sense of why two men had tried to kill him. There was no shortage of people who would like to see him dead, but they were the same people who would want all paparazzi dead. The two men were obviously under orders, working for the spook who called himself John Smith—if indeed that was what Smith was. Graham's job should have made him a professional unbeliever, and yet he had never questioned Smith's bona fides. Smith had poleaxed him by knowing things about him, the kind of intelligence Graham had thought only a governmental agency might be privy to. Graham's fear of being exposed had done his thinking for him.

Now that he was legally sober—or close enough—maybe he should go to the police. But there was always the possibility that Smith—whomever or whatever he was—had the kind of juice that could get him jammed up. Besides, without Graham's admitting to what had happened in Paris, there were huge gaps in his own story. He couldn't very well explain the jobs he had done for Smith without some compelling reason. Even if he came up with some plausible story, the police investigation might tie him up for days, and he couldn't afford that, at least not now. He was potentially sitting on his biggest story in years.

It seemed like weeks had passed since Graham caught Lanie trying to commit suicide, but it was less than eighteen hours ago. Before doing anything else, he needed to see how his pictures from the night before had turned out.

From a pay phone at a service station, Graham called for a cab. He paced around, going over the plan in his head. It was fifteen minutes before the taxi arrived. Graham walked up to the driver's window, leaned over, and said, "Go ahead and start the meter. I just need to make a quick call."

He dialed 9-1-1. When asked about the nature of his emergency, Graham said, "Yes, I live at the Los Arboles Apartments on Rivera Street. That's 1100 Rivera. Anyway, I'm in 4B. The unit next to mine is 4A, and I just heard gunshots."

"What's your name, sir?" the dispatcher asked.

"I'm Jason."

"Your last name, Jason?"

"Look, I really don't want to get involved."

"It's just for our records."

"Did you hear that shot?" Graham asked. "Someone's screaming!"

He hung up the phone, and walked over to his cab. The dispatcher would have to put it out as a hot call. Graham expected that in a very short time LAPD would be knocking at Apartment 4A. His apartment.

The taxi driver was a young black man. Graham looked for his name on the license: Rashid Jackson. While the cabby waited for instructions, Graham fished out his wallet. He knew Hollywood sorts who regularly handed their waiter a hundred-dollar bill even before their order was taken. Said or unsaid, the message was, "Take care of me, and I'll take care of you." From what Graham had observed, the pre-tip was an effective means of getting the best of service. Ben Franklin tended to get a server's attention. And what was even more important in Hollywood, it made a statement to the other diners.

"Rashid," Graham said, "I'm going to be doing some apartment hunting in this area. That means you're going to have to do some sitting and waiting. I hope this will make your waiting worthwhile."

Graham passed over an Andrew Jackson. It didn't produce the genuflecting of a Ben Franklin, but at least it got Rashid to nod.

"Where to?" he asked.

For form's sake, Graham had Rashid drive him to an apartment complex a few blocks away from where he lived. He nosed around for a few minutes, wasting time while doing his prospective tenant imitation, then directed Rashid over to Los Arboles. Two patrol cars were parked on the street.

"Not a good first impression," Graham said, getting out.

He walked over to his unit, and heard Mrs. Kerr long before he saw her. Mrs. Kerr and her dog Rex lived next to him in 4B. Mr. Kerr had died a decade earlier. He had, Graham often thought, taken the easy way out.

One officer was talking with Mrs. Kerr, or at least trying to talk, while the second officer was scouting the area. "I wasn't the one who called this time," said Mrs. Kerr, "but I've called other times, believe you me. I didn't hear any gunshots, but that doesn't mean there wasn't shooting going on. It's getting so I don't even want to leave my apartment."

"Do you know your neighbor in 4A?" the officer asked.

"Him?" she said. "I should say not. He's an animal-hater. I caught him trying to abuse Rex." Mrs. Kerr patted the small dog protectively.

What she didn't tell the officer was that Rex had been using Graham's front door step as a litter box for some time. Mrs. Kerr had caught Graham trying to dissuade the dog from his habit through tennis ball therapy. The balls had missed the dog, but Mrs. Kerr had never forgiven him.

"Do you know where he works," the cop asked, "or what he does?"

"I'm a photographer," Graham said. "My name is Graham Wells."

He announced himself not so much to the cop doing the interview, but to the second cop, who had picked up the FedEx package that Graham had mailed to himself. Graham held out his hand, and the officer passed over the package. They were rejoined by the other officer, who seemed only too happy to take his leave of Mrs. Kerr.

"What's going on?" Graham asked.

Mrs. Kerr's cop, a well-built Hispanic man, seemed to be the designated speaker for the day. "We had a call about shots being fired from inside your apartment," he said. "Do you know if anyone is inside?"

Graham shook his head. "It should be vacant." He scratched his whiskered chin. "I've been away on assignment since yesterday afternoon, though."

"Do you mind if we look inside?"

"Not at all." In fact, if the offer hadn't been made, Graham would have insisted on it. He reached for his keys, found them missing, then remembered they had been abandoned with the van. He walked over to a planter whose flowers were perpetually brown and neglected, reached under it, and pulled out his spare set of door keys. The cop took them from him.

"Better let us open the door."

Graham stepped aside. While the Hispanic cop opened the door, the other covered him with his drawn gun. Eye signals passed between the officers, then both made their way inside. Graham was left waiting outside with Mrs. Kerr, whose curiosity outweighed her long-standing indignation of him. Graham's apartment was all of 750 square feet, and it didn't take long for the officers to go through it. They came out shaking their heads.

"It's empty," said the speaker. "We're going to look around the complex, though."

That suited Graham just fine. The longer the cops were around, the better. He still felt as if he were wearing a bull's-eye target on his back. He stepped inside and dead-bolted the door behind him. Years of last-minute assignments had made Graham an efficient packer, allowing him to hurriedly throw together a bag. Instead of listening to his messages, he pulled out the message machine and tossed it into his suitcase. He shaved in less than a minute, long enough for him to take in his bumps, bruises, and bags under his eyes.

Mrs. Kerr was the only person around to see him off. She looked at him, and his bag, suspiciously. Graham half expected her to start screaming for the cops. Rex was hiding behind her legs. The dog would probably make a beeline—make that peeline—for his doormat as soon as he was out of sight.

Graham took the stairs down to the parking garage, clicked his keyless remote, and dashed over to his T-bird. This time no one materialized from behind a pillar. Once on the street he pulled up alongside of the parked cab and lowered his passenger window.

"What's the fare?" he asked.

Rashid barely blinked at his sudden appearance in a vehicle. Maybe he thought Graham was boosting it. If so, he didn't ask any questions, merely read the meter and quoted a fare of $8.40. Graham passed over a ten-dollar bill, and drove off.

Having the rolls of film in his hand gave Graham a rush. It was rare to finally catch up with the carrot that kept you going. He drove around the block, checking his rearview mirror to make sure he wasn't being followed, then headed over to a commercial photo plant on Sepulveda.

A young, white-coated Asian tech took in his film. Management must not have heard that even scientists had given up on white coats. The tech recognized Graham as a regular.

"You want to put it on your account?"

Graham nodded, then searched out the tech's name. It was stitched with blue lettering onto the white coat: *Adrian.*

"I'm in a rush here, Adrian," he said. "How long do you think?"

"I can make it one-hour service if you'd like."

Graham looked at his watch. "I'd like it even better if it was half-hour service."

"Got a couple jobs ahead of you."

"See what you can do," Graham said.

From the sitting room, Graham could watch the development process. Henry Ford would have liked the setup. Human involvement was at a minimum. Staff never bothered to look at the film other than a cursory glance to check the color of the prints. That was how Graham liked it.

He kept watch on the door, on his film, on the street, and kept impatiently checking his watch. Graham kept rethinking the shoot, second-guessing himself on everything he had done. He'd be lucky if any of the pictures came out. Lanie would probably just be a blur, indistinguishable from anybody.

Even with the ventilation system going full blast, the place reeked of chemicals. The smell always brought on a memory that Graham could do without: an embalming. The chemicals smelled the same. He had been covering the death of a big name actor and had done a butter-up job on the mortician. One thing led to another, and the mortician had invited him to come do a shoot of the embalming. Because this violated all sorts of professional ethics, the mortician arranged it to look as if Graham was taking the pictures unbeknownst to him. The mortician had preened like a peacock while he went about with his embalming. He was proud as could be of his work.

Graham wished he could say the same thing about his job. He sniffed the air. Pictures and death.

His negatives were hanging like laundry on a line. Graham looked at his watch. The hour was ticking down. He got up, walked over to the counter, and in his worst Stallone yelled, "Yo, Adrian."

Adrian looked up, raised his index finger to signal one minute, then went back to his work.

He should have raised five fingers—or his middle finger—for the five minutes it took before he raised himself. At least Adrian managed to package the photos without doing any rubbernecking. But maybe, Graham thought, there was nothing to see.

Graham took the packages out to his T-bird. His heart was racing as he unsealed the envelope. This could be a huge payday. He stopped breathing, pulled the pictures out, then loudly exhaled.

It was Christmas, New Year's, and Independence Day all wrapped into one. The shots were better than he could have hoped. Lanie Byrne's dance with death was there for all to see.

He flipped through the photos. There was no doubt about it. You could read the lettering on the Courvoisier bottle. Even her pill bottle was clearly visible. There were a few good shots of Lanie's lips opening, swallowing death. And in all of them were Lanie's celebrated eyes, but these eyes were glassy and full of despair, not the eyes the world knew. Betty Grable's gams had been insured for a million dollars. Lanie's eyes were worth about a hundred times that. But not in these shots. All he'd captured was the dying of the light.

Graham's ebullience vanished. He tried to jolly himself up, then got mad that it wasn't working. What the hell was wrong with him? He was holding his future. The main reason he had become a paparazzo was that there was no money to be made in legitimate photography. He'd been on staff for newspapers and magazines, and done stringer work. The wages had been pitiful, the assignments mundane. He had thought of himself as only a short step up from a department store photographer. Squeak toy work was how he described it. Squeak the toy and get the shot. But looking at the photos of Lanie made that work somehow seem noble. He thought of his mother that he had barely known. "Shit!" he said, then pushed the photos back into the envelope.

Graham put off calling his film agency and telling them what he had, even though he wasn't sure why. These were the kinds of photos that were auctioned. In a few hours they would have bids from around the world. Lanie had that kind of juice. She had worldwide appeal. Graham knew he was sitting on gold, but he told himself it was just one vein of gold. With a little digging, he tried to convince himself, a whole potful could be uncovered.

He stopped at an electronics store, and paid cash for a new digital phone. This might put them off his track if they were monitoring the numbers of calls he was making. Graham got Estelle Steinberg's number and phoned her. Around town she was known as "Estelle from hell." An assistant who identified herself as Carrie Farnham took down his name and number.

"What's this concerning, Mr. Wells?" Carrie asked.

"Tell her that I'm Lanie's little helper from last night," Graham said. "Tell her that I'd like to see Lanie this afternoon to see how she's doing."

Graham knew that in the best of circumstances, Estelle was stingy with Lanie's time. People in the business said it was easier getting an audience with the queen than five minutes with Lanie. But he was holding certain cards that would be hard for her to ignore.

He continued to make other calls while driving around. Between conversations, he thumbed through the photos. Every time he looked at the pictures, he came away feeling bothered, but he couldn't stop staring at them. Nothing he heard made him feel better.

Graham called Estelle a second time. He got a different assistant, a man named Donald, but the same promise. He made more calls while waiting to hear from her. Graham didn't know exactly what he was searching for, but he kept poking and talking. Like any good celebrity photographer, he knew that if you only looked for dirt, you often missed the bigger picture. In this instance, Graham knew his story went well beyond an actress trying to kill herself, even if he didn't know where it went.

Estelle had done a good job protecting her hen, had managed to keep Lanie's suicide attempt off the radar screen. There wasn't even a hum out there. Estelle had put out the word that Lanie had the flu. Her cover story was easy to believe, helped by Lanie's reputation as a workaholic, an actor's actor that gave her all. Besides, the flu *was* going around, like always.

The afternoon was ticking away when Graham made his third call to Estelle. Carrie was being her buffer again, and Graham gave up any pretense of diplomacy. "Tell Estelle I expect her to call me within five minutes. If I don't hear from her, I'll be on the horn to some people describing what Lanie had for dinner last night. We're talking about her Last Supper diet."

Three minutes later Graham's phone rang. Estelle didn't waste time: "Who the hell are you?"

"I'm the guy who saved you from having to dress in black today, and having to put in the longest day of your life. My name is Graham Wells. I drove Lanie to Dr. Burke's last night."

"What do you want?"

"I need to see Lanie. Now."

"Impossible."

"I'm sure Lanie would prefer seeing me to the alternative."

"Her flu—"

"Cut the flu crap. She OD'd and had her stomach pumped. I was there.

I'm sure she doesn't feel like doing cartwheels, but we talked last night when she was much worse. A little conversation won't inconvenience her too much."

"Why do you want to see her?"

"That's between me and Lanie."

"You try and blackmail her, and before we're through with you our lawyers will be cutting you a new asshole."

"I'm happy with the one I have, thanks."

"Don't try and jerk me off, scumbag. What were you doing at the Grove last night?"

"I was saving the life of Miss L."

"You were trespassing. What are you, a stalker?"

"No. I just happened to be at the right place at the right time."

"That sounds like bullshit to me. If your story doesn't check out, I can have you brought up on charges."

"I didn't know that saving a life was a felony offense."

"Do the words 'trespassing,' 'unlawful entry,' and 'reckless endangerment' mean anything to you? If I get wind of you trying anything, I'll have you arrested and thrown behind bars. Step out of line and you'll be playing French Maid to a gorilla named Bubba."

"Thanks anyway, but I think I'll pass on your matchmaking. You can expect me at the Grove within an hour."

Estelle delayed committing to anything. "What do you do for a living, Mr. Wells?"

"I'm in public relations."

"That's the kind of answer a hooker gives."

"I guess you'd know."

The long silence that followed didn't fool Graham. Estelle ached to tell him to go to hell and hang up on him, but she couldn't. She had to protect Lanie from him making good on his threat.

"I'll clear your name with the guard at the gate," Estelle from hell said. She didn't say good-bye, but he got the point that their conversation was over when she slammed the phone down.

It was half a minute before Graham's hearing returned to his left ear.

Twenty

Graham made his return to the Grove in the late afternoon. The view from Vista de la Ballena was much different this time. It was pretty enough, he thought, that you could even make a case for the prices people paid for Malibu real estate. The still potent November sun was about to disappear on the horizon and cast a red glow on the Pacific.

Lanie's staff was back on duty. An armed guard stood up and greeted Graham at the gate. He cleared him for admittance, opened the gate, then directed him to where he should park. As Graham drove slowly along the winding flagstone driveway, he had the feeling that he was on a set. The grounds were too manicured, too perfect. There were streaming fountains, ponds that abounded with koi, and between stately trees were beds of blooming flowers.

As large as the house was, its boxlike structure somehow blended into the hillside. The whitewashed villa would have looked at home along the coast in the Mediterranean. Trellised bougainvillea followed the house around, offering a palette of pinks, reds, oranges, and purples.

Graham parked his T-bird under the canopy of a huge coast live oak. He awkwardly held a bouquet of flowers that didn't appear nearly as colorful as those outside the house. He hadn't wanted to come empty-handed, but it was hard to know what to bring to a woman who had tried to commit suicide. When he was still ten steps away from the front door, it was opened by a greeter, L.A.'s answer to a butler. The man was young, wearing nice clothes, but not formal wear.

"This way, Mr. Wells."

Graham was led in the opposite direction of Lanie's wing of the house. Everywhere there were objets d'art that looked as if they belonged in a museum. He passed by two floral arrangements of a size usually only displayed in five-star hotels. With every step, the bouquet he was holding was feeling smaller and more insignificant. Eventually he was deposited in a sunroom. As he took his leave, the greeter told him, "Company will be joining you very shortly."

Company turned out to be Estelle Steinberg. Estelle was five feet tall, but small like a pit bull. Her hair was dyed a shade of red not found on any living organism, the same shade of red she used on her lips. Her face had been lifted so many times Graham doubted whether she could smile, but apparently that wasn't a hindrance in her line of work.

"You," she said, as if identifying a contagious disease. "Take off your coat, unbutton your shirt, drop your pants, and kick off your shoes."

Graham faked umbrage: "But we hardly know one another."

"I know all about you. You're a fucking paparazzi."

"Paparazzo. 'Paparazzi' is the plural."

"You're a fucking parasite no matter how you say it, and you are not going to get anywhere near Lanie until you prove you're not carrying a camera."

Graham sighed, then removed his sports coat and handed it to Estelle. She ran her hands through it, then dropped the blazer to the ground. "Keep going."

He emptied his pockets, pulled his shirt from his pants, and unbuttoned it. Then he did a full turn for her, displaying his hands to her like a magician, showing there was nothing in them.

"Shoes and shirt off and drop your pants."

"You've got to be kidding."

"I know about those spy cameras and miniature recorders."

"I promise you that I'm not carrying a camera or a recorder."

Estelle shook her head. What was once her face tried to look amused. "Think of me as Missouri. Show me."

Graham would have bet that Estelle had never been within a thousand miles of Missouri, but he could see there was no compromise in her challenge. He kicked off his shoes and took off his shirt, but even that wasn't good enough.

"Drop 'em," said Estelle, signaling his pants.

"If the camera's in my pants, how exactly do I go about snapping pictures? Do I just keep casually raising and lowering my fly?"

"You could be hiding a camera in your pants and pull it out later. So either drop them or leave."

Graham reluctantly reached for his belt, loosened it, then lowered his trousers to the ground. Estelle stared at his boxers, but stopped short of frisking him. Graham pulled his pants back up.

"What happened to your face?" she asked.

"I walked into something."

"More like you put your nose where it didn't belong."

"According to your definition, that would probably be anywhere."

"You're damn right about that. Were you taking pictures here last night? If you were, that's fucking illegal. The California courts aren't allowing that kind of invasion of privacy."

"I'm here to talk to Lanie, not to you."

"My job is to protect Lanie from people like you."

"In that case, she would be dead."

"I haven't told Lanie about you because she's been napping, but she is under the misguided impression that you are some kind of Puritan—"

"Pilgrim."

"Whatever. She thinks you're the Salvation Army. She doesn't yet know you are one of those pricks that jumps out from behind bushes and thinks life should be one never-ending episode of *Candid Camera*."

"I saved her life."

"You want a reward? That can be arranged. It comes with strings, though."

"What strings?"

"A confidentiality contract that includes all aspects of last night, including any photos you might have taken."

"How much?"

"As much as your scandal sheets would pay you. This is predicated on your not having talked to anyone yet."

"I haven't."

"We got a deal then?"

"I'll think about it."

"You think about doing it any other way and our lawyers will drag you through the mud for years."

Graham never did well with threats. "The mud bath goes both ways. I doubt you'd want Lanie subjected to the same."

Estelle shook her head in disgust. "I forgot that wallowing in the mud would appeal to you."

"As fun as all this has been, I'd like to talk to Lanie now."

"You'll talk to the both of us."

"That isn't what we agreed upon."

"Our agreement was voided when I learned what you do for a living."

"I have no intention of keeping my work a secret from Lanie."

"Good. I'll be there when you tell her."

Graham could see it was fruitless to argue further. He waited on Estelle while she called over on an intercom and announced that she would be taking Mr. Wells to the guest cottage. Then, without looking back to see if he was coming, she opened the door to the backyard and walked outside. Graham followed her down a pathway lined with birds of paradise.

The so-called guest cottage was a self-contained house on the northeast side of the property. Most guests probably never wanted to leave. The cottage had its own spa and gardens, and a private deck that looked out to the ocean. As Graham walked inside, he saw that it was a good spot to hold a controlled interview. There were no personal mementos of Lanie's, nothing to allow insights into her life. But that still didn't stop Graham from doing an inventory of the living room.

Estelle didn't trust his snooping. "Sit," she said, pointing to a chair.

Instead of taking a seat in the chair, Graham chose to sit down on the sofa. That left Estelle with the choice of sitting next to him, or taking the chair and leaving Lanie in his near proximity. She was spared that decision by the entrance of Lanie.

"Hello," she said, standing tentatively at the entryway. Lanie was dressed simply, in jeans and a white sweater, and was wearing no makeup. Still, she was Lanie Byrne. Some stars the camera loves, but offstage they blend in with the woodwork. Lanie was that rarity, even more beautiful off-camera. She was pale, but not as pale as she had been the last time Graham had seen her. Lanie raised her eyes and looked at Graham. He could tell that she wondered what had happened to his face, but didn't ask. She was still vulnerable. He had seen her at her most exposed. Her cheeks reddened, and she averted her eyes to a wrapped package she was holding. Not an actor's blush, Graham knew, but the real thing.

Speaking to the package, Lanie said, "I wanted to find a way to thank you, Mr. Wells."

"Graham. I'm Graham."

They had never been formally introduced. He awkwardly offered his right hand to her, just as she started to hand him the present. Each regrouped, he retracting his hand just as she reached for it. After a second false start, both of them laughed.

When they finally shook hands, she said, "I'm Lanie."

"Pleased to meet you. I mean—"

"I know what you mean."

There was that awkwardness of having shared an intimacy together, something much more personal than even sex, that both bonded and embarrassed them. Each carried a mutual shame.

"I brought these," Graham said, remembering his flowers. "They're just, uh—"

"They're beautiful. I am going to go put them in something."

Lanie went out to the kitchen, found a container, and ran some water. "Open your present," she yelled.

Graham fumbled with the wrapping, tore it off, then opened the box. He carefully brought out a very old book. The leather cover was from another age, and the bound pages were thick and uneven, more like parchment than paper. Gilded lettering spelled out *The Pilgrim's Progress*.

"It's supposed to be a classic," said Lanie, returning to the room and taking a seat next to him on the sofa. "I never read it, though."

"Nor I."

Graham carefully flipped through some pages, pausing to look at the illustrations. Then he closed it, gently, but with finality.

"I can't take this. It's too precious. And as I told you, I'm no pilgrim."

"I know that."

"What you don't know is that I am a celebrity photographer."

"He's a paparazzi," Estelle said.

Graham didn't bother correcting Estelle again. He looked up at Lanie, expecting her to be angry or disgusted, but she didn't appear to be either. "I suspected it had to be something like that."

Estelle acted as if Graham wasn't in the room. "We're negotiating with him for his silence."

"I didn't come here to negotiate," Graham said to Estelle. "That was your doing. I came to talk with Lanie."

"What about?" asked Lanie.

"I have some questions I wanted to ask you in private."

"No way," said Estelle. "The first two words you should say to this joker are 'No comment.' And the second two words are, 'Good-bye.' His kind twist everything. He's just fishing for a banner headline for the *Enquirer* or the *Star*."

"What I'm looking for are answers."

"What do you want to know?"

"For starters, why?"

Estelle answered, "Miss L was practicing for a part. No one gets into character like Lanie. As she is taking on the role of a substance abuser, she needed to get in touch with that character's state of mind. She very much regrets her accidental overdose."

Graham shook his head. "I hope you're not starting to believe that kind of press release, Lanie. Everyone around you might want to sweep all this under the rug and forget it, but they shouldn't. I saw how serious you were."

Their eyes met. He tried to keep her looking at him.

"You're right," said Estelle. "She was serious. Serious about her acting."

Graham ignored Estelle and kept looking at Lanie. "Your next role is to play Elizabeth Barrett Browning, not Janis Joplin."

"She is considering an interim part," said Estelle.

Lanie didn't look comfortable with her publicist's explanation and chose to change the subject. "Last night you talked about your walk through Spain. Was that just a story?"

He shook his head. "I walked more than five hundred miles."

"I've always dreamed of doing something like that, going on some kind of adventure where no one knows me."

"It would have to be on another planet."

"I am afraid you're right. I could wear a disguise, though. That's how I often get away from your sort."

She didn't say her words to hurt, but just as a fact. Still, they reminded Graham of Paris, and the couple who hadn't successfully escaped his "sort."

"Did your long walk change you?" she asked.

Graham shook his head. "It gave me a daily goal of putting one foot in front of another. At its end, I don't think I came away with any great insights other than how to tend to some very sore feet."

Lanie tried to smile at what he said, but it was almost as if Graham could see her front crumbling right in front of him. She wanted a miracle in her life, or short of that, a much needed dangling carrot to keep her going. He sensed she was despondent, and not only because she had tried committing suicide. Something about her pain resonated within him. It was all too familiar.

Graham said, "You shouldn't judge by me, though. Others walking the Camino seemed to get lots out of it. I wasn't there for miracles."

"Why were you there?"

"Exercise."

His one-word answer was an obvious lie and put a momentary pall on their conversation. Estelle stepped in, glad for the chance to interrupt their talk. "Lanie, you need to rest. Doctor's orders."

"Why is it the more I rest, the more tired I get?"

"You're probably catching something, dear."

Or she had caught something, thought Graham, and couldn't shake it. Or maybe he was just projecting. He needed answers—both of them needed answers.

"You've probably noticed the state of my face," Graham said. "Two men tried to kill me late last night after I left the Grove."

"Shame they didn't succeed," muttered Estelle.

"I've been thinking about the attack all day. It wasn't random. They knew I was at your house last night. I can only assume that they've been monitoring you as well.

"The men closely resemble one another. I am sure they are brothers. They have a medium build with dark hair and complexion. I'd put them in their late twenties or early thirties. Both have slight accents. Do they sound familiar?"

"You say they tried to kill you?" asked Lanie.

Graham nodded.

She shook her head in disbelief. Then it was her turn to tell an obvious lie. "No, I don't know them."

"These men bid me bon voyage off of Mulholland Drive. They also stole the equipment I left behind when I helped you, which makes me believe they're the ones that called Dr. Burke trying to determine whether you were alive or dead."

"Didn't you hear her?" said Estelle. "She doesn't know them."

Graham kept his eyes on Lanie's. "I'd advise you to have your phone and house swept for bugs. It's possible you're under some kind of surveillance."

"Of course she's under surveillance," Estelle said. "People like you never let her alone."

"I'm not talking about paparazzi. I'm talking about something more dangerous."

Estelle started wagging her finger. "Ask Arnold Schwarzenegger if he doesn't think your kind are dangerous, what with the way he was forced off the road just after he had heart surgery just for the sake of getting his picture. And I just wish you could ask Princess Di about the danger paparazzi pose. Or think of the anguish Jackie Kennedy, a first lady mind you, had to suffer when they published those pictures of her sunbathing nude. She thought she had the whole beach to herself. She didn't think that some boat she could barely see had a photographer with one of those huge lenses. You make people prisoners in their own houses."

Graham refused to be sidetracked. "These men aren't interested in photography. I don't know what they are interested in, but if they're the ones that drove you to despair, then you need to get some help."

"Say nothing, Lanie," said Estelle. "He's fishing for you to say something controversial. Or he's trying to drive his price up through some conspiracy theory."

"Think about it," Graham said.

The publicist put her arm around Lanie. "Let's go, dear."

"Thank you," Lanie said to Graham, then she let herself be walked away.

Graham watched her. He couldn't explain it, but he knew her hurt like it was his own. It didn't make sense, of course. Lanie was Hollywood royalty, and he snapped sneak pictures. Besides, he was no bleeding heart. He looked out for himself. But something was tearing Lanie apart enough that she had chosen to stop the pain by killing herself. He knew how much hurt that was. Over the past few years, especially early on after the accident, Graham had considered suicide. He wasn't sure if he was stopped by cowardice, or whether he still found reasons to live.

At the doorway, Estelle turned and said to him, "I'll send someone to see you out. Call me tomorrow morning at nine and I'll patch in a conference call with the lawyers."

Graham said nothing. When they left the cottage, he rose and walked to the door and watched them make their way up the path. Lanie was known for her perfect carriage, and a long, graceful neck rivaled only by Audrey Hepburn's. Her head, always held high, was down. She sneaked a look back, as if feeling his eyes on her, then continued walking. A few moments later she turned around again. This time she said something to Estelle, then hurried down the path back to him. As she came toward him, Graham couldn't help but feel that for the first time in a long time he had done something right. But Lanie still needed to decide upon life, and he wasn't at all sure she had made that decision.

Then Lanie was standing in front of him. "You don't need to worry," she said.

"I think I do."

She didn't argue, as Graham would have hoped, but only clarified what she meant. "I mean about those two men. I'm sure they didn't mean to kill you. They only wanted it to look that way. And they're no threat to me."

"Who are they?"

"They probably thought they were helping me."

"I still don't understand."

"They're friends," she said.

Graham spoke from instinct: "They're no friends of anyone."

"I promise you, they meant you no harm."

"Who are they?" Graham asked again.

"They're Mossad," she whispered, then ran back up the path.

Twenty-one

Mossad. As he drove away, Graham kept chewing on the word and its implications. Why would the Israeli secret intelligence service have any dealings with Lanie Byrne? And could she be right? Had his two assailants just meant to put the fear of God into him? Graham wondered if his attempt to escape had endangered his life or saved it.

Hollywood had attracted more than a few former Mossad agents working as security consultants. At Michael Jackson's wedding to Lisa Marie, the head of security had been an ex-Mossad agent who seemed to take great pleasure in foiling the paparazzi.

Mossad. Maybe he hadn't heard Lanie correctly. Graham searched his mind for an alternate interpretation and fell short of one. No, he had heard her distinctly. And though she was an actress, he didn't think she was trying to misdirect him.

Graham pulled out his new phone, then thought better of it. Maybe they were already on to his new number, and he didn't want to put his friends in any more potential danger. He stopped at a pay phone and dialed a number. It popcorned a few times, until its call-forwarding hit the mark. When it did, Graham said, "How is your brother Dan?"

"Who spells his name D-O-N," said Ran Jacobi, an Israeli paparazzo who Graham sometimes worked with.

It was a stupid joke, but one they both persisted in. Since Ran pronounced his name Ron, Graham figured he had to have a brother named Dan who spelled his name Don. Ran had never Americanized the spelling of his name, and was constantly having to explain it. Sometimes his attempts to clarify the spelling almost became a "Who's on First" routine. Wrong Ran, Graham called him.

"When did you get back?"

"An hour ago."

"You working now?" Graham asked.

"Yeah, I'm doing Pottygate. I keep trying to sneak into this woman's shitter to snap some photos. Problem is that it always seems to be occupied. I should have just dressed in drag."

Ran was hairy and squat. His face and hands were thick and imposing, his beard invariably heavy.

"I don't even want to conjure up that image."

"I'd look like my grandmother, 'cept she has a thicker mustache. Wait a second. The coast just got clear."

Ran apparently dropped his cell phone into his pocket, letting Graham listen in to his movements. A door opened, and a few seconds later Graham could hear the familiar sounds of a camera and flash working in sync. But then the sounds stopped.

"Excuse me," Graham heard him say.

A very indignant woman's voice asked, "What are you doing in here?"

"We're going to be redecorating the woman's cra—bathroom, ma'am," Ran said. "I needed to get a few shots. I'll just get out of your way."

He really was in a woman's bathroom. Graham started laughing. The image of Ran, whose idea of color sense began and ended with his collection of garish Aloha shirts, trying to pass himself off as an interior designer gave Graham his first good laugh in days.

"Shut up," said Ran, coming back on the line. "I don't want security following the trail of your laughter."

"Did you ever think about carrying a plumber's helper and putting up a sign on the door?"

"I didn't think the place was going to be Grand Central Station."

"Where are you?"

"Scene of the crime. Westwood. They had this chi-chi screening of Quentin's new film here last night."

"And something happened in the ladies' room?"

"Yeah. It was a real hot ticket event. The studio only allowed their muckety-mucks to attend. The premiere won't happen for another two weeks, and apparently Quentin's still working on the final cut. Anyway, the film clocks in at just over two hours. When the lights go up, there's this mad dash for the bathrooms, which results in a major logjam of the ladies' facilities. Now we know damn few things in this world are democratic, but toilets come close. First come, first served. But not in Hollywood. Bambi Spellman, wife of Jack Spellman, the studio head that's distributing Quentin's film, makes a point of walking to the front of the line without so much as an 'excuse me.' Apparently this isn't the first time she's made such a power play either. Bambi and potty politics are old friends. We're talking some considerable egos she's stepping on when she walks to the front of the line, but because Jack's the studio power broker, no one dared to say anything out loud."

"Oh, if those stalls could only talk."

"Exactly. The ladies are lined up to bad-mouth her—off the record of course."

"Getting a picture of an empty bathroom isn't exactly gripping photography."

"Oh, I got a few shots of Bambi in a lah-di-dah kind of pose. And one of her so-called friends supplied me with a picture of Bambi showing off her bare ass. Apparently she was demonstrating the results of a new trainer and diet at a party in Newport Beach."

"I don't want to detain you from your Pulitzer. The reason I called is that I need a favor."

"Name it."

"I'm hoping I can crash at your place tonight."

"No problem. What's wrong with yours?"

Graham wasn't sure what, if anything, he should tell Ran. "It's being fumigated."

"They got one of those tents up?"

"No."

"Termites or vermin?"

"Rats."

"I got a friend who's got an exterminating company. He tips me off when he's doing any big name house. I dress up in overalls and act like a hired killer of bugs. I've gotten a few good shots that way."

Mr. Moto, the Man of a Thousand Faces, had nothing on Ran.

"You'd be surprised at how many rats there are in this town."

"No," said Graham, "I wouldn't."

Ran lived in a Santa Monica house just three blocks up from the Strand. He couldn't afford the place, but Jackie, his live-in for the last three years, could. Jackie was a stylist who set up photographic and commercial shoots for some of the biggest advertising accounts in Los Angeles. She was basically a producer, even if none of her work ever ran more than sixty seconds. Jackie arranged locations, props, actors, and scripts. Even photographers. Lately, she had been pushing Ran hard to leave "gutter photography" and join her in the business. She detested his work, and anything to do with it—including Graham. If he hadn't been afraid of Smith tracking him down through his credit card, he would have taken a hotel room.

Ran slapped him hard on the back with one arm, and waved him in with the other. Graham only caught one glimpse of Jackie as she escaped into the bedroom, shaking her head and rolling her eyes.

"Jackie's had a long day," Ran said, looking away. He knew the words sounded lame, but they were the best he could offer.

"I hope you're not in the doghouse on my account."

"No more than usual. Want your usual bourbon rocks?"

Graham nodded. Just that morning he had sworn off booze forever, but a hair of the dog that bit him might help his headache. As Ran went off to get the drinks Graham felt his old cell phone vibrating. He stared at the readout and saw the words "Number Is Restricted." That warning had been coming up all night. Since the caller wasn't willing to be identified, Graham wasn't willing to talk. His gut told him Smith was on the line. If his suspicions were correct, he didn't want to speak to him, at least not until he knew more. It was possible U.S. intelligence was working with Mossad. From what Graham had heard, they had a history of being in bed together.

Ran returned with the drinks. He was drinking red wine—obviously Jackie's influence. As he was handing Graham his bourbon Ran suddenly took notice of his face.

"What the fuck happened to you?"

"Car wreck. The van was totaled."

"Jeez. Anyone else hurt?"

Graham shook his head and took a long pull of the drink. Once wasn't enough. He went back to the well.

"Maybe I should just give you the bottle," said Ran.

"Maybe you should."

"You're not telling me everything."

"No, I'm not. Get me drunk and maybe I will. In the meantime you can tell me about the Mossad."

"Why's a *goyim* like you interested in the Mossad?"

"I'm doing some fishing. I'm curious if James Bond has infiltrated Hollywood."

"You mean *Chaim* Bond? Not that I've heard. You know how some Italians say there is no Mafia? It's the same way some Jews say with a wink that there is no Mossad. There's never a mention of it in the Israeli budget, and no prime minister ever talks about it."

"But it is Israel's version of the CIA?"

"The bad boys in the Mossad would be insulted by that comparison. The Mossad's full name is *Ha Mossad, le Modiyn ve le Tafkidim Mayuhadim*—the Institute for Intelligence and Special Operations."

"Would there be any reason for the Mossad to be in Hollywood?"

"Anything's possible. They track their enemies around the world. But this would be way off their usual haunts."

"Which are?"

"They got deep cover going in all the Arab countries, but from what I hear most of their agents are in Europe. Here in the U.S. they concentrate on New York City and Washington, D.C. I got a second or third cousin who's in the Institute. That's what they call it. The guy's a real prick."

"Runs in the family, huh?"

"Fuck you. Now what's this all about?"

"I don't know yet. Right now I'm just following a rumor."

"Watch out that the rumor doesn't start following you. The Mossad doesn't fool around."

"I'll tell them I know *krav maga*."

"Yeah. They'll *show* you *krav maga*."

Krav maga is Hebrew for "contact combat," and is the preferred form of down and dirty fighting utilized by the Israeli police and military. Graham had gotten his first taste of it when he and Ran had teamed up for a shoot in Venice Beach. They had heard that Prince was trying out new material while disguised as a street performer. To while away the time, Ran had shown Graham some of his martial-arts moves on the sand. The rumor about Prince never panned out, but Graham came away from their long weekend of fruitless surveillance with a few deadly combinations. Occasionally he even took some classes at the *krav maga* martial-arts studio in West Hollywood.

Ran said, "I always thought we should steal the Mossad's motto for our own profession."

"What is it?"

" 'By way of deception, thou shalt do war.' "

"It sounds too biblical for the likes of us. We're closer to 'Say Cheese.' "

Graham took another drink and found himself chewing ice at the bottom of his glass. Ran got up, returned with a fresh glass of ice and the threatened bottle of Jim Beam.

"Tell me about it," he said, refilling ice and drink.

Graham turned his head and made sure Jackie was still boycotting him. "I'm not going to tell you the whole thing," he said. "It would take too long. But I will tell you what happened last night after a shoot."

Without mentioning Lanie, he described the late-night drive, and how he had been force-fed vodka. He fudged his source by saying that the two men alluded to being Mossad just before they tried to kill him. Ran listened without interrupting him. When Graham finished, both men were silent for a time.

"Some story," Ran finally said.

"I know it sounds crazy."

Ran shook his head. "Not crazy if you were a terrorist. It's no secret that the Mossad carries out assassinations, what's euphemistically called the 'long arm of Israeli justice.' They literally are given a license to kill by the prime minister. You ever hear about the '72 Munich Olympics when the Black September terrorists massacred members of the Israeli team?"

Graham nodded.

"The Israelis didn't mind when the Germans exchanged their seven Black September prisoners for the release of hostages taken in a Lufthansa hijacking. It gave them a chance to hunt down and assassinate each one of them. And that's what they did for many years. It wasn't until 1991 that the Mossad killed the seventh and last terrorist."

"Long memories."

"You better believe it."

"What I can't figure out is why they set up the portable bar for me, making me drink vodka every few minutes."

"That's easy," said Ran. "Your autopsy would have shown that you didn't do your drinking all at once. That way it would look like you were doing some binge drinking instead of being force-fed the booze."

"Just another alcohol-related death."

"You got it. But the Mossad did not do this to you."

Ran spoke emphatically, announced himself as certain beyond any doubt.

"How do you know that?" Graham asked.

"Because you would be dead."

Twenty-two

Though Graham had been up for two days, sleep didn't come easily to him. He tossed and turned. Tucked under the mattress were the photos he had taken of Lanie. It was almost as if he could feel her pain even through all the material and fabric that separated him from the pictures.

Princess and the pea time, he thought. The fable made Graham think about royalty, about Lady Godwin.

He didn't want to get caught up in that mind loop again, so he turned on the light. Usually he kept a book on his nightstand, but in his haste to pack he hadn't brought any reading material. But he did have one book, he remembered. Lanie's gift to him.

Pilgrim's Progress wouldn't have been his first reading choice. The language was arcane, and the book dated, but he still stayed with the Pilgrim through the Slough of Despond, the Valley of Humiliation, and the Mountain of Death. When the Pilgrim reached Vanity Fair, Graham felt at home. He figured that in his own life he had settled somewhere between the Slough of Despond and Vanity Fair, but the Pilgrim didn't give up as easily. He persevered through Bypass Meadows, the House of the Interpreter, the Palace Beautiful, in the end making it all the way to the Delectable Mountains.

Graham carefully put the book away. No star had ever given him anything before, if you didn't count a clenched fist, the finger, or a restraining order. In the throes of pain, Lanie had thought of him.

Maybe she just wanted to butter me up, thought Graham. She knew he was holding the cards, but she wouldn't have known that until after he arrived at the Grove to meet with her. By then, the gift was already waiting for him.

He thought about her suicide attempt, and mulled over what could have driven her to such a desperate act. Over the years Graham had heard a lot of AA patter. People in show business were always drying out. But one phrase in particular kept playing in his head: "You are as sick as your secret."

In this case, the secret wasn't an alcohol problem. But whatever the secret was, it had made Lanie very, very sick.

Graham knew all about trying to carry the weight of a debilitating secret.

You are as sick as your secret.

Maybe he and Lanie were both terminally ill.

Estelle Steinberg was taking his calls now, but she wasn't intent on easing his way. "I need to see Lanie today," Graham said.

"Like hell you do," said Estelle.

"I want a neutral location."

"Then get a one-way ticket to Switzerland."

"She can bring me the legal papers."

"The lawyers need to draw them up. They're the ones you need to meet with, not Lanie."

"I only talk with lawyers when I have to. This isn't one of those times."

"It is if you want to get paid."

"You want Lanie to get screwed?"

"What are you talking about?"

"Lawyers talk even when they're not paid to talk. Lawyer-client confidentiality? It's a joke. And even if the attorneys are tight-mouthed, what about their staff? Half my tip-offs come from legal offices. If you want things buttoned up between us, keep the lawyers out of it."

"We just hand you unmarked bills, is that it?"

"Don't make it like I'm blackmailing you."

"Is there another name for it?"

"You're the one who wants to buy the pictures."

"Mysterious pictures that no one has ever seen."

"For Lanie's sake, I think that's how it should be. They need to be for her eyes only. And that's why I want to meet with Lanie alone. These pictures are very"—he struggled for the right word—"private."

"Then why the hell did you take them?"

"That's my job."

"You would have made a good Nazi."

Another voice came on the line. "He's right, Estelle. I don't want a go-between."

"With all respect, Lanie, you don't know what you are talking about. It takes a snake handler to handle a poisonous snake. That's what we are dealing with here."

"He saved my life," said Lanie.

"He didn't want the Golden Goose to die."

"I'll take over from here." There was no compromise in Lanie's voice. Estelle sighed, then hung up, putting the receiver down decisively, but not with the vehemence that Graham knew she possessed.

"Are you there, Mr. Wells?"

"Scales, fangs, and all."

"When do you want to meet?"

"As soon as possible. I'm going to give you a number, and I want you to call me from a pay phone along the way. We'll make arrangements at that time."

"Why can't we make those arrangements now?"

"Because I'm not certain your line isn't tapped."

Forty minutes later his new digital phone rang. "Where are you?" Graham asked.

"Just outside of Topanga Beach."

"You got your Praetorian Guard with you?"

"Only Nurse Ratched. Dr. Burke still has me on a short leash."

"Is the nurse in her whites or in civvies?"

"Street clothes."

"We'll be meeting in Santa Monica. Park near the pier. I want you to make a loop around the carousel area. I might or might not join you at that time."

"You won't know me. I'm disguised."

Graham laughed. "Let me guess. You're wearing large dark glasses and either a hat or a shawl, or both."

Surprised: "Yes."

"Next time just wear a neon sign that says, STAR. It's the worst disguise in the world, but every name in the business still wears it. When I catch sight of that kind of outfit I reach for my camera."

"I'm sure you do."

"If I don't join you, a half block south from the pier on Ocean Avenue is a restaurant called Chez Jay. We have a reservation for a quiet table in the back under the name of Bunyan. You can tell the nurse it's a table for two."

Graham was sitting on a bench and had his face in a newspaper when the two of them walked by. Lanie clearly wasn't used to being out in public. She looked uncertain, tentative, out of place among the other passersby who were enjoying the sights or getting some exercise. The nurse, built like a fireplug, looked as if she could have come out of central casting for a prison matron. Graham studied the sports page until the two of them were some fifty yards off, and even then didn't look their way. He stretched, craned his neck as if there was a crick in it, and looked all around. Nothing suspicious stood out.

His hair was combed back and down, not parted on the left as usual. He was wearing wire-frame reading glasses that he'd picked up that morning from a drugstore, glasses that were giving him a slight headache. He had on a blue herringbone jacket and gray slacks. All Graham was missing were pony shoes for the ultimate preppie outfit, but his penny loafers would have to do. He looked at his watch and gathered up his briefcase.

Graham walked in the opposite direction Lanie and her nurse had traveled, then made his way over to Ocean Avenue. He set up his second observation spot from a bus stop catty-cornered from the restaurant. The women arrived before his bus. For an actress, Lanie didn't have the insouciant pose down very well, looking nervous as she entered the restaurant. Graham waited several minutes before he was certain they weren't under observation, then crossed the street. A pretty blond hostess greeted him at the door with a smile. Graham spoke before she could.

"My name's Bunyan. I have a reservation for two, but I imagine my friend's already here."

"Yes, Mr. Bunyan, if you'd just follow—"

"No need," he said, walking by her.

Per his reservation request, Lanie was seated in the back. The nurse, four tables away, seemed to be the only one looking her way. Lanie was studying her watch and not appearing happy with what she saw. At his approach, Lanie looked up for a moment, took him in at a glance, and turned her head. She probably figured he was a diner heading toward the rest room. When Graham sat down in the booth she looked at him a second time and registered surprise.

"You clean up well," she said.

"I molted."

"Estelle was just being protective when she described you as a snake."

"I know."

This was the first time, Graham thought, that they'd been alone together. Death had been hovering around them their first meeting, and Estelle was there for the second. With a camera in his hands, Graham was never intimidated by star power. Without his equipment, he felt at a loss.

"I hear the food's good here," he said.

"I'm not hungry."

Graham motioned with his head. The nurse was monitoring both of them. "If you don't eat, I get the feeling she's going to come over and force-feed you."

"I'm afraid you might be right."

Lanie picked up the menu and started scanning it. Graham followed suit. They finished their looking several moments before a waitress approached.

"We can skip hearing about the arugula and lentil special," Graham said.

"Very good," said the waitress, and turned to Lanie.

"I'll have the arugula and lentil special," she said.

The waitress's pen hung in the air. "I'm sorry—"

Graham tried to unsuccessfully suppress a laugh. "I think that was directed at me," he said.

"I'd like the Caesar salad with chicken," Lanie said. "Dressing on the side. And iced tea, please."

"Make that two iced teas," said Graham, "and I'll have the grilled shrimp and swordfish brochette."

As the waitress left their table, Graham said, "I shouldn't have spoken for you."

"I didn't take umbrage. I think I just wanted the opportunity to say the word 'arugula.' "

"Feel free to slip it in the conversation anytime."

Lanie reached into her handbag and brought out a mini-tape recorder. "For my protection, I need to record some things on tape. Is that all right with you?"

Graham shrugged and nodded.

"You'll need to respond verbally, Mr. Wells."

"Yes. And if you don't want to draw undue attention to us, I'd move the recorder next to the flower vase."

Lanie did as he suggested. "Now," she said, "can you please give your full name for the record, as well as the date, time, and location where this meeting is taking place."

"You're good at this," Graham said.

"Thank you."

"That wasn't a compliment." He moved his head slightly closer to the microphone, and answered all that was asked of him. When he finished, he added, "For the record, let me state that I am not now, nor have I ever been, a member of the Communist Party."

"What I'm more interested in knowing is whether you currently have me under surveillance, and whether you are taping this conversation."

"You are the only one doing any taping."

"I also need to be assured that during this meeting I will not be photographed surreptitiously either by you or one of your associates."

"I get the feeling you're going to be reading me my Miranda rights any moment."

"I'm sure you are familiar with those words."

"I come unarmed. I don't have a camera. Okay? And I don't have any partner shooting pictures from behind a menu."

"Thank you." She reached for the tape recorder and turned it off.

"Remove the tape," Graham said.

"Excuse me?"

"It's a voice-actuated model with a multidirectional microphone. The only way to be sure it's not recording is by removing the tape."

She popped out the microcassette and slipped it in her pocket.

Graham said, "Anything you say can and will be used against you."

"What?"

"You got me thinking about Miranda."

Their iced teas arrived, and Lanie seemed to take refuge in her drink. To get her eyes out of its russet well, Graham said, "Arugula."

She looked up, but she didn't look amused. "Why don't we get down to business? Show me the pictures."

"I'd rather wait until after our meal."

"I'm not hungry. The only reason I am here is because of what you have, or don't have, in your briefcase."

There was no compromise in her expression. Graham reluctantly reached over, opened his briefcase, then handed her a sealed manila envelope. She used a bread knife to cut it open, then withdrew the first glossy. Graham couldn't see which picture it was, but he did see her reaction. She paled. Her lips trembled and her eyes watered.

"Why don't I hold that package for a little while?" Graham said.

"Why? I'm sure you have copies."

"Because the pictures don't get any prettier. Because in a few minutes you might be better ready to view them. Because if you get any more upset, I'm afraid Nurse Ratched is going to come over here and deck me."

Lanie replaced the picture in the envelope. She looked up to see the nurse's scrutinizing eyes. Almost instantaneously she transformed her appearance, somehow even managing to get color in her face. Her sorrow vanished from view, replaced by a relaxed, even happy visage. Still, when Graham retrieved the envelope, she didn't object.

He needed to stop her ruminating, distract her somehow. "That's a neat trick," Graham said.

"What is?"

" 'Doing the Janus face,' as my father calls it. He is quite practiced at it as well."

"Is he an actor?"

"No. He's a recently retired foreign service officer."

Incredulous: "A diplomat?"

Graham nodded. "At the moment he's living in England, but he'll be moving to India soon. I'm afraid his retirement is going to be more like the country du jour. I thought he'd settle down after all these years, but old habits are hard to break. The two of us lived around the world while I was growing up."

"What happened to your mother?"

Graham fudged the truth. "She passed away when I was a boy."

"That must have been hard."

He shrugged.

"A foreign service officer's son turned paparazzo. That's hard to believe."

"No one's ever accused me of being a chip off the old block."

"Maybe you took after your mother's side."

"No." His answer was too quick and vehement, but he hoped she didn't notice.

Lanie was looking at him, but he couldn't tell how deep her scrutiny went. "Have you set a price for your pictures?"

He shook his head. "And I'm not being coy. It's just that I have been too busy trying to stay alive."

"You seem to have succeeded."

"I was lucky. I can't count on that. Those two men I told you about filled me up with vodka, and then tried to make a crispy critter out of me before sending me off the road. I need to know who they are and why they wanted me dead."

"They were just scaring you."

"I've tried to believe that. It doesn't wash. Tell me about those men. You said they were with the Mossad."

"I was mistaken."

"Why did you think they were with the Mossad?"

"I don't remember saying that. It was probably the meds speaking."

"Do those two men have something to do with your attempting suicide?"

"I don't know what you are talking about."

Graham's eyes strayed down to the manila envelope, then looked back at her. "Yes, you do."

"What I did, I am responsible for."

"Are you talking about your suicide or something else?"

"I didn't come here to have this conversation."

Graham had a sudden insight. "Did you think by killing yourself you could atone for something?"

Lanie reached for her purse.

"Don't go," Graham said. "I won't push it any further."

She hesitated for a moment, but then pushed her chair back and stood up.

"It's personal for me," Graham said. "My mother committed suicide."

He watched her weighing his words, deciding whether to believe him or not, and what to do if she did.

"It's true." Graham rose to his feet and pulled back the chair closest to him. "Sit down and I'll tell you the story."

He gestured again, and she took a seat in the offered chair. Graham fiddled with the silverware in front of him. "Uh," he said, thinking where to begin. When he finally started, he didn't look at her, choosing instead to talk to the empty seat in front of him.

"It happened when I was almost ten. It was the second time she abandoned me.

"The first time was when I was three. My mother had the acting bug. She said she left me to pursue her destiny. My father described it as 'moth syndrome.' She was attracted to the brightest lights on the planet: Hollywood.

"My mother was very young, and very beautiful, when she married my father. He was ten years older, urbane and sophisticated, but he still had to use all his diplomatic persuasion to win her over. You see, even then my mother had her dream to be in pictures. She was only nineteen. I am sure she thought her life was going to be exciting, almost like the movies, but it didn't turn out that way. Money was tight, and when my father got his placement overseas she became homesick. Their young marriage was further complicated when Mother became pregnant with me.

"We were living in Denmark when she announced to my father that she wanted a divorce so that she could go back to the States and pursue the acting career she always wanted. My father says the biggest failure in his diplomatic career was not convincing her to stay so that they could work out their situation.

"She didn't give him much of a chance, though. When she made her announcement, her bags were packed. Only one other matter needed to be attended to. She told my father that he would have to raise me. She also left it up to him to explain everything to me."

Graham took a sip of his iced tea, then put the glass down. He seemed in no hurry to say anything else.

"You were three?" Lanie asked.

He still didn't look at her. "Three and a half."

"Did you see her again?"

A nod. "Every other year I flew to L.A. for a two-week visit. She was always at a new house with a new man, usually some producer who was going to make her a star. Toward that goal she was willing to do anything. She took acting and voice lessons, and worked out. And she tried to find a shortcut to the top through the casting couch, but the only thing it got her was the reputation of being a very pretty pass-around piece of ass. A Blue-Page girl."

Lanie knew the term. Every year thousands of young women travel to Hollywood hoping to become a star. People in the industry prey on them, promising them parts, or saying they will get them a reading. The quid pro quo is that they are supposed to go to bed with the person arranging this. The real tragedy is how seriously they prepare for their lines, for their big break. Their part comes out of the so-called blue pages. They never knew that when they do their reading there is no film in the camera. Later, they are told their part was "cut," or that someone else got it.

"She ended her life at a party in Newport Beach," said Graham. "Over the years she had gone to hundreds of similar parties, hobnobbing with film people, auditioning as it were. In the days leading up to the party she came to the realization that her dream wasn't going to happen. While the champagne flowed, she walked out into the surf beyond the breakers and took a midnight swim."

Graham stopped talking for a moment. His voice changed, became a little less matter-of-fact. "There was no moon that night. When it's dark on the beach, you don't see the horizon. I wonder what she was swimming toward."

"How can you be sure it was suicide?"

"She left an envelope. There was no note, just a list of people to be contacted."

Their food arrived. "Saved by the bell pepper," Graham said.

"Can I get you anything else?" the waitress asked. "Perhaps something to drink?"

The waitress directed her question, and her eyes, to Lanie. She was smiling, being overly exuberant. Lanie had been recognized.

"A martini suddenly sounds good," Graham said.

When the waitress reluctantly left, torn between her duty and asking for an autograph, Graham turned to Lanie and admitted, "I don't even like martinis. But it was my mother's drink of choice."

Lanie said, "I always remember what Dorothy Parker wrote about martinis: 'Three I'm under the table, four I'm under mein host.' "

Graham shook his head. "I envy people who can pull verse like that from the top of their head."

"In my case, you can spare your envy. I played Miss Parker onstage. For six months I recited her lines. But I should have remembered them a little better."

"What do you mean?"

"Her verse was often morbidly funny. She wasn't afraid to crib from her own pain. She attempted suicide several times, and lived to write about it.

> *"Guns aren't lawful, nooses give,*
> *Gas smells awful, you might as well live."*

Graham's martini arrived. Lanie kept her eyes on the table, her body language making it clear that she didn't want to be disturbed. The waitress lingered for too long. She obviously wanted to tell Lanie what a fan she was. When she finally left, Graham raised his glass, and Lanie reached for her iced tea. With their backs to the rest of the restaurant, to the rest of the world, he proposed a toast:

"You might as well live."

"You might as well," Lanie said, clicking glasses.

Twenty-three

Jaeger stretched out, his first-class airline seat allowing him plenty of room. He was dressed in a Savile Row suit, complemented by a Turnbull & Asser shirt. His clothes were as stylishly conservative as they were expensive. By appearances, he was a successful young businessman, an entrepreneur shaping the new world. And just like them, Jaeger was out to make a killing.

He hadn't expected to be returning to Los Angeles so soon, but circumstances dictated that the brothers keep out of sight for a few days. As slim as the possibility was, they could be identified by *both* the paparazzo and the actress. That wasn't a chance they could take.

It was also why the paparazzo had to die.

"Would you like some sparkling wine, sir?"

The flight attendant flashed her dimples and tilted the bottle invitingly toward him. It was covered with a white cloth that hid its label.

On this trip, Jaeger was using his public school English accent. It was good enough imitation that even when he employed it in Great Britain no one ever suspected he was anything but an upper-crust native.

"What kind is it?"

"A Taittinger Brut."

Jaeger returned her smile, and took notice of her name tag. *Angelica.* She was attractive, petite enough to look good even in an airline uniform. Her dimples reminded him of someone.

"Taittinger," Jaeger repeated, then shook his head reluctantly. He never deviated from his brand. "You wouldn't have some Veuve Cliquot, would you?"

A shake of her head. "I'm sorry."

"Then I'll just have a bottled water."

Angelica opened her mouth to offer him a selection, but Jaeger raised his hand to ward off her question and smiled. "I'm not particular about what kind of water you bring me. I am only fussy about my champagne."

The flight attendant laughed. "That's a good thing to be particular about," she said. "I must make a note to try your champagne. What name did you say?"

"Veuve Cliquot. It's a sentimental favorite of mine."

Angelica had already noticed he wasn't wearing a wedding ring, but with men you could never tell whether they were married or not. "Let me guess: it was the champagne served with your wedding toasts."

He shook his head. "But should I ever get married, that will certainly be what is served at my wedding."

Each appraised the other. Angelica found herself beguiled by his speech and looks. Even his scar fascinated her. It covered much of the left side of his face, but made him that much more masculine.

"If you don't mind my asking, what's the sentimental association?"

Jaeger paused before saying, "I guess you'd call it my first love."

"Ah. That's sweet."

He was rugged, yet romantic, thought Angelica, well spoken, but not effete. Belatedly, she remembered her work. "I better get you your water."

She moved with alacrity, quickly returning with the sparkling water and a napkin. "There you are, sir."

Jaeger's eyebrows wrinkled. "There's something missing."

"What?"

Only she heard his reply: "Your telephone number."

In the almost three years Angelica had been a flight attendant, she had been asked for her telephone number hundreds of times. Up until that moment, she had never considered giving it out.

"I'll get it for you right away, sir."

A minute later, she brought a pillow to Jaeger. As she handed it over, she slipped him her number. He watched her walk away, admiring the way her nicely rounded ass moved. The view had an unexpected effect; Jaeger found himself getting hard. He could have aborted his hard-on by thinking of any number of boring things, but decided the pillow had a use after all.

He put it atop his lap, covering up his erection. His condition prompted Jaeger to remember who the flight attendant reminded him of: Greta Reineke.

Or maybe it was just his erection and their talk of the Veuve Cliquot.

Jaeger closed his eyes and remembered.

"It will never be done," announced Karl Witt at the smoke- and drink-filled party that followed the weekly Convent of the Corps Normannia. The drinking had worked its usual magic in loosening tongues. Only Jaeger wasn't taking part in the discussion, but everyone was still aware of his presence. He was the youngest of all the corps brothers, but no one wielded a sword like Jaeger.

"Never," repeated Witt.

He was referring to a challenge that had been thrown down generations earlier, a challenge much discussed throughout all dueling fraternities, but one never taken up. It had been the Holy Grail of many a late-night drunken talk. To win the challenge, a duelist would have to enter the *Mensurboden* with an erection, and maintain it during the match.

Jaeger listened to the alcohol-fueled discussions about whether it could be done. Why anyone would even want to attempt such a thing was never addressed. Men who willingly faced sharpened steel, who dueled, did not ask such questions. Among his peers, the thought of entering the ring with both *Schwanz* and sword held aloft was considered the ultimate in male expression.

"For starters," said Witt, "consider the clothing constraints. When I enter the ring, I feel like a baby who has been swaddled."

"And when you leave, you look like a baby who needs to be changed," said Hildebrand, a brother known more for his cutting wit than his cutting sword.

Witt ignored the resulting laughter. "The weight of all our protective gear would prevent any *Mannerfahne* from waving. Except, of course, Herr Hildebrand and his two-meter *Steifer*."

Hildebrand put his elbow on his crotch and waved his arm around to the cheers of corps brothers.

"The apron alone," said Witt, "would make it physically impossible to walk into the ring with a *Hammer*."

Oberman, a serious engineering major, shook his head. "Not if you repositioned it," he said, "or if you cut a strategic hole in the leather."

Witt nodded in mock agreement. "Yes, and as you stepped into that small ring and stood an arm's length away from an opponent wielding a razor-sharp blade, I'd like to see the *Steifer* that wouldn't turn into a very tiny *Nudel*."

In a *Mensur* fought according to the rules of the Berlin Corps, the sword blows were aimed above the chin, but sometimes during the upward cuts the blades dipped dangerously low.

Witt spoke over the nervous laughter. "Self-preservation would make anyone's *Prengel* fall."

"Reminds me of something I saw in the pisser yesterday," said Hildebrand. "At eye level on the urinal someone wrote, *Your life is in your hands*."

The great debate sparked something in Jaeger. He had always liked being dared. As a child, he climbed up to the top of trees that the other boys feared to scale, and as he grew older, he had excelled at all sports, especially those deemed dangerous, becoming expert at rock climbing, hang gliding, and downhill racing. The greater the difficulty or danger, the more Jaeger enjoyed it.

He believed in *rising* to any challenge.

Jaeger had refrained from fucking Greta for a week. Three hours before his *Mensur*, he took her to bed. Their lovemaking had been going on non-stop for over two hours.

"Oh, God, oh, God, oh good, good, good, God, God, God, God."

Greta was coming again. Almost with dispassion, Jaeger watched as she writhed and bucked. "Come with me," Greta said, "come with me."

Her panting was rapid, her words shrill. Then her groans cascaded to cries of pleasure. Pistonlike, Jaeger kept moving. Greta's cries lessened in intensity, then changed in tone. "No more. Please, no more."

In the relative quiet, Jaeger heard the banging on his door. He pulled out of Greta and made his way across the room. Insensate, Greta rolled over, not caring about her nakedness, not caring about anything.

"Jaeger," yelled Hildebrand. "Time to get you ready for the match."

"I am ready," said Jaeger, opening the door.

Hildebrand turned his head away. "For God's sake, get some pants on."

"I'll be dueling for champagne today," said Jaeger.

Priapism had set in sometime after the first hour of fucking. Now his cock was completely vertical, pressed up against his belly button. He could no longer even feel it. He had withheld from coming until all sensitivity had been lost.

Hildebrand suddenly understood what Jaeger was talking about. "You can fight the first match!" he said excitedly. "We can hurry things along!"

Supremely confident he could defy gravity, and whatever came with it, Jaeger said, "There is no need to rush."

The emperor had no clothes, and he was proud of it.

When Jaeger walked into the *Fechtsaal*—the fencing hall—of the Corps Normannia in Berlin, heads turned. Usually a *Mensur* draws an audience of no more than a hundred people, but word of his endeavor had gotten out, and more than three hundred people filled the *Fechtsaal*. The quiet of a *Mensur* match is akin to the silence of a gallery while watching a golfer standing over a putt, but the normal etiquette of dueling was disrupted by Jaeger's condition. For a long moment everyone stared, and then the hall filled with noise and ribald laughter.

Jaeger ignored the crowd. He had eschewed the oblong apron and trousers that duelists traditionally wore, opting instead for a skintight leotard. When a German male waxes poetic about his member, he refers to it as *Mannerfahne*—a man's flag. Jaeger's flag had everyone's attention. In a way, Jaeger was saluting himself. He had further accentuated his condition by attaching a blue-silver-black ribbon, the colors of the Corps Normannia, to the end of the stretched-out fabric.

His was the fifth and last duel of the day. There was no love lost between Normannia and Guestphalia, two Berlin fraternities with a long-standing rivalry. The two clubs had split the previous four matches.

Witt hurried forward to speak with Jaeger. He was wearing a butcher's chain-mail glove. His job would be to inspect and disinfect Jaeger's sword between rounds. Jaeger had requested that Witt be an attendant doing the work usually assigned to a *Schleppfuchs*—an assisting pledge—so that he could be a close-up witness to what he had so vehemently termed as being "impossible."

Slapping Jaeger on the shoulder, Witt said, "*Waffenschwein!*" The word's literal translation was "weapon swine," but in the dueling world it was the traditional greeting of good luck and a protection against evil spirits.

Centurionlike, Jaeger answered, "It's a good day to die."

"You're going up against Meyer," said Witt. "He's their best, but you wouldn't know it to look at him now. It appears your tumescence, and your reputation, have quite unnerved the boy."

"What's delaying the match?"

"The Guestphalia mafia think if they drag their heels long enough gravity will win out over your *Steifer*." Witt took a quick look at the situation, and then laughed. "That apparently isn't the case. I'd say it's more likely that Meyer will run out of the *Fechtsaal* before the steam runs out of your dick. Look at him. He looks more like a pledge than someone with ten *Mensuren* to his credit."

Jaeger didn't bother to look across the fencing floor at his opponent. Soon enough, he knew, he would see him up-close.

"So how do you feel?" Witt asked.

"Thirsty for champagne," said Jaeger.

The promised reward—the long-standing prize that most had thought would never be collected—was a case of Veuve Cliquot Grande Dame to the fighter who dueled with an erection.

Witt laughed again. "You are the ice man, Jaeger."

Jaeger knew that even seasoned duelists entered a *Mensur* afraid. Some attempted mock-bravado, with poses and forced smiles, but those were fronts for butterflies, and dry mouth, and nausea. Most duelists entered the ring with one goal only: to come out unmaimed. They wanted to leave with both ears, to have a smile not extended several inches by the slice of steel. Jaeger never had those fears. The only thing he ever felt was anticipation.

"God, Jaeger, you almost look comfortable."

He was different that way as well. His corps brothers hated being "mummified" for battle. Dressing for a *Mensur* was as daunting to some as the swordplay itself. Silk bandages were wrapped incredibly tightly around the neck, causing severe shortness of breath; bodies were weighted down by heavy padding, chain mail, and Kevlar clothing; vision was inhibited by the *Paukbrille*—heavy, protective goggles with steel ridges around the eye openings, and a metal mesh curtain coverlet. The eyes were protected, but at the price of steel cataracts.

"I *am* comfortable," Jaeger told Witt. And it was true.

"Don't worry," said Witt. "Fritz the Cat is about to get this thing going."

Local fencing master Fritz Fehrensen—nicknamed Fritz the Cat—would be the umpire for the match. As any of Fritzie's students could tell you, he had the look and prickly demeanor of an alley cat. His eyes were feral, untamed, and his face was crisscrossed with the scars of his youthful *Mensuren*.

Witt was right. Fritz shooed away all the seconds, and then in a voice that brooked no argument announced to the assemblage, "*Silentium!*"

The hall hushed, but the silence didn't mask the energy that was there. Jaeger walked out to the middle of the fencing floor with his second and two attendants, Hildebrand, Witt, and Gross. They were joined by the contingent from the Corps Guestphalia. Pro forma formalities and instructions were offered and received, and then Hildebrand measured a blade's length between the sternums of Jaeger and Meyer, the distance of how far they would stand from one another—and each other's swords.

The *Bestimmungsmensur*—rules of the match—called for forty rounds at six cuts each. Each round would take between two and three seconds, with the combatants cutting and parrying simultaneously.

At a gesture from the umpire, Jaeger raised his right arm and angled his *Schläger*. Meyer did the same. Each man observed the ritual of the *Ehrengang*—the round of honor, standing motionless in a pose referred to as *steile Auslage*.

Meyer was the larger man, both in height and weight. He would have the advantage of a longer reach. But sweat was already pouring from him. Through his fencing goggles, Jaeger watched Meyer's eyes drift downward to his crotch. Nothing had changed there. Meyer raised his eyes, and was confronted by Jaeger's smile.

"First blood," whispered Jaeger.

"Fuck you," said Meyer.

With combat only moments away, the music started up in Jaeger's mind. He never told anyone about the music, how before every *Mensur* he heard movements from Wagner's *Der Ring des Nibelungen* playing in his head. The chorus was quickly building to a crescendo; Siegfried was reforging Notung, his father's famous sword. Jaeger listened to Siegfried's hammer pounding away: Boom boom-ba Boom boom-ba Boom—

Hildebrand crouched, locking Jaeger's hilt with his blade. "*Auf die Mensur!*" he announced.

The Guestphalian second offered the ritualized reply: "*Fertig!*"

On Hildebrand's barked "*Los!*" both seconds tumbled out of the way. Blades clashed and flashed; the hiss of metal made the arena sound like a snake pit. In an instant, sharpened steel rose and fell six times.

Neither Jaeger nor Wagner missed a beat.

"*Halt!*" both seconds yelled, then jumped in between the duelists, intervening with their *Schlägers*, locking their swords under the hilt of each combatant. Their arms were so heavily padded they had a gorillalike look; a hockey goalie's pads looked anemic in comparison. As the swords lowered, other attendants jumped in. Like trainers working a boxing match, they all had a particular job, some attending to the equipment, some to the combatants.

And one to clean away the blood.

Jaeger had scored a hit. *Rote plume* was his. The vertical cut along his opponent's left cheekbone flowed, and didn't look inclined to stop.

Another movement from Wagner, this time a chorus from *Die Walküre*. Brunnhilde and the Valkyries were singing as they gathered the warriors killed in battle. The dead were going to Valhalla. As the Valkyries' voices rose to a crescendo, blood pounded in Jaeger's head. He couldn't wait for the next round.

Jaeger opened his eyes, aware of a presence. Angelica was hovering nearby.

"Would you like a refill of your sparkling water? Or another pillow?"

"Nothing, thank you."

"I hope I didn't wake you."

"I wasn't asleep. I was just daydreaming."

"Are you sure? You had a big smile on your face."

"I always smile when I slay dragons."

Her smile matched his. "I'll let you get back to your dragons then."

The pillow was still on his lap, covering his erection. It was a convergence of things past and present. Jaeger wasn't sure if she knew what the pillow was hiding, but there was something almost tangible in the air between them. He wanted to rut with her right there—take her in the empty seat next to his and become a member of what the Americans called the Mile High Club—but there were those dragons to vanquish first.

When Angelica walked away he closed his eyes again and let his thoughts return back to those days in Berlin. He could feel the corners of his lips rising on their own accord. Angelica was right. He was smiling. In his mind, Wagner started playing again.

The white-haired doctor stepped in to look at Meyer. He was an unsympathetic old man the students called "the Butcher." One thing was certain—the Butcher never ended a match prematurely. A combatant had to be bleeding profusely, or cut open to the bone, before the Butcher ruled *Abfuhr*—the termination of the *Mensur* due to what was deemed an incapacitating wound.

"Will he live?" asked Hildebrand.

"He will if he isn't subjected to your so-called witticisms," said Braun, the apparent spokesman of Meyer's attendants.

The infighting between opposing attendants was sometimes almost as furious as the swordplay itself.

"I'm hoping he can go another round," said Hildebrand. "We have some very special champagne on ice for our boy, but it's not properly chilled yet."

Braun parried back: "I'm glad you have that ice handy. You know how it is when one loses a finger—or body part. You have to put it on ice in the hopes it can be reattached."

The barbs thrown out by the attendants were meant to be overheard by the duelists. Each side was always working for an advantage.

The Butcher finished his examination. "He's fine. Get back to it."

Fritz the Cat lined up the combatants. Standing at the ready, Jaeger experienced an epiphany: he was born for combat. It made him feel alive.

"*Auf die Mensur!*"

"*Los!*"

Jaeger swept his bell-guard *Schläger* across in a crushing *moulinet*. The blow staggered Meyer. He tried to recover, but overcompensated, leaving his guard too low. Jaeger punished his mistake with an incredibly quick and hard horizontal *quarte*, followed immediately by another. The audience gasped. To them, it almost looked as if Jaeger were whipping his opponent.

"*Halt!*"

The two cuts were so close to one another that they looked like one—even if they bled like two. The gash—gashes—were just above Meyer's left cheekbone. While attendants scurried about the fencing floor, the Butcher examined the wounds, squinting at the obvious.

Hildebrand announced to the opposing second: "I hope you will remind the gentleman from the Corps Guestphalia that parrying with the blade is considered more acceptable than parrying with the face."

"Not in the case of your face," said Braun.

The Butcher took a step away from Meyer. "You and I will be getting to know one another very well after this match," he said, referring to the stitching he would have to do, "but you're all right to go on."

Jaeger had known the Butcher wouldn't call the match this soon. He liked blood too much. His music switched again. It was *Götterdämmerung* time—the twilight of the Gods—the last of Wagner's four operas. Death and more death was playing in Jaeger's ears. The Norns, the Fates, were weaving out destiny. The Gods were being toppled and were falling hard.

Time slowed down for Jaeger. He would open his opponent as an offering to *Götterdämmerung*. He would give blood to the old gods.

Jaeger started in a high *quarte*, his blade beating *quarte* against Meyer's cuff, then with a quick turn of his wrist he shifted his *Schläger* to a high tierce. For an instant, his recovery seemed incomplete—and it was.

His deceit was purposeful.

The maneuver was called a *Stirnzieher*. His misdirection froze Meyer's blade for the instant that was needed.

There—there was the opening. For the audience, it happened too fast, but for Jaeger, there was all the time in the world. Meyer's scalp was his. All Jaeger had to do was claim his prize. He reached out and cut, his blade a silver bolt of horizontal *quarte* that sliced his opponent's forehead from one side to the other.

Blood showered down Meyer's face. His *Paukbrille* turned red. He started shrieking, bad etiquette for a *Mensur* where pain is supposed to be greeted with a stoic's reception.

There was enough blood for even the Butcher. *Abfuhr* was called.

Later, his corps brothers, in a ceremony of pomp and circumstance, presented Jaeger with his case of Veuve Cliquot. He didn't bother with a glass, just drank down two of the bottles in one sitting and got gloriously drunk, his immense pleasure counteracting the pain. He had done it.

Jaeger removed his pillow from his lap and put it on the seat next to him. A minute later the flight attendant came along and noticed the pillow.

"May I take that?" Angelica asked.

He nodded, and she reached over him, their skin almost touching. As she straightened with the pillow, he lifted his index finger as if reconsidering. "I'd like a raincheck, though," said Jaeger. "Can you return it to me a little bit later?"

"When?"

Jaeger looked at his watch, a platinum Patek Philippe wristwatch with a perpetual calendar and moon phase worth fifty thousand dollars.

"Say eight o'clock?"

"You'll need to readjust your watch. This flight lands at just past four Pacific standard time."

"I know. I already have my watch set to California time. But if you and that pillow aren't busy later, I was hoping the two of you could join me at a restaurant of your choice."

Angelica smiled. "I am afraid this particular pillow will have to stay on board," she said, "but I'm sure an appropriate substitution can be arranged."

Twenty-four

From his car, Graham spent the day working on the Lanie Byrne puzzle, starting with charting out a timeline for her. Her movements from the previous weekend, beginning on Friday the fifteenth, interested him most. Graham was sure something had happened then. That was the first of two weekends that Tina Wiggins and the other live-ins had been told to vacate the Grove for a few days and find other lodging. What happened the second weekend was obvious: Lanie tried to commit suicide and didn't want any witnesses. It was possible the first weekend had been a trial run for her grand finale, but Graham didn't think so. The pills had been prescribed just four days prior to Lanie's suicide attempt. Something had happened to send her on a downward spiral.

Graham used one hand to dial numbers, and the other to turn pages. He leafed through magazines and papers and tabloids—from *Variety* to the *L.A. Times* to *Entertainment Weekly* to *The Globe*—while making a string of calls, fishing the usual sources for gossip, and throwing out the bait of Lanie Byrne to see what was biting. Graham just finished talking with a "nail artist"—for some reason her industry clients always seemed to open up to her when she gave them pedicures—when a story in the *Times* headlined HOLLYWOOD POCKETS DEEP FOR VEEP caught his attention. Director Carl Camden had hosted a very exclusive party at his Malibu estate to help raise money for Vice President Brett Tennesson's run for the presidency.

Lanie Byrne had been among a guest list that included Tom Hanks,

Steven Spielberg, Meg Ryan, Warren Beatty, Annette Bening, Whoopi Goldberg, Robin Williams, and Barbra Streisand.

The article said it was Tennesson's third visit to California in the last two months. The gathering of stars netted the veep some serious change, putting almost two million dollars into his campaign coffers. It had been a very lucrative day for Tennesson. His stumping had started early with a 6:00 A.M. breakfast with Silicon Valley executives, followed by a meeting with the governor in Sacramento, a luncheon fund-raiser in San Francisco, a midday address on the campus of the University of California at San Diego, and finally the Malibu party. Tennesson had spent the night in California, staying at The Palms, an exclusive Malibu resort hotel.

Hollywood, Graham knew, was always fund-raising for one thing or another. There seemed to be a strange symbiotic relationship between ranking politicos and stars, a basking in the mutual glow.

The Camden fund-raiser had been held the Friday before last, on a night when Lanie Byrne had the Grove to herself. Though the media had not been invited to the fund-raiser, that didn't mean the media was absent from it.

Graham decided to call Libby Byrd. Some of the celebrity photographers in town specialized in a particular line of photos. Libby's signature work usually involved getting a team into exclusive parties. Though Graham didn't remember seeing any nonsanctioned photos from the fund-raiser, he was sure it wasn't for her want of trying.

Libby picked up on the first ring. Her growl didn't put Graham off. She smoked constantly, and her voice reflected it.

"I'm disappointed in you, Libby."

She hacked up some phlegm without bothering to put a hand over the phone. "Join the crowd."

"I'm working on a Hollywood-Beltway assignment, and figured you for getting inside shots on the Camden fund-raiser for Tennesson, but everything I've seen from that party makes it look as if it was staged by Norman Rockwell."

"That's because there was only one official photographer working the party, a stiff who should go apply for a job at the coroner's office because he shouldn't be shooting the living."

"Where were your people?"

"Getting all but cavity searched."

"You're kidding?"

"I wish I were. I had the staff lined up in place weeks before the party. That was necessary because the Secret Service was doing background checks on everyone working it. I guess they didn't want another presidential hopeful like Bobby Kennedy dying in L.A. I got commitments from three of the banquet staff to do some undercover photography. Because they were rookies, I spent half a day setting them up with mini-cameras in their cummerbunds.

"Since I knew security would be tight, I figured the staff might have to go through metal detectors, so I took my three to LAX and had them stroll through the detectors with their camera cummerbunds. Not a peep out of those machines.

"Everything should have gone like clockwork at the party. The Feds had the metal detectors just like I figured, but the problem is they brought in this new gizmo, our fucking tax dollars at work, a laser designed to pinpoint any kind of optical sight. The first of my would-be photographers walked through the detector, and suddenly these Buck Rogers lights go off, and these Secret Service goons charge at him. My guy was a little jumpy to begin with, and Tennesson's hired muscle pushed him over the edge. As they're jumping him, he's so scared he wets his pants, and that causes a short in the camera's wiring. The Feds act like some kind of goon squad. They push him down on the ground like he's an assassin, and then they start ripping off his cummerbund, and all the while this poor kid's got volts running up his nuts, and pee running down his leg.

"My other two plants see what's happening, and they're smart enough to lose their hidden cameras. So I'm out over three grand in expenses, and that's even before Mr. I-Need-Depends tries to hit me up for another grand because of what he describes as his 'disfigured scrotum.'

" 'Disfigured scrotum?' I say to him. 'It can't be too disfigured if you've got the balls to try to scam me.' So he goes teary on me and I end up throwing him a couple bills for missing out on working that night and for his getting canned from the service that throws him the banquet work. The man definitely can't hold his water on either end."

Libby stopped her story long enough to cough again.

"A camera-sniffing laser," Graham said. "When I hear about people bringing in equipment like that, it makes me wonder what they're trying to hide."

"Maybe they should have been hiding the artichokes Benedict. I hear the Hollandaise sauce had a canary-yellow glow."

"The first rule of politics," said Graham, "is to line up any photo ops. You wouldn't think Tennesson would care if anyone snuck in a camera."

"Is that what you're really calling about?"

"What do you mean?"

"Don't bullshit a bullshitter, Wells. You're not doing any Hollywood-Beltway assignment."

Graham's silence was answer enough.

"Care to ask me what's really of interest to you?"

"I want to know what happened at that party, Libby. It might not have anything to do with what I'm working on, but then again, it might. I'd like to talk with your two insiders and ask them some questions."

Graham listened to Libby's hack. When she regained her breath, she gave him two names and telephone numbers, then said, "Welcome back, Wells."

"What are you talking about?"

"It sounds like you've got some fire in your belly again. It's been absent for a long time."

"I wish I could say it was good to be back, Libby."

The first telephone number Graham called was disconnected, and there was no forwarding number. L.A., thought Graham, the world's capital of disconnected numbers. He managed to reach his target at the second phone number, but it took Graham several minutes of fast talking before C. C. Crane decided she would answer any of his questions.

C. C. had a high-pitched, breathless voice, a patois of Valley Girl, Mall Doll, and some art courses at a community college.

"I don't know why I ever even agreed to try to take those pictures," she said. "It was like that lady cast a spell on me. Something about her frog voice made it impossible for me to say 'no.' But even if that poor guy in front of me hadn't been busted, I doubt whether I would have been able to take any pictures. It was hard enough just delivering plates to *those* people. It felt like I was in one of those mind-blowing museums where everywhere you turn there's a Monet, or Picasso, or Degas, or Van Gogh, but instead of paintings there were all these name-brand kind of people. I had to pinch myself from stopping and staring."

Graham didn't interrupt C. C. much, just let her ramble on with her memories of the night. It was clear she had told her stories to a host of people; it was also clear she enjoyed repeating them.

Robin Williams had a comment for every plate brought out; the mussels were a "Rorschach test from the chef," the artichokes "were not quite potty-trained." Whoopi Goldberg tried to show Warren Beatty how to do the

Charleston, and finally announced that he had "two left legs, two left arms, two left everything," to which he replied, "All I want is to be *left* alone." Tom Hanks was seated next to Meg Ryan, and C. C. said they looked "just like they did in all their movies together."

Unsolicited, she mentioned the name of Lanie Byrne. "Miss L was like this princess or this angel," C. C. said. "She had on a beautiful silk designer dress, and had this strand of gorgeous white pearls. She was probably the quietest person there, but her eyes were glowing, and she had this serene smile that was happy and content, sort of Buddha-like."

Graham questioned C. C. about the arrival and departure times of some of the guests. It wasn't a carpooling kind of crowd. As far as C. C. remembered, all the guests arrived separately, and all came in limos. Tennesson, and his Secret Service contingent, left right after Streisand sang "America the Beautiful" just before midnight. The rest of the guests soon followed his departure.

C. C. rather abruptly decided it was time to depart as well; she was late for an appointment.

Graham mulled over their conversation, then dialed Celestial Motors. He told their operator: "I need to talk to someone about a car we rented."

"One moment," she said. After the operator put him on hold, Graham regretted his not dropping Lanie Byrne's name, an omission that resulted in his getting a long earful of elevator music.

Celestial Motors sold, leased, and rented the best driving machines the world had to offer, both contemporary and vintage. It had picked the right town to set up shop. "Keeping up appearances" was one of the oldest and greatest of Hollywood games. It didn't matter if you didn't have a pot to piss in—you still needed to show up in style. One director had managed to convince most people in town that his car collection was the Eighth Wonder of the World, when in fact most of the vehicles he was seen driving were rentals from Celestial Motors.

"This is Bernadette, may I help you?"

"Yes, this is William Foley," said Graham. "I work for Lanie Byrne." He paused to let that sink in, as did most underlings who wielded power through the boss's name. "We recently rented an XJR Jaguar from your establishment. I'm calling to check on extending that rental."

"Let me pull that up on my computer," Bernadette said. "Do you have the invoice number?"

"I'm afraid my paperwork is incomplete. I do have the car's license number, however."

"May I have it please?"

Graham recited the plate number he had memorized, and heard Bernadette tap in the entry. "According to our records, Mr. Foley, there is no specified return date for the rental."

"That's what I'm calling about. We're currently being charged a daily rate for the rental, aren't we?"

"That's correct."

"And we've had the car now for what, two weeks?"

"Since Wednesday the thirteenth."

He jotted down the date, the information he had wanted, while keeping up his end of the conversation. "Well, is there any way we could pro rate the original agreement, and get the monthly rental rate?"

"I'm afraid not. The Jaguar was supposed to be returned on Monday the eighteenth. We called on Tuesday the nineteeth, and were told by a Vera Grady—she signed for the vehicle—that the car would be needed for at least another week. However, if you have some firm dates at this time, and would like to switch over to a monthly rental—"

"Let me get back to you on that," said Graham.

It was one of those little things that had nagged at him. In a garage full of cars, that one rental had stood out. It was the only car with keys in it, the car that Graham and Lanie had raced death in. But why had Lanie rented the Jaguar when she had her own personal fleet of cars?

There might be some simple explanation. She could have rented it for a relative or a friend. Or she could have rented the tinted window luxury car to allow her some anonymity. Her other vehicles could easily be identified with her; in the Jaguar she could go incognito.

Graham wondered if there was some reason the car hadn't yet been returned. Maybe when you're contemplating suicide, that's not one of the things you think about.

Or maybe that's exactly what you think about.

Graham dialed Tina Wiggins's number. Without identifying himself, he said, "We need to meet tonight."

"I've been trying to call you," she said. "Don't you even have a message machine?"

"Yes. It's packed in my bag. Is seven good for you?"

"I was just leaving to work out with my girlfriend."

"Tell her your uncle is taking you to dinner at The Palms."

Surprised: "The hotel?"

"That's right."

"Which restaurant? They have two."

"We'll meet in the lobby. I'll let you choose."

"In that case, my sweat can wait until tomorrow."

Tina chose Crystal, the hotel's "fusion" restaurant. The menu selections claimed to combine cooking elements of East and West. Graham looked at the prices and thought the chef should have called the result nuclear fusion.

The interior designer apparently thought the ocean view wasn't enough. The restaurant lived up to its name, with strategically placed crystals reflecting colorful prisms of light around the restaurant, the rainbow will-o'-the-wisps magically appearing and disappearing.

Tina had forsworn her sweats for a short and sheer black dress. She was unabashedly freckled, her exposed arms and legs putting her pontilism on display. Her brown hair was dyed dark red, setting off her pale skin. While Tina gushed over items on the menu, Graham tried to find something familiar. The closest thing to a shrimp cocktail appetizer was shrimp in a papaya/lime sauce with macadamia nut shavings. He ordered it with trepidation. Animal-thin Tina decided to start with soup, salad, and an appetizer. She was apparently one of those animals who could eat most of her body weight given an opportunity.

It didn't take Tina long to devour the soup and salad. Her appetizer, wontons with an apricot glaze stuffed with crab and lobster, apparently agreed with her. She was all but doing a "When Harry Met Sally" number over it.

Graham eased into his questioning. "So how's life at the Grove?"

"It's been crazy. Lanie came down with the flu, and it's like they've opened up a hospital wing at the house."

Graham didn't see any need to tell her anything differently. It's a good cover story when even the staff believes it.

"So," said Tina, "was my lead a good one? Did you get some pictures?"

"I got some pictures," Graham said. "But Lanie wasn't entertaining anyone last Friday. She was by herself."

He changed the subject, honing in on a request he'd made of her when they had talked on the phone earlier. "Did you get a chance to talk with Vera?"

Tina nodded, swallowing a bite of the pot-sticker. "Lanie told her she was thinking of buying a Jag, and wanted to test one out. She gave Vera a company credit card to rent it, and told her to make sure it had tinted windows for privacy."

"Did Lanie have any other requests?"

Tina shook her head, then reconsidered. "Vera said she had to wait an extra fifteen minutes for them to get a second pair of keys."

"Two sets of keys?"

"That's what Lanie wanted."

Graham mulled that over. "Does Lanie often drive by herself?"

He kept catching Tina with food in her mouth. She nodded. "She's always driving around in her Prius. That's her favorite car. She likes it because it's half electric and barely pollutes. Lanie likes to go easy on the environment."

"Did either you or Vera ever see Lanie drive the Jaguar?"

Tina seemed to like the nonverbal answers. She shook her head and speared another wonton.

"There was a big fund-raiser for the vice-president on the fifteenth," said Graham. "Since all of the staff was given that day off, do you have any idea how Lanie got to the fund-raiser?"

"Probably through the studio. She could have asked for a limo and driver and they would have provided it."

Graham made a mental note to check on that. He had a contact at Warners who could find out for him.

"When Lanie asked you and your housemates to vacate the Grove," said Graham, "did she give you much advance notice?"

"She did for the first weekend. We knew well ahead of time. But not last weekend. That's why I was so pissed. She only told us the day before."

The waiter approached them. He was in his early thirties, and had a Steven Segal ponytail. His greeting, whenever he came to the table, was eastern by way of California, a clasping of hands and a slight bow of his head.

"Have you decided on your entrees?" he asked.

While Graham looked in vain at the menu again, Tina ordered. Though he had lived around the world, and sampled food from scores of countries, Graham was in the mood for something uniquely American. "I wonder if you could hold the horseradish teriyaki and radicchio, reconstitute the marinated filet strips, and just give me a New York steak medium rare with a baker."

Graham got the bow: "Certainly, sir."

When the waiter left, Graham sighed in relief. "For a moment there, I was afraid it was going to be a scene right out of *Five Easy Pieces*."

Tina didn't understand his reference.

"The movie," Graham said. "You know, where Nicholson tries to work a side order of wheat toast out of a chicken salad sandwich because of an inflexible menu and system."

A hint of memory, a vague remembrance, revealed itself on her face.

"I might hate the bullshit process that surrounds them," said Graham, "but I love nothing more than a good movie."

A prism of light danced around Graham's head. He looked up, and had to smile.

"You've got a halo," said Tina.

The lights from the crystal vanished.

"Short-lived," said Graham.

"So," said Tina, getting down to her own business, "am I going to get some money from those pictures you took?"

Graham nodded. "But I haven't sold them yet, so I don't know how much they will bring."

"Did you get some good shots?"

Graham didn't look at Tina. He stared instead at the ocean. Though the restaurant had lights shining out to the water, it was still hard to make out what was beyond the sand. From their table the ocean looked more like a great, enveloping shadow than a reassuring vista. Graham knew his own view was tainted. Whenever he looked at the Pacific, he was reminded of his own mother's suicide.

He suddenly realized that Tina was looking at him and expecting an answer. It took him a moment to remember her question.

"The pictures of Lanie came out much more fuzzy than I would have liked," he said.

Without telling her, Graham used Tina as his beard to survey the hotel and schmooze the staff. Hotel employees are typically gregarious sorts, and their mouths get that much more lubricated by generous tipping.

They drank in the hotel's lounge and learned what room the vice president had stayed in, and how the Secret Service had taken the rooms on either side of Tennesson's, as well as above and below.

"His arrival was all hush-hush," the bartender said. "He came in late at night and left early in the morning. I don't think anyone on the staff even saw him. His limo pulled down into the garage, and I hear the Secret Service hustled him up the stairway to his room on the second floor."

The bartender's words, and eyes, were mostly directed at Tina. It never hurts to have a pretty woman at your side.

On the pretense of taking a walk with Tina around the property, Graham was able to chat up the night auditor and the bellman, learning more about the veep's stay. They strolled around the exterior of the hotel; Tina's eyes were on the ocean, while Graham was more interested in the layout of the inn and the location of Tennesson's suite.

They slowly made their way back to the hotel's courtyard. Tina said, "One of the best things about working for Lanie is that sometimes I travel as part of her entourage, and I get to stay in some wonderful hotels."

"I suppose that's one of the perks of my job too," Graham said, "though the jet-set spots are usually wasted on me."

"Why is that?"

"While the rich and famous play, I work. They cavort on the snow and the sand, while I get frostbitten or sunburned."

"Oh, come on."

Graham raised his right hand to swear to the truth. "I became a human icicle while staking out Donald Trump a few years back. That was the vacation when he had his wife and family in one condo, and his girlfriend in another. But the frostbite wasn't as bad as the sunburn I got covering Brad Pitt and Jennifer Aniston. They were staying at this resort where clothing wasn't very much in evidence. I did my 'When in Rome' routine, shucking my swimming trunks, and paid the price. I was peeling where no man should ever peel."

Tina didn't hide her laugh very well. "I suppose Brad and Jennifer would say you deserved it."

"I suppose they would."

"You're good at blending in, aren't you?"

"My father was a foreign service officer. That made me a glorified version of an army brat. There was always a new posting, a new country. I learned how to be a chameleon."

"You change colors, do you?"

"In a manner of speaking. You would be amazed at how some people never see beyond a change of clothes. When I track a star to a luxury hotel like this one, I'm a regular cast of characters."

"What do you mean?"

"Depending on the situation, I pose either as staff or guest. Most resorts make it easy. The staff usually wears the same kind of polo shirts they sell in the gift shop. I get close to my target by dressing the part. No one notices the guy picking up the trash or cleaning bird shit off the balconies. If that doesn't work, I go into guest mode. It's like hunting, you look for the right game trail, and the best spot for an ambush. If I'm at the pool drinking a mai tai and reading the *Wall Street Journal*, everyone dismisses me as the vacationing businessman who can't quite get away from work. They never notice my briefcase with its aperture. That's how I regularly catch couples at play."

"Don't you ever feel bad about deceiving people?"

"Who am I deceiving? I *am* a businessman, just not the kind they think. Besides, a star and his publicist conspire to put a certain face out to the public, even if it's not a real face. Sometimes that face has more than a few warts on it. Like the star who has a clothing line that's produced in sweatshops by little kids, or the country singer who comes across in public as being all God and country, while in private he's really just a bully who wraps himself in red, white, and blue. There's one supermodel—you know her, the one who married the pop singer—who refuses to flush after herself. She thinks it's beneath her. She calls in her assistant right after she finishes and has her do it, and she's teaching her daughter to do the same thing. In her case, when I shoot her in a less than flattering light, I know that I'm getting the true picture."

"But not everyone's guilty. To use your word, you *hunt* these people. That means you target the innocent as well as the guilty."

"Yes, I do."

"Sometimes your pictures hurt people."

And sometimes I hurt them just trying to get the picture, he thought, nodding.

Tina shook her head. "I wouldn't want your job."

"I'm fond of saying the same thing."

"Why do you keep doing it?"

"Because I do it very, very well. And I like to beat the odds."

"What odds are those?"

"Everyone likes to root for the underdog, except when it comes to paparazzi. And we really are the underdogs. Our resources are next to nothing. We have to rely on smarts and perseverance to get the shots."

"And deception, and lying, and trickery."

"I'm not justifying those things, but I will say the other side does more than their share of the same. And when you consider we're going up against the studio, the star machine, and the publicist, not to mention all the resources available to the television camera, we really are the underdogs."

They walked across the tiled courtyard. Tina slowed as they approached a huge, decorative fountain. Nymphs and dolphins gamboled along the well.

The Little Mermaid rested on top of the fountain. Water splashed down from her tail.

"Do you have a coin?" asked Tina.

Graham dug out a quarter and handed it to her. She turned her back on the well, closed her eyes, and tossed the coin over her head.

"Your turn to make a wish," Tina said.

"What more could I wish for than your company?"

Tina seemed pleased at his answer, not recognizing it for the evasion it was. He didn't want to offer up a wish. He didn't want to think about once upon a time. Paris had changed his life forever, and he had learned to accept its consequences. To his thinking, contemplating a wish would just be setting himself up for a fall.

"Wherever Lanie goes," Tina said, "they treat her like royalty. She gets these huge gift baskets, with chocolates, and champagne, and treats of all sorts. Sometimes she just hands them over to us. Tim calls it 'trickle-down economics,' but we really score with the goodies."

They made their way over to a railing overlooking the ocean, and Tina breathed deeply of the sea air. She'd had wine with dinner, and several after dinner drinks, and was relaxed. As she leaned her elbows on the railing, Graham realized she had the posture of someone who wanted to be held.

For a long moment, he thought about doing just that. Tina had probably thought his taking her to dinner was a prelude to romance. He had probably even encouraged that notion, what with the way he had prattled. Their talk had surprised him. For a little while Graham had forgotten there were people out there who wanted him dead.

Graham hadn't been in a steady relationship since Paige, another man's wife. After that, Paris had done a job on his libido. He had been with a few women since the accident, but had felt as if he was just going through the motions with them. Nothing was as he remembered it before the crash, not food, or sex, or life. Nothing. That was his curse. It was hard for him to be passionate about anything anymore.

The light of a half-moon shined down on them. He ran a hand through his hair, and when he did, it looked as if his shadow reached for Tina and touched her freckled arms. But Graham knew taking her in his arms wouldn't help him escape his shadows. It would probably only bring them home to roost. And besides, he had work to do.

"I am so glad you could join me for dinner," Graham said. "It's a shame I have to go out and ask people some questions before they turn into pumpkins."

His retreat surprised her. "You're really going to work this late?"

"It's actually early for my line of work. May I walk you to the valet stand?"

Tina nodded at his offer, though she seemed a little put off at the abrupt end to their evening. Graham did his best to charm her as they walked, and that seemed to mollify her a little, but Tina also came to the late realization that she had been little more than that evening's camouflage. At the entrance of the hotel, a valet took her ticket.

"After I called you that first time," Tina said, "I felt bad. On the whole, Lanie's been a pretty good boss. I didn't want to see her get embarrassed or anything. I wanted to call the whole thing off, but it was too late. I'm not going to turn down the money from your pictures, but I don't think you should count on me ever contacting you again. And I would appreciate your not calling to ask me any more questions about Lanie."

"I understand."

Tina's car pulled up to the curb. The valet opened the door, and then closed it behind Tina. Graham tipped him, then leaned his head into the opened window.

"I know I haven't told you much about those pictures I took that night. I can't give you specifics, but you should know that instead of hurting Lanie, you actually helped her."

Graham surprised himself, and Tina, by reaching for her left hand and kissing it.

Before leaving The Palms, Graham went on a self-tour down to the parking garage. Valets were supposed to drive all cars in and out, but there was nothing to prevent a guest from driving away other than the valets controlling the keys. Security stood at the entrance to the garage, but not the exit. Angled metal spikes prevented any unwanted traffic, a sure blowout to any tires going the wrong way. Large warning signs were posted warning of tire damage.

Though he looked for security cameras, Graham didn't see any. Luxury hotels were famous for splurging on ornamental items, while stinting on security. Flower displays generally ranked higher on budgets than security cameras. Though he tromped around the garage, and made his nosing about obvious, Graham didn't capture the attention of anyone on staff.

It was one in the morning when Graham drove away from the hotel. He was afraid to go to his apartment, and didn't want to use his credit card to get a hotel room for fear that all of his transactions were being monitored. Graham wished he had arranged to stay at Ran's for an extra night, but it was too late for that. The backseat of his T-bird would have to do for the night. At least he had a blanket, essential equipment for a celebrity photographer.

Graham drove up into the Malibu hills, looking for a spot where he might park undisturbed from traffic, curious residents, or the police. Being homeless wasn't to his liking. He finally parked on a quiet street a block from an elementary school, then tried to settle into the backseat. Though he was very tired, sleep was slow to come. He kept trying to find the right fit to all that had occurred, but the puzzle still had too many missing pieces.

As was usual when he couldn't sleep, Graham started thinking of the two people who had died, the Lady and LeMoine. He wondered how he would have felt had the victims been ordinary and anonymous people. Would he still be up ruminating, or would he have put the accident well behind him?

Graham tried to think about something else. That never worked, of course. It was like attempting to will a tune out of your head. The more he tried to push it from his thoughts, the louder it played.

He cracked open a window. In the silence, he thought he could just hear the sound of the ocean. It didn't lull him, but instead added to the chorus of the dead. His mother joined with the others. Graham knew his tiredness didn't help. Tomorrow, he thought, I'll try and get a gun. Armed, he could return to his apartment. He was tired of being on the run. Always running from accidents, he thought. That, more than anything, was his Paris legacy. He had fled the scene of the accident, and nothing could erase that from his mind. He had run, but he couldn't hide, especially from himself.

That had to stop.

He needed to find a way to make his enemies visible. Lanie had some answers, even if she didn't think she did. He could squeeze her for the information, blackmail her.

Just like they had blackmailed him.

Coercion wasn't anything new to him, but he knew how fragile she was. Push her hard enough, and it would be the same thing as yelling "jump" to someone on the ledge of a building. Somehow he would have to get her to trust him. Given their adversarial roles, that would all but take a miracle.

He thought about Lanie's suicide attempt. Maybe someone had pushed her buttons the way Smith and company had pushed his. One of his would-be assassins had called him "Pilgrim." Lanie knew his two captors. Everything was interrelated somehow. It was possible she had balked at being blackmailed, and had embraced death before dishonor.

No, that didn't feel right. Lanie's sickness was similar to his own. He knew that, without knowing how. It was obvious to him, painfully obvious.

You are as sick as your secret, he thought, once again remembering the AA canon.

It kicked in then. He didn't call it intuition, or sixth sense, or a leap of faith. Sometimes he just *knew*.

Lanie had been involved with something that had very bad consequences. Whatever it was, suicide had seemed a viable answer.

He wondered if she had somehow caused someone's death.

Graham had no evidence of that. A shrink would probably call his assumption blatant displacement, a reading of his own feelings of guilt into her pain. But it seemed right to him. He believed, even without any proof, that was their connection.

In a selfish way, he wanted to believe it was so. Misery loves company.

He tried to tear down his theory. It didn't stand up to any true scrutiny. There was nothing in the way of hard facts to support it. But Graham was still not willing to put it aside.

Eventually, he slept. Usually he was a light sleeper, but not this time. His exhaustion was so complete that he fell into a deep, deep slumber. He dreamed of a phone ringing for the longest time before he finally awakened. Even then he was disoriented, foggy, almost drugged.

It was almost like that time he had awakened on the oil rig in Santa Barbara.

The phone. Graham reached for his digital phone, flipped it open, then wished he hadn't.

"Pilgrim," said a familiar voice. Smith.

"How the hell did you get this number?" Graham asked, but he didn't wait for an answer.

He slammed his flip phone shut. He tried to remove the phone's battery, but it took him several tries. His hands were trembling, a combination of rage and frustration. Graham wondered if they had somehow gotten a fix on his location just by his answering the phone. His own medicine tasted bitter. How many times had he been the one doing the tracking?

Graham huddled in the darkness, but the cloak of night didn't help. He felt exposed and vulnerable.

His enemies, whoever they were, were close.

Twenty-five

Under Blackwell's orders, Monroe continued to try calling Pilgrim back. Even with an auto-dialer, he had long grown tired of attempting to reach the paparazzo. Blackwell didn't seem to realize that Monroe had a business to run, not to mention having a life of his own.

But you did what Blackwell said if you wanted to keep having a life.

The number was ringing, but Pilgrim wasn't answering. Monroe suspected he was scared, and for good reason, but he believed that eventually Pilgrim would break down and talk to him—the man he knew as Smith. And even if he didn't, Pilgrim wouldn't stay hidden long. He didn't have the funds to escape, and it was unlikely he had the patience to stay concealed. But in the meantime, every moment of his continued existence posed potential problems. According to Blackwell, he had already told others about the Brothers' attempt to kill him.

Jaeger was on his trail, so it was just a matter of time. In a day or two he would get him, though Blackwell was already chafing at the delay. They knew things about Pilgrim, were aware of his habits, his haunts, and his acquaintances. That was the way they did business. It eliminated surprises.

Monroe wished Blackwell hadn't involved him with Pilgrim. He always preferred staying in the background, and not being put in the field. But because their organization was so small, Blackwell sometimes insisted upon Monroe's involvement. From his first meeting with Pilgrim on the oil rig, to the last time they had talked on the phone, it had been his job to keep him off balance. Because Pilgrim's past and present were so well documented, it meant his future would be very brief.

Monroe tried both of his numbers again, but Pilgrim still wasn't answering. The son of a bitch wasn't making this easy. Blackwell had told Monroe to schedule a face-to-face meeting with the paparazzo where they could discuss "all the misunderstandings." He would propose "one last job" for Pilgrim, and offer him the carrot of a completely clean slate. Naturally, Monroe would never show up to the meeting. Jaeger would be there in his stead. And knowing Jaeger, he would quickly make his *point*.

He suspected Jaeger enjoyed his work even more than he did the money. The two men had little personal contact, which was just as well. Not that Monroe had any complaints about Jaeger's job performance. He never failed at his work, even under the most difficult of circumstances. On several occasions, Monroe had tried to praise him for a job well done, but even to himself his words had sounded false. It was difficult to condone murder, let alone sound like a cheerleader. The money was what Monroe loved, and he tried to turn a blind eye to the rest.

Despite his reservations, Monroe had to admit that Blackwell could not have done better in choosing his team. They all brought something to the table, and that made for symbiotic relationships. Blackwell was the leader, though he kept himself insulated from the fray, and his identity a secret from everyone except Monroe and Jaeger. The firewalls went down the line. Blackwell provided the information, Monroe had his established company with its money and resources, and Jaeger did whatever dirty work needed to be done.

Monroe even paid much of Jaeger's salary on his company's books. It was laughable, actually. At his firm, Jaeger had the reputation of being a workaholic, of always doing work on the road. He handled the "foreign markets." That helped explain his exorbitant salary, as well as his travels around the world. For appearance's sake, Jaeger attended several large conferences every year representing the firm. Surprisingly, judging from the feedback Monroe had gotten from others, the man did very well—especially considering he was a stone cold killer. Men and women alike found him charming. Still, Monroe was glad Jaeger rarely occupied his office at the firm. Truth be told, Jaeger scared him. Monroe knew what lurked behind his polished exterior. But the man had his uses. He spoke half a dozen languages with virtually no accent. He was smart, and he was creative. And he was utterly ruthless.

Monroe was glad he wasn't the paparazzo.

Twenty-six

With a laugh, Angelica plumped a pillow for Jaeger—a man she knew as John Hunter. He stuck his elbow down on it, and with his arm propped his head. She ran her hand along his naked, firm flesh, pausing at his face. With her index finger she traced the line of his scar.

"How did you get this?" she asked.

"When I was a little boy I fell off my bicycle and my face landed atop some glass."

Angelica kept stroking the scar. "It makes you look that much more intriguing."

"That's why I never had a plastic surgeon do away with it. I knew someday I'd find a woman who found my old scar intriguing."

He had actually kept it as a physical reminder of the way of the world. The story he'd told her about falling off a bicycle was a lie, of course.

Jaeger had been a student in Berlin on November 9, 1989, the day the Wall came tumbling down. He had helped take a sledgehammer to it, and had danced along Checkpoint Charlie Boulevard. Little did he know what the Wall's absence would bring.

Like a polluting stream, a flood of Eastern Europeans had descended upon his beloved Berlin. In his own city, German became almost a second language, what with the influx of Albanians, Poles, Serbs, Czechs, Romanians, and Russians. Various mob factions set up shop in town, bringing prostitutes and drugs. Within eighteen months of the Wall's coming down, Jaeger had first one car, then a second, stolen. It was well known that a Polish car thief ring was stealing everything not cemented down. Garbage begets garbage. Illegal workers came and plied illegal trades.

Honor became a forgotten concept.

Honor was the reason Jaeger had joined a dueling fraternity. Before taking up the *Schläger*, he had excelled at the foil and epee, but had found that swordplay lacking. There had been no true consequences in crossing blades. The *Mensur* stood for much more. In Jaeger's young mind he saw it as the closest equivalent in modern times to being a knight. You might not be fighting for a maiden or a just cause, but you entered the ring and faced up to steel. As your hands wrapped around the sword's hilt, you grasped upon an ancient tradition. Somehow it all seemed noble to him.

The Wall had been down less than a month when the Corps Normannia fought a match against Corps Marchia. It was expected to be another hard-fought contest between two Berlin fraternities with a long rivalry of swords crossing. The story of Jaeger's Godiva-like exploit had circulated throughout the fencing world, making him a minor celebrity. What Jaeger didn't know was that in many ways it made him a marked man.

Jaeger entered the *Mensur* overconfident. He had done what no duelist had ever accomplished. What else was there to conquer? He knew he was the best, and he let it show in the way he walked into the ring.

His opponent looked at him with clear disdain. Oskar Freiherr von Saxe was a descendant of royalty, and he didn't like pretenders to the throne. The English royal family of the so-called House of Windsor, German expatriates really, had much the same blood in their veins that Saxe had in his. His family had managed to maintain land, titles, and fortune throughout the centuries, through whatever means necessary. Given the ever-shifting political climate in Germany, that was no mean feat. Their good fortune was not accidental. His family had a reputation for treachery. At Saxe gatherings, stories of familial duplicity were brought out like old heirlooms. Instead of being ashamed, the men winked and laughed at tales of the "old family habit."

Saxe had been drinking brandy steadily for hours before his match. He had worked it out among his corps brothers that he would be the one to face "Pretty Boy," his constant reference to Jaeger.

"Pretty Boy needs some red in his cheeks," he told a few of his brothers.

If Jaeger heard any of his talk, he didn't show it. He entered the match looking exceedingly nonchalant. While the umpire talked to the two duelists, Jaeger yawned directly in Saxe's face. Saxe took that as an affront. A commoner was trying to show him up. Whether it was the brandy or the stirred-up blood of his ancestors, Saxe felt the need to right the wrong offered him.

He showed nothing in his face, gave no hint of what he was thinking. Generations of his forebears had been served by acting suddenly, without warning.

"I've never dated a passenger," Angelica said. "And this—well, this certainly isn't typical of me."

"Don't apologize for this evening," Jaeger said. "It was special. It was almost perfect."

"Almost?"

"It was only missing one thing. Now, what was that?"

He pursed his lips and pretended to be thinking.

"Stop it." She lightly slapped, then caressed, his chest. "What are you talking about?"

"Oh, yes," said Jaeger. He reached over the side of the bed, opened his valise, and pulled out a space-age-looking container.

"What is it?"

"Open it."

Angelica took it and unsealed the top. "It's cold."

"It's a wine cooler."

"How ingenious." Angelica reached inside and pulled out a bottle of Veuve Cliquot Grande Dame.

"You are amazing!" she said. "Let me get some glasses."

"No need."

He took the container from her, twisted a compartment at the bottom, and pulled out two chilled champagne glasses. Angelica clapped her hands.

"It is said that Marie Antoinette's bosom was so exquisite, champagne glasses were modeled on her chest."

Jaeger reached over with a glass and rolled it along Angelica's nipple. "But the queen's chest could not have been as exquisite as yours."

"Thank you." Her smile was a little bit forced. "That glass really *is* cold."

He didn't immediately withdraw it. "It's properly chilled," he said. With some satisfaction he watched her plum-colored nipple harden.

She took the glass from him, her way of stopping his play. Jaeger stifled his impulse to reclaim the glass and take up his game with her other nipple. If he saw her again, she would learn not to deny him his play—any of it. But he smiled as he popped the champagne cork, and then poured. As they both sipped from their glasses, he found himself getting hard again.

Angelica noticed. "I think I'll invest in a few cases of this," she said, laughing.

It was like drinking victory, Jaeger thought, which to him was the ultimate aphrodisiac.

They both drained their glasses, and then started touching each other anew. Her eyelashes and lips worked their way up his chest, feathering him in their gentle touch, then continued up his neck. He stopped her at his chin, taking her head in his hand, and then firmly directing her lips over to the left side of his face.

"Follow the trail of my scar," Jaeger said, his voice husky, even rough, "and we'll see where it leads."

"Auf die Mensur!"

"Fertig!"

"Los!"

Jaeger started with a *quarte*, took his opponent's return low on his forte, then riposted with two more lashing *quartes*.

"Halt!"

At the seconds' command, Jaeger's guard relaxed, and he began to turn toward his attendants. Though his *Paukbrille* severely limited his peripheral vision, he sensed or saw his opponent's blade coming his way. It was too late to raise his own *Schläger*. His second had already interceded with his blunt blade, blocking his *Schläger*. The second should also have been in position to protect him from his opponent's blade, but he was moving too slowly. All this Jaeger saw in an instant. Though he didn't even have time to blink, his reflexes were such that he still managed to jerk his face back.

It would have been far worse if he hadn't moved. His lips would certainly have been split apart, and he would have lost teeth. But still, it was bad enough. Saxe's *Schläger* sliced open his cheek almost to his lips. In disbelief, Jaeger looked up and saw Saxe staring at him with no little satisfaction. Jaeger tried to pull his *Schläger* away from his second, but his blade was locked.

The umpire was screaming that Saxe was disqualified, and Jaeger's corps brothers were screaming bloody murder.

"I did not hear the command to halt," insisted Saxe.

His performance seemed genuine, except for his eyes. Jaeger knew what he had done.

"You are a fucking disgrace!" screamed Hildebrand. "I hope you get kicked out of the corps with *cum* fucking *infamia*, you shit!"

"I apologize, of course," said Saxe. "It was a terrible mistake."

C.I.—*cum infamia*—meant "with infamy." In the world of *Mensur* there could be no greater stigma attached to your name. But Saxe had known what might result from his actions. His ancestors had not let their ill deeds interfere with their appetites or their sleep. They had murdered, cheated, and connived, and because of that, they had thrived.

Yes, Saxe had lost the match, but that's not what the mirror would say. For the rest of his life that arrogant prick Jaeger would stare into the looking glass and know what he had done. That was enough for Saxe.

Jaeger stifled his impulse to strike back. He was hustled away for medical attention, and while the Butcher worked on his face, he had time to think about what had happened to him. It had been his fault. Rules or not, he shouldn't have relaxed his guard. And he never would again—in the ring or out of it.

The world was amoral. To be idealistic was to ask to be blindsided, much as he had been. Honor was a handicap. The immigrants overwhelming his Germany knew that. To succeed, he would do whatever was necessary, much like Saxe.

But Saxe had made a mistake. When you stab a lion, you should stab to kill.

"Yes, yes, yes . . ."

Angelica's eyes were closed. She wasn't watching the man who was pushing in and out of her. She didn't see his face, had no idea that he was reliving another rhythm, didn't know the rapture of his thrust came not from their sex, but a particular memory.

Among most who have dueled, there is a certain pride that comes from scars earned in a *Mensur*. Those who belittle such dueling think of the scars as anachronistic marks, things that don't belong in the modern world. But in most tribes throughout the world scarification is an important ritual, a way to signify the warriors from the boys.

The night after his match, with his face sewed up, Jaeger's corps brothers rallied around him.

"Where there's scar tissue," said Frankie Obermann, pointing to his own prominent *Schmiss*, "no pimples will grow!"

"That's right," said Witt. "Now you have a badge of pride."

Jaeger wasn't buying it. "I think of what Bismarck said to a corps student who was proudly brandishing his scars: 'In my day we parried with the *Schläger*, and not with the face.' "

"Yes," said Hildebrand, "the Iron Chancellor did say that, but if you look at any of his portraits or pictures you can see he had a *Schmiss* or two of his own."

"You're not a virgin anymore," said Witt.

That was one thing Jaeger could agree with. "You're right. I've lost my innocence."

A part of his mind registered that Angelica was a talker. She liked to speak during sex. It didn't seem to matter to her that Jaeger didn't say anything back. That was just as well, for his mind was elsewhere.

"Oh, that's it. Oh, yes. Oh, you feel so good. That's it. That's right. There, there, there."

Over time, Jaeger's face healed. At first his scar was red, but gradually it turned lighter. Over time, it became white, blending in with his skin. Now, only on very cold nights did the red show itself.

It was on just such a freezing, cold night that he tracked down Saxe.

Jaeger had never spoken of revenge to anyone. He had seemed to accept what happened to him with equanimity. Saxe had received the ultimate in punishment, had been thrown out of the corps *cum infamia*. That meant his own corps brothers turned their backs on him.

But that wasn't enough for Jaeger.

He had waited just over a year, long enough that the memory of their *Mensur* and Saxe's betrayal had faded from the minds of most people. Unbeknownst to anyone, Jaeger had made Saxe his little project. He had trailed him on countless occasions, had come to know his routines and his haunts. The anticipation of their eventual meeting had been a great source of pleasure for Jaeger.

Saxe left his girlfriend's house at just past midnight. She had taken a very cheap apartment in the Oranienburger Strasse area in East Berlin. At that time, the area hadn't been redeveloped. Most of the neighborhoods were dark, and not altogether safe. There had been a rash of skinhead attacks, disenfranchised young East Germans attacking people. Since the fall of the Wall there had been numerous stabbings. Jaeger had read the accounts with great interest.

It was a cold night. A slushy rain had fallen and driven everyone indoors.

The temperature bordered on freezing. Jaeger had waited patiently. His scar throbbed in the cold.

Jaeger intercepted Saxe on the way to his car, a new BMW.

"I'm sure your family has warned you against slumming," said Jaeger. "Do you make her call you Herr Graf? Do you play bed games, the Lord of the Manor visiting his peasant?"

Saxe tried to hide his surprise, tried to cover up his look of alarm. He did his best to exude royal disdain.

"I am a baron, not a count," Saxe sniffed. What Jaeger had done was the equivalent of addressing a general as a captain.

"My apologies, Baron. But does it really matter? Do not blue bloods bleed red? Let's put that to the test, shall we?"

"Step aside," Saxe said.

"We have unfinished business."

Jaeger opened his overcoat, showing two *epees de combat.* "I borrowed these weapons of honor from my corps," he said. "They are relics from a time when differences were resolved in a definitive way."

The epees had deep bell guards of polished steel, with blades shaped like a "V" that tapered to a finely honed and deadly point. These were killing weapons.

"You have your choice of weapons. Both are identical."

"You are mad."

"Mad to even give you a chance? I suppose you are right. But I am not like you. It is the right thing to do, and truth to tell, I would have it no other way. I suspect the pleasure of this duel will erase the memory of the other."

"I want nothing to do with this."

"Are you sure? Are you absolutely sure?"

Jaeger pulled both swords free. The French-style epees were called "*Parisers*." The same word was German slang for "condom."

"I would have thought you would like a *Stobmensur auf Pariser,* Herr Graf."

In one sentence Jaeger made a double entendre, slighting Saxe's nobility. Then he tossed one of the epees in the air. Saxe reached out, catching it by the hilt.

"Your hands are warm," said Jaeger. "Mine are cold from waiting for you."

He raised his hands and blew on them. The point of his foil was facing the frozen ground.

"I will not duel with you," said Saxe. "As you can see, I am tossing the sword aside."

He moved as if to fling it away, but instead of releasing it, he came across with a vicious lunge.

Jaeger had been expecting as much. Like a matador who has manipulated a beast into charging, he stepped away, allowing Saxe and his blade to lunge past, but not before his own blade tunneled through Saxe's chest.

From *quarte*, he twisted his hand into a *tierce*, widening the wound before pulling out.

The sword dropped from Saxe's hand. He didn't scream, just stood in a state of shock. Jaeger made sure their eyes met before he died.

Jaeger used a stiletto to finish the job. They would assume the stabbing was the work of skinheads.

He took the knife, and plunged it in again, and again, and again . . .

"Don't stop!" said Angelica. "Don't, don't, don't stop!"

He pushed hard into her, each thrust a vivid memory. They climaxed at the same time, though Jaeger's thoughts were some dozen years earlier.

When their breathing steadied, Angelica said, "Oh, God, that was wonderful."

"Yes, it was," said Jaeger.

He felt warm all over, especially his scar.

Angelica wanted him to stay the night, but Jaeger demurred. "I have to work," he said.

"Work? But it's so late."

"I have to go crunch numbers," he said.

Twenty-seven

Gut instinct told Graham to keep running. Ever since his unwanted wake-up call he had been on the move. Maybe, he thought, he was just trying to justify his cowardice. But he didn't think so. His personal radar was on full alert. He had covered wars and military conflicts as a photographer, and by trusting his feelings had come out of some dangerous situations alive. Having walked away from one death trap already, he was willing to err on the side of caution. Until there was proof to the contrary, he was assuming there were people out there who wanted him dead.

Again, he debated going to the police. He could request protective custody. It would be a relief to involve some higher authority. But they wouldn't look at his case carefully unless he incriminated himself. Even now, years later, dying was almost preferable to facing his shame. He hadn't been willing to own up to his sins in 1998, and he couldn't now. Better to go it alone. Besides, that was how he was used to working.

Like a shark, he needed to keep moving or die. But he wasn't the predator now, but the prey. Still, he wasn't helpless. Graham's office was mobile. He worked from his car using his laptop and cell phone. There weren't very many people whom he had given his new telephone number. He spent hours eliminating those who might have told Smith his number, until only one name remained.

Lanie Byrne was already back to work, but getting a message to her on the set proved impossible. No one even went through the pretense of taking a message. Graham tried to find a back door, but his attempts were quickly rebuffed. When he tired of working the maze, he changed his focus. Estelle Steinberg proved a little, if not a lot, easier to reach.

"What the hell do you want now?" she asked, finally coming on the line.

"I need to talk to Lanie."

"She's on the set."

"Tell me something I don't know."

"That would take the rest of my lifetime."

"Does she have a private number to her trailer?"

"If you knew anything about Lanie, you'd know she doesn't like to be bothered on the set. Someone like you probably can't understand this, but when it comes to her art, Lanie doesn't compromise. She gives it her full attention."

"I need a few minutes of her time."

"A few months ago Barbara Walters asked for the same thing, and I'll tell you exactly what I told Babs: we'll get back to you in a few days."

"Did Babs have pictures of your girl trying to off herself?"

"I better not be hearing what I'm hearing. Are you trying to fucking blackmail me?"

"I'm trying to tell you this is important."

"Gee, I've never heard that one before."

"Why don't you let Lanie decide if it's important or not?"

"Here's your news flash: she decided years ago. Everyone including me has standing orders not to bother her on the set unless it's goddam life or death. Lanie doesn't think anything's more consequential than the film she's working on."

"When is she going to be home?"

"Late. Production's trying to make up for the days she lost. She'll put in a fifteen-hour day minimum, and tomorrow's going to be the same. That's your hint not to bother her. She doesn't need your kind of stress."

"I was her ambulance driver," Graham said. "I wasn't the one who put her in the ambulance."

"Like hell you didn't. You and your kind are as responsible as anyone."

It would be easier to lie, Graham thought, than argue. "I have to meet with Lanie tonight. We need to conclude our business ASAP."

"You're willing to hand over all the photos and negatives, and agree to complete confidentiality?"

"Yes."

"How much money are you asking?"

"That's between Lanie and me."

"The hell it is. You got your claws in her, and she's in a state of duress. You're all but holding a gun to her head."

Graham had to think of a price tag. There was always a big market for the "last living photos" of stars like Monroe and Belushi, but he wasn't aware of any precedent for celebrity suicide pictures. Still, anything Miss L did was tabloid fodder. Estelle would know that more than anyone.

"I want half a million dollars."

"I'm smelling fucking sulphur in the air."

"What are you talking about?"

"A deal with the fucking devil, that's what I'm talking about. You want her soul too, right?"

"I want what's reasonable."

"Reasonable is half that amount, and not a penny more."

"What are you, her business manager now?"

"I'm looking out for my client and friend."

"And I'm looking out for me. I am asking for a conservative amount. I could probably get a million for those pictures on the open market."

"That's possible. But you don't take our deal and I promise you this: every penny you get from those photos you'll have to spend on legal fees."

Graham mulled that over for a long moment. "You're right," he said.

"About what?"

"I'm suddenly smelling sulphur in the air."

Twenty-eight

The tall, well-built black guard had the look of a moonlighting Marine. He directed Graham to park just in front of the gate at the Grove. He was as vigilant as he was polite, punctuating all of his requests with the word "sir" while he pleasantly but thoroughly inspected both Graham and his car. Graham wondered if the scrutiny was usual, or a little treat Estelle Steinberg had cooked up.

It was late, approaching midnight. Lanie had stayed on the set until almost ten o'clock. She hadn't been the only one working. Graham had been studying his own lines all day. The problem was, his script still had blanks in it. He would have to perform based on the responses of his leading lady. That was usually a recipe for disaster, though it had worked in *Casablanca.* Toward the end of the film none of the actors had known what was going to happen. Even the director wasn't sure. The screenplay was a constant work in progress, but the movie turned out all right. Graham had seen it maybe a hundred times.

The guard wished him a good night, and Graham decided Estelle wasn't behind the inspection. She would have insisted upon a cavity search.

The Grove's penitentiary lighting softened beyond the gate. Graham followed the flagstone driveway around. He rolled his window down, taking in some deep breaths. The air was fresh, with a coastal scent, but the house was far enough away from the sea that there was only a hint of brine.

Graham parked under the coast live oak, but this time there was no greeter at the door. Lanie was there, looking pensive and vulnerable and alone. She was wearing worn cotton sweats and broken-in Ugg Boots. As Graham got closer, he saw her face wasn't made-up, and she wasn't sporting any jewelry or adornments of any sort. Somehow that made her all the more attractive. Graham knew of two different actresses whose husbands said they had never even seen them in private without their makeup.

Neither Graham nor Lanie appeared comfortable in the other's presence. Graham might have saved her life, but he was still the enemy. They offered each other a cautious greeting, amicable sounds that weren't exactly words, and then Lanie motioned with a tilt of her head for him to follow her.

The recessed lighting in the hallway was dimmed, perhaps because of the lateness of the night, or perhaps to prevent Graham from getting too close a look at Lanie's world. There was a clear demarcation between the designer showcase part of the house and Lanie's area. Her living space was more personal and warm, with lots of plants, old pictures, colorful paintings, and pottery. She liked masks; visages of all sorts hung from her walls. For a moment, Graham flashed on the Abbot and his figurines of the Seven Sins. But Lanie wasn't limited only to sin. She had masks for every occasions. It was appropriate for an actor, Graham thought. Her profession was often represented at theaters or on playbills with two masked faces, the one showing joy, the other sadness. But the masks might have been mere decoration more than a statement of her profession. It surprised Graham that there were no signs of Hollywood in Lanie's personal space, no movie pictures or memorabilia, nothing to indicate Lanie's profession or status. People in the business usually made a point of putting such items on display. Around town, those who have Oscars usually create shrines. Genuflecting to Oscar was optional, but encouraged. Lanie's Academy Award was nowhere to be seen.

She led him into a large den that was about the size of Graham's apartment. The room was warm; a fire burned in the fireplace. Real wood, not designer ceramic logs. Lanie took up a poker and stirred the fire. The flames cast an orange pallor on her face and accentuated her dark circles.

"It's not really a cold enough night to have a fire," Lanie said, "but I thought I would indulge myself anyway. Sometimes I burn a log or two even in the summer."

"You and President Nixon," Graham said. "He used to have roaring fires going in the Oval Office in the summer, even on muggy, miserable days."

"The Oval Office must have been a sauna."

Graham shook his head. "While his fire raged, he kept the air-conditioning going full blast."

"How clever. Pollute the air and diminish resources at the same time."

Graham had told his Nixon story any number of times before, but had never heard that response. People either commented on how quirky Nixon was, or they expressed admiration for his managing to get the pleasure of a fire in July. Maybe Lanie's lending her name to environmental causes wasn't done only for the usual Hollywood show.

"I understand he sat in front of the fire a lot more after Watergate," Graham said. "With his world tumbling down around him, the fires were one of the few things that comforted him."

"That sounds like an updated version of Nero's fiddling while Rome burned."

Graham shook his head. "I have the story on good authority, and I'm not talking journalese here. My father worked for an ambassador who was a friend of Nixon's. The ambassador visited him several times during his dark days. He said Nixon sat in front of his fire for hours at a time."

"Thinking," she said, "about how everything can change so quickly and so drastically."

Graham wasn't sure if Lanie was talking about Nixon or herself.

"I was surprised to learn you went back to work today."

She shrugged her shoulders. "Work is supposed to be therapeutic," Lanie said. "Besides, my guilt was kicking in. Whenever the director called to see how I was doing, there was a certain desperation in his voice."

"The production must have been idled."

"It was detoured. I don't ever want to wield what an actor friend of mine calls the 'John Wayne Status.' "

"What's that?"

The question brought a small smile to her face. "Wayne never performed until he finished his morning's business. Usually, he was regular. But every so often, he was stymied. Sometimes there would be hundreds of people on the set milling about for hours waiting for one man to do a bowel movement."

"At least he didn't have to ask the director, 'What's my motivation?' "

"That's true," she said, still smiling. "His motivation was quite basic. Wayne said he didn't feel right until he unburdened himself. When he'd make one of his late exits from his trailer, he would often be greeted by loud cheers."

"Only in Hollywood."

Lanie hung the poker back up and dusted her hands. "Drink?" she asked.

"Only if you'll join me."

She walked over to a portable bar. "What would you like?"

"Anything over ice." Graham thought for a moment, then reconsidered. "Except vodka."

Lanie made his drink, then poured her own, some watered-down cranberry juice. Both took up chairs near the fire. Lanie sat with a foot underneath her backside, as if it was the most natural position in the world. It was a position Graham had never attempted, and doubted he ever would.

"Estelle had the lawyers working late," said Lanie. "You're supposed to review the contract, and then sign on all the pages they color-tabbed."

She reached with one hand for the folder, then decided two hands were in order. Graham reluctantly relieved her of the burden. He hefted the stack of papers, as if weighing them.

"I think the thicker the legal document, the more fear it's supposed to induce."

He put the pages aside, making no move to look through them. Lanie took note of his inaction.

"After you sign, I have a check for you."

A quarter of a million dollars. Graham had never had a payday like that before. That was real money, not the dribs and drabs that the photographic agency filtered through to him. He hadn't really had a chance to consider the money. His negotiation with Estelle had just been a ploy to have this conversation with Lanie. Graham supposed he was more interested in getting answers than getting the money, because he wanted to live to spend it.

"My lawyer's going to have to review it before I sign anything."

Lanie looked disappointed. "Estelle said you wanted to conclude our business tonight."

"I was prepared to look over a contract, not a book." When in doubt, blame the lawyers.

"I see."

"But I brought you all the pictures that were developed." He didn't tell her that the negatives were in safe storage, but she was aware of his omission.

"That's a start, I suppose."

He handed her a manila envelope. She didn't look inside, but instead walked over to the fireplace, opened the screen, and fed the envelope to the flames. The fire liked the offering, immediately sprouting up.

"I need you to give me something as well, Lanie," he said. "I need you to tell me who you gave my number to."

She kept her eyes on the torching fire. "What are you talking about?"

"Did the men who tried to kill me contact you, Lanie?"

Lanie didn't say anything for several seconds. "They didn't try and kill you. They were only scaring you."

"They were going to murder me, Lanie. Did you give them my number?"

She didn't answer.

"Your boys are somehow associated with a man I know as Smith," said Graham. "Before last week I thought Smith was in intelligence. Now I'm not sure. The only thing I can say for certain is that Smith is a blackmailer. He didn't want money from me, though. Over the last eighteen months Smith has called on me twice to shoot some photos to embarrass or discredit others.

"He sicced me on Joseph Cannon and Haley Robinson. You probably remember their scandals. She had the sticky fingers, and he was with a minor. I looked, but couldn't find any connection between the two. I kept playing the Six Degrees of Kevin Bacon game, but there didn't seem to be any link. Did you ever act in a movie with Kevin?"

She shook her head.

"But you know about the game?"

A nod this time, and then some reluctant words: "It's something like Six Degrees of Separation. Kevin can supposedly be linked to anyone in Hollywood within six steps."

"Right. For example, I know you costarred with Geena Davis in *Fire Walking*, and she acted with Susan Sarandon in *Thelma and Louise*, who was with Julia Roberts in *Stepmom*, who starred with Kevin Bacon in *Flatliners*. So in four degrees you have your connection with Kevin Bacon, and I'm sure we could have named that tune in less."

"What's your point?"

"I kept playing the Kevin Bacon game with Cannon and Robinson. It wasn't hard finding connections, but they didn't seem to be the right ones. It's no secret that Hollywood's an incestuous town, with all sorts of ties with or without Kevin Bacon in the picture. The only obvious connection between Cannon and Robinson was that he had directed films with other actors she had worked with. But my mistake was that I was looking for something that was there, instead of something that wasn't there. You."

"I have no idea what you're talking about."

"Last year you were supposed to be in a film directed by Joseph Cannon. He had to bow out because of his difficulties. As for Robinson, both of you were up for the part in *Mrs. Lincoln's Bedroom*. When Haley dropped out of contention, you got that role. Most of that film was shot in Washington, D.C."

"So what?"

"I assume in the not too distant past that someone—some organization—noticed your burgeoning friendship with the vice president. Maybe they were privy to information that the relationship even went beyond that. They decided your proximity to Tennesson was in their best interests."

"That's ridiculous."

"You saw the vice president when he visited less than two weeks ago—"

"Hundreds of people saw him."

"You rented a Jaguar and left it at The Palms. The night of the fund-raiser you had the studio limo at your disposal. You were discreet, neither getting picked up nor dropped off at The Palms. My guess is that you used a third car, parking it in a location where the limo picked you up and dropped you off. What I know for sure is that you took the Jaguar using a second pair of keys. That allowed you to bypass the valets at The Palms and permitted you and the vice president to slip away unnoticed."

Lanie was shaking her head and rolling her eyes. Her body language told him he was being ridiculous, no, crazy. But she was waiting to hear what he had to say. "You missed your calling as a fiction writer."

"Something happened with you and Tennesson that night."

"I suppose we had a three-way with Elvis. That's about par for the tabloids you work for, isn't it? Or maybe the vice president and I were abducted by aliens. Isn't that one of the tabloids' take on my interest in astronomy? They said I was abducted at the age of twelve, and that's why I keep looking up to the skies waiting for my *friends* to return."

"Something *bad* happened."

She tried to hide the pain, but he saw it in her eyes. He knew that look from his own mirror, and felt her hurt. Even after all this time he knew it wouldn't take much for his own stitching to tear away. Without even knowing the particulars, he still knew her pain.

Lanie assumed a pose of hauteur. "I suppose you have a witness to this *bad* thing. No. Witnesses. Probably a convention of nuns saw the whole thing."

"No witnesses," said Graham.

She didn't seem all that relieved by the news. Graham remembered how there were times when he had wanted to be caught, when the idea of punishment seemed not only right but appealing. He had waited for the other foot to drop, and then had learned it didn't need to drop; every day the wait ground him down that much more.

"Get out." She said the words softly, with her eyes closed. Graham would rather she had screamed them.

Lanie started shaking. Her body tensed in an effort to regain control, but her hands seemed to have a mind of their own. She opened her eyes, and saw that Graham was watching her.

"Leave—or—I'll call—the guard." It took her three breaths to complete the one sentence, to keep control.

"Believe me, I know what you're feeling."

Lanie walked toward the phone. Graham knew he couldn't leave. For once, he wasn't thinking about himself. If Lanie was left alone, he was afraid she would kill herself.

She picked up the phone. Graham reached around her shoulders, cradling her hands and the phone between his fingers.

"Unhand me."

Graham didn't let go. He could feel her civil war. Her body was rigid from trying to hold in her raging emotions. Graham had been there. He remembered his own struggles.

It was never his intention to tell her anything. Any kind of admission would weaken his position. But he remembered how he had felt when Smith dangled his secret in front of him. He had wanted to throw up; he had wanted amnesia; he had wanted to run away. Time was supposed to heal all wounds, but it hadn't.

"I told you that Smith blackmailed me. A few years ago I did something bad, something wrong. My actions resulted in the deaths of two people. Not a day goes by that I don't think about what I did. I would give anything to relive that one act and take back what I did, and I know it's the same with you. I've heard that men who have gone to war and been in battle can sense that same pall in others. It's an experience that marks people in a certain way. That's how it is with us. We have that connection. There are very few people who can tell you, 'I know what you're going through.' I can."

Lanie stopped trying to pick up the phone. With his arms still encircling her, she turned around and looked up at him, staring at his face to see what was there. Her scrutiny unnerved him. He hadn't felt that exposed since being on the oil rig with Smith. But she wasn't looking at him critically. Tears welled up in her eyes. Together, they were secret sharers of each other's pain. She started sobbing, and he felt her chest and stomach convulse against his own. His eyes started watering, and Graham bit hard on his lip, drawing blood. The physical pain was easier for him to deal with, and prevented his tearing.

She burrowed her head deep into his chest. Graham didn't think; he reacted. Someone else needed comforting. He started stroking her head with his hand and nuzzling it with his mouth. He couldn't forgive himself, but forgiving her was easy. He kissed her forehead, then kissed the tears on her cheeks. Their lips brushed, separated, and came back together.

It started more as mouth-to-mouth resuscitation than a passionate kiss. Both were breathing life into the other. But the comforting quality of their kisses suddenly changed.

This isn't happening, Graham thought, kissing her. This can't be real. But it was. He kissed her again. It was as if something had been switched on inside of each of them, something that had started with a little spark and was now flaring. They held each other tightly, afraid to let go. With no conscious thought of direction they swayed and moved, dancers in search of a rhythm. Step. Kiss. Step. Gasp. Their mouths locked, and they accelerated forward, rolling out the doorway. They pinballed along the hallway, his back against the wall, then hers. It was a Tilt game, each of them out of control, each of them free-falling. Together, they fell through an open doorway and dropped onto a bed.

Buttons loosened and zippers fell. Their hands groped each other. No words passed between them until Graham raised himself to enter her. She reached out with her hands to welcome him into her, but then with tensed arms delayed his entry.

With shortened breath, she gasped, "My real name is Elaine Bernsdorf."

"What are you telling me?" Graham asked.

"I am telling you who you're going to bed with. Not Miss L. Not somebody you have seen on the screen. Elaine Bernsdorf."

"It's nice to meet you, Elaine."

Clarifying that point seemed important to her. For a moment, Graham wondered if they should shake hands, but he remembered her fingers were already occupied. So did she. Lanie guided him into her, and for a time they were able to escape their thoughts.

Graham took a deep breath. He was physically at peace, felt about a hundred pounds lighter. He resisted consciousness, did his best to just hold on to his feeling of contentment, but his mind was surfacing from its cave. Lanie Byrne was lying next to him, naked and still. He had just made love to Miss L. Graham wanted to pinch himself, he who prided himself on never being starstruck, who thought he was impervious to Hollywood's glitter. But God she was beautiful.

Lanie felt him stirring. She raised her head up, and took stock of the room. The blankets were on the floor, as were the pillows. The sheets were still clinging to the bed, but they were wet and askew.

She shook her head.

"What?" asked Graham.

"Believe me when I say that what happened is very, very out of character for me. I have to be emotionally involved with a man before I get intimate. I don't even know you."

"I think a part of you does know me. We've been shaped by the same crucible."

"Shaped or warped?"

Graham answered with a question of his own. "Is that why you introduced yourself to me? Because you didn't think we knew each other well enough?"

"Partly," she said, not choosing to elaborate beyond that.

The glow from their lovemaking was already fading on Lanie. On her face, he could see her shadows were coming back to roost. The silence between them grew, at odds with the noise that had shook the room minutes before. Graham tried to reach out to her with a story.

"When I was in Kosovo," he said, "I holed up for a night in this little village. Another photographer and I—I think his name was Jack—ended up having to share a room. We also shared a bottle.

"We started telling stories. It's odd how sometimes you open up more quickly with a stranger than you do a friend, and that's how it was. Jack told me about a funeral he had attended a few years back. He was friends with both the man who died and his wife. The man's death was a shock to everyone. He was one of those fitness types, and wasn't even forty when he died of heart failure.

"After the funeral, Jack consoled the widow. He said they were crying in each other's arms one moment, and the next he was hiking up her black dress and they were making love. Jack said it was the strangest thing that ever happened to him.

"I was a bit skeptical of the story at first. I asked Jack if he'd ever been intimate with the woman before, and he told me that the one and only time they were ever together was after that funeral.

"I asked him about the widow, and her marriage. I figured she had to be

"From the Brothers?"

"They're the tip of the iceberg that I know. I am afraid that what's underneath scares me even more."

"If I could assure you that you were no longer in any danger, could you just take the money and forget everything?"

"I'm listening."

"This is off the record. Do you swear to that? Can you make a vow to whatever is holy to you?"

What was there that was holy to him? Graham wondered. Lanie was looking him in the eye when he said. "Yes."

She didn't seem to know how to begin. Finally, she said, "My real name is Elaine Bernsdorf."

Again, she made the pronouncement as if that should explain something.

"I decided I wanted a simplified stage name, so I changed it to Lanie Byrne."

That was an old thespian tradition. Marilyn Monroe, John Wayne, Tony Curtis, Natalie Wood, Kirk Douglas, Winona Ryder, Rock Hudson, and countless others had also changed their names.

"By blood, I am a Jew, though not a practicing one. My mother is more of a Buddhist than anything, at least when it suits her, and my father is an agnostic. He says that when it comes to religion, he's too indifferent to even be an atheist.

"My father is a geologist, a hired gun for the oil companies. His job takes him around the world. I was only eight when my parents decided to send me to a year-round boarding school. According to them, they did that to provide me with a more stable environment.

"When my parents were out of the country for the holidays, which seemed to be most years, I went and stayed at my Aunt Miriam and Uncle Hi's. It would be hard to find two more different people than my father and his brother. Uncle Hi—his real name was Hiram—was outgoing and loud. He couldn't seem to give enough hugs. Uncle Hi also had very firm beliefs. Family, community, and religion were all very important to him. It was through my uncle's family that I learned about Judaism.

"One of the things my uncle was proudest of was his being a *sayan*."

After a moment's pause, Graham asked, "What's that?"

"A *sayan* is a Jewish volunteer who assists the Israeli intelligence service."

"The Mossad?"

A nod. "My uncle owned commercial and residential real estate in New York City that he allowed the Mossad to use for their own purposes."

in a loveless marriage, or had wanted to get posthumous revenge against her husband for some reason. Jack said I was way off the mark. He said she loved her husband, and that they had a good marriage.

"So I asked the obvious: how could the two of them be screwing each other on the very day of the funeral? Jack asked me if I had ever heard of people laughing at funerals. I told him that I had, but I said I thought *that* was understandable. Extreme emotions produce extreme responses. But what they had done, I told him, went far beyond that.

"Jack said that he had given a lot of thought to what happened. He said that he and the widow were both numbed by the death, though he knew that didn't justify what occurred. Jack could understand how others might view their actions as debased or grossly misappropriate, but in his own heart he said that what they did felt right. Grief brought them together. For a time, each was the other's life preserver. They felt like they were drowning inside, so they grabbed onto what they could. Jack said they came together to prove they were still alive. Sex was a way of keeping death at an arm's distance."

Lanie thought about the story before responding. "Is that supposed to make me feel better?" she asked.

"I don't know," said Graham. "Maybe there was something to what Jack said. Maybe both of us needed a reminder that we're alive."

"Or maybe," she said, almost sounding playful, "all of you photographers are a little strange."

"Don't let me get started about actors."

"I'll concede you that one."

Lanie slid off the bed and walked over to a walk-in closet. It was dark enough that she wasn't much more visible than a shadow; it was light enough for Graham to appreciate what he could see. She pulled down two terry robes, draped one over her back and brought the other back to Graham. While she picked up the strewn pillows, he put on the robe.

"I'm afraid to look at the time," she said. "I have to be on the set early. Very early. Makeup's going to have a hard time trying to make me look presentable."

"I doubt that."

"I'm not fishing for compliments. You've heard how a camera puts ten pounds on you? Sleepless nights put ten years on you."

"Is that my cue to leave?"

"I am explaining that I'm very tired."

"That's two of us. I haven't been home in days. I've been on the run."

"In what way?"

"All sorts of ways, and all of them secret. When the Mossad went through my uncle there were no paper trails. No deposits. No governmental red tape. Sometimes Uncle Hi was able to entice certain enemies of Israel to rent a particular apartment or building. Naturally, the Mossad was given full access to those rentals which allowed them easy monitoring. My uncle said his 'special friends'—that's what he called the Mossad—sometimes used his office space to set up phony businesses that allowed them to target their enemies. 'Friends you keep close,' my uncle always said, 'but enemies you keep even closer.' He and his network helped Israel however they could."

"Network?"

"The *sayanim*. Around the world there are tens of thousands of *sayanim* like my uncle. They offer financial, professional, and material support to the Mossad. As a resource, they're invaluable, like the *sayan* ticket agent at the airline counter who magically eliminates any record of a Mossad agent's passage, or the *sayan* gun-shop owner who provides weapons without paperwork or a waiting period, or the anonymous *sayan* doctor who treats those kinds of injuries that hospitals might be nosy about. Without the *sayanim*, Israeli intelligence would not be nearly as effective as it is."

"You were recruited as one of those?"

"Yes."

"To do what?"

"To tell you would be a betrayal. I can say that nothing I ever did was anti-American."

"But you spied nonetheless?"

"I assisted."

"Why?"

"Maybe to atone for not being a very good Jew. Israel has enemies on all its borders. It is an island under siege. I decided to be its friend."

"You could have been its friend by writing a fat check to B'nai B'rith instead of being Mata Hari."

"I was no spy."

"Then what were you?"

Lanie didn't answer.

"Did you tell anyone of your involvement?"

She shook her head. "No. I was under strict orders to keep silence."

"Not even your uncle?"

"He died several years ago. Part of the reason I decided to work with the Mossad was that I knew Uncle Hi would have wanted me to. He considered his contributions as a *sayan* to be one of the crowning achievements of his life."

"How did the Mossad approach you?"

"One of the Brothers—Ari Cohen—was attending a Hollywood function and came up to me."

"The Brothers are the men that abducted me?"

"Yes."

"Did this Ari identify himself as being with the Mossad?"

"Not at first. Ari told me he was a friend of my Uncle Hi's, and that his death had saddened him greatly. He said my uncle was a great man who had saved countless lives and contributed to the state of Israel in more ways than anyone could ever imagine. Without being too obvious, it was clear Ari was talking about my uncle's being a *sayan*."

"How did he put his hooks into you?"

"I don't like that phrasing."

"How did you begin working for him?"

"Ari asked me to do a minor favor. I complied."

"The favors escalated?"

"I helped out several times."

"Doing what?"

She shook her head. "No details."

"How did this Ari contact you?"

"He called me here on my personal line."

"And how did you contact him?"

"I didn't. The communication was one-way. As I told you, I really didn't do too much work for them."

"Did you meet or talk with anyone besides Ari?"

"His brother Yitzhak."

"Who was also with the Mossad?"

A nod.

"How did you know that?"

"Yitzhak had also worked with Uncle Hi." A moment later, as if to rebut her own doubts, she added with not a little defensiveness, "The Brothers always spoke Hebrew to one another."

"Do you know Hebrew?"

"A few words."

"Whom did you give my number to?"

"Ari."

"When did he call you?"

"Last night. He told me how he and Yitzhak had tried to scare you, and that while you were resisting things got out of hand. They were only protecting me, you know."

"Why did you need protecting?"

"They knew I was upset. The week before I had told them not to contact me anymore, that I was through with being their *bat leveyha*—their female agent."

It was clear that Lanie believed everything she said. But she was omitting more than she was admitting.

"By telling me everything," he said, "it would make it easier for me to help you."

"I don't want your help. You're in this for the money. You are not Gregory Peck and this isn't *Roman Holiday*."

"Peck was the reporter," Graham said. "Eddie Albert was the photographer."

In the movie, Peck had gone from being the opportunistic journalist to the altruistic person, in the end sacrificing his big story. Audrey Hepburn had portrayed a princess playing hooky from her onerous responsibilities. Graham suspected that like the princess, Lanie had recently tried to escape the fish bowl. But she hadn't experienced a happy ending like Hepburn.

" 'Rome, by all means, Rome,' " quoted Lanie. " 'I will cherish my visit here in memory as long as I live.' "

"It's a classic film."

"I wouldn't have thought you enjoyed movies."

"Why is that?"

"Your profession. It throws dirt and grime and worse on the film industry."

"That's not how celebrity photographers look at our work. I think of Hollywood as great and powerful Oz. It does special effects wonderfully. It hides behind spectacular veneers. It blusters and it blows and it poses. Sometimes I shoot those things. But every so often it needs a Toto like me pulling its curtain back."

"Toto, huh?"

"It was either that or admit I lack a brain, a heart, or courage."

Wistfully, she said, "We're not in Kansas anymore, Toto."

"Ain't that the truth."

Their hands reconnected, and then their bodies. They sidled up next to each other. Lanie covered up a yawn. She was clearly exhausted. It was a good time to go for the jugular, thought Graham. People who are tired make mistakes. Graham needed to know more about her role as a *sayan*, and wanted to ask about the Brothers. But instead of prodding her with more questions, Graham asked, "Is there any way I can sack out in an open bed tonight?"

She said, "How about this one?"

Twenty-nine

They were still holding each other, fast asleep, when the phone rang.

"Don't answer it," Graham said.

"But what if it's—"

"We know who it is." He reached over her and disconnected the phone.

Both were too tired to talk anymore. They fell back into each other's arms and then fell asleep.

Later, Graham awoke to Lanie's moving about the room. She was already dressed.

"Keep sleeping," she said.

"I'd rather look at you."

"You're not usually this nice this early in the morning, are you?"

"Not usually."

"Good."

"Is it possible," asked Graham, "that we can meet for a late dinner?"

Lanie hesitated, and Graham was annoyed to realize he wasn't breathing while waiting for her answer.

"I don't mean to be pushy," he said. "I know last night was a—fluke. But we still haven't finished our—"

"Business," she said, a frown on her face.

"I was *going* to say conversation."

She appeared to like his word better, but still wavered. "I don't know if dinner will work. It's likely I'll be on the set until very late."

"The sooner we talk, the better. I'll hand you the negatives tonight, and if you want me to sign that contract right now, I will. It's not about money anymore."

"My business manager says that whenever anyone says those words, I should run away."

"That's probably good advice."

"What is *it* about?"

"I don't know. But what you told me last night didn't make me feel a heck of a lot better."

"But everything ties into the Mossad. It all fits."

"Maybe that's why I don't feel better."

"That story about your being blackmailed—that was true?"

"Yes."

"I'm sorry."

Her apology took Graham aback. He didn't deserve her sympathy, but then she didn't know what he had done.

"I'll call you tonight sometime between seven and eight," she said. "By then I should know whether dinner's possible."

"You need a ride to the studio?" Graham asked.

She shook her head. "Limo's waiting."

"Silly me."

"Security knows you're here. My part of the Grove doesn't get cleaned until the afternoon, so you shouldn't be bothered. If you want to linger, it would be best if you used the guest house."

"Should I sneak out there and muss up one of the beds to make it look as if that's where I slept?"

"Why? Are you afraid your reputation might be sullied?"

"Mine is beyond redemption."

"You saved my life. That must count for something in some ledger. I know I won't forget it soon."

"Is that what last night was about?"

Lanie shook her head, and then leaned close to him. She didn't kiss Graham, just put her middle and index fingers on his cheek and lightly touched him.

"Bring a hat tonight," she said.

"Why?"

"To cover your face. You always have to watch out for the paparazzi."

It was a stupid time to be feeling goofy about someone. Graham knew he was being a fool if he thought he had a chance at a relationship with someone like Lanie. A proper suitor for her would be royalty, or a billionaire, or an artistic genius. Or the future president of the United States.

With the likes of him, she was slumming. Lanie would realize their one night together was a mistake. She had told him last night wasn't a mercy fuck, but he found that hard to believe. He needed a clear head, but she played on his mind. He kept flashing back to their making love. Their heat had been so intense. Just thinking about it made him feel echoes of it on his forehead, and neck, and groin. Her skin was toned, but soft and feminine. She had kept surprising him; in word, in thought, and in bed.

Graham was feeling things he hadn't felt in years. He didn't expect things would ever be the same again, but it was still nice to be touched by sunshine.

There was work to be done, though.

Before leaving, he stopped by the garage. He didn't look at the other cars housed there, just went directly to the Jaguar rental.

When Graham had raced away with a comatose Lanie as passenger, he'd had to move the seat back. Lanie was a half foot smaller than he was. The driver's seat would have been positioned for someone of her stature.

There didn't seem to be any good reason that the Jaguar hadn't been returned to the rental agency. Lanie had enough money to not worry about its running meter, but there was staff aplenty to see to its return. There had to be an explanation for its being housed in her garage.

The Jaguar was unlocked. Graham carefully went through its interior. The rental agreement was still in the glove compartment. That was the only evidence of human occupation. The rest of the car was so clean he barely came away with dust.

He started an inch-by-inch search of the exterior of the car. Because he began with the front bumper, it wasn't long before he noticed the scrapes and scratches. They extended along the right bumper of the car, across the grille and up the hood. The right headlight was cracked in several spots, but the glass had remained intact. Someone had rubbed down the scrapes, applying a coat of wax that all but made them blend in with the car. When Graham had driven the car, he had never noticed that it had been in an accident.

Graham was willing to bet that no police report had been filed.

Thirty

Graham knew that Ran had no shortage of uniforms in his closet. The UPS and FedEx outfits were his standards, but he had costumes for every occasion.

"Maintenance man," Graham said, "for my apartment."

"I got blue polyester or tan polyester. The blue polyester has the name of Roy, and I think the tan has Alberto."

"I think the guys at my place wear blue."

"Roy it is."

"In that case, I suppose I should call you Ray."

"And I'll just stay with your usual standard of calling you Asshole."

"Can't improve upon a classic."

"The surprise isn't that someone wants to kill you," Ran said. "The surprise is that there isn't a line."

They met at a prearranged spot in a Vons Supermarket parking lot, and drove in Ran's car over to Graham's apartment. Graham opened a bag and pulled out two EXIT signs and two motion detectors. "You ever do camera trap photography before?"

"A little. But I'm not Mr. Gadget like you."

"I got into it after watching a nature show where some researchers and biologists were using an infrared system between a transmitter and receiver to photograph any animals crossing the beam. The animal tripped off the system just by walking across the infrared beam. I figured what worked for the four-legged would work even better with the two-legged."

He tapped an EXIT sign and motion detector. "These are the fronts for our transmitters and receivers. Everything is already in place. I'll go first. I already have motion detectors in the front and back, so it's just going to be a matter of changing the casings. After I get back you can be the officious maintenance man replacing the exit signs around the property. On the front side of my apartment is an exit sign about sixty feet away. It's a straight line between the sign and the motion detector. The back of my apartment faces the garage. That's where another EXIT sign is. It's about eighty feet off."

Ran looked dubious. "Where do you get the juice to operate these things?"

"They're self-contained. Each has two C batteries."

"If your Buck Rogers beam gets tripped too often, you'll go through your roll."

"It can store up to a thousand events, and the program is designed to key into your game of choice. It doesn't matter if a biologist is out to shoot a mouse or an elephant, because he can specify the range of the beam. I've set it up so that anything approaching the front or back of my apartment will break the active infrared beam and get nailed on film."

"Golly gee, Batman," said Ran.

"All you have to do is replace the EXIT signs without getting electrocuted."

"I might be able to do that. Seems to me you forgot one detail though. Your pictures might come out during the day, but you'll get shitty shots at night."

Graham shook his head. "The sign illuminates. So does the motion detector. Between the two of them, the area around my apartment should get some half-decent lighting. Just make sure the camera end of the garage EXIT sign is pointed toward the back of my apartment. You don't have to worry about the one in front. Just set it up as is."

"What kind of shots you get out of these things?"

"Pretty good. Over four hundred lines of resolution."

"What kind of film?"

"I've set it up with two kinds. In the front EXIT sign I put in some high-speed color film. The back EXIT sign has high-speed black and white infrared."

"Won't that give you a distorted image?"

"Not really. There's a surreal look, but you get incredible details. If you shoot it close enough, sometimes you even get the veins through the skin.

With the infrared, the eyes will look dark, and the skin will look a little different, but like I said, you get some bonuses in the clarity."

"Spoken like a true artist."

"Yeah, that's it."

Graham had Ran circle the area twice before parking out of sight down the street. He approached his own apartment cautiously, surveying the area with professional eyes. Graham had done enough surveillance to know how it was done, and how many ways it could be done.

Before working on the motion detectors, he did a quick inspection of his apartment. Nothing looked as if it had been touched. Graham changed that. He turned on some lights, opened shades, threw back the covers, and tossed the mail on a table. If someone was checking up on him, he wanted to make it appear he was back at the apartment again. That might bring them in for a closer look.

Camera trap photography was nothing new to him, and it didn't take long to replace the two motion detectors. Graham was glad about that. It might have been his own apartment, but he still felt uneasy. His fenced-in back porch allowed him some privacy, but on the front stoop he was exposed. He used his back to shield what he was doing, and hoped that if anyone was looking they would think he was replacing the light in the motion detector.

Even the notion that someone could be looking made him self-conscious. Finishing was a relief. He walked down the street and found Ran reclined on the hood of the car catching some rays.

Graham tapped him on his work shirt. "All set for you, Roy," he said.

Ran stretched, slid off the hood, and reached inside the car for his work belt and a stepladder. He wrapped the belt around himself and arched an eyebrow in Graham's direction.

"Perfect," said Graham. "Other people wouldn't think to have their butt crack showing, but damn if you didn't go the extra yard, and I don't think I'm exaggerating that detail by much."

"Glad you noticed."

While Ran worked, Graham read from a book he had picked up that morning. *By Way of Deception* was Colonel Victor Ostrovsky's account of his time as a Mossad agent. It was like many kiss-and-tell memoirs Graham had read: part bitter, part informative, and part braggadocio. What interested him most was Ostrovsky's section on the *sayanim*. It was much as Lanie had described. Before doing their recruiting, the Mossad made sure that potential *sayanim* were one hundred percent Jewish. No Israeli citizen was a *sayan*—that would be too obvious. The Mossad used a gathering officer—a *katsa*—to manage his stable of *sayanim*. The *katsa* kept in regular contact with his helpers. By using the volunteers, the Mossad was able to supplement its rather meager, at least by international spy standards, workforce.

Ostrovsky described various manipulation and enforcement tactics used by the Mossad. One assassination scenario Ostrovsky related struck close to home with Graham. He described how Israeli agents had performed a hit by funneling vodka down the throat of an unconscious target, and then sending the "inebriate" over a cliff in a flaming car.

Reading about his own brush with death, Graham looked around, then locked the car doors. That still didn't stop him from jumping in his seat when Ran tapped on the car's window.

"How did it go?" Graham asked.

"No problem. It was hard to get away, though."

"What happened?"

"Your next-door neighbor, an old lady, came out and saw me working. She had a whole list of things she wanted me to do. I promised I'd be back a little later. Only thing that was harder to shake was her dog. That little bastard thought my leg was his love connection."

"His name's Rex in case you want to give him a call sometime."

"You're the one who will probably be calling him something. He was visiting your doorstep when I left. I'm hoping we don't end up with too long of a documentary detailing his stay."

"Shit."

"That's about the size of it. He was definitely tripping your infrared beam. Yeah, it was almost like the little bastard knew what he was doing. He kept positioning his backside to the camera. He was really doing a job of cracking you a smile."

"If the pictures come out, I'll be sure to get you a framed copy."

"I'd like that," Ran said. "I really would."

Thirty-one

Blackwell flipped through the news stations. It was laughable, really. The so-called breaking news was mostly old hat. The real news of the world rarely aired.

He knew that information was power, but also knew that information was like gold. It needed to be mined, and dredged, and sifted before the riches emerged. No one panned for gold these days. Gold-mining operations were huge operations with expensive equipment, and sluices, and power hoses. Tons of rock and earth had to be moved before they would yield minuscule quantities of gold. Mother lodes were ever elusive.

That's how it was with most treasure. You knew it was there, but you couldn't get to it. Blackwell had thought long and hard on how he could mine that gold. To draw on those riches, he needed to be a part of that elite that was handed the earth's wealth every day. They were given all of the news that those in power believed was not fit to print, were handed an opportunity for riches by having a subscription to the most informative newspaper on the planet, a paper published every day but Sunday. Insiders called the President's Daily Brief (PDB) "the most expensive, least circulated, newspaper in the world." On any given day, it had a readership of less than fifteen people. It was a paper without bylines; its editorial staff consisted of the sixteen thousand employees of the CIA, and their many contacts throughout the world. To get a copy of the PDB, you had to be one of the very select: the president and the vice president, the secretary of state and attorney general, the national security adviser, and the head of the Joint Chief of Staffs. Being a member of Capitol Hill didn't get you a subscription; only the ranking member of the Senate Select Committee on Intelligence and the House Permanent Select Committee on Intelligence received copies.

Though the CIA's President's Analytical Support Staff (PASS) published the PDB, even they didn't know its contents. The staff produced the paper "blind," going through protocols to *not* read the copy. Only one member of the CIA had a subscription: the director.

The paperboy, thought Blackwell. It was the director that delivered the newspapers to the rest of the inner circle.

PASS produced other very secret, very classified documents, including the Senior Executives Intelligence Brief and the Economic Executives Intelligence Brief. Like the PDB, the information was published in such a way that one hand purposely didn't know what the other was doing.

It was all there in writing. Politics. Economics. Business. For the most part it was *finished intelligence*, intelligence that had gone through the rinse, wash, and dry cycles, information that had been taken, evaluated, analyzed, and confirmed to a reasonable degree. Gold. Not that fool's gold didn't occasionally get paraded around as the real thing. The CIA and their army of analysts and agents were certainly fallible. They liked to pretty up information to justify their existence, and support the public till they fed from. The Agency was good at supplying position papers that would support whatever way the administration was leaning at the moment. Maybe that explained their failure in the past to accurately predict what had happened in Iran, Iraq, and the Soviet Union, not to mention September 11, 2001. Sometimes it seemed like the CIA was more in the lobbying business than the espionage business. But Blackwell knew how to read between the lines better than anyone. He was good at picking out what was smoke and what was fire. In the hands of the right person, the CIA's finished intelligence could prove very, very valuable. There were three types of finished intelligence: basic, current, and estimative. That was a fancy way of saying past, present, and future. It was the ultimate insider information, the headlines of the future delivered in advance.

Everyone wanted a crystal ball. Corporations and individuals paid huge money to Henry Kissinger and his ilk to try and position themselves and their companies in a changing world. Fortunes were there to be made and lost. Reading the world's tea leaves was a big business.

The SEC was about the only governmental agency that knew just what a big business it was. There was no currency so valuable as insider information. Knowing U.S. policy ahead of time could yield enormous financial gains, both short term and long term. Blackwell wanted that foreknowledge, and the power that went with it. Being in the inner circle would give him hundreds of ways to parlay that information into a huge windfall, including stocks, options, futures, commodities, and foreign exchange markets. And those were the quasi-legal ways.

That didn't even take into account the much more profitable, and much more interesting, illegal methods to get rich beyond imagination.

Thirty-two

Usually getting to the bottom of things was the fun part, but this time it felt more like pulling teeth. The harder Graham dug at the roots, the more nerves he exposed. His *and* hers. Getting emotionally involved with Lanie had affected his thinking. He wanted to be protective of her, but what he had uncovered wouldn't allow that.

Graham didn't like having to take her into consideration. He was sure she wasn't thinking about him. You could dress up their night together, put it under the category of mutual emotional comforting, but it still amounted to a one-night stand. That's all it was, and all it would be. Still, he didn't want to be the messenger delivering her the bad news.

He had to confront her, though. He was involved in all of this as well. It would just be easier if he didn't give a damn. That's how it usually was. He snapped pictures, and didn't look back. But this time was different. Their secrets intersected. No, they did more than that. They traveled the same bloody road.

His digital phone rang at quarter past seven. The number on his readout was a local one.

"Still up for dinner?" Lanie asked.

Graham pretended to be upbeat: "You bet."

"Is nine o'clock too late? I should be able to get away by then."

"That's fine."

"Do you like Italian?"

"It's my favorite."

"Good. There's this wonderful restaurant just outside Brentwood called La Dolce Vita."

Graham didn't comment on the irony. It was, he thought, an appropriate place to have dinner with a paparazzo. Fellini's movie, *La Dolce Vita*, featured a persistent photographer named Signor Paparazzo who was always trying to shoot the stars. Because of Fellini's Signor Paparazzo, celebrity photographers were forever tagged with the name paparazzi. He doubted that was something he would tell Lanie. There was no need to give her a bad association with one of her favorite restaurants.

"One of the things I like most about the restaurant," Lanie said, "is that it has these old-fashioned booths with high wooden dividers. And the manager is very accommodating. He lets me slip in through the kitchen and reserves the back booth for me."

"Assuming I enter through the front door, what's my story?"

"That you will be joining Elaine Barnes in her booth."

You just didn't get into a restaurant like La Dolce Vita. It wasn't a private club, but like other cachet L.A. restaurants it acted like one, catering to the Hollywood crowd. There were certain nights that you basically needed a secret password to get in. You had to be connected to get a table. Money wouldn't do it, and being willing to wait all night wasn't enough. You had to be a Hollywood insider. Stars liked being among their own and not having to look over their shoulders.

"I'll look forward to seeing you," Graham said.

Maybe he had inherited some acting skill from his mother. She never picked up on his lie.

After talking with Lanie, Graham turned the ringer back on both of his phones. He only had to wait fifteen minutes before his digital phone rang again.

"Pilgrim."

He had expected Smith's voice, had mentally prepared for it, but that didn't stop his heart from racing.

"I'm listening."

"You've been rather hard to reach."

"I was afraid for my life."

"But now you know better?"

"Let's say I am somewhat reassured."

"It was regrettable that we had to use scare tactics on you, and even more regrettable when matters apparently got out of hand. But you know that if we had truly wanted to remove you from the scene, we would have gone about it differently. A word to the French would have been enough. Your next stop would have been jail. They haven't forgotten the accident."

"Nor have I," Graham said. "You haven't let me."

"We are prepared to do that now."

"I want a face-to-face with you," Graham said. "And I want fifty thousand dollars in cash to pay for the loss of my van and equipment. But this time I don't want to meet on an oil rig, and I don't want a tranquilizer dart in my ass."

"Fine. I'll call you back with the date, time, and details."

"No," said Graham. "My trust only goes so far. This time I'll be the one in charge of arrangements. We'll meet tomorrow at one o'clock in the afternoon at the George C. Page Museum on Wilshire. You'll find me in front of the entrance to the museum."

"I'll have to see if I can rearrange my schedule—"

"Do it," Graham said, talking over his objections. "Just the two of us. I better not see any sign of the Brothers or anyone else."

"I'm not sure—"

"Bring the money."

"Pilgrim—"

"I never liked that name," Graham said, and hung up.

Thirty-three

Graham parked in an alley with a view to the back of the restaurant, and waited in his car for Lanie to appear. The chef who grabbed a hurried smoke, and the busboy and dishwasher who hauled trash out to the Dumpster, had no idea he was watching. Graham had arrived early, and for the last half hour had listened to the clatter of dishes and calling of orders. Periodically he inhaled the drifting scent of garlic, basil, and olive oil. On this night, it didn't make him hungry.

Lanie was late. Graham wondered if he was being stood-up. He had turned off his phones again. It was possible she had called and tried to leave a message for him at the restaurant. He had decided it wouldn't be fair to sit down to dinner knowing what he was going to say and ask. That would be like sucker-punching her. He had followed the trail of her damaged rental, focusing on the Malibu area. He needed to ask her about a hit-and-run.

Graham noticed a movement in the shadows. Someone was waiting at the side of the building, someone who didn't want to be seen. Graham could only see an arm. The figure was crouched down, his back to the wall.

Car lights suddenly illuminated the alley. The unmistakable outline of a limo showed itself. As it neared, the figure in the shadows started to move. Graham turned on his brights, surprising the man. He raised an arm and shielded his eyes. Graham saw he wasn't holding a gun. In his hands was a camera.

As the limo drove toward the back of the restaurant, Graham continued to flash his brights, strobing the photographer. He started his engine, drove forward, and pulled aside the limo. Graham pushed open the passenger door while he continued to flick his brights on and off. Lanie emerged from the limo, looking mystified at his light display.

"Get in," yelled Graham.

She hesitated for a moment, said something to her driver, then sat down next to him. The photographer cursed loudly as Graham pulled away.

"Friend of yours?" Lanie asked.

"Not anymore."

"I hope I don't sound ungrateful, but I'm not usually scared off by a lone photographer. In fact, I am sort of surprised there was only one."

"I panicked," Graham said. "He stayed out of sight until just before you pulled up. I thought he might have had a gun."

"There aren't that many Mark David Chapmans out there, thank God."

"It wasn't a stalker I was worried about."

"But you kept blinding him even after you knew he was a photographer."

"I didn't want to take any chances."

"Why were you out in the alleyway anyway?"

"Because we need to talk."

While waiting for her, Graham still hadn't figured out how to begin their talk. His father would have known how to finesse the whole thing. Graham once told him that he had missed his calling as a funeral director. He had this way of making people feel better even at the worst of times.

"Domingo Avila," Graham said.

"Oh."

She made more of a sound than a word. It came from deep inside of her. It wasn't a voicing of surprise, but more a chord of pain and guilt and sadness that she didn't try and hide. Even now, years after his own accident, there were times when Graham felt like making that very same sound.

"One paragraph in the local paper," Graham said. "He was a Mexican national out riding his bicycle, a dishwasher in a Malibu restaurant."

Lanie didn't say anything.

"Your rental was slightly damaged. That's why you couldn't return it."

Next to him, she started wringing her hands.

"All this time you probably thought that the police were running tests. It's amazing how much they can figure out with just a speck of paint or a shard of plastic. There are only so many Jaguars, so you figured it was only a matter of time before they tracked you down. The wait was the hard thing. I know. I've been there. It's like waiting for a bullet to find you, and there's nothing you can do about it."

"Oh."

That sound again.

"You couldn't act responsibly," Graham said, "because of who you were with at the time of the accident. There couldn't be a police report because of the scandalous implications. Politicians have survived sex scandals before, but this would have transcended that. There was a death involved. That's something that would stick to even a Teflon politician. Teddy Kennedy still hasn't removed the stain of Chappaquiddick, and that happened more than thirty years ago."

Lanie was still now, no hand wringing, no sounds.

"I remember how bad it was for me, but it was even worse for you because you're so visible. There was no place you could escape, and no one you could talk to. I'm not Catholic, but I had my own personal confessor, and I know how much that helped me. You felt guilty because you were the driver, and the man you were with was married. Both of you had several glasses of champagne at the fund-raising party. You were by no means legally drunk, but in retrospect you've wondered if that might have played some role in your accident.

"You hit Domingo just as you were emerging from the tunnel. Even when your own life was in the balance you couldn't stop thinking about that. When we were racing to see Dr. Burke, and you were almost comatose from taking those pills, you suddenly grew alert when I hit that possum. The accident was still in your thoughts. That's why you were trembling and had your eyes closed when we entered the tunnel. Domingo Avila was haunting you then, just as he haunts you now.

"Some people wouldn't be able to understand that. You are a movie star. He was a dishwasher with a green card. The world takes note of what you wear. When you change your hairstyle, it makes headlines. All Domingo Avila's death rated was a paragraph in the local paper. He didn't even make the *L.A. Times*. But none of that mattered to you. You saw his dead body. You probably held him. Maybe some of his blood stained your party dress.

"The police would certainly have ruled the accident wasn't your fault, but their vindication wasn't an option. You were someone who wanted to pay penance, but because of the situation you were denied that opportunity. You could only grieve in private. I know that you're a stand-up person. From the first I'm sure you made it clear to the vice president that if the police came knocking, you, and you alone, would take all the blame. You were probably prepared to lie and say you were driving by yourself. Your guilt would have prompted you to do all of that; guilt that he was married; guilt that you were driving; guilt that there was a certain taint to your friendship because of your being a *sayan*, or *bat laveyha*, or whatever it is they called you. What else would the Mossad have asked of you other than to get close to Tennesson? I am sure your handlers encouraged you to be his good friend. They would have told you that you could best serve Israel's interests with a timely word here or there. What possible harm, I am sure they emphasized, could come out of doing that?

"You already were his friend, his lover. Each of you admired the other. Your paths crossed at social events, at fund-raisers, at celebrations of the arts. The two of you were akin both politically and personally, and it's no secret that Tennesson and his wife's marriage is more of a business relationship than anything else.

"It's said that Tennesson is the most charismatic politician since Jack Kennedy. He's certainly one of the most photographed. Your mutual attraction must have been powerful indeed. I suspect the affair started several years ago. The miracle is that there has never been a whisper of it. There are some secluded mansions not far from the Beltway, mansions that are sometimes unused for months at a time. Both of you have influential friends. Discreet getaways could have been arranged, especially while you were on location in Washington, D.C. You probably thought that no one knew. But someone always knows."

Lanie didn't acknowledge any of his allegations. The silence built until she finally said, "Take me home."

"You can't hide behind the walls of the Grove, Lanie. You should know that by now."

She didn't answer, so he prodded her a little more. "Don't be thinking you can escape this by courting death again, Lanie. You try and commit suicide, and I promise you, I'll put a trumpet to my lips and tell all."

"Damn you."

"Damn me."

He hadn't enjoyed torturing her. There was no other name for it. But now she would be ready to hear the rest. "You know what tunnel vision is, Lanie?"

She didn't respond.

"Tunnel vision is like seeing the world through a small tube," he said. "You don't get the whole picture. You get just this small area of vision.

Someone can be standing right next to you, but unless you turn and get them in your narrow line of sight, you can't see them.

"We both suffer from tunnel vision, Lanie. But I think there might be some light at the end of your tunnel."

Her mouth didn't move, and her face said nothing.

"Because of what happened to you," Graham said, "you've never been able to see beyond Domingo's body. That's understandable. But now I want you to open your eyes. I want you to see beyond the tunnel.

"Do you know what happened to Domingo's body?"

She didn't respond.

"I'm asking you a question, Lanie."

She sighed, made the briefest eye contact, then shook her head.

"Did you hear about the explosion at the coroner's office?"

"Someone planted a bomb. That's really all I know."

"It was big news."

"I was preoccupied at the time."

"Domingo's body no longer exists. It was vaporized."

"I wondered," she said, then stopped talking for a moment to consider her words before continuing, "about that."

"Wondered why the police hadn't come to arrest you?"

No nod, but that was clearly her answer.

"The body of a man named Frank Kurtz was stuffed with Semtex, a plastic explosive. Kurtz was a huge man. His body was taken into the coroner's office just a few hours after Domingo's was. The detonation wiped out better than half a floor. It was a major explosion. The miracle is that it didn't kill any of the living. But it did a hell of a job on the dead.

"The three cold storage rooms that housed the dead were obliterated. I'm not talking about the structure being blown into chunks and pieces. The explosion went way beyond that. Walls and windows disappeared. Flesh and blood and bone were liquified. What the bomb didn't erase, the fire did.

"There have been a lot of theories put forth on the bombing. More than a dozen individuals have purportedly called to claim responsibility. The explosion has been linked to everyone from the Klan to the Mexican Mafia. Frank Kurtz had a history of dealing drugs. Some believe that his being made into a human bomb was a warning to the DEA. Kurtz was also a biker. Some think the Hell's Angels used his death to strike out at the government's crackdown against them. And, of course, there is no shortage of people with axes to grind against the coroner's office that might have used a bomb to strike back at them. Those are among the more rational theories.

There are a few dozen Web sites devoted solely to the bombing. If you want to see paranoia taken to the extreme, you ought to check them out. But nowhere among all the theories is the explanation for what I think happened: Frank Kurtz was murdered not because he dealt drugs, or was in the Hell's Angels, or was a member of the Aryan Brotherhood, but because he was a big, big man who could be stuffed with a lot of plastic explosive. And the bombing had nothing to do with terrorism. It was not an Oklahoma City or Twin Towers type of statement. What occurred was overkill in every sense of the word. The dead do tell tales. The forensic team working the L.A. coroner's office is among the world's best. Someone didn't want the dead to talk."

Graham had thought Lanie would be excited by what he had to say, but by appearance she remained impassive.

"Do you understand what I'm saying, Lanie? There were over fifty bodies in the cold storage rooms. After the bombing, they were mostly gone. There was no Domingo Avila, and no corpus delicti."

Graham turned his head from the road and tried to take a read of her eyes. Tired eyes looked back at him, eyes that didn't reflect any hope, eyes that still only saw the tunnel.

"Someone," he said, "some group, didn't want Domingo Avila to be autopsied."

She finally spoke: "If you are hoping for some kind of admission, you're not going to get it."

"What I'm hoping is that you see this goes far beyond you and the accident. Why else would anyone go to these lengths to manufacture such a gruesome bomb?"

"I will deny everything."

For a moment, Graham couldn't understand what she was saying. Then he realized she was once again being protective.

"You think your Mossad did the bombing, don't you?"

"Your words, not mine."

"Tunnel vision, Lanie. You only see Domingo's death and nothing else. He dominates your perspective. But let me throw out some *what if*s to you.

"*What if* the Brothers aren't Mossad agents at all? *What if* you were being used to get close to the real target, the man who will likely be our next president?"

Her defenses were up. She kept shaking her head, not buying any of it.

"*What if*," Graham said, "you didn't kill Domingo Avila?"

She continued to shake her head. Even in the darkness, Graham could see the wetness of her eyes.

"I went to the scene of the accident, Lanie, and I think I figured out how they did it. Domingo came at you right as you were emerging out of the tunnel, didn't he? It was the same tunnel where Warren Beatty's character in *Heaven Can Wait* had a car come at him while he was riding a bicycle. Maybe that's what gave them the idea. I am sure you didn't have time to react. I suspect you didn't see Domingo, and suddenly he was there. But *what if* he was pushed? Or more likely, *what if* he was already dead? An autopsy would have shown that. An autopsy might have revealed that he died in a very different manner than being hit by an automobile. An autopsy could have shown that death occurred much earlier that night.

"Behind the tunnel, there's the creek. Someone could have brought Domingo's body and bicycle up that way. And just outside the tunnel there's a perfect spot to wait. They probably had a transmitter on your car. They might have even subtly suggested you get a rental for privacy. And there they waited, knowing you and your passenger would be coming along. The tunnel's not that large. They would have rolled Domingo and his bicycle out just before you passed.

"I can even take all this beyond a *what if*. The night he died, the last time Domingo's friends saw him on his bicycle was around nine o'clock. That was almost four hours before you supposedly hit him. And there were no witnesses that came forward to say they saw Domingo riding up Malibu Canyon Road that night."

It wasn't conclusive. The police investigation, brief as it was, revealed that Domingo was known to ride his bicycle at odd hours, and that he was one for wooing the senoritas, no matter how far the ride or how late the night. But Graham didn't tell that to Lanie.

He couldn't, not with the way she was suddenly sobbing for joy.

Later, in her bed, she whispered to him, "When I was younger, I used to have this terrible nightmare that I murdered someone. I can remember waking up two or three times from that nightmare, and being absolutely distraught. I think my victims were people I was angry at, and my subconscious was letting me vent my feelings. It was always so real to me. I would always awaken in tears and despair at the thought of what I had done. I can't tell you the feeling of indescribable relief that came over me when I realized it was all a dream, and that I hadn't killed anyone."

Graham knew that was Lanie's way of telling him that she now had some hope that she hadn't done that "terrible thing." They had talked little since her cry in the car, but it was clear that Lanie was rethinking all that had occurred.

"You told me they were blackmailing you," she said. "If I was set up, isn't it possible that you were set up as well?"

"No," said Graham. "I only have myself to blame for what happened."

There was no one to lift his nightmare from him. He responded without inflection, but what she heard made her draw closer to him.

"Thank you," she said.

"For what?"

"For saving my life."

"You're welcome."

She was warm in his arms. They hadn't made love. Each was content just to hold the other.

Graham asked, "When you took your pills, did you have a near-death experience? See a white light? Anything like that?"

Lanie shook her head. "At one point I had this feeling of drifting off, though. You'll never guess what brought me back."

"What?"

"The thought of me being the feature of one of those awful True Hollywood Stories. I didn't want my life to end on that kind of a note."

"First saved by a paparazzo, then saved by tabloid TV."

She laughed. "I suppose you're right."

Their fingers found one another and intertwined. "You would have given her a ride to the gas station," Lanie said.

"What are you talking about?"

"A few weeks ago some paparazzi were following Gwyneth Paltrow when she went out for a drive. She ran out of gas, and instead of helping her, the paparazzi took shots of her walking to the service station. I know you would have given her a ride."

"No," said Graham. "Would you want a picture of a star in a car, or a picture of a star holding a gas can? The human element is her running out of gas."

He thought about it another few moments, then reconsidered a little. "Yeah," said Graham, "I would have offered her a ride, but not before she walked at least a block."

"That's not so bad," said Lanie. "I've lost a couple of roles to Gwyneth. I probably would have made her walk two blocks."

Thirty-four

Both of them slept deeply and well, something neither had done in too long of a time. Chin propped on hand, Graham watched Lanie get ready.

"I was hoping you would keep sleeping," she said.

"This is better than sleep."

"I thought you were jaded."

"I am. But I'm not blind."

There was a bounce to her step, and her inimitable eyes gleamed. Her long neck was once again held straight and high, her carriage defying Newton's laws of gravity. Graham hoped he was right in his belief that she hadn't caused Domingo's death. He was setting her up for a very hard fall if he was wrong.

Lanie came over and sat on the bed. "I wish I could linger."

"So do I. But I need to get an early start as well."

She didn't have to ask him what he was working on. "Do you have any idea who's behind all this?"

"No, but I'm going to find out."

"Be careful."

"They're the ones who should be afraid. I'm one of the dreaded paparazzi, remember? We're supposed to be worse than marauding Huns, Visigoths, Mongols, or Vandals. Knowing what I am should put fear in the heart of my enemies."

"I'm not kidding."

"Neither am I," he said, with more than a little steel in his declaration.

She leaned forward, kissed him on his nose, then on his lips. He couldn't tell if she was kissing like a friend, or a lover. Either way, he didn't mind it.

"My driver's waiting," she said.

"Star treatment."

"I usually drive myself. But on long shooting days, the studio sends a limo. I think it's their way of keeping me captive from start to finish."

"You ever feel like Cinderella being taken in her carriage to the royal ball?"

"Yes. But most of the time I feel like Cinderella hearing the clock tower chime midnight, and knowing my carriage is about to turn into a pumpkin."

"Have I told you that my car's pumpkin-proof? Most people don't spring for that option, but I did."

"That's very reassuring. Will you and your squash-free vehicle be available tonight?"

"Just call."

"There's just something about a man in uniform," Graham said, whistling.

"Fuck you."

Ran, aka Roy, was dressed in his maintenance blues. He got into the car and dropped the film into Graham's waiting hands.

"Did I tell you what your payback's gonna be for all this?" Ran asked.

"I've been afraid to ask."

"You like a man in uniform? That's good. My friend Dave, the one who manages that security company, is throwing us a great gig. Next week you and me are going to be rent-a-cops at an exclusive party."

"I've told you before, I don't do well in polyester."

"Poor boy. We'll be part of this team of about twenty rent-a-cops, and get this, our assignment's going to be to keep people like us well away from the talent. They're going to put the foxes in charge of the henhouse."

"You're not serious, are you?"

Ran nodded. "The best thing is, we'll be double-dipping. We'll be getting paid for the guard shift, four hours work at ten bucks an hour, while doing our own work. By the way, I got dibs on your boutonniere camera. Maybe you should use that necktie jobbie you got. Anyway, here's the deal: I get half the money from any pictures you sell that night. The rent-a-cop money will be all yours."

As a rule, Graham didn't do that kind of work, and Ran knew it. Occasionally Graham resorted to a disguise, but usually he chose to get his shots in other ways. Ran actually liked going in character, and couldn't understand Graham's reluctance to do the same. When they sniped at one another, Ran liked to paint him as being a snob.

"You really don't even need me, do you?" asked Graham. "The only reason you want me at that function is to demean me."

Ran couldn't hide his smile. "I'll probably take as many pictures of you in your guard outfit," he said, "as I will of Angelina Jolie's chest and Courtney Cox's backside."

Both of the men waited for the pictures to be developed. It was a long shot, Graham knew, but he needed to bring Smith and his confederates out in the open.

With Ran looking over his shoulder, Graham started to flip through the camera trap shots. Ran hadn't been kidding about Rex's posing for the camera. There were half a dozen pictures of the dog in action. But there were also pictures that interested him. Two of the shots taken from the front of Graham's apartment showed the same man in profile approaching his door. The man was wearing a hat, dark prescription glasses, and a bulky sweatshirt, clothing that would make it difficult for anyone to get a good look at him. Graham had never seen him before.

"Is that a scar on his face," asked Ran, "or is the film just grainy?"

Graham touched the picture, running his finger along the man's face. "Scar," he said. "You can see it in both pictures."

He opened the second packet of pictures. The garage EXIT sign camera had captured a number of his neighbors passing by. It had also caught Scar.

"What's he doing in that shot?" Ran asked.

The man was leaning down for something, that much was clear. In the other shot, he was looking away from the apartment. Graham studied the two pictures, and tried to figure out the sequence.

"He's picking up a rock," Graham said.

"Looks more like he's tying his shoe."

"That's what he would have wanted any onlooker to think, in the unlikely event he had any witnesses. The shot we're missing between the two pictures would have shown him throwing the rock at my bedroom window."

Ran shook his head. "I don't see it."

"Then look again. You can see that a few seconds passed between the photos. In the second shot he's already tossed the stone. He would have done it casually. Someone watching him might not even have noticed."

"You got a good imagination," said Ran. "If he tossed that rock, what's he doing looking away from where he supposedly threw it?"

"More misdirection for any onlookers." Pointing, Graham said, "Look at the window in the first picture. Then check it out in the second."

Ran examined the pictures closely. He almost needed a magnifying class to see. In each of the shots, the bedroom window was in the background, something easy to overlook. "Son of a bitch."

In the first shot the window was intact; in the second, it was broken.

"He moved outside of infrared beam range," Graham said, "and there he would have gauged the response to his rock throwing."

Ran was still looking at the two pictures. "Dammit. In all the pictures, this guy seems to be at an angle or looking down. The camera never got a good bead on him."

Graham flipped through the rest of the packet. Toward the end, he was rewarded. There was a picture of Scar walking along the pathway out back. He still managed to have his head averted downward, but it was the best of all the shots. The black and white infrared film even held a surprise bonus.

The film had penetrated the dark barrier of Scar's prescription glasses. His eyes were clearly visible. They stared out from his sockets, unblinking and unrelenting. It was probably just a by-product of the infrared image, but Graham had this feeling that death was staring at him.

Thirty-five

Curson Street was blocked off because of some filming going on. It was a common event in L.A., with studios appropriating neighborhoods for their productions, but it put Graham that much more on edge. He went east a block to where the set trucks weren't set up like blockades, and then drove north on Masselin Street. Passing by the Museum Square Building, home of the Screen Actors' Guild, he thought about Lanie.

He turned west on Wilshire. Around him were buildings that were regularly featured on television shows and movies. For Angelenos, suspending reality was sometimes difficult when your own turf was always up on the screen.

The area he was navigating was part of the so-called Miracle Mile, a name coined by one of its developers. The mile part was about right, the approximate distance one traveled when going along Wilshire between Highland and Fairfax. As for the miracle, no shrines had been built on its path, unless you wanted to count the nearby CBS Studios, or some of the production companies housed in buildings along Wilshire.

Ran had wanted to know why Graham picked La Brea Tar Pits for his meeting with Smith. "It's the right place," he had told him, "to draw in the Dire Wolves."

Ran had looked at him as if he was crazy.

The tar pits were one of Graham's favorite visiting places. His familiarity with the Museum Row area, and Rancho La Brea and the George C. Page Museum in particular, had made the spot an obvious choice for the meeting place. If L.A. was New Age, the tar pits were Ice Age. On display were remains of animals that roamed the Los Angeles Basin in the last ice age between ten thousand and forty thousand years ago. Over two hundred tons of fossil bones had been removed from the tar pits. The most common remains were those of dire wolves; almost four thousand had been excavated. The wolves were drawn in by their entrapped prey, and they themselves became victims.

Now it was Graham's turn to play lamb to the wolf.

Even from half a block away, he could smell the methane from the tar pits. Some of the buildings in the area still had methane detectors. The 1986 Fairfax fire had alerted many to the dangers of the methane permeating the soil. Fueled by the underground gas, a large area of sidewalk on Fairfax Avenue had burst into flames. The methane still surfaced along the Miracle Mile, sometimes quite dramatically. An olive tree had recently exploded into flames when a lit cigarette was thrown into its hollow trunk.

Instead of turning on Curson for the museum parking, Graham continued on Wilshire past the Los Angeles County Museum of Art. He turned right on Ogden, found a metered parking space, and fed it quarters.

As Graham set out toward the tar pits, he wondered if he was already being watched. It was easy being paranoid; everyone was a potential suspect. He could be in someone's crosshairs at that very moment. Graham figured he would be safe though, at least until they found out what he knew.

He walked along Wilshire and opted to bypass the museum's western entrance. It was the least traveled part of the grounds, and Graham was looking for safety in numbers. There were those in plenty at the active loading zone. School buses were letting children out. Graham stepped around teachers trying to establish order, made his way through the schoolchildren, and started down the main path to the museum.

The Lake Pit was bubbling up in a number of spots, methane rising from the fissures below the lake. Oddly enough, Graham had come to like the odor. On more than one occasion he had even mouthed the line from the Robert Duvall character in *Apocalypse Now*: "I love the smell of napalm in the morning."

Graham took some deep breaths, but not to breathe in the scent. He needed to look and act normal. If he was being watched, they didn't have to know his heart was racing, and his mouth was too dry to even wet his lips.

At the east end of the Lake Pit, Graham stopped on the path to ostensibly take in the life-sized figures of an imperial mammoth family. But before looking to the past, he took stock of the present, swiveling his head in all directions. There were no familiar faces, and no one appeared interested in him.

His eyes drifted back to the mammoths. On shore papa mammoth and baby mammoth were safe. Their attention was riveted out to the water, where mama mammoth was trapped. Huge as she was, she couldn't escape the grip of the tar. It had her in its hold, and it wasn't going to let go. Her alarmed trumpeting wasn't going to help, and the plaintive calls of her little one, at least relatively speaking, weren't going to free her.

For thousands of years the pools of asphalt had claimed countless victims. In the heat of the summer, the asphalt melted to a viscous glue. Small animals became stuck like flies to flypaper. Larger animals sank two to three inches into the liquified asphalt, enough to entrap many forever. Typically, it only took a little more than an inch of the liquified asphalt to trap an animal the size of a cow. To a small degree, Graham knew the entrapment process still continued at the tar pits. Liquified asphalt oozed to the surface, trapping insects, lizards, birds, and small mammals. Inside the museum, one exhibit challenged children to test their strength against the pull of asphalt. Firsthand, they learned of its grip. They were allowed to escape its consequences, but the tons of bones in the museum reminded them of those that never did.

Graham looked around again. No sign of the Brothers, or Smith, or Scar.

He continued down the path, stopping in front of a stone sculpture at the entrance that showed two saber-toothed cats fighting. Graham didn't know how accurate that portrayal was. Some paleontologists believed the cats were social animals that lived and hunted in packs, even caring for the old and infirm. What the sculptor did get right was how large and deadly the cats had been. They were the size of modern African lions. With their huge canine teeth, the cats sliced open the stomach of their prey.

The teeth were enough of a grim reminder for Graham to survey the area around him once more. As far as he could tell, he was still alone.

Near to him was another statue that showed North American lions, and on the west side of the grounds Graham knew there was a statue of a prehistoric bear.

"Lions, and tigers, and bears, oh my," he whispered to himself.

The L.A. Basin had been a tough place during the last ice age. Some things never changed.

Graham looked at his watch. It was ten minutes after one. His underarms were already soaked, and he had only been on the grounds for ten minutes.

Time had never gone by so slowly. By now, he was sure they had him under surveillance. All he had to do was wait.

Wait while the dire wolves closed in.

That was the plan. His plan. It didn't seem very inspired at the moment. But he had to get them out in the open, and the only way to do that was to use himself as bait. He was just another animal trapped in the asphalt.

Half a dozen times he withstood the urge to check his watch again. When he broke down, only another two minutes had passed. Graham stayed on the alert. He continued to study all the adults around him, but he still almost overlooked the wolf in sheep's clothing.

The man was dressed like a tourist, had the obligatory camera around his neck and guidebook to Los Angeles in his hands. The book was written in French. The cane in the man's hands, and his stoop, accentuated his years, made him appear to be about seventy. He was wearing sunglasses and a black beret covered his head. Graham would never have given him a second look if not for his scar.

Graham tried to hide his look of recognition. Scar wasn't eyeing him, at least not directly, but he was staying close. Had Scar wanted to talk, he would have just walked up to Graham. He was up to something else. Graham edged away, pretending interest in some murals. Two could play at being tourist. Scar followed him, almost imperceptibly closing the distance.

For the kill? There were people around. But would that stop him? Dying wasn't part of Graham's plan. The tar pits had seemed like the right place for him to play tar baby. His enemies would come to him, show themselves, and then he'd stick to them.

He slowly retreated down the steps and headed west. From the corner of his eye, Graham tried to keep sight of Scar. For whatever reason, he didn't seem to be following. At the bottom of the steps, Graham paused and surveyed the area around him. There were no visible threats, unless you counted the horde of elementary school children. He looked behind him. Scar was still at the top of the steps, pretending interest in a graphic.

Graham waited to see what would happen. If it was an ambush, it was slow to close in on him. Almost fifteen minutes passed, and no one drew near. Even Scar maintained his distance, perhaps sensing he was spooked.

For his own purposes, Graham decided enough time had elapsed. Smith wasn't going to appear for their meeting, but that was no surprise. He had figured Smith for a no-show, had been certain he would stay safely in the background while others came for him. Scar was the only enemy Graham had identified. He wondered how many others there might be. Unhurriedly, he set out along the path that led to the western entrance, stopping to pause at the working dig. Every year scientists drained the pool and dug into the past. One of the paleontologists had described the animals as being "trapped in time." That was much like his own condition ever since Paris.

Behind him, Graham heard approaching footsteps. Scar had reappeared, and was walking at a brisk pace. Graham's digital phone rang. He suspected Smith was calling. This was where they wanted him to stop.

Graham reversed his direction. His move surprised Scar. For a moment, their eyes met, and then Graham was past him, suddenly running in an all-out sprint. In a footrace, there were few who could catch him. Besides, it was his home field. He had choreographed his escape route, and was ready to shake the pursuit. One look back was all he allowed himself. Scar was watching him, but not following.

He ran through the side gate that led to the art museum. Graham raced along its patio, cut through its dining room, then exited through the gift shop.

The bike Ran had dropped off that morning was waiting for him outside in the bike rack. Graham felt like a Chippendale's performer shedding his garb. He wasn't quite wearing Velcro clothing, but his loose Polo shirt and chinos were shucked and in his backpack in a matter of moments. Underneath he was wearing a form-fitting biking outfit. A flick of one digit, and he freed the lock. He threw on a bike helmet, one of those Jetson's designs that hard-core cyclists used, and doffed some metallic shades. Even his father would have had a hard time recognizing him.

From start to finish, Graham was off in less than twenty seconds. It had been like a hurried pit stop. Now he was going for the checkered flag.

He pumped hard at the pedals, and in a few moments was flying. Anyone trying to get a good look at him was only going to see a blur.

Thirty-six

You should have seen them," said Ran. "They looked like bridegrooms left at the altar."

Graham had been waiting for Ran's call for more than an hour. After hurriedly leaving Rancho La Brea, he had cycled five miles over to the posh Century Plaza Hotel where he had picked up his car rental. The rental clerk had been surprised at his appearance. Most of those who came to the counter wore business suits and didn't wheel their alternate transportation up with them.

"What happened?"

"Scar made a few calls, and then he split out of there but fast. Like you figured, they had your car staked out. They were waiting for you to come back for it."

"Who was there?"

"I assume it was the Brothers, but the way they were dressed up, it wasn't easy seeing their resemblance. One was watching from the lawn of the museum. He had his nose in a book and had on this long wig that gave him a surfer look. That didn't hide the burns on his face, though. The other one had the jogging detail. He had on a fake mustache and was wearing a bandana. The guy kept jogging up one side of the street, and then down the other. He looked pretty winded by the time I left."

"Speaking of disguises," said Graham, "I never made you. What were you wearing?"

"I was the homeless guy with a very evident drinking problem. I kept tipping my brown paper bag up. Thing is, I wasn't sipping, I was snapping. My brown bag had a hole at the bottom."

"You get pictures of everybody?"

"Multiple shots of everyone. First-class close-ups even."

"How did you manage that?"

"You ever notice Hancock Park's got a lot of trash barrels? I got an up-close and personal experience with most of them. I went all over digging through the barrels. It paid off, though. I got the shots. And I must have collected sixty or seventy aluminum cans."

"You finally found your calling in life."

"Fuck you very much."

"I need those pictures as soon as possible."

"I'm taking them to get developed now."

"Don't let 'em out of your sight, okay?"

"Stop worrying."

"Let's meet up at four, have a drink. You choose the place. I'll set up an open tab for you and Jackie. You can be the last of the big-time spenders, get her a dinner with all the works."

"You going to join us?"

"I've got plans."

"Seems to me you've had a lot of plans lately. You finally getting a social life?"

"I don't know. I'll fill you in over drinks. Where do you want to meet?"

Ran thought for a long moment: "Ivy at the Shore on Ocean Avenue."

"I don't know it."

"Neither do I."

"Then why did you pick it?"

"Because the food is supposed to be good. But that's not the most important reason."

"Which is?"

"You're paying, and it's expensive."

"In that case, you want to loan me some of your aluminum cans?"

"The more you talk, funny boy, the more it's going to cost you."

"I'll see you at four."

"You got it."

"Oh, and, Ran?"

There was something in his tone that made Ran suspicious. "What?"

"Do shower before you show up."

Ran dropped off the pictures at Wolf Camera. They would be ready in an hour, and so would he. Ran knew Graham would have preferred he stay with the film, but he wasn't the one who had been rooting around in garbage for most of the afternoon. The wise-ass had told him to take a shower, and that's just what he intended to do.

There were no neighbors around, which was just as well. Ran didn't feel like explaining his look, and smell, and all the aluminum cans he was hauling in. That reminded him—he was going to have to crush the cans and put them away before Jackie came home. To him, the cans were trophies of his work. To her, they would be a disgusting reminder of his disgusting work. Jackie couldn't understand why he got such satisfaction out of a job she considered demeaning. The more he explained to her, the less she seemed to get it. She couldn't understand the thrill of the hunt and how it gave him a rush outsmarting people. Jackie thought he could best show the world how smart he was by bringing home a fat and steady paycheck. But where was the fun in that?

Maybe she'd give him a little more slack after their night out. Ran had called Jackie from the road. She had been excited to hear where they were having a night on the town. He would surprise Jackie by dressing up, put on a blazer, maybe even a tie. The bum look was about to be a memory.

Ran entered the apartment, went straight to the bathroom, and started the water running in the shower. In a minute it would be nice and hot. He stripped off his clothes, opened the hallway closet, and dumped them in the washer. The amount of detergent he tossed in probably would have killed off the bubonic plague. Better to be safe than sorry. He wasn't about to throw out the worn clothing, though Jackie had been lobbying him to do so for years. They were an essential part of his costume collection.

He always liked the water to be just right before getting in. Ran reached out with a finger and tested it. Perfect. He stepped into the shower, drew the curtain behind him, and started soaping up. God, the hot water felt great. He let it pelt him for a minute, a mini-massage that he reveled in. Now it was time for the shampoo. Usually he used baby shampoo, but decided instead to use some of Jackie's expensive gel that smelled like cherries. The scent was enough to make him hungry. He was going to bring a big appetite to the restaurant.

The gel sudsed up real nice. He was lathering his hair when he felt the draft behind him. The damn bathroom door had worked its way open. Ran always hated when that happened. It was like waking up in the middle of a wet dream.

But this was worse.

The shower curtain wasn't pulled back, it was pulled off. The violence of its removal almost broke the rod. Half-blind, Ran had to wipe away suds to see the silenced pistol pointing at him. His eyes stung from the shampoo. They hurt even more when he recognized who was standing there.

Scar was smiling at him.

Ran tried to bluff it out. "Who the hell are you?"

Instead of answering, Jaeger said, "Push the stopper down."

"What?"

His English was monotone and without accent. "Fill the bathtub."

Ran didn't immediately react. He was close enough to Scar that he considered lunging at him.

"I wouldn't do it," said Jaeger, leveling the gun in his right, gloved hand at Ran's privates. "I never miss even small targets."

"Fuck you, asshole."

The gun didn't waver. "Push the stopper down."

Ran reached out with his foot, tripping it. The shower water started to accumulate in the tub.

"What do you want?"

"Oh," said Jaeger, "I pretty much have what I came for. It was nice of you to leave the claim check for the film in your wallet."

"I don't know what you are talking about."

"Of course you do. It took me a while to figure out your game. The two of you must have thought you were so clever. The one paparazzo acting as bait, the other hiding in the bushes. By the way, where is your partner?"

"I think he's *shtupping* your mother."

"I've been checking on all his friends and acquaintances, you see, figuring he would show up at one of his usual haunts. The last few nights I've stopped by here, but alas, he was elsewhere. Did you know that you snore?"

"I know you probably enjoy talking with naked guys in the shower," Ran said, "but it's not my thing."

The water continued to fill the tub.

"How were you able to identify me?" Jaeger asked.

"I have an asshole detector. The thing just about went tilt when you walked by."

"Perhaps I should ask your woman that question. Jackie looked so nice last night in her black negligee."

Ran's face reacted to his words. Scar really had been in his apartment. And he knew things, like Jackie's name. He tried to keep the panic out of his voice. "She doesn't know anything."

"I'm listening."

"It's not like I know much either. Graham's been working on this thing by himself. A few days ago he told me that two men took him for a ride and almost killed him. He was tipped off that they might be Mossad agents. Then he got a call from this guy and they arranged today's meeting. Graham wanted some bargaining power, so he asked me to photograph anyone who came anywhere near to him. Hell, I must have shot ten rolls. The only reason I recognized you just now is because of your scar. I remembered seeing a man with a scar like yours at the museum."

The water was halfway up Ran's calves.

"When was he going to get your film?"

"Five o'clock at his place. I ordered doubles of the pictures. He wanted me to put one set in a safe place, and the other set I was supposed to hand off to him at his apartment. He figured the film would be his insurance that nothing happened to him."

"Your friend is paranoid."

"Yeah, he's silly that way. He probably wouldn't like a gun held on him either."

Jaeger shrugged apologetically, then lowered his pistol. "Your friend has stumbled upon some matters of national security. Today, had he not run, we would have explained that to him."

The water was now getting dangerously high in the tub. Jaeger motioned with his head. "You're about to have a flood," he said.

As Ran reached for the faucet handles, Jaeger struck. He moved so quickly Ran didn't even have a chance to make a sound. With one gloved hand he grabbed Ran by the hair, with the other he cradled his chin. Jaeger yanked his head back with what appeared to be a minimum of effort, but the force of the impact shook the walls. Limp and unmoving, Ran sank into the water, his nose and mouth falling beneath the surface. For a minute, bubbles rose from Ran's nose and mouth. Then they stopped.

Jaeger was willing to bet the coroner's office would rule the death as accidental. The injuries would be consistent with a bad fall. Besides, the coroner's office hadn't yet recovered from the bombing. They were operating, but nowhere near peak efficiency.

It was a good time to get away with murder, thought Jaeger, and that was a good thing. The night was still young.

Thirty-seven

Graham sipped at his Ivy gimlet. The drink was the house specialty; tamped mint leaves at the bottom of the glass topped by crushed ice, Skye vodka, and lemon juice. He would have enjoyed the drink a lot more with Ran sitting next to him. His friend was almost half an hour late. That wasn't like him, especially when Graham was buying.

The Santa Monica version of the Ivy was less ostentatious than the one in West Hollywood, which was frequented by celebrities and the incumbent stargazers. The movie *Get Shorty* had featured Danny DeVito and his omelet scene there. DeVito's display was Gatsby updated: stars are different from you and me. Menus were something for ordinary people, not stars. Stars order whatever strikes their fancy, because they can.

"Can I get you another?"

"Not yet," Graham told the bartender, who nodded, then went back to cleaning some glasses.

The drinking crowd was light. At another time Graham might have better appreciated the water view, tropical plants, and Gauguinesque artwork, but he'd already crossed the line from impatience to concern. He flipped open his phone and dialed Ran's number, waiting while it rang and rang. Night or day, no matter where he was, Ran always answered his phone. It was his lifeline. This time he didn't pick up.

Unbidden, the thought struck Graham: He's dead.

I'm overreacting, he told himself. Ran's just late. Or he needs to replace the batteries to his phone. But the morbid thought clung to him, and wouldn't be beaten back. As the minutes passed, Graham's fears continued to grow. A drumbeat in his mind started beating, a continual pounding of the words "What the hell have I done?"

When Ran still hadn't appeared after forty-five minutes, Graham scrolled through his Palm Pilot. Jackie's cell phone number was there. With a very heavy hand, he dialed her number.

Graham had never thought he could feel worse than he had in Paris. One of his few consolations over the years was that what happened there was an accident, and that the other driver's aggressiveness was the main cause of the deaths. But he couldn't point his finger at anyone else this time. As little as he knew about his enemies, he did know they were ruthless, and he should have taken that into account. Somehow they had clued in that Ran was helping him, and now he was dead.

Just like in Paris, he felt overwhelmed. Body and mind roiled in turbulence. There was no relief for him. And like he had in Paris, Graham ran from his crime—not the crime scene, but the crime itself.

A detective had interviewed him, but only briefly. "So when he didn't show up for our meeting," Graham told him, "I called up Jackie."

The detective didn't press him further, accepting his story. No one seemed to think Ran's death was anything but a tragic accident, and Graham didn't tell them anything different.

Surrounded by strangers, Jackie turned to Graham's shoulder to sob on. Grief made her forget how much she disliked him. Every time she cried, Graham was reminded of his guilt. For hours he remained captive. It wasn't until Jackie's sister showed up at eight o'clock that he was able to leave the apartment.

Once outside, Graham bent down and sucked in air, but still he couldn't seem to get enough breath. There wasn't enough air in the world for him.

After a minute, he straightened up. They could be watching him now. He was vulnerable, out in the open. Graham looked around and didn't see anything. But there were a hundred spots where someone could be stalking him without being seen. What Graham did professionally with a camera, someone else could be doing with a weapon. If he hoped to get payback for his friend's death, he needed to stay alive.

Graham thought it unlikely that the murderer or murderers would have lingered after killing Ran. They probably didn't know about his rental. As a precaution, Graham had removed all the telltale Hertz clues. It was just another Camry. But he didn't take any chances. He walked half a block away from the car, then suddenly turned around and sprinted to it. No one jumped out with a gun.

Inside his car, he activated the locks, started the engine, and jackrabbited off. He checked his rearview mirror, and didn't see any pursuit. Safe, he thought, but he didn't feel safe. And his friend was dead.

"Bastards," he yelled, the word an explosive sob. "Bastards."

Graham wiped hard at his nose. Grief would have to wait. He needed to think, to plan. But the more he tried to concentrate, the more his ghosts kept surfacing. They were all driving with him, Ran and Le Croc and Lady Godwin and her just begun baby.

His digital phone rang. He looked at the display, and saw it was a local number. When he picked up the phone, Graham heard someone crying. At first he thought it was Jackie, but she didn't have his number. It was Lanie.

Her words were tremulous, and she could barely hold them together: "Did you hear about the accident?"

For a moment, Graham wondered if she was talking about Ran, but then realized she didn't even know him.

"No."

Her answer was jumbled in one long run-on sob: "Therewasabadaccident—mylimo—mystand-in—myfriend—Ineedyou."

He understood her last three words, and those were enough.

For once, Graham didn't mind having to deal with the security at the studio lot. He hoped they were as vigilant to everyone trying to gain entry. Graham was even escorted over to the set. Lanie was waiting for him behind the locked doors of an office. They didn't say anything to one another, just held each other in a tight hug. Graham's already wet shoulder got another workout before he hustled her away.

In the car, she told him about the accident. It had occurred in Malibu on a quiet stretch of road just a few miles from the Grove. Two of the limousine's tires had blown out, and the limo had gone over the side of the road. There were no survivors.

"Piper had a fight with her boyfriend," Lanie said, "so I offered to put her up at my place. Since you were going to pick me up, Piper took the limo."

Piper Francis had been Lanie's stand-in for five years. A stand-in does a lot of the star's dirty work. Directors often figure out how they want to shoot a scene using a stand-in. Lighting and camera people block their shots with the stand-in. Usually a stand-in bears a resemblance to the star. According to Lanie, Piper could have been her sister. She had the same complexion and hair, and was the same height and build. Piper hadn't only been Lanie's stand-in. Over the years, they had become good friends.

"Maybe it was just an accident," she said. "But when I heard, I panicked. The police say it was an accident, though."

She said the last words as if trying to convince herself that was the case.

"Let me tell you about Ran's *accident*," Graham said.

When he finished, Lanie said, "What will we do?"

"GALA," Graham said, then explained his shorthand. "Get away from L.A."

"I have a getaway home in Ojai," Lanie said. "No one knows about it."

Ojai was a town off the beaten path about two hours north of Los Angeles.

Graham voiced his doubts: "No one?"

"Not even your sort. My property is up in the foothills of Upper Ojai Valley. It's surrounded by the Los Padres National Forest and is very secluded. I don't know my neighbors and I can't see their homes. And I never take visitors. You'll be my first."

"What about staff?"

"The gardener comes every Thursday. That's it."

Graham still wasn't convinced. "People in town would have seen you and talked."

"I don't go into town. The property is my Zen retreat. It's very Eastern in a very Western setting. Trees, rocks, and nature are my companions. There are no phones, and no power lines."

Maybe it was just his frame of mind, but to Graham, her retreat sounded more like a cemetery than a home. He didn't say that aloud, though. Without a better alternative, he got on 101 going north. The farther they traveled, the quieter each of them seemed to get, both of them lost in their own grief. Traffic on the freeway was slow, and the cause eventually became apparent. On the side of the road were two damaged cars, a California Highway Patrol cruiser and the paramedics. Traffic accidents were a daily event on L.A.'s freeways, but it was always as if no one had ever seen a wreck. Drivers slowed down and rubbernecked. No one, it seemed, could look away from an accident.

Graham hated the slowdowns. They always made him think about his own crash.

As she stared at the accident, Lanie asked, "Why?"

Graham knew she was talking about the accident that had claimed the life of her friend. "I would guess it was an ambush. They identified the limo as the same one driving you back and forth to the Grove. Mistaken identity killed Piper. You were the one who was supposed to die."

"Why?"

"You're a loose end. I am a loose end. And so was Ran. Today the loose ends were supposed to be tied up."

Lanie said, "Maybe—maybe I should—make some calls."

"To the vice president?" Graham asked.

"Don't ask me any questions."

"Excuse the hell out of me."

"You're still looking for your goddam story."

"No, I'm looking to keep us alive."

"I won't betray a trust. If you were in my position, would you put a secret into the hands of someone like you?"

Graham wished he could be insulted, but she was just turning the camera on him and what he did.

"To stay alive," he said, "yes."

"Staying alive isn't enough."

Lanie had proved that during her suicide attempt. They had slept and wept together. He had saved her life, but he still hadn't earned her trust.

"I need to tell you a story," said Graham.

He took a deep breath. He had never thought he would tell his secret to anyone but the Abbot. It was the five-hundred-pound gorilla he was always chained to. It moved him, he didn't move it. The very notion of telling another being made him feel as if he were stepping through an opening, with no idea of how far he would fall.

Graham started talking anyway.

Thirty-eight

Even after two hours of lovemaking, Jaeger couldn't quite shake his feeling of annoyance.

He didn't make mistakes. He was a craftsman at his work. And yet he had erred: Lanie Byrne still lived.

Jaeger wondered if she had gone into hiding. Lanie had taken the day off from work. If she was in mourning for her friend, she was doing her grieving away from the Grove. Jaeger thought it possible she was with the paparazzo. The man had balls. He had used himself as bait, and somehow had identified him as the enemy. The Israeli had lied to Jaeger when he said that he only recognized him because of his scar. His pictures had told a different story. He had keyed on Jaeger and to a lesser degree the Brothers. The photographer had known what to look for, but how?

It was small consolation to Jaeger that he had gotten to the pictures first and destroyed all of them. He should have been anonymous to the paparazzo. Pilgrim must have known that someone like Jaeger would be coming for him. Maybe he had seen him from a distance while Jaeger had been working his trail. The tar pit meeting had been designed to bring Jaeger in close. Photos would have provided the paparazzo with something tangible in the event he tried to take any of his speculations to the authorities. Without them, he had nothing, or nothing that could ever be proved.

The paparazzo was in a maze he would never find his way out of, but it bothered Jaeger that he had played tag with him, and was still alive. Soon, though, he would have to surface. And when he did, Pilgrim would find that Jaeger had the exits to all of his holes covered. Every contingency had been planned for. Pilgrim would be dead before he got any closer to figuring out the puzzle.

The woman next to Jaeger nestled closer. Angelica looked up at him and smiled. She had no idea that he was the least bit troubled. In her presence, he kept a fatuous smile on his face, as if he were smitten. Angelica ran her hand along his firm chest.

"This is what I call a layover," she said.

Jaeger nodded, feigning total agreement. Angelica's eyes went a little cross-eyed looking back at him. He could tell that she was already beginning to think she was in love. His English businessman persona was rather irresistible. Earnest, yet boyish, wealthy, but not snobbish.

"More champagne?" she asked with a giggle.

"Perhaps in a few minutes, darling."

While she had thrashed under him, Jaeger had been thinking about ways to make Pilgrim surface. Everyone had their pressure points. All Jaeger had to do was ratchet them up. The Israeli's death would be plaguing him now. He would know that they could easily strike at someone close to him. Jaeger considered using his father as bait, or that former girlfriend they had uncovered. Guilt worked well with Pilgrim. It wasn't an emotion you would associate with a paparazzo, but it was clear he had never gotten over Paris. What a fool.

Tomorrow, Jaeger would begin turning up the pressure on him. The only problem was, Pilgrim wasn't taking calls again. But there were always ways to get messages to people, thought Jaeger. Strong messages.

"Are you all right, John?"

Angelica was looking at him again with her cow eyes, her expression one of too tender concern.

"Why, yes."

"Because you've been quiet."

"Perhaps because I am satiated beyond words."

"It was special, wasn't it?"

"Oh, yes."

"It feels so right being here in your arms."

Jaeger made some appropriate sounds of agreement, but he was tired of her drivel and looked for a way to end it. He reached for the remote control on the bed-stand.

"Do you mind if I turn on the telly for a few minutes, dear? The Tokyo and Hong Kong markets are open now, and I need to get a read on their activity."

Her head bobbed up and down in quick agreement, and Jaeger started channel surfing.

"CNN's Channel 30," Angelica said.

Jaeger entered the numbers. Lanie Byrne materialized on the screen looking upset.

". . . he came at me," she said, "swinging a knife. I started running away, and that's when he pulled a gun and started shooting. I thank God I'm alive."

The face of a talking head appeared on the screen. "Ms. L was able to escape her attacker, the same man she believes has been stalking her for months."

The correspondent's face was replaced by another. Jaeger found himself looking at his own picture on television. The shot was dark and blurry. It was unlikely that even people who knew him, and there were few of those, would be able to recognize him from the photo. He was wearing a hat and dark prescription glasses, but somehow his eyes were visible in the picture. And so was his scar.

Jaeger tuned in late to what the talking head was saying: ". . . allowed them to get a picture of the suspect. Last week Ms. Byrne's security cameras at her estate captured her stalker on film as he tried to gain entry to her property. Los Angeles police are asking your help in locating this man. He is described as about five-foot-eleven, one hundred eighty pounds, with well-groomed sandy blond hair, and has a scar running down the left side of his face. Police warn you that the suspect is believed to be armed and dangerous."

Jaeger's picture finally disappeared from the screen, replaced by footage of a distraught Lanie Byrne. With tears running down her face, she spoke to the camera.

"I'm terrified," she said. "The man looked and sounded absolutely normal, and then he tried to kill me. I want him caught, and I am offering a one-hundred-thousand-dollar reward for information that will lead to his capture."

The fucking paparazzo had done this, Jaeger thought.

He felt a body tensing next to him. Jaeger turned and looked at Angelica. She froze even more under his glance. As bad as the picture was, it was easy to see the resemblance when you were lying down next to the suspect.

"Just my luck," Jaeger said. "Because of my scar, everyone in Los Angeles is probably going to think I'm that crazy person."

Angelica appeared to relax a little.

"He does look a tiny bit like you," she said.

Because the story involved Lanie Byrne, Jaeger knew his face was going to be plastered everywhere. Bad picture or not, it was a face people were going to be looking for. There was a bounty on him.

"If you really think so," Jaeger said, "then you're probably not alone. Maybe I should go visit the constabulary tomorrow and have them write something exonerating me."

Angelica let out some pent-up air. For several moments she had been very frightened, but, of course, it had just been a case of mistaken identity. She should have known.

"You really did think I was that man, didn't you?" asked Jaeger.

"Maybe a little," she said, giggling.

Jaeger shook his head in mock disbelief.

"Kiss and make up?" she asked.

"That sounds like a capital suggestion."

Jaeger knew that Angelica was a woman who closed her eyes when she kissed. He leaned toward her. As expected, her lids dropped and her lips slightly opened.

She died waiting for a kiss.

Thirty-nine

Graham had never thought he would willingly return to Paris. The night before, after talking with his father, he had reconsidered.

There was a reason the gendarmes had never tied him to the Citroën. Graham always assumed the Thierrys had reported their missing car as stolen, and that somehow the concierge must have lost the paperwork that showed him signing for the keys to their apartment. That was the only explanation, he was sure, to his not being linked with the car. It was easy to tell himself that his falling through the cracks was his one stroke of good fortune, and that he shouldn't dwell on it lest he jinx himself. But he had finally looked back, this time without a blind eye, and realized he wasn't the only one who might be impacted by the disappearance of the Citroën. There was only one explanation for the Paris police not investigating the Thierrys' missing Citroën: they had never reported the car as being stolen.

He needed to somehow confirm that, and had thought to call his father. A few months before his father had stayed with the Thierrys in Paris. After waking him up in London, Graham had steered the conversation to his father's Paris visit, and after having to patiently endure hearing details of the trip he finally managed to ask whether the Thierrys still had their loaner car.

"Odile would never get rid of her old Citroën," said the senior Wells. "She calls it her baby."

Of course she wouldn't get rid of it. The replacement Citroën's paperwork might turn up some discrepancies. His father had kept talking, but Graham stopped listening. He knew he had to return to Paris.

As Graham slipped out of Lanie's arms into an LAX terminal, he said, "We'll always have Paris." Bogey's farewell to Bergman in *Casablanca*.

Now, many hours later, he disembarked from the Métro's Line 8 at Place de l'École Militaire. Taking the subway had been one of his many precautions. He had switched lines, had gotten on and off several times to see if he was being followed. Of course it also allowed him to avoid seeing the roads he had traveled on August 28, 1998.

So many years ago, his rational mind told him.

Yesterday, his other senses said.

In his nightmares, Graham had returned to Paris many times. Now he had to confront the past. Graham had never willingly dwelt on what had happened, but after unburdening himself to Lanie he realized he could no longer avoid the past. His answers were still waiting for him.

Graham studied a map for a moment, more for something to do than out of directional need. He knew the lay of the land. That was one of the things he had always loved about Paris. The city was accessible, less than forty-one square miles. The Seine traveled through ten of its twenty arrondissements, or districts. It was almost impossible to get lost.

The Métro station was crowded with people. It was morning, and Paris was coming alive. Graham was still trying to awaken from his jet lag. There was a nine-hour time difference between L.A. and Paris. He hadn't slept on the long flight, had spent the time thinking of the questions he needed to ask. They were questions he should have thought about years before, but he'd been too busy running from the accident.

His destination was the middle of the seventh arrondissement, less than a ten minute walk from the Métro. The apartment was close to the American University, in a central location between the École Militaire and the Eiffel Tower. Around him was the kind of history that gave Parisians the right to have airs, old buildings lovingly renovated, a past embraced by the present. There was tradition on every corner. Paris was a symphony, L.A. was Muzak. Still, Graham wished he were back in his City of Angels. He could lip-sync a top forty song; he didn't know if he could fake classical.

Graham walked quickly. The neighborhood where they lived should have given him pause for thought on his last visit. It was an upscale setting, an avenue of trees and quiet wealth. Their first-floor apartment had five rooms and was extremely large by Paris standards. Their building even afforded them the luxury of having two car spaces in a garage, something few Parisians had. No one, except perhaps an American, would ever ask where they had gotten the money to afford such a place. That wasn't an acceptable inquiry. Most people probably assumed the couple had come into an inheritance. A civil servant wouldn't have been able to afford such an apartment otherwise.

Just as Aldrich Ames should never have been able to afford his upscale house on his CIA salary. But no one at the Agency ever questioned his home or his fancy car.

Graham approached the Thierrys' art-deco building. It was seven stories high, with a decorated facade trellised by gardens and greenery. The structure had old world looks and new world conveniences, with its own concierge, elevator, and security code.

He hadn't called ahead, hadn't warned the Thierrys of his imminent arrival. Graham wanted to come at them unannounced. His father would have been aghast. A diplomat's son should have known better. You don't just drop in on people, especially in France.

Graham bypassed the concierge. He pressed the buzzer to their apartment and waited. The seconds passed, and he began to think they weren't home. He had come all this way, and now it was possible they were out of town.

The box suddenly came alive: "*Oui?*"

"Madame Thierry?"

"*Oui*."

He knew her English was better than his French, but Graham persevered, apologizing for his intrusion.

"*Je suis désolé de ne pas telephoner en avance. Mon pere m'a dit de vous voir.*"

Graham hoped, was betting in fact, that their good manners would make it impossible to refuse him entry. He wanted that element of surprise. There was no immediate reply. Graham wondered if his French had deteriorated to the point of not being understood. But in asking to see them, he had forgotten to offer the basic information.

"*Qui c'est?*" Who is this?

"Oh, I'm sorry. It's Graham. Graham Wells."

In the background, he heard a quick conversation between the Thierrys. The unsaid conversation was that he was an American, which to the French meant you had to take that into allowance, like anyone else would a slow child. Only an American cretin would show up in just such a manner.

"Come in!" she said. "Come in!" He was buzzed inside.

Graham walked down the tiled hallway. The spacious interior showcased marble arches and fixtures and ornate moldings. In Paris, room meant money.

A door opened. The diplomatic training of the Thierrys showed itself. Pierre and Odile were doing their best to smile even as they were touching at their hair and pulling at their clothes.

Pierre was in his mid-seventies, Odile five years younger. Both were still handsome, had somehow survived close to half a century of receptions and official dinners and parties without being bloated by drink and food. Graham kissed Odile on each cheek, and grasped Pierre's extended hand. They had known him as a boy, and then years later as a young man. His father and the Thierrys had ended up being posted to two of the same countries at overlapping times.

Graham was shown to their dining room where an antique table rested on an oversized oriental rug. Ornate Lalique lamps decorated the corner. The room was well lit without the lamps, light coming through the French windows. Outside, there was a balcony and a small table.

The Thierrys tried to interest Graham in café and a baguette, but he declined. It would be better, he thought, if no one got too comfortable.

"You were out of town the last time I was in Paris," Graham said. "That was the latter part of August in 1998."

"We always go to the country in August," said Odile.

"Paris is a foreign country in August," said Pierre.

They both laughed. Graham didn't.

"The concierge gave me the keys to your apartment. In addition to offering your accommodations, you told my father that I could borrow your Citroën. But when I went to the garage, I found that it was missing."

Even now, Graham couldn't tell the truth. He wasn't alone. The couple didn't look at each other. Their expressions remained frozen in a smile.

"Information has reached me that your Citroën was in a car accident," Graham said.

Pierre was shaking his head. Odile copied his lead. "You are mistaken."

Graham said, "I am not mistaken."

To be a diplomat, you have to be a wonderful liar. Pierre did his profession proud. "Then how is it that we still have our Citroën?" he asked.

"They provided you with a duplicate. I am sure they picked up the car in Italy or Spain. They would have made sure of getting an exact match of your old car."

Pierre raised his hands, blew out through his lips in a manner unique to the French and to horses.

"They? Who is this *they*? I do not know what you are talking about."

"The CIA," said Graham. "Your other employer."

Pierre shook his head. "What are you saying?"

"I'm saying that you were a CIA informant. The Cold War must have been very good to you. If I remember, you had some very unique postings. You would have been privy to information the CIA wanted. I imagine they kept you on their payroll for many years."

Graham looked around their apartment. "It looks like the double income came in very handy."

"Why do you think—"

Graham interrupted. "Your Citroën was involved in the accident that took the lives of Georges LeMoine and Lady Godwin."

If Graham had not been watching the Thierrys so closely, if he hadn't been so absolutely attuned to their every facial expression, their every utterance and sound, he would not have heard the noise that came from the hallway off the dining room.

The sound was muffled. It was its suppression that Graham noticed more than the noise itself. At any other time, he would have assumed it was just another creak from an old building.

There was a back door, Graham remembered, just off the kitchen. The delivery door. Someone could have entered through there.

He had no time to think. Instinct made him react. In an instant, he made his decision. The Thierrys didn't look as if they were expecting another visitor. While talking with them they had kept their eyes on him, never looking beyond him as if they were expecting someone else. Graham silently rose to his feet, then gestured out in the direction of the hallway. That only drew puzzled looks from the Thierrys.

"You came back from your vacation," Graham said, "and found your Citroën missing."

He moved without sound across the room. Thank God for the cushioned oriental carpeting. Their eyes followed him. Graham motioned for them to keep talking, and to direct their stares into the far corner. Anyone entering from the hallway wouldn't be able to see to that spot without turning the corner into the room.

The Thierrys continued to look at him. Graham was adept at charades and could always make himself understood through gesture. When words failed him in other countries, he resorted to hand language. So when the Thierrys didn't immediately respond, Graham knew he had guessed wrong. They were in on it.

Odile Thierry opened her mouth. He knew she was going to yell a warning to the visitor. But then she turned away from Graham, directing her gaze to the imaginary guest in the corner, and spoke.

"We don't understand what you're saying, Graham. The car you speak of is garaged right in this building. We have no idea of what you claim."

Odile gave her husband a quick, sharp look, then turned her head back to the empty corner and smiled. Pierre, looking somewhat mystified, still decided to follow her lead.

"Believe me," said Pierre, "that we know nothing of what you say. We returned from the country and our Citroën was garaged as always."

The gun preceded the assailant. He came into the room firing, and got two shots off into the corner. An antique vase shattered and Odile screamed. The silenced pistol only made a little coughing noise. The shooter almost instantly realized his error. He was already turning when Graham attacked from behind, kicking hard at the man's instep and then smashing his knee. The crack of bone was the only sound. As he fell, the assassin twisted, but dropped in such a way as to still have the shot.

The shooter's left shoulder hit the ground hard. He bounced on impact. It didn't stop him from getting off several more rounds, but his aim was thrown off. The glass window behind Graham shattered. But instead of running from the gun, Graham came at it. His foot came at an angle, shattering the gunman's wrist and knocking the gun away.

The assassin dove for the weapon with his good hand. Graham was on it as well. The gun was like a loose football, squirting out of each of their hands. With the prize denied, each turned on the other. Graham had the better position, and two working hands and legs.

It was barely enough to make the playing field even.

The assassin smashed his head into Graham's, and then swung an elbow into his ribs. Half-conscious, Graham's hands seemingly moved on their own accord. His thumbs stabbed at his assailant's eyes. With his good hand, the man pulled at his belt buckle. Graham reacted just before a knife entered his ribs, pressing down with his left arm and the weight of his body.

The man's arm countered the weight. One good arm seemed to be all that he needed. He pushed upward, the blade of his knife inexorably edging toward Graham's flesh. With his free hand, Graham struck at the man's throat. The blow wasn't as powerful as he hoped; fending off the knife diluted the effort. The blade was already pressing into his flesh.

Graham struck at his Adam's apple again, but the blow didn't seem to have any effect. He hit him a third time. The cumulative blows worked.

The assassin dropped his knife, and stopped fighting for anything but tortured breath.

Graham's breathing sounded almost as ragged. He grabbed the knife, noticed its red tip, but didn't pause to assess the growing stain on his shirt. He stretched for the gun, reached it, then turned it on his assailant.

The man's face was bright red. Some air was making its way into his lungs, but only at great effort. He was breathing like a fish out of water. Every gasp made it sound as if he had the croup.

Graham wasn't much better himself. His hands were shaking, and his head felt as if someone had taken a baseball bat to it. The cut on his stomach didn't appear too serious, but the Thierrys looked sickened by his seeping blood. Maybe it was because he was dripping on their prize oriental rug. He made no effort to move. Graham thought of Ran for a moment. He would be dead if it weren't for him. Ran had taught him the basics of *krav maga*, given him the chance to survive. It was one more debt he owed his dead friend.

His gun hand steadied, and so did his breathing. Graham studied the man who had tried to kill him. He had never seen him before. He was wearing a deliveryman's uniform, had probably come in with a bag of groceries.

"I'll need some rope," Graham told the Thierrys.

"Rope?" asked Pierre.

"Or cord, or chains. Something to tie him up. Do it now!"

As Pierre hurried out of the room, Graham gave Odile a quick look.

"Walk out to your balcony, Odile. Some of your neighbors are probably curious about the breaking glass. Give them an explanation."

Graham was left in the room with his assailant. He kept the gun centered on him. As long as the man had breath, he was dangerous. His lungs were still straining for air, but his breathing didn't seem quite as desperate.

Pierre returned with some monofilament fishing line. "This is all I could find—"

"It will do," said Graham. "Use it."

"I don't—"

"Wrap him tightly. Very tightly. We don't want this fish to get away."

"I can't—"

"Now!" said Graham.

Pierre started in. In the background Odile was finishing up her apologies to the curious. Her excuse was something about a heavy lamp that had fallen while it was being moved.

"Tighter," Graham instructed Pierre, as the line went around the man's wrist.

"It will stop the blood from circulating."

With his left hand Graham touched his bloody shirt. "My blood will do enough circulating for the two of us." The gun never moved from his right hand.

When Pierre started wrapping up his ankles, Graham spoke again: "Tighter."

"But I think his leg is broken," Pierre said.

"After he finished killing me, he was going to kill you and your wife. Given any opportunity, he will still do that."

Pierre worked the line with renewed vigor. As he finished up, Odile returned to the dining room. Their prisoner was breathing more regularly now. His face had gone from being bright red to ghost white. The pain from his injuries showed itself on his face.

"Now," said Graham, "I think it's time the four of us had a little chat." He turned to the prisoner. "What's your name?"

The man shook his head. Graham leaned over, and grabbed his injured wrist. The man turned even whiter, if possible, and gasped in pain.

"We will not condone torture!" Pierre shouted.

"If your ethics were so stringent," Graham said, "he wouldn't have been sent here to kill us." He asked his question again. "What's your name?"

"Bernd."

The man had a slight accent.

"Where are you from?"

"Germany."

"Who do you work for?"

"Myself."

"Who hired you?"

"I don't know."

Graham stood up, lifted his foot to kick the man's bad knee.

"That won't help," said Bernd. "I don't know."

Graham kept his foot raised for several moments, then reluctantly lowered it. "What were you hired to do?"

"Watch for you."

"And how did you do that?"

"Electronically. This apartment's bugged."

"How did you get over here so quickly?"

"I have an apartment in the building next door."

"How long has your surveillance been going on?"

"A few days."

"How many others are you working with?"

"I work alone."

"You work twenty-four hours a day without a break?"

The man shrugged. "They sleep, I sleep. He didn't want anyone else on the job. He didn't even think you would show up here."

"He?"

"The man who hired me."

"What's his name?"

"I told you, I don't know."

"How very strange to be working a job for someone you don't know."

"In my work, that's not strange at all."

"So you were hired to kill me, and then kill the Thierrys?"

Bernd didn't answer, just gave Graham a defiant look.

"Call the police," Graham said to Pierre. "I'm willing to bet some agency somewhere will have a line on our Bernd here."

Bernd eyed both Graham and Pierre and shook his head. "You don't want to do that."

"Why not?"

"I will admit to breaking in here, but nothing else."

"I get the feeling the gendarmes will want to talk to you about more than this break-in, Bernd."

He shrugged. "That will still not benefit you."

"Are you wanted for another murder or two, Bernd?"

"The only thing you should care about is that I can help you. I think you need help."

"How can you help me?"

"I know things."

"And what do you want for telling me those things?"

"Freedom."

Graham laughed.

"Is it so funny?" asked Bernd. "I don't think any of you want me talking to the authorities any more than I want you talking to them."

No one said anything. Everyone seemed to be taking the measure of the other's eyes. Bernd was the only one who smiled.

"You see, in this room there is plenty of guilt to go around."

"You are nothing but a hired killer, Bernd. You said so yourself. And if you don't know who hired me, you can't be of much help."

"But I know things about the man who hired me. I met him only the one time, and that was a few years ago, but in my former profession I was taught to be very attentive and not miss a thing. I am quite good at my work, and I have not forgotten my meeting with Herr Narbe."

Narbe. The German word for "scar." Graham tried to keep a poker face, but Bernd saw through it. The S.O.B. was observant.

"Oh, you know Herr Narbe," he said.

Forty

Jaeger studied the picture on his portable computer's monitor. Pilgrim's eyes were closed, and his face was pale. About time, Jaeger thought. The paparazzo had proved surprisingly adept at staying alive, but his luck had finally run out. There was something apropos about his dying in Paris. Years ago he had gotten a reprieve from the car accident, but the crash had finally caught up with him. Still, Jaeger had to admire his persistence. Even with his death sentence hanging over him, Pilgrim never gave up trying to put together all the pieces in the puzzle.

He died a few pieces short.

Jaeger severed his connection and turned off the computer. The site would self-destruct behind him. It was designed so it would leave no "ghost," no electronic image that could be lifted afterward.

Would that he could get rid of all images so easily. It was galling that the paparazzo had gotten that picture of him, though he considered the circulation of his blurry photo to be more of an irritant than a problem. Jaeger blamed himself. He should have gone out better disguised. The paparazzo duped Monroe in their last telephone conversation, acting as if he was ready to negotiate. Monroe told Jaeger he was a meek lamb ready to be led to slaughter. That same lamb had attempted to fleece them.

After the fact, it was easy for Jaeger to figure out where and how he had been photographed. He had gathered up the infrared camera setup at the paparazzo's apartment complex and been impressed by the system and its quality. You no longer had to be connected to get top drawer surveillance equipment.

His scar would now have to go, of course. He should have removed it years before, but vanity kept it on his face. In his profession, there was no place for vanity. The scar was a physical reminder of his first kill. Jaeger remembered the death of Saxe like other people remembered their first love, but even without the scar, he would still have the memory. At the first opportunity, he would visit a plastic surgeon. It was a shame he couldn't do it in Los Angeles, the cosmetic surgery capital of the world. Along with losing the scar, he would have a full makeover. That was overdue as well. He had been killing for long enough that it was time for a change of face. He was used to altering his appearance anyway, though not permanently. Jaeger usually went out into the field disguised, just as he was now.

But even without a plastic surgeon it was no problem making his scar vanish. He never went anywhere without carrying his "disappearing act"—a cover-up cosmetic that made his scar disappear. There were lifts in his shoes. He now stood almost three inches taller than the man who arrived in Los Angeles. To the untrained eyes, he was also packing about forty extra pounds. Padding under his clothes fleshed out his body. He packed his gums with shipping material and denture adhesive to give him jowls. The result made him look and sound something like Brando's Don Corleone. He also thinned his hair, giving himself the look of male pattern baldness by pulling out thousands of hairs. The self-applied tonsure made him look something like a cross between a monk and a Rogaine poster child. He darkened his remaining hair and added to his face a thick black mustache that seemed to compensate for the lack of follicles on his head.

He looked nothing like the bounty poster that was supposed to represent Lanie Byrne's stalker.

But now he could go out and be that very person.

By phone, John Hunter checked out of the airport Hilton. He never went anywhere without multiple sets of identification. It was Dan Turner that checked into the Westin Bonaventure.

Jaeger hadn't left his room at the Bonaventure since his arrival. His time was spent researching Lanie Byrne. The Brothers had helped in that search, though from a distance, getting their hands on every article ever written on Lanie Byrne and scanning it into a file that Jaeger downloaded. The German was sure that by finding Lanie, he would find the paparazzo. Pilgrim's death had been a very pleasant surprise. He supposed the actress hadn't accompanied him to Paris because her face was too recognizable. She was in seclusion now, but not at the Grove. Lanie wouldn't know her knight was dead. Bernd had cleaned up so that no one would learn about the deaths for at least a few days. That meant Lanie was waiting for a dead man to return to her.

But where was she waiting?

Jaeger methodically searched for that answer. Reading the countless articles made him realize how much time America spent kneeling at the altar of stardom. By dying young and leaving a beautiful corpse, Lanie would get that much more written about her.

For all the articles though, there was very little of substance. Lanie was no Greta Garbo, no recluse, but she had managed to maintain some semblance of a personal life. She gave freely of her image, being one of the most photographed people in the world, but not of herself.

Still, among all the articles, Jaeger gleaned some things that interested him. In one interview, Lanie confessed that several times a year she became a "runaway." Lanie said she escaped "to her place in the mountains." The spot wasn't identified, save that it was "a few hours drive outside of L.A."

In another interview she discussed the "pressure cooker" that was Hollywood. "You know how Superman always gets away to that Fortress of Solitude of his?" she said. "I sort of have the same thing. There are times when I need to be by myself and commune only with nature. When I am ready to jump out of my skin, I know it's time for a vacation, time to recharge my batteries and return to Eden, to Shangri-la."

Mountains, not too far from L.A., and Shangri-la.

It was nice of Lanie to provide Jaeger with the next best thing to a road map.

Forty-one

Graham looked down to the city below. His Lufthansa flight was on a holding pattern over Berlin's Tegel Airport. The city looked gray and uninviting, but maybe his own doubts were coloring the picture. Berlin was shrouded in a yellow-gray smog. Graham reminded himself that few cities looked good from the air, but he couldn't shake his foreboding.

As his plane began its final approach, the cloud cover cleared some and Graham got a better look at the extended urban landscape. He wondered if there was any chance of finding what he was looking for. He was going on the word of a hired assassin. Bernd said West Berlin was where Schmiss was born and raised. That's what both of them were calling him now: Schmiss. It was the name of a particular kind of scar. All Graham had to do was look for the needle in a haystack.

Or something just as pointed, if not more visible: a sword.

"Tell me about Schmiss."

"You ask a lot of questions for a dead man," Bernd said with a laugh.

Odile's pain pills had kicked in and were making Bernd talkative.

"The news of my death was greatly exaggerated," Graham said.

"Let's hope Schmiss doesn't think so," said Bernd.

Odile had lightly powdered Graham's face; his eyes were closed, his face slack. In less than a minute the picture came to life, but Graham's image didn't. He was supposed to be dead. They had scanned the picture, then downloaded the file by modem. Bernd had said that would be message enough. If Schmiss believed he was dead, that might give Graham the time he needed.

It helped that Pierre Thierry had spent most of his life negotiating minefields and was used to dealing with factions that totally distrusted the other. It also helped that his own ass was on the line, and that he had a vested interest in all of them coming to some accord.

In the end, an agreement was ironed out. It was probably fair, because no one was completely satisfied with it. Bernd would tell what he knew, but only if the police were kept out of it. He readily admitted to being a former Stasi agent, an East German intelligence officer. German unification had ended his livelihood.

"For someone like me," said Bernd, "work is hard to find. Nothing about this job was personal. When I was offered the assignment, I took it. But it was never more than a job."

"Just following orders, is that it, Bernd?" asked Graham.

"Are there any saints in this room?" asked Bernd.

He knew damn well—everyone knew—there were not. None of them would be there if that was so.

Herr Hartmann was an official in the Immatrikulationsburo of the Freie Universität in Berlin-Dahlem. He stayed seated as Graham approached him at his desk and gave him his biggest smile. A Texas twang suddenly emerged in Graham's best aw-shucks good old boy routine.

"Herr Hartmann?"

The man, immaculate in a dark blue suit, nodded. He was a balding, middle-aged man with pursed, thin lips.

"Do you speak English?"

Another nod.

"Say," Graham said, "I was told that you're the man who might be able to help me. You see, I'm in town on business and my wife asked me if I could swing out here. See, she's big into genealogy and she's trying to track down all of her relatives in Germany for this big family reunion we're going to have. Now, Rebecca has a second cousin who went to school in Berlin, and she wanted to see if I could get his address."

Herr Hartmann considered what Graham had said. His face gave away nothing. As much as Graham was smiling, the man showed no teeth in return.

"Which university?"

There were five universities in the Berlin area with dueling fraternities. Graham took a stab at one of them. "Guestphalia."

"What is his name?" he asked.

"I'm feeling real stupid here," Graham said. "His name just fell out of my head. It's one of those long German names—no offense, of course. I have it back at the hotel."

Herr Hartmann said nothing.

"You know what, though? My wife said he was one of those fencers. No, that's not quite right. One of her relatives said he was a dueler. Guess there's some kind of special swordplay that goes on at that university, is that right?"

Herr Hartmann gave him a slight nod.

"So all I'd need is an album, or a yearbook, or some records of when that boy was *auf dem Haus*. He went there about fifteen years ago, give or take a few years."

"We have no yearbooks," the man said, emphatically shaking his head as if the very idea was reprehensible. "And without a name, I cannot access any records. And even with his name, I am afraid those records are closed."

Before his very eyes, Graham could sense the Berlin Wall arising anew.

"I've come a long way," Graham said.

Hartmann looked at him impassively, even coldly.

"There's nothing anywhere with pictures?" Graham asked. "I met him a few years ago. I'd recognize his face in a picture."

Graham was all but holding a cup out and asking for alms. Hartmann breathed heavily through his nostrils, as if sniffing out the request.

"At most of the corps houses," Hartmann finally said, "there are some photographs."

Herr Hartmann flared his nostrils, seemed to smell out the situation one more time, then lifted his hand to the phone. "Let me see if someone over there can help you."

The woman didn't speak English. For Graham, that was a blessing. He'd used up his allotment of smiles while trying to tell his cover story. Over the phone, Herr Hartmann did the explaining to Frau Mueller. Apparently she was a sort of house mother to the Corps Guestphalia.

She led Graham into the banquet hall and pointed to a wall. There, row upon row, were the pictures. Hundreds of them. Graham thanked the woman, and walked up to get a closer look.

Hanging in small frames were face shots of the current members of the corps. The past was not documented nearly as well, though there was no shortage of alumni pictures and reunion shots. There were also black and white group photos from years past. Those interested Graham the most. Some of the pictures had names, and some didn't. The gaps in documentation meant Graham was in need of luck, and lots of it. He was supposed to extrapolate a face from the past, and find a match with the Schmiss he knew. And his starting point had been determined by a Stasi agent who had tried to kill him. His chain of investigation was made up of one questionable link after another.

Graham had no other option but to study the pictures.

"Schmiss is a Berliner," Bernd had told him. "Born and raised in West Berlin."

"How do you know that?"

"My work," said Bernd, tapping his head. "Schmiss is very good at hiding his accent. He speaks Hochdeutsch, upper crust German without the accent, but that time I met with him his Berliner came out."

"How can you be so sure?"

"Instead of pronouncing 'what' as 'was,' Berliners pronounce it as 'vut.' "

"That's all?"

"There were a few other things. Most Germans pronounce 'that' as 'das,' 'da,' or 'dies.' Berliners say 'det,' 'dit,' or 'ditte.' "

"How do you know he's from West Berlin?"

"On the western side the 'ich' is more emphatic. They pronounce it as 'ick' or 'icke.' If he was from East Berlin, it would sound like 'iche.' "

"I'll accept that he's a West Berliner," Graham said. "He and a million other men. What else?"

"His scar is interesting, isn't it?"

"You tell me."

Bernd adjusted himself a little and grimaced. He was sitting in a high-back chair. His bad leg was elevated. After coming to their agreement, Bernd had been untied. He also demanded the return of his gun, but that was one condition that wasn't met. Graham was doing his interrogating across the table from him, the gun at his side.

"I have seen its like before, but not so often on the face. It is more common to see that kind of scar above the hairline. That usually means the man has to be balding before such a scar can even be noticed."

Bernd seemed to find that funny. He laughed to himself.

“On rare occasion, though, I have noticed similar horizontal cuts. They’re almost always on the left cheekbone. And the recipient is invariably a West German or Austrian male.”

“So what the hell does all that mean?”

“It means you’re looking for a Turn-und Rasierverein.”

Graham tried to translate the words. “Gym and barber association?” he asked.

Bernd shook his head in amusement. He was smiling as he passed his index finger in a cutting motion across his throat: “A gymnastics and shaving club.”

“I still don’t understand.”

“A dueling fraternity. Swords.”

“A fencing club?”

Bernd was even more amused. “Not a fencing club. Not even close. Fencing clubs have blunted blades with a protective covering on the end. They swing thin little foils and wear protective masks. The shaving club boys fight for real blood. They win their match by making schnitzel out of their opponent’s cheeks and forehead.”

Graham looked at the Thierrys. Both of them were nodding, apparently familiar with the custom.

“How many of these fraternities are there?” asked Graham.

Bernd shrugged. “Probably, two, three hundred.”

It wasn’t what Graham wanted to hear, and his face showed it.

“It’s not so bad as that,” said Bernd. “Our boy did his dueling in the Black Circle. Schmiss was in the Kosener Corps.”

“That’s the name of his fraternity?”

Bernd shook his head. “There are different dueling associations. The Weinheimer Corps are usually attached to technical universities, while the Landsmannschaften are town or community groups. If you belong to the Deutsche Burschenschaft, you probably enjoy goosestepping and reminiscing about the Third Reich. They hold nationalism in one hand, and the sword in another. The Kosener Corps are the most serious of the duelists. They are associated with a university, and their traditions go back for centuries. They have their dueling colors and sayings, their own little brotherhood really. I’d guess there are about seventy-five universities that have their Kosener Corps.”

“How do you know Schmiss was in the Kosener Corps?”

“The one time I met with him, we each had a beer. Old habits die hard. It is tradition for those in the Kosener Corps to never drink alone. Each of the drinkers

is expected to raise their glass to their companion before drinking and say, 'Prost.' *Then, after drinking, they lift the glass from chin to eye level in a kind of salute before setting it down."*

"And Schmiss did that?"

"He tried not to. Most of his stein was empty before he reverted to his old habit. And he only did it the one time. But I had seen that gesture before and knew where it came from."

Graham nodded with grudging respect. The man who had tried to kill him was observant. He had doubted whether Bernd would be of any help, had figured his negotiations with Pierre were conducted for the sole purpose of escaping incarceration. Instead, he appeared to be assisting him as much as he could. Bernd seemed to read Graham's thoughts.

"We are on the same side now," he said. "I want you to succeed. I want you to kill Schmiss."

"Why is that?"

"Because if you don't kill him, he will hunt us down and kill us."

"I'll do my best to give him your regards," Graham said.

Bernd found that funny. The pain medication must have really been kicking in by that time.

The day was waning, and so were Graham's hopes. His search seemed to be going in slow motion. It didn't help that he wasn't familiar with the city, and drove with one eye on a map and the other on the streets. His German had been getting a workout. There were five Berlin universities with active Kosener Corps, but the number of dueling fraternities had declined over the years. Getting the opportunity to have your face cut open apparently wasn't as popular as it used to be. It was possible Schmiss had been a member of one of those corps that had disbanded. If that was the case, there was little chance that Graham could track him down. He had struck out at Guestphalia and Marchia. Three corps were still on his list: Normannia, Borussia, and Vandalia-Teutonia.

"Third time's a charm," Graham said to himself as he made his way toward the *Kneipe*, the banquet hall, for Corps Normannia. He expected their setup would be much the same as he had encountered at Guestphalia and Marchia, the two fraternities he visited earlier in the day. Both of their display areas had been in their banquet halls. Behind glass were swords, ribbons, trophies, and old photographs, and hanging on the walls were framed pictures. The mottoes and corps colors changed from school to school, but little else was different.

Graham arrived at the Corps Normannia banquet hall without an escort. Now that he knew the corps setup, he decided it would be better to trespass and beg forgiveness rather than chance being denied permission to visit. The *Kneipe* was locked, but one of the doors had an encouraging jiggle. Graham pulled out a credit card, looked around in both directions, and worked on the latch. It took him less than a minute to spring the door open.

The room wasn't overlarge, maybe fifteen hundred square feet. Blue, silver, and black ribbons decorated one wall, the apparent corps colors. The ribbons accented large, bold letters, which read: *Durch Kampf zum Sieg, durch Nacht zum Licht.* Graham came up with the translation: Through battle to victory, through night toward light. It wasn't the kind of thing he heard people in L.A. saying very often.

Graham went to the display area and skipped over the current pictures. He needed to look at the windows to the past. Schmiss didn't strike him as the kind of individual who would be paying alumni dues to the *Alte Herren*. Unfortunately, only dues-paying graduates had individually framed photos. Graham also thought it unlikely that Schmiss would attend the *Stiftungsfest*—the foundation anniversary and reunion gatherings—but he took a close look at all those group shots anyway. The face of Schmiss didn't jump out.

For much of his adult life, Graham's work had forced him to study pictures. He had scanned countless proof sheets and had a trained eye for detail. He could pick out one face among many as few others could. But now he also had to imagine a younger Schmiss, had to remove fifteen years off his features, perhaps even had to find him without his scar.

Graham studied yet another older group picture. The corps brothers looked like any other sporting team, young men posing for the camera. There seemed to be an unwritten rule in all the Kosener Corps that smiling for any picture was verboten. Graham went down the line of faces. He was about to go on to the next picture when one face stopped him.

The young man had left a space between himself and the rest of his brethren. He was posed more casually, wasn't throwing back his shoulders or sticking out his chest. He wasn't smiling, but showed a hint of an arrogant smirk. Though he was off to the side of the picture, he somehow seemed to be center stage. It was probably his eyes. They bored into the camera.

His eyes hadn't changed.

The young man in the picture had a face that was smooth and unlined.

He barely looked old enough to shave. The picture had been taken before his own close shave. His body type hadn't changed much over the years. He had probably put on twenty pounds, all of it muscle.

Graham didn't have any doubts. It was Schmiss.

He even came with a name. According to the picture, Graham was looking at Hans Jaeger.

Forty-two

After the lights were dimmed, and everyone in the airliner settled down around him, Graham made his phone call. The flight was less than half full, and the nearest passenger to Graham was either asleep or had the ability to snore while awake.

He wasn't the only one who was sleeping. Pierre Thierry sounded positively groggy.

"His name is Hans Jaeger," Graham said, speaking softly.

Graham could hear the phone being repositioned. He imagined Pierre was now sitting up straight and a light was being turned on. The Thierrys were staying about an hour outside of Paris at the house of friends who were out of the country. They had taken Bernd with them. In the background Graham could hear Odile whispering to her husband in French. "*Oui, oui,*" Pierre impatiently answered, then rattled off something in French about getting him a pen and paper.

A few moments later, when he apparently had the necessary implements in hand, Pierre cleared his throat and said, "Spell it."

Graham did. Then he said, "The day after tomorrow, in the early morning, I want you to take that name to your friends."

"Friends," said Pierre, making the word sound the opposite of that. "Why the day after tomorrow?"

"Because I need the time."

Graham had spent the night buying dinner and drinks, lots of drinks, with a former corps brother of Jaeger's who lived in Berlin. Jaeger had dropped off the radar right after college, and he hadn't turned up at any of the reunions, but one of his old dueling chums had run into him a few years back. Herr Jaeger had left the old country and gone west. Graham had a line on where he supposedly worked.

"Remember," Graham said, "you don't want a one-on-one. I want you to do your presentation in front of a committee."

Pierre didn't sound happy about that. "Confess to a den of thieves."

His reluctance was obvious. If word of Pierre's activities got out, the French government would likely throw him and his wife in jail. All of them, thought Graham, had that unpleasant reality in common. The French did not tolerate spying, even if it was for a supposedly friendly nation. Graham thought about Lanie, and how she had been compromised. Ideology, not money, had done her in. Agents in the Directorate of Operations were adept at recruiting informants. That was their job. Graham knew the system. To get pictures, he often did much the same thing.

Even though there didn't appear to be any prying ears around him, Graham continued to speak cryptically. "They'll understand the need for sensitivity. It matches their own. It can't be like last time."

Pierre's last contact with the CIA had occurred on August 30, 1998. That was when he and Odile returned from the country and found their Citroën missing and the French police looking for just such a car. Pierre called the man who recruited him thirty years earlier when both of them were young, the same man who had been his contact for many years. Back in the sixties Walter Carey was a junior case officer in the CIA's Directorate of Operations division. His main job was the recruiting of foreigners for the purpose of gathering intelligence. Getting Thierry was his big coup. Over the years, both of the men had risen in their ranks. Carey had promised his old source that he would replace the Citroën in a "hush-hush operation" that would save both Pierre and the Agency from any embarrassment. Everything, Carey said, would be kept between them. He knew just the man who would confidentially "tidy up everything."

Carey asked for pictures of the car, and as many details about it as the Thierrys could provide. Pierre said that Carey inquired about his retirement, and mentioned that he would soon be joining him in "the good life." That never happened. Carey died in a car accident several months later, but not before he made good on his promise. According to Thierry, within five days of his call to Carey an identical Citroën suddenly appeared in his garage. It was a carbon copy of the old one, even down to a few small dents. Only a few small giveaways clued Pierre that it wasn't the same car.

"Tell them to search the waters where I told you," Graham said. "There, they will find your Citroën."

"I will."

"How is our friend?" Graham asked.

"He whines like a baby, eats like a pig, and expects to be pampered like royalty."

The ex-Stasi agent was making the best out of the situation.

"I'll try and call you tomorrow," Graham said.

He cradled the phone back in its slot, then tried to think through all his weariness. It was possible he had just thrown Pierre to the wolves, but he didn't think so. The cover-up didn't feel like a sanctioned CIA op. Iran-Contra proved you could have a rogue operation going on without the Agency's official blessing.

Graham thought it a shame that no matter how tired he was, he could never sleep on an airplane.

A few moments later, he fell asleep.

Forty-three

Though he had gotten little sleep in the past week, Blackwell arrived at work in a good mood. Pilgrim was dead, and Jaeger was tying up the other loose ends. His plan was going to work. Polls showed that Tennesson was a shoo-in. After he was elected, Blackwell would arrange a meeting. He would tell him about certain information that had reached him and how he had taken it upon his own to suppress it. Blackwell wouldn't need to resort to blackmail. Tennesson would want him close by. The vault would be opened to him, information and power for the taking.

Blackwell opened the door to his office, what he referred to as his "rabbit hutch." For as long as Blackwell had worked at the CIA, space at Langley had always been at a premium. At least he wasn't an analyst working out of one of those endless rows of six-foot by six-foot cubicles. The average grave was larger than a CIA work area.

He sat down in his chair and leaned back. At least he had that much room, if only barely. Blackwell even had a window to look out of, but he knew his office was still a long ways from the seventh-floor spacious accommodations of the director.

That had been one of the good things about being out in the field. You had elbow room out there. For his own purposes, the less time he spent in Virginia, the better. Blackwell had started as a case officer in the Directorate of Operations, DO as everyone in the Agency called it. His primary job had been the recruiting and running of foreign agents, work that had taken him around the globe. Learning how to deal with the CIA's stifling bureaucracy had been a long lesson in patience. Jumping through those hoops had killed the initiative of many case officers, but not his. Blackwell had understood the need to learn the rules of the game.

If the CIA was a business, Blackwell thought, it would have had to declare bankruptcy long ago. Because the Agency was cloaked from outsiders, it got away with its many sins of omission. By and large, it was the incompetents who rose to the top, because they buffered the bureaucracy. As a fledgling case officer, Blackwell watched others get promoted because they had recruited more agents. It didn't matter that their agents were incompetent and poorly placed. Higher-ups saw it as a numbers game. The more "scalps" you could show—recruits that were supposedly working and supplying information to you—the better job you were deemed to be doing. By and large, most of the case officers Blackwell worked with didn't know the language, customs, or history of the area they served, and they had no desire to learn. They all but begged to be hoodwinked, and their superiors were no better. It was enough to get him thinking . . .

The system also interfered with getting good finished intelligence from analysts. To get promoted, specialization was a bad thing. You rose up the ladder by moving around. It was unusual for a DO analyst to spend more than a few years in a given country or area.

Time and time again, Blackwell had seen the best and the brightest quit the Agency, beaten by the bureaucracy. Half of his "class" was gone within a decade. The survivors were probably more like Aldrich Ames than they would have cared to admit. Ames was disenchanted with his work for many years before he did anything about it. He was a drunk who was indifferent about his job and suspicious of his fellow agents. Ames was an incompetent senior case officer, but that didn't stop him from being firmly entrenched in the bureaucracy as a mid-level officer.

When he had first started working for the CIA, Blackwell had assumed his skills and Ivy League credentials would soon catapult him into the top ranks. He hungered to be privy to the world's secrets, and dreamed of running one of the CIA's fiefdoms, or even being in charge of the entire game. But he was never accepted into the Club. Oh, higher-ups gave him glimpses of it, but he was like a gardener trimming the shrubbery around the clubhouse. His rise through the ranks was not meteoric, but merely steady. Along the way, one or more of his superiors decided he was a hardworking drone, smart enough to be sure, but not fast-track royalty.

Professional limbo hadn't sat well with Blackwell. Though he had no stomach for office politics, and seemed incapable of glad-handing or brown-nosing, he never lost his burning ambition. He transferred around the Agency, looking for the right opportunity for him. Eventually he settled in the Directorate of Intelligence. It was obvious to Blackwell that his best chances for "personal growth" were with the Counternarcotics Center, especially after it expanded its mission to deal with international organized crime.

Blackwell turned on his computer. It was a shame, really, that he even had to report to Langley, but former Director John Deutch's use of his personal computer had caused a bit of a shakedown of the troops. The director had stored some of the nation's most sensitive secrets on his computer, the same unsecured computer that was used to access pornographic Web sites, as well as send and transmit E-mail. Since then, antennae had been raised to make sure sensitive information remained on the grounds. For Blackwell, that meant his monitoring had to be done at Langley.

Not that he was worried. Even after Ames, there was still virtually no in-house policing. Police forces in all major cities in the country had their version of an Internal Affairs Division, but that was something the CIA had never instituted. Maybe that explained how for nine long years Ames had blatantly passed on information. You would have expected that heads would have rolled, but the bureaucracy covered all asses. No one in the Agency lost their job because of Ames.

Blackwell had a theory about Ames's ability to operate without anybody noticing. The longer you stayed at the Agency, the more invisible you became. Channel the right reports and paperwork, and it was easy to disappear right in front of everyone's eyes.

That's what I am, thought Blackwell. The invisible man. Unseen, but with long fingers.

Blackwell tapped out his identification, then entered a series of passwords that allowed him to access a series of restricted handling files. He was careful in the way he did it. The in-house computers left trails, and though it was unlikely anyone was looking over his neck, Blackwell always made sure he had a logical explanation for everything he did. That was why he waited almost an hour before pulling up Pilgrim's file.

The man had been lucky for too long. They should have had him in their sights the moment he left De Gaulle Airport, but Blackwell had accessed his credit information too late. Pilgrim had bought his ticket at LAX, and while Blackwell had slept, he had flown across the ocean. Not that it had done him any good.

Blackwell looked at his computer screen. As a rule, the CIA doesn't keep tabs on American citizens, but those with suspected drug and mob ties garnered the interest of Counternarcotics. Pilgrim was on his watch list. He wasn't "high tier," wasn't numbered among those who merited constant scrutiny, but he was designated for monitoring.

According to the latest information, no one had reported Pilgrim dead yet. Good. Maybe the ex-Stasi agent had been able to make him vanish without a trace.

Blackwell looked at the screen again. Something was wrong. There had been credit card activity since the time the paparazzo had died. But what he had in front of him didn't tell him enough. He started tapping at the keyboard, his fingers stabbing the keys. It took him two minutes of pounding and probing to get into the right area. Unblinking, he stared hard at the computer screen and tried to decipher what was in front of him. Maybe the East German had decided to use the dead man's credit cards. After all, the first charge was for a flight to Berlin. But the second charge wasn't so easy to explain. Another flight had been booked, this one to New York City.

Blackwell called up for the flight's manifest. The more he learned, the less he liked it. He looked at his watch. The ticket that had been charged on Pilgrim's credit card was for a flight due to arrive at JFK in an hour.

He stared at the screen, and thought hard about what it told him.

Pilgrim was alive.

Blackwell had to assume the worst, that Pilgrim had gone to Berlin, and then New York, for a reason. Jaeger's roots were in Berlin, and Monroe worked in New York City. It was possible Pilgrim knew that. If that was the case, he had reversed field on them. Instead of being on the run, he was tracking them down.

How much did he know?

Blackwell couldn't take any chances.

Forty-four

In a few minutes Graham's flight would be making its approach to New York's JFK airport. He had been lucky so far. Against all odds, he had found the old photo of Hans Jaeger. After that, everything had fallen into place. The president of the fraternity's *Alte Herren*, which was much like an alumni association, had given him the name of Karl Witt, who lived in Berlin. And Witt, over drinks and dinner, had told Graham how he had run into Jaeger in New York City.

Witt had told him much more besides that, none of which made Graham feel any better. Even as a young man, Hans Jaeger had shown how determined he could be. When he set his mind on something, he accomplished the task.

And the luck that had sustained him so far, Graham knew, had a way of quickly changing.

Graham was worried about Lanie. Despite her assurances that no one knew about her getaway, Graham had his doubts. There was always a trail, and Jaeger struck him as a two-legged bloodhound. At first, her going into seclusion had seemed like a good thing. Now it felt wrong. And he couldn't even call Lanie with his worries, at least not yet. There were no phones at her retreat. They had made arrangements to communicate, but those weren't supposed to kick in until tonight.

If Jaeger was after her, Graham needed to throw him off Lanie's trail. For the second time in the flight, Graham unlatched the airline phone. He looked up a number and dialed it. The continent and time zones didn't seem to matter. Graham kept catching people deep in sleep.

"Who the fuck is calling at this hour?"

Estelle Steinberg had a way of getting right to the point. "You need to do something for Lanie," Graham said.

"You," Estelle said. "I knew it was some major league asshole calling. I should have figured it was you."

"You need to hold a press conference today. It can't be too early, though. I want it as late as possible, but not so late that it doesn't generate stories for tonight's news and radio shows on the West Coast."

"Would you like me to part the fucking Red Sea while I'm at it?"

"Any miracle would be greatly appreciated," Graham said. "We need one."

"The miracle is that I'm still listening to you."

The miracle continued for long enough for Graham to explain what needed to be done.

Forty-five

Monroe paced around his office. Hearing from Blackwell did that to him.

He didn't like the news. All this time Blackwell had assured him that he was untouchable. Inviolable. And now he told him there was a possibility that their security had been breached and that he was a potential target. Pilgrim was not only alive, he was in New York City.

Blackwell was downplaying the threat, of course. It wasn't his ass that was on the line. It never was. To Blackwell, this was their "opportunity." All Monroe had to do was be the lure. That wasn't to his liking at all. He wanted to hunker down in his office, not go strolling around Manhattan. But he had to do it Blackwell's way.

It was true the man hadn't led him wrong yet, but Monroe was still uncomfortable. Blackwell knew how to push his buttons, though. Once Pilgrim was dead, he said, they would be making the real money. Not millions, but billions. They would be privy to the insider information that would make them rich, not minor league rich, but robber baron rich. But before their dream could be realized, they needed to take care of the "vexing problem."

Blackwell's euphemism for murder didn't make his part in the scheme any easier for Monroe. He always tried to distance himself from that area of the business. Now he was expected to be the Judas goat. The blood would be on his hands. There would be no getting around that.

He had no choice. Blackwell put his balls in a vise years ago, and had steadily ratcheted up the pressure. The spook had been following the Russian money and traced it to New World Financial. Monroe was desperate at the time. Bad hedge fund investments had turned his portfolios into mincemeat. To stay afloat, he acted on Russian mob overtures to "handle" their money. Subsequent deals with them proved easier. Monroe figured he might as well be hanged for a sheep as a lamb. When Blackwell came calling, he had him dead to rights for laundering drug money, mob money. But instead of shutting him down and having him thrown into prison, Blackwell offered him a proposition. He needed a money man, a front for what he had in mind. Blackwell said he was privy to the kind of information that could make them rich.

Time proved him right. Their enterprises, legitimate and illegitimate, were wildly profitable. With the green rolling in, it was easy for Monroe to turn a blind eye on any qualms he had.

If only Blackwell had kept to the tried and true. Over the last two years his ambition had outweighed his senses. The easy pickings of Russia and Eastern Europe weren't enough for him. He wanted a seat of power beyond what he called "their little pond." Seduced by his vision, and dollar signs, Monroe went along with his scheme.

There never really was a choice, he told himself. Almost thirty years ago Monroe had started as an assistant to a trader. He had all the trader's shit work, done his apprenticing, and learned. When he was given his chance to be a trader, Monroe ran with it. For years he put in hundred-hour work weeks and glad-handed enough to make Dale Carnegie puke. It didn't stop at building up a clientele. Monroe became a fund manager, and then started his own business. New World Financial never took off like Monroe hoped, and when he was threatened with losing it all, with seeing all his sweat and work go forever south, he compromised.

Compromised. Hell, he sold his soul to the devil.

And now the devil was asking for payment in blood.

Forty-six

While in Berlin, Graham only had time to confirm that New World Financial was still an extant New York firm. As he turned the pages of a Manhattan phone directory, he felt like a rider barely holding on to his mount. His only option was to cling tight a little longer. He was living the Chinese saying: "If you ride on the back of a tiger, you can never dismount."

New World Financial's listing showed it was located on the Upper East Side on Lexington Avenue. Graham dialed its number. An automated answering system advised him that if he knew the extension of his party, he could dial it at any time. His other options included talking to an operator, or entering the first three letters of his party's last name.

Graham tapped in J-A-E.

An atonal voice with no discernible accent came on the line. It was hard to tell if it was Jaeger or a computer-generated voice: "This is Hans Jaeger. I am away on business. Please leave a message."

Graham hung up and called New World Financial again. This time he went through the operator, asking to speak to Hans Jaeger.

"I am sorry," the operator said. "Mr. Jaeger is out of town on business."

"Do you have any idea when he will return?"

"I don't have that information," the operator said. "Mr. Jaeger does check in for messages, however. If you would like, I'll connect you to his voice mail."

"Please."

A moment later, Graham heard the start of Jaeger's atonal message. There were a lot of things he would have liked to say to him, but he hung up instead.

The building was a skyscraper sandwiched between other skyscrapers. Its lobby had six elevators, a concierge, and a security guard who used one eyeball to survey the foot traffic, and the other to study several security monitors.

Graham walked past the concierge and guard as if he knew what he was doing, and where he was going. He hit the up button and had time to quickly scan the marquee. New World Financial was located on the fourteenth floor. Graham didn't see any other businesses listed on that floor, so it was apparently not a small operation.

He let a woman in a business suit precede him into the elevator. She pushed nine, and he reached out and pushed fourteen. As his hand came away from the button, he realized that he was really going up to the thirteenth floor. Not having a thirteenth floor accommodated the superstitious, but it accommodated the landlords even more. They charged more rent for the higher floor. That, more than anything else, had eliminated the thirteenth floor from most New York buildings.

The ride up was silent and fast, speedy enough that Graham felt as if his stomach was going down while he was going up. Maybe it was his tension speaking more than the ascent. The woman exited on the ninth floor. Graham continued his ride on the tiger.

When the door opened, Graham was faced with two hallways, both leading to a reception area. The company's veneer was serene; large plants, big paintings, oversized floral arrangements, and expensive furniture. It offered its window to the world much like the front desk of a five-star hotel. Stately gold lettering that announced New World Financial was inlaid into the black marble reception area. The calm exterior belied what was going on behind the scenes. A man with a tie hurried through the hallway door, flinging it open on his way to the back. Graham caught a momentary glimpse behind the facade. Sitting in a long, rectangular room were mostly young, mostly male employees positioned in front of computer screens. They wore hands-free headsets that allowed them to punch in their trades while feverishly talking.

Graham made a slow approach to the reception area, stopping to pick up several of New World's brochures that extolled the virtues of investing with them.

The receptionist, a young Latina wearing a name tag that said Marta, didn't look like she had to handle phones or typing. Marta was there to greet. Most of her face appeared to be made up of large, milk-white teeth. Her smile should have been registered as a weapon. "May I help you?"

"I was hoping to catch Hans in," Graham said. "Hans Jaeger."

Marta didn't need to consult a chart. "Mr. Jaeger is out of town on business."

Thank God, thought Graham. But he said, "He's always out of town on business."

Marta laughed and nodded.

"I wish I had his frequent flyer miles," Graham said. "Where's he this week?"

"I am afraid I don't know."

"And I suppose you don't know when he will be back?"

Marta shook her head. "As you said, Mr. Jaeger is often away."

Graham rolled his eyes and shook his head while stalling. He was fishing around, but he didn't know for what.

"Last time I saw him," Graham said, "he had a very nice tan. You don't get that kind of bronzing by working all the time. I asked him his secret, and he pretended not to understand. So I said, 'Hans, give me copies of those pictures.' And he said, 'What pictures?' And I said, 'Those incriminating pictures of your boss. They must be doozies.' "

Marta was doing her nodding and laughing again, albeit self-consciously. Her eyes shifted momentarily to a wall of photos, the corporate lineup that companies often put on display. Graham supposed it was business's attempt to come off as extended family. In his experience, the more executive the position, the easier it was to picture that same face on a post office wall. He scanned the suits for Jaeger's picture, and found not one, but two familiar faces.

Jaeger was three rows down. But looking out from the top of the pack was a face he wasn't expecting. For a long moment, Graham remembered being on the oil rig. The tranquilizer dart had been unpleasant, but nothing compared to the psychological torture he had been put through. Smith had made him relive the accident, had forced him to swallow the poison of his shame.

Mr. Smith. On the oil rig, he had mentioned the name Adam. Adam Smith as in *Wealth of Nations* fame. Graham kicked himself for not picking up on the clue. There was a different name, of course, below the face shot. Mr. Smith was New World Financial's CEO Jefferson Monroe.

Graham awakened to Marta's talking to him. ". . . a message for him?"

He turned away from the picture. From his anger. "No, that's all right."

"Perhaps someone else could help you?"

Graham was already backing away. "I will catch him another time."

After making another two calls to New World Financial, Graham was reasonably sure Jefferson Monroe was in. He had used different voices when calling for Monroe, and been stonewalled each time by his secretary. In his gut, Graham knew he was up there. It would be just a matter of time before Monroe came down. There were two ways he could exit from the building though, and short of planting himself in the lobby, Graham couldn't cover both spots. He was also faced with the problem of not standing out. At first glance, that didn't seem a likely problem. There was no shortage of pedestrians on Lexington Avenue, and never a time when people weren't milling about on the sidewalks. He could kill some time with vendors, pause over a hot dog or pretzel, but it was possible he would have to wait for hours.

Graham flagged down a cab, got inside, and took a look at the driver's license: Vlatr Rjdskvy. If Pat Sajak had been around, Graham might have tried buying the driver a vowel.

"Pull over to the curb," Graham instructed. "I'm waiting for someone. They might be a while."

"The meter have to run," Vlatr said.

Graham handed him a twenty. "I know."

Over the next hour, several more twenties passed between them. Vlatr didn't seem to mind not driving. He also didn't feel the need to spend the time talking. From behind a newspaper, Graham watched everyone coming and going from the building. His attention didn't lag. He had time to think about Smith/Monroe's nod, and the resulting tranquilizer dart. He remembered him hanging the Paris deaths over his head, and his being forced to gather dirt. He thought about Ran's death, and his own near-death experience.

At a little past one o'clock, Graham began to believe that Monroe had either left for lunch from the other door, or was eating in. Maybe the building even had a private elevator for the big-wigs. Graham considered reentering the building. He could try to sweet-talk Marta. Or maybe from the stairwell he could monitor anyone entering or leaving New World Financial. It was possible he could fake a delivery. Or he could just sit tight a little longer.

Every minute that passed made the waiting that much harder. Time was getting short. He had already set the dominoes in motion and needed to get to Monroe before the afternoon was out. He needed to surprise him. Otherwise, a man like Monroe could pull a John Ramsey and insulate himself with a phalanx of lawyers that would make him all but untouchable.

Graham scanned another group of emerging faces. They walked quickly, immediately finding a place within the rhythm of passing feet. All except one.

Jefferson Monroe paused at the doorway. He took a long breath, adjusted his tie, and seemed to consider which way to go. Instead of flagging a cab, Monroe started to walk. Graham threw Vlatr a tip that made his long wait worthwhile, and jumped out of the car.

Monroe walked up the block and turned West on Fifty-seventh Street. Graham stayed about twenty feet behind him, always leaving at least half a dozen people between them. He didn't want to make his move prematurely. In his pocket he had a Sharpie marker. Pressed up against Monroe's back, it would have to pass for a knife or a gun. The threat of imminent danger stimulated the imagination. Slowly, Graham closed the gap between them.

Jefferson Monroe tried to loosen up. He wanted to look casual, wanted to appear as if he were just strolling to a luncheon destination, but everything felt unnatural. It was easy to smile for the camera, but this was the opposite. He had to pretend the camera wasn't there, pretend an insouciance he didn't feel. Being so exposed wasn't to his liking. His nerves were on edge. It was like knowing a balloon was being overinflated, and having to wait for the resulting explosion. You know the pop is going to happen, but not when.

Blackwell's plan was not to his liking. The way he had set things up, Monroe needed running shoes, for God's sake. It was seven blocks to the restaurant, all the way to 150 West Fifty-seventh. And then afterward, he would have to trek another two and half blocks to Central Park. Apparently, Blackwell wasn't prepared to act until then. Monroe was glad he didn't know the details.

Given his choice, Monroe would have picked another restaurant, but Blackwell loved the Russian Tea Room. He had made his acquaintance with it on the job; the Russian mob often dined there. Monroe imagined how Blackwell had watched the mobsters stuff caviar into their mouths. It had evidently been enough to make him think.

Monroe slowed down a little, remembering that he was supposed to be strolling. The restaurant was still a few blocks off. Monroe wondered what he should do or say if Pilgrim approached him on the way to the restaurant. Or inside it. He inhaled and exhaled. Damn. He was almost hyperventilating.

There were four floors at the Russian Tea Room. Monroe's favorite dining area was the second floor, with its revolving bear aquarium filled with sturgeon, and its colorful glass walls and ceiling. But maybe he should stay out in the open on the first floor. It annoyed him that Blackwell hadn't been more specific. They had communicated through a secure E-mail box, but it had been clear Blackwell was rushed for time. There had been no mention of how long he should stay at the restaurant.

No more than an hour, thought Monroe. Russian food wasn't his favorite. It was too heavy. To him, borscht had the look of congealed blood, and the way his stomach was already flip-flopping, the idea of *kakusa* or *karsky sashlik* was not appealing. First he would order a very large scotch. After downing that, he might be able to stomach a little *blini* with smoked salmon.

Monroe had never liked the idea of being Pilgrim's handler, but Blackwell had insisted he pose as a spook. The acting job had seemed to go well. Playing the Lady Godiva and Le Croc card had put a major pin in the paparazzo's balloon. It was always exhilarating having that kind of a whip hand. He never would have guessed the beaten dog could turn on him, and be trying to track him down. Or at least that's what Blackwell suspected he was doing.

Monroe resisted the urge to turn his head and look around. He pulled a handkerchief from his pocket and wiped down his forehead. After this was done, he and Blackwell would have to talk. Monroe wasn't cut out for spy stuff. And he particularly didn't like being bait.

Never again, he thought. Never again.

As the two men crossed over Fifth Avenue, Pilgrim moved in two steps behind Monroe.

It was a good place for Pilgrim to make his move, thought Blackwell. He had trailed the two men for four blocks. During that time Pilgrim had remained fixated on Monroe, never aware of what was behind him.

Amateur, he thought. He would pay for the mistake.

Blackwell suddenly picked up his pace. He would strike at the same time Pilgrim did.

Closer now, and still closer. Pilgrim was only a step behind Monroe now. He was all but breathing down his neck. Monroe might have sensed his approach, but it was hard to tell. The man had been stiff as a board ever since leaving his building. By trying to appear relaxed, he had come off as the opposite. The man was a terrible actor. They were both lucky that Pilgrim hadn't picked up on that.

The paparazzo was apparently going to come up on Monroe's left and press up against him. He had his hand in his pocket. It looked as if he planned on getting Monroe's cooperation by faking that he had a gun in his jacket.

Blackwell hit the catch on his briefcase that released the safety. At close range, the briefcase rifle was very effective. By pressing the latch shut, he activated a small pump that pressured the trigger into firing. It would take little more than a second, just a heartbeat really, for the entire magazine to empty. Blackwell tucked the briefcase under his arm, sighting on the target. He had practiced with his briefcase rifle enough to be confident in its use. The device was an efficient assassin's tool. It had been designed to muffle the gunfire, capture the gun's escaping gas, and collect all the ejected casings. The only thing Blackwell intended to leave behind was a body.

He tilted his head right and left. No one was looking at him. New Yorkers weren't big on eye contact, and besides, Blackwell appeared to be just another suited businessman.

Just ahead was an alleyway. There, thought Blackwell, was where Pilgrim would make his move. He would force Monroe into the alley, and try to intimidate him to get his answers.

In three seconds, thought Blackwell.

Two.

One.

Pilgrim shoved his hand in Monroe's back. The man put a lie to the theory that white men in Bruno Magli shoes can't jump. Pent-up anticipation gave him good spring. By the time he returned to earth, Blackwell was already in position to shoot. Monroe's hop, skip, jump, and yelp had gathered in all of the eyes around him. That didn't dissuade Pilgrim. He gathered Monroe in by the elbow.

Briefcase firmly braced at his side, Blackwell closed the latch. As the firing began, he swiveled slightly.

The bullets entered their target. Fabric separated and bone shattered. A line of red appeared along the man's upper chest. The bullet entry wounds were spaced no more than an inch apart.

The man didn't fall immediately.

It only took a moment for his blue, pinpoint Oxford shirt to turn red. He looked at his chest in disbelief.

And still he didn't fall.

Pilgrim's hand was on his elbow. Maybe that was keeping Monroe up. Pilgrim looked even more surprised than the dying man he was supporting.

The crowd started screaming. Everyone was staring at the paparazzo and Monroe. Half the people were running away. The other half were frozen, watching in horror.

Pilgrim eased Monroe to the ground. He took his hand away from him. It was covered in blood. "I didn't," he said to the crowd.

No one said anything back.

Pilgrim's mouth opened and then closed. People stared at his bloody hand.

Without warning, he suddenly sprinted away. Several people took off after him, but it was clear to Blackwell that they couldn't match his speed. The paparazzo had run again. He was predictable.

Half a minute later, police sirens were everywhere. From over a hundred yards off, Blackwell took one look back. A huge crowd was already forming around the body.

Blackwell flagged down a cab. He had a flight to catch.

Forty-seven

Graham kept his arms folded. He didn't want his sports coat opening up, or his hand exposed. Hours before he had used the lining of the jacket to clean the blood off his hand. Ever since he had felt like Lady fucking Macbeth. The blood was nowhere in sight, but it still felt as if it were there.

He was out of his league. In Graham's profession they talked like hit men. Among themselves the job was "going after the target," and "getting the shot," and "closing in for the kill." They were hunters tracking prey. They scoped and stalked and got hits. But people didn't die. At least not until Paris. That was where his life had started its descent into hell.

Monroe had been shot down in broad daylight in the middle of crowded Manhattan. His blood had stained Graham's hand red. Any number of people witnessed him pressing his coat pocket into Monroe's back. All of them had stared at him in horror. They were sure they were looking at a murderer.

Instead of explaining, he ran.

He should have stood his ground. There were tests that could prove he didn't fire the gun. It wasn't too late to give himself up. He could tell the police what he knew about Monroe, but that would mean telling them about the oil rig.

And about the tunnel in Paris.

And his role in Ran's death. He wouldn't even be able to protect Lanie. Everything was too interconnected.

It was possible the killer *wanted* him to surrender to the police. If the intelligence community was involved in this, they might be able to put a muzzle on things. Custody might not mean safety. People died in prison all the time. And Jack Rubys had a way of turning up. It was easy being paranoid after seeing someone shot down right next to him.

What Graham couldn't figure out was why he was still alive. Whoever or whatever was behind this had wanted him dead before. They had tried to kill him in L.A., and then Paris. It didn't make any sense letting him walk away in New York.

Graham expected to be shot down as he ran away. He assumed a sniper had gotten Monroe, and that he was the next target. But the bullet never came. He escaped underground, his head in constant scanning motion, and grabbed the first subway. After two stops he got off, and flagged down a cab. His first impulse was to fly out of La Guardia or JFK, but instead he had the driver take him to Port Authority. There, he caught a bus to New Jersey. As far as he could determine, no one had followed him. If the New York police were looking for him, maybe they hadn't extended their search as far as Newark Airport.

But it wasn't the police that worried him the most.

Over the loudspeaker, Graham heard the last call for his flight to L.A.

He waited another thirty seconds, and just as they were closing down the gate he ran up waving his ticket. After boarding the plane, the door was closed directly behind him. Graham took his seat. He had this superstition about flying. Whenever the plane took off, he watched the runway disappear below him. He thought by just watching the takeoff he would be safe.

The plane gathered speed, and lifted off the ground. Graham watched the plane leave the runway, but he didn't feel safe.

Paris, L.A., and then New York, Graham thought. Each time death made him run.

I won't run again, he promised himself. I won't.

Forty-eight

Jaeger drove up Sulphur Mountain Road again. The Brothers had used his information to track her down. The one who didn't look like an overcooked lobster had gone and researched Ventura County records. Lanie had tried to bury her name among the corporations that fronted her investments, but knowing which aliases she regularly hid behind made her attempt at subterfuge all too transparent. She thought she could hide amid all her land, but that was what gave her away. In all those interviews she must have imagined herself so clever, never realizing her cryptic comments would lead him to her.

Shangri-la, she had said. In English, the word has come to mean a utopia. But for residents of Ojai, the word is more personal. Much of the 1937 film *Lost Horizon* was shot in Ojai. Ronald Coleman traipsed around the Upper Ojai Valley's Dennison Grade, and residents of Ojai hadn't forgotten. They still occasionally referred to their community as Shangri-la. In a way, Lanie was betrayed not only by her incautious remark, but by the film industry. She was going to die in Shangri-la.

He wished there was time to better investigate the 250 acres she owned in Upper Ojai off of Sulphur Mountain Road. Her house was hidden from the road. Jaeger guessed it was at least a half mile from the imposing entrance gate. It was a good location to build a castle, a spot hard to reach and potentially easy to defend. An unpaved road wound up the hill, falling out of sight behind a blanket of red-berried toyon, scrub oaks, and laurel sumac.

There was no viable back-door entrance to her property. The mountains prevented that. Given a full day and night, Jaeger could have crossed that terrain and surprised her from behind, but he didn't have the luxury of time.

Jaeger continued driving until he was stopped by a U.S. Forest Services gate and the end of the paved road. He had seen no sign of Lanie, or a security detail, but that didn't mean guards weren't patrolling closer to home. As far as he could determine, there weren't any cameras in and around Lanie's property, but it was still possible the road was being watched. The traffic was infrequent enough for a single car to stand out on the road, but there was another way to travel and be inconspicuous.

In his eight-mile drive along Sulphur Mountain Road, he counted five mountain bikers. Over the course of six miles the incline rose upward several thousand feet. The grade, switchbacks, and scenery apparently made it a popular route for bicyclists.

The Purloined Letter, thought Jaeger. Be obvious, and not be noticed.

He drove back into Ojai, paid cash for a mountain bike and various supplies, then visited two other stores, coming away with several changes of clothing. Two miles from Lanie's house was a pull-out for a hiking path. Jaeger parked there and began his ride. On his upward climb, he spent as much time looking as he did cycling, especially when he drew near her property. Sulphur Mountain Road overlooked the Ojai Valley. Her house, Jaeger figured, probably had a 360-degree view that took in Lake Casitas to the west, the mountains of Los Padres National Forest to the north and east, and Ventura and the distant ocean to the south. Closer to home, it was likely she would be able to see anyone's approach up the road to her house.

Jaeger turned his mountain bike around. The turns were fast, requiring him to turn hard into them. He only braked when absolutely necessary. If it came down to it, Jaeger knew he could outrace a car. It had taken him close to fifteen minutes of hard cycling to get up the pass; in less than three minutes he was back down at the pull-out.

He changed outfits and helmets, and added some tape to his bicycle. Anyone looking would see a different cyclist going back up. Jaeger pushed back up the hill. He was several hundred yards past Lanie's turnoff when he pulled to the side of the road.

Upturning the mountain bike, he set it seat down, then leaned over a wheel. Anyone driving by would assume he had a flat. To complete that picture, Jaeger pulled out a patch kit from his pack and made a show of fumbling around with it. Lanie's house wasn't visible, but his vantage point allowed him a good view of her long driveway.

Darkness wasn't far off. Jaeger would wait until then. His equipment was in the car. He would replace his cycling outfit and sunglasses for black clothing and night-vision binoculars. There was enough shrubbery to afford him more than adequate hiding spots. It wouldn't matter if she had an army of security. He would still find his way in. She had said in interviews her place was a "remote getaway from it all," with no telephones and no distractions. Jaeger knew better than to believe all that he read, but it would be nice if she didn't have a way to communicate with the outside world.

The sun was setting when he saw dust rising in the distance. His spine started vibrating like a tuning fork. His hunter's instinct told him his prey was coming out. That surprised him. He had been all but sure she would stay holed up.

The brush lining the driveway obscured his view, and he waited to catch a glimpse of her. When the car emerged into open space he got the look he wanted. Lanie was out for a solo drive. Jaeger was glad she was alone. That would make things easier.

Jaeger jumped on his bicycle. Though he had a gun in his backpack, he decided not to ambush her at the gate. It would be too easy to spook her, and shooting her outright didn't fit within his plans.

He was already past her gate and sailing down the road. The gate would take half a minute to open, giving Jaeger at least a minute's lead on her. He leaned right, then left, looking for just the right spot. When he came to a tight switchback, he braked hard. Sometimes the old methods were best, he thought. He had taken out her limo in much the same way, and then removed the incriminating evidence. Luck had been with the actress on that day. Her stand-in hadn't been so lucky.

Ancient armies used caltrops. The device was simple, yet effective. It consisted of four spikes. Toss the caltrops down, and three of the four spikes rested on the ground, while the fourth raised its ugly head. Caltrops stopped horses in their tracks and slowed armies. When trucks replaced horses, they fared little better against well-placed caltrops. The four-legged and the four-wheeled both pulled up lame.

Jaeger's caltrops were specially designed. They were dark and nonreflective, with hollow points that would disable even so-called puncture-proof tires in a matter of minutes. Six caltrops in hand, he hunched down and rolled them along the grooves marking where tires were forced to bite hard into the asphalt. The caltrops tumbled end over end, coming to a pointed stop in the bend.

Just like playing jacks, Jaeger thought.

Lanie bounced along in Graham's rental, wishing she had driven her Land Rover to the retreat. She had bought her four-wheel drive out of necessity, not as part of southern California's love affair with vehicles on steroids. When it rained at the retreat, you needed an SUV to get around. Luckily, the skies had remained clear.

The car was shaking so hard it felt as if it were going to fall apart. The earth looked hard-packed, but it was full of holes and ruts. Lanie wished she had brought along a mouth guard for the ride.

She checked her cell phone, and saw it still registered as being out of range. Her retreat's remoteness was a blessing, but it did make any communication difficult. Closer to Ojai she would be able to pick up Graham's call. He had told her he would phone at seven o'clock Pacific time. More than anything, she wanted to hear his voice. She remembered his promise that he would come back to her as soon as he could. All paparazzi are resourceful, she thought. That had never seemed endearing before.

During his all too brief visit to her retreat, she had sensed that Graham had felt the magic of the property. "So this is your Zen garden," he had said.

She could see his amusement. "What's so funny?"

"The Zen gardens I've seen usually have a rock stream, a few bonsai plants, maybe a koi pond, and a serene statue or two. They haven't been the size of Montana."

"There's a lot I've been meaning to contemplate," she said.

They had both laughed. She liked the way Graham spoke his mind without weighing the words. To other people, even those who knew her well, she was Miss L. That was a stumbling block most people could never get over. Lanie believed that was one reason she had ended up seeing the vice president. She and Bret had their celebrity in common, and high-profile people had a way of finding one another. Rock stars married supermodels. Professional athletes married actresses. Going into the relationship, celebrities were mutually aware of the pressures of public life.

Most men were intimidated by Lanie. Not Bret. He might have been only a heartbeat from the most important job in the world, but until the Malibu accident he had told her his heart beat only for her. She had never been comfortable with their relationship, though. Arranging their rendezvous had always taken monumental planning, and once together, it was never easy to relax. And even had he not been in the limelight, Bret was a married man. Though he and his wife's physical relationship was long over, that didn't matter. But she had been in love. Regardless of your station in life, love makes you stupid. They had been peripatetic lovers for over a year before she was approached by the Mossad, or what she had thought was the Mossad. But it wasn't love that seduced her into being a spy. Oh, they never even used that word. They cloaked her duties in all sorts of nice wrapping, and made the pill easier to swallow by calling her a "friend of Israel" and a "patriot to Jewish people everywhere." She never really did anything more than follow her heart, but merely the idea that she was supposed to be currying favor with Bret never felt right to her. She wasn't her uncle, and she should have found a better way to pay homage to his memory. It didn't matter that it wasn't really the Mossad that had approached her. She consented to the work, and that wasn't something she found easy to forgive.

The dirt road, and her physical bouncing, finally came to an end. Lanie stopped the car twenty-five feet from the gate and pressed the remote control. The gate opened slowly.

Lanie reached for the radio. She pushed the scan button, and hit on a country station. Her nerves already felt twanged enough, so she scanned some more. KNX, a news station, came in. Lanie was listening with half an ear when a familiar voice captured her attention. She reached for the volume and turned it up all the way.

Nothing, not even the elements, could mute Estelle. Lanie was listening so intently she never noticed the slight bump of her tires going over something. Two miles down the road Lanie was still considering what Estelle had said. Now, more than ever, she wanted to talk to Graham. She reached for her cell phone again, but was diverted by a *thump-thump-thump* on the right side of her car. Go away, she thought in silent prayer, go away, but the thumping got ever more insistent.

Lanie looked for a good place to pull over. The road was narrow, and there really wasn't a safe area to park. On a straightaway, she pressed over to the right as far as possible, leaving little space between the vehicle and a rock outcropping.

For a long moment she sat, thinking of what to do. It was all but dark now, dammit, and she had no flashlight. The main road was still miles off. She opened the car doors, using the interior illumination to see better. Once outside, the problem immediately showed itself. Shit. She had a flat. Another look, and the problem got worse. Shit, shit. Two flats.

Maybe she would have to pave her dirt road after all.

Lanie considered her options. She had never changed a tire before, but with two flats and only one spare it wasn't a good time to learn. She checked the time. It was quarter past six. Graham would be calling within the hour. She had to do something. If memory served her, she needed to travel at least two more miles to get in cell phone range. It was either that or introduce herself to neighbors she had assiduously avoided for years.

Drive, Lanie decided. She would stop once she was in range of the cell tower. And after talking with Graham, she would call a tow truck.

She started the car and began inching it along. It didn't begin well, and as the rubber shredded the exposed axle began grinding into the asphalt. Though Lanie kept her speed at under five miles an hour, sparks flew, metal shrieked, and the steering wheel acted as if it were possessed. After two minutes of driving, Lanie was screaming as loud as the remains of her wounded tires.

Lanie was slow to register the approach of the headlights coming from the opposite direction, and overreacted when she did. She flashed her brights and hit the horn. The other car slowed, and the driver's window was lowered.

"Got a problem, ma'am?" he asked. His accent was western and friendly.

"Two flat tires," she said.

"I'll come around and take a look."

He drove forward, made a U-turn up the road, and left his brights on as he pulled up behind Lanie's car. Lanie had to shield her eyes, seeing him only in silhouette. He was tall and on the heavy side. The man came around, silently appraised her tires, and shook his head.

"Rims don't look good, ma'am. Could be the axle's bent, too. You shouldn't have been driving on those tires."

"I'm sure you are right, but I am expecting an important call and I'm out of cell phone range. I hate to impose, but I wonder if you could drive me down the road."

"My pleasure, ma'am."

Lanie followed him back to his sedan and settled in the passenger seat. The car was new, and smelled like it. On these roads, she thought, it wouldn't be new for long.

Her Good Samaritan started the car, but waited a moment before putting it in gear. "There's a wasp on your arm," he warned. "Don't move."

His right hand shot out, flicking at the insect.

"Ow!"

"Did it sting you?"

Lanie was rubbing her upper arm. "Yes," she said.

"Sorry about that." The man reached over to the dashboard and raised the yellow jacket's corpse into the air.

"You're not allergic, are you?" he asked.

"I don't think so."

As he started to drive, Lanie rolled her window down. She felt hot and suddenly unbalanced, and hoped the stream of cool air would revive her, but it didn't. Lanie reached for the dashboard to steady herself.

"Are you all right?"

The driver looked concerned. "I'm feeling a little dizzy," Lanie admitted.

"Probably the sting," he said.

Lanie could only remember being stung once in her life, and that was when she was a girl. It hurt enough that she cried, but it hadn't felt anything like this. She wasn't feeling any pain now, but her mind didn't seem to be functioning quite right. The last time she felt like this, Lanie remembered, was when she was trying to kill herself, and Graham ended up rescuing her.

Graham . . .

She reached for her purse, and frantically felt around. Her phone was there. She flipped it open, squinted to see, then wanted to shake it. Still out of range.

"Dammit." It felt like she had walnuts in her mouth, and her curse sounded slurred.

"What?"

She concentrated on saying the word clearly: "Nothing."

Her Good Samaritan was looking over at her. He had on a John Deere baseball cap that covered his head. She should have asked him his name. In a minute, she would. He was clean-shaven, and very tan. His blue eyes stared at her. There was something hypnotic about them. Lanie found herself drifting.

Good, Jaeger thought. She was nodding off. They would never find the needle mark. It was a liquid form of Nembutal. He liked the irony. The actress thought she had been stung by a yellow jacket. In a way she was right. That was the street name for the drug that was going to kill her. He was going to prescribe her a cocktail of Valium and Nembutal with an

Everclear chaser. The actress had already tried to kill herself with pills and booze. This time she would succeed.

A star like Lanie Byrne couldn't die without a huge investigation. They would uncover her previous suicide attempt and conclude she had just finished what she started. There would be no shortage of speculation as to why she killed herself, but all the theories would be wrong.

Lanie was humming to herself. It was an old song with the refrain "It's in his kiss." The tune was catchy, but Lanie didn't believe the words. Lips did lie. There were some men who were great kissers and even better liars. She had known a few of them intimately. Lanie thought the true barometer of the soul was in the eyes.

Her thoughts drifted. Everyone was always going on about her eyes. Any caricature of her featured huge doe eyes and a giraffe's neck.

She liked Graham's eyes. His words and manner might be hard, but his eyes weren't. His eyes were always alert, as if he were measuring up some picture.

Lanie shifted in the seat. She couldn't quite get comfortable. Something was eating at her.

The driver's eyes. She had seen them before. They were the eyes caught by Graham on film. No, that couldn't be. This man was taller and heavier. He had no scar.

She turned her head his way. Lanie knew what could be done with makeup and wardrobe. She tried to focus, tried to strip away the veneer. What she saw made her throat tighten. She was in a car with the killer. The yellow jacket, Lanie remembered. That's when he drugged her, shot her up with something.

She had to get away before it was too late. Fighting unresponsive muscles, moving as imperceptibly as possible, Lanie reached for the door handle. If she could throw herself out of the car, he might not find her in the darkness. Without breathing, trying to will herself to be invisible, Lanie pulled on the handle. It didn't seem to give. She pulled again, then leaned closer to the door. It wouldn't open. She tried again, pushing harder.

"I disabled that door," said Jaeger. "You can huff, and puff, and blow as much as you want. It won't open."

He slowed the car, and turned it around. There was no more need for pretense. He saw that her eyes were glassy, and she was already all but immobilized. He would drive back to her car, fix her flat tires, then go back to her ranch. In the quiet of her retreat she would commit suicide.

Jaeger watched the actress open her mouth. Let her scream, he thought. But she was saying something instead.

Lanie bit her lip. The words were eluding her. But she was an actor. Delivering lines was her business. She focused on her character. If her character didn't make herself heard and understood, she would die.

Motivation, an actor's best friend.

She spoke clearly, loudly, and her enunciation was perfect: "Hans Jaeger."

He turned toward her, not believing what he had heard. Could this woman somehow know his name? "What did you say?"

Second take, Lanie told herself. It didn't matter that she was drugged. She was playing someone sober and needed to hit that mark. It needed to be done in just one take, like one of those special shots they set up for all day.

Her eyes were rolling back into her skull when she said with perfect clarity: "We need to talk, Hans Jaeger."

Cut. Edit. Wrap.

Lanie lost consciousness.

Jaeger braked hard. "How do you know my name?" he asked.

The bitch didn't answer.

"How do you know my name?" Jaeger was screaming the question now.

When she didn't respond, he slapped her face. That didn't help. She was unresponsive. Her words taunted him. Before killing her, he had to know how she knew his name.

Jaeger wanted to slap her awake, but he couldn't chance leaving a bruise. He clenched his hands into fists. Oh, how he wanted to slap that smirk off her face.

Forty-nine

Jaeger considered aborting his plan. It would be easier just to kill the actress, dispose of her body, and make sure it was never found. Doing that would ensure Lanie a spot as this generation's Amelia Earhart. But her disappearance would put the rumor mill into overdrive. Leaving a body was the better way. Besides, before acting rashly, he needed answers. His cover might be blown, but that didn't mean his plan was compromised. He was prepared to abandon his old life, but that didn't mean he had to run.

Lanie would tell him what he needed to know. He fixed the flat tires while she was incapacitated, and then drove around Upper Ojai until she raised her head and started looking around dazedly.

"Ah, Sleeping Beauty awakens," he said.

Lanie took some deep breaths, trying to clear her mind. She took stock of the surrounding landscape, and wondered how much time had passed. Judging by how dark it was, Lanie imagined she had slept for an hour or two.

Graham's call, Lanie remembered. She had missed it. Maybe, she tried to convince herself, that wasn't necessarily a bad thing. Graham could have assumed something was wrong and called the police. Help might be on its way.

Jaeger seemed to sense her hope. He lifted his left hand from the steering wheel, revealing a gun. The comfort with which he held it made the gun seem a natural extension of his hand.

"How many security people," he asked, "do you have stationed around your property?"

"Hundreds," Lanie said.

Jaeger shrugged. She was soft. Hadn't she tried committing suicide at the mere thought of killing the bicyclist? "Your choice," he said. "Anyone I encounter, be it gardener, caretaker, or even passerby, I will be forced to treat as the enemy."

Lanie knew what that meant. She didn't want to chance another innocent dying. Besides, cooperating might buy her the time she needed. "There's no one else at the retreat. I am staying there by myself."

"Where's the paparazzo?"

"Long gone."

More gone than she knew, thought Jaeger, but he didn't tell her that.

"How did you know my name?"

"Everyone knows your name. They've identified you as my stalker."

Jaeger reflected on her news. It still didn't tell him how they knew his name. He wondered if someone had identified him from the grainy photograph taken by the paparazzo. Tying him into the actress complicated things. Even in the case of an apparent suicide, he would be wanted for questioning.

"I don't know how much you are getting paid for doing this," Lanie said, "but if you let me go, I promise I will pay you more."

Jaeger appeared to consider her offer, then said, "Any and all negotiations will have to wait until we're safely inside your house."

He made himself sound agreeable. She wasn't the only one who could act. Hope would keep her docile.

As they drove up Sulphur Mountain Road, the streetlights were few and far between. Jaeger seemed to approve of the shadows. "It's harder and harder to find remote spots like this," he said. "Civilization seems to think it has a duty to provide illumination. It acts like a parent providing a night-light to the child."

Lanie used the opening to ask: "Do you have any children?" Her survival might depend on connecting with him. When he didn't answer, she said, "I've always dreamed of having kids."

Instead of responding, Jaeger flipped off the headlights, and for several seconds it was almost as if they were driving in a huge, dark tunnel. He laughed aloud. "Like one of those rides at Disneyland, yes?"

Jaeger turned the headlights back on and eased up on the gas. They approached the gate, and Jaeger reached for the remote, activating it with the barrel of his gun.

"Why no security cameras?" he asked.

"This is supposed to be a retreat."

Her answer was measured, even chiding. Lanie was doing her best to not show how scared she was. It was important she stay alert, and be mentally ready to act once she got the opportunity. Her hands were tied, but she would offer up some ruse to get him to remove her bonds. If she could just get a moment in the kitchen alone . . .

Lanie studied her captor, watched him lower the window and actually sniff the air. He reminded her of a watchful animal, all of his senses on alert. He stopped the car, listened, moved forward a hundred yards, and braked to listen again. His eyes never stopped scanning the road, constantly looking right and left. Turning a corner, the car lights picked up on two points of reflected light that glowed like embers. Jaeger's gun was immediately on the target. When the dark shape was better revealed, they saw a raccoon staring back at them. Instead of running off, the animal stood its ground.

"Arrogant, isn't he?" said Jaeger. With his gun, he casually sighted on the animal. A head shot, that's how he would take him. One bullet only, of course. That was how he hunted game.

The privacy that Lanie had so desired, the remoteness once so appealing, now seemed oppressive. Her house was more than half a mile from the main road, and her neighbors were even farther away. In the distance she could see the lights from her granite lanterns. She had only recently put a name to her retreat, calling it "Tama," the Japanese word for "jewel." She wondered what the Japanese word for arrogant was.

"How do you power the house?" Jaeger asked.

"Solar panels. And a reserve generator, if necessary."

Jaeger turned the headlights off again, but this time not for fun. He eased the car along, driving it off the road and then cutting off its engine far short of the periphery of the lights. Stone lanterns lined the pathway leading from the house. Jaeger looked at Lanie, and signaled for her to be silent by touching the gun to his lips. For a minute he watched and listened. The breeze kicked up wind chimes and caused a slight ringing.

"What's that?" he whispered.

"Garden bells."

He wanted anything unusual, or out of the ordinary, explained. "What are those wavy things you have running around the house?"

"They're called rain chains."

"Which means what?"

"They're a Japanese alternative to rain gutters."

He raised a pair of night-vision binoculars to his eyes and methodically scrutinized the area around them. Several varieties of bamboo were planted around the enclosure. The landscaping wasn't to his liking.

"Bamboo curtain," he said, shifting in his seat to try to see better.

At last he seemed satisfied with what he saw, or didn't see. "Let's go."

This time the gun prodded her to go left. That was how he communicated directions to her in their circuitous route around the house. Lanie turned, lost her footing on a rock, tried to keep her balance, but couldn't. Without the use of her hands, she couldn't soften the impact of her fall. All she could do was hit the ground. "Shit."

"Silence."

Her shoulder hurt, dammit, and he was telling her to shut up. From the ground, she said, "I told you there's no one here. I'm tired of these army games—"

"Shhh."

His gun pressed into the back of her neck. She inhaled sharply, sucking down the rest of her words. He scratched the back of her neck with the gun, then withdrew it.

"We'll crawl toward that strand of bamboo," he whispered.

The bamboo was about fifty yards off. Crawling without the use of her elbows or arms would be difficult at best. She opened her mouth to protest, but he anticipated that, and poked the back of her head with the gun. Bastard. She wanted to bite his hand. But instead she crawled on the ground, inching forward with her shoulders and knees. The shrubbery and rocky earth dug into her, shredding her blouse. He stayed at her side, using her as a potential shield until they reached the shelter of the bamboo.

Her house was now only a stone's throw away. They had made almost a complete circle from where they had parked, but Jaeger was still cautious. Grabbing Lanie by the elbow, he forced her to run to a window at the side of the house. He took a quick look through the glass, saw nothing, then pulled her along until they reached the entry door. With his body directly behind hers, Jaeger opened the door and pushed her inside. He found a light panel, and extinguished the interior and exterior lights.

Using Lanie as a shield, he did a rapid search of the three bedrooms. No one was waiting inside.

He let Lanie drop down on an oversized floor pillow, but didn't sit himself, choosing instead to go to a corner that was out of sight of the windows.

He sat on his haunches. The room was dark but there was still enough light coming in from the windows to see. He looked around, and seemed amused by what he saw. With a tilt of his head, he pointed toward a brass Foo Dog.

"Nice guard dog."

"He's housebroken. Are you?" Lanie hoped he didn't hear the quaver in her voice.

"What is this, some kind of a geisha house?"

"It's my retreat."

"The floor's all spongy."

"Tatami mats." Lanie kicked off her shoes. "The rule of the house is that you take your shoes off before entering. There are some slippers next to the entry door that might fit you."

"You know what they say about rules being made to be broken."

"And wisdom being lost on fools. The mats are made of woven rice. It's easy to catch a shoe on the edge and slip. You'll have to watch your step."

"I always do."

"My hands hurt," Lanie said. "How about untying them?"

"Soon."

He was busy doing his visual scouting of the house. It was a simple design, and Lanie loved it all the more for its understated elegance. The posts and beams had been joined using no molding or trim, true old world workmanship. *Furoshiki*—wall hangings—adorned the rooms, along with dried flower arrangements. There was little in the way of furniture. Instead of chairs there were *zabuton* pillows with Japanese motifs. In the living room, a hibachi table served the dual purpose of coffee table and tea warmer. There were no cupboards in the kitchen. Instead, there were *tansu* chests that could be stacked as needed. They served as storage containers, counters, and even a stepladder when the need arose.

Lanie never looked at the kitchen or the chests. That's where her gun was, hidden inside a box of green tea. Philosophically, she never liked having a gun in her retreat, but she had reluctantly purchased it for her protection. Better to have it and not need it, she decided, than to need it and not have it. She was afraid to even think about the gun, scared that Jaeger might somehow read her mind. But his interest wasn't on her.

"Are those swords the real thing?" he asked.

They rested on a table in the corner.

"Yes," she said. "They're from the Edo era, about two hundred years old."

He left his corner to get a better look. Lanie had thought the swords weren't in keeping with her retreat, but the designer convinced her to look at them as historical relics and not weapons. "Refined ornamentation," she called them. Lanie had been won over by their elegance.

Jaeger removed one of the swords from the rack. He looked at its *tsuba*—handguard—and admired the design work of dragons. He took off the heavy gold foil *habaki* and hefted the blade, appreciating its fine balance. It wasn't as long as a *Schläger*, but it would do very, very nicely. He cut the air with the sword, enjoying the feel of it in his hands. A true craftsman had created a work of art. Jaeger lightly touched the steel. The blade was still sharp. There were no nicks or chips, no *kizu* or flaws. Still, it was apparent the sword hadn't been removed from its scabbard for some time.

"You should have been tending to the blade," Jaeger said.

Her designer had warned her the swords would need regular care. "I've been meaning to."

Jaeger shook his head in disgust. He carefully returned the sword in place, then took off the wrappings of the second sword. It looked identical to the other.

"Another *katana*," Jaeger said.

"Are you a collector?" Lanie asked.

He attacked the air, doing a *passe avant* and then a Russian lunge.

"No," Jaeger said, the blade stopping just shy of her body. "I'm no collector."

Fifty

Jaeger was holding a glass of water and two pills. He wanted her cooperation. The autopsy would look better if there were no bruises, and no signs of struggle.

"If you want your hands untied," Jaeger said, "you'll have to take these."

"What are they?"

"Sleeping pills. I understand you have more than a passing familiarity with them."

The gun, thought Lanie. She needed to have her hands free to get it.

"One pill," said Lanie.

Jaeger shook his head. "I need some sleep myself. I wouldn't want you waking up in an hour or two and planting one of those swords in me."

Lanie appeared to deliberate before saying: "Okay."

One at a time, Jaeger put the pills on Lanie's tongue and watched her swallow. "Very good," he said, "save for the fact that the pills are still in your mouth."

"I don't know—"

He pressed his thumb into the side of her mouth, grinding clockwise into her flesh. It wasn't enough to leave a bruise, but enough for her to capitulate.

In obvious pain, she said, "All right."

Jaeger looked more satisfied with her second effort. What he hadn't told her was that the pills were far more potent than over-the-counter prescription barbiturates. She had just taken the equivalent of four times the recommended doses of Valium and Nembutal. Soon, he would have her drink a glass of Everclear. That, and some more pills, would do the job.

He removed her hand restraints. She started rubbing her wrists, trying to regain her circulation.

"If you don't mind," Lanie said, starting to rise, "I would like to make myself some tea."

"I'll make it for you."

"I'm rather particular. And the hibachi is quirky."

"I think I can handle it."

There was no compromise in his voice. "On second thought," she said, "tea and the pills might not be the best combination. I'll just get some bottled water in the refrigerator."

"I'll get it for you."

Lanie reluctantly dropped back down to her pillow. When he returned with her water, she asked, "How much will my freedom cost me?"

"We'll discuss that later."

"You said we could talk about it once we got here."

"But you'll soon be asleep. I don't want you nodding off during our negotiations. There is one thing we need to discuss, though. Where were you headed tonight?"

There was almost no hesitation in her answer: "I was going on an ice cream run. I had this craving for mocha almond fudge like you wouldn't believe."

Jaeger knew she was lying. The actress hadn't been disguised, and he knew she had managed to maintain her anonymity in the community. She wouldn't have exposed herself for a mere craving. From what he could determine, she was planning to return to her retreat, which meant something important motivated her going out.

"You were either going to meet someone," he said, "or you left to make, or receive, a telephone call."

"You obviously don't have a thing for ice cream the way I do."

"You scream for ice cream."

Lanie shuddered. She didn't like the way he said it.

Jaeger said, "Had you been making a business call, I assume you would have left earlier in the day. And since you were—what's the word?—incommunicado today, that means your call, or your meeting, was prearranged."

It was almost as if he could read her mind, Lanie thought. And there was one thing she most definitely didn't want him tuning in on. She tried to make her mind a blank.

"The question is," Jaeger said, "would your absence have caused any sort of alarm?"

He stared at her. Lanie met his eyes, or at least appeared to. What she was really doing was staring at his nose. It was an acting trick she used, a way of looking inward instead of outward. The camera, and her fellow actors, never knew that she wasn't staring directly at them.

But somehow he did.

"You're praying for a visitor tonight, aren't you?"

She didn't answer.

"Beware of what you pray for."

Graham's flight from Newark landed at L.A. International Airport just after midnight. It was a good time to beat the traffic in Los Angeles, and he managed to catch the California Highway Patrol napping. By breaking every speed law, by going warp speed on the 101, 33, and 150, he made it to Ojai in just under one hundred minutes.

Lanie had given him an extra controller to the gate, but Graham chose instead to park on the street and trek in. Without a weapon, without a plan, he didn't want to drive into a potential trap.

Graham scaled the gate and started running up the road. There was barely enough light for him to make out the path. That was good, he thought. It would make it difficult for anyone to see him coming.

His breath was ragged. He hadn't realized how high up Lanie's retreat was. Every step was harder than the last. He was exhausted, had lived on a diet of stress and caffeine for too long. His legs grew heavier until he couldn't even pretend he was running. Panting, it was all he could do to just keep going. He wished he had some grand scheme in mind, but he was all out of ideas. Nothing made sense anymore. Getting to Lanie was the only thing he could think about.

When he caught sight of the retreat's lights, he stopped to catch his breath. Everything looked quiet and normal. Graham wiped the sweat from his face. Even though there was a chill in the air, he was hot and his body was drenched with perspiration.

It was possible, he tried to tell himself, that he had just failed to reach her by phone. The airplane phones were always quirky. Or the problem could have been on Lanie's end. But it had felt wrong, just as it had felt wrong when he called up Ran and there was no answer.

Graham moved just off the dirt road, keeping low and close to the brush. He stifled his urge to run to the house. Now, more than ever, he needed to exercise caution. Lanie's bedroom, Graham knew, was in the back of the house. If all was well, she would be sleeping there. Using the bamboo as cover, he moved forward. He froze several times, unnerved by the sounds of the wind chimes coming from her Zen garden, but at last he made it to her window. Afraid of what he might see, Graham cautiously raised his head and looked through the glass. He almost laughed at the sight of Lanie asleep on her futon. A small glow of light highlighted her, making her look like some kind of ethereal being. The camera loved her. And maybe, Graham thought, so do I.

He exhaled all of his pent-up breath, and was still looking at Lanie when he was struck from behind.

The paparazzo had more lives than a cat, thought Jaeger. "Wake up, Pilgrim. Wake up."

Graham felt his nose being tickled. He tried to reach out to scratch it, but he found he couldn't move his hands.

"Wake up."

His nose was being tickled again. Graham opened his eyes and visibly started, his head bouncing on the mat. A sword was pointed not two inches from his face. Jaeger smiled at his reaction.

"Have I made my point?"

Lanie spoke to him over Jaeger's laughter: "Are you all right?"

Graham turned to her. Judging by her pale face and glassy eyes, he could have asked that same question of her. But Lanie was staring at him with an intensity that made him realize she wanted to communicate something.

"My head hurts like hell," Graham said. "How are you?"

"She's all tied up and no place to go," Jaeger said.

"He forced me to take some sleeping pills."

Almost imperceptibly, her head and eyes tilted toward the kitchen, then returned back to Graham. With Jaeger looking at the two of them, it was the only signal she dared give.

"This isn't the time for auld lang syne," said Jaeger.

He used his sword as a pointer, tapping Graham on the side of his nose to get him to look up, but not before Lanie got a last signal in. With Jaeger's attention on Graham, she mouthed the word "gun," and again tilted her head toward the kitchen. Graham understood what she was trying to tell him. Her gun was still there.

Jaeger said, "You've been a busy boy, haven't you, Pilgrim?" He asked the question with the sword pointed at Graham's face.

"What makes you think that?"

"Why don't you tell me about your travels?"

"There's really not much to say."

"Refusing to answer is not an option."

Jaeger moved the sword from Graham's sight, but there was no mystery about where it went. As it pricked his finger, Graham cried out.

"Now that I have your attention," said Jaeger, "I expect your complete cooperation. Each and every failure to comply will result in your losing a finger. Do you understand?"

Graham nodded.

"I thought that you would. Let's start with your telling me about Paris."

"Your man tried to kill me. He didn't succeed."

"And he compounded his failure by helping you fake your death."

"He saw the error of his ways."

"No, but he will. Where did you go from Paris?"

"Berlin. Bernd clued me into your dueling scar. I traveled to several universities. In one of them I found an old picture of yours."

"Clever. And so was your broadcasting my identity as Lanie Byrne's stalker. But as you can see, it didn't dissuade me from continuing my mission."

"If anything happens to Lanie, you'll be the prime suspect."

"Will I? The poor girl already has a history of suicide attempts."

"There's no point in continuing this thing. This is your opportunity to run. It's all over."

"Nothing is over."

"The Thierrys will have contacted the authorities by now."

"And said what?"

"They'll have told them about their missing Citroën."

"Do they have proof of that? All they'll be able to show is that their so-called missing car is magically back with them now."

"They'll tell how I investigated its disappearance, and how I suspected their real car was involved in the Paris car accident that killed Georges LeMoine and Anne Godwin."

"You are a paparazzo. That makes you as credible as a used car salesman. And that's before you've been examined under a microscope. Something tells me you won't fare very well under official scrutiny."

"Pierre and Odile Thierry are witnesses to Bernd's attempt to kill me."

"Further proof that a former Stasi agent and a questionable paparazzo might have had a falling out over some dubious activity."

"Bernd will tell them about you."

"He'll say nothing. Bernd's left his bloody fingerprints too many places. He has probably slipped away already."

"What about you? You've been identified as Lanie Byrne's stalker. You won't be able to just waltz back to New World Financial."

"Why, you have been a busy boy, haven't you?" Jaeger flicked out with the sword.

Both Graham and Lanie cried out. Graham tried to crane his neck to look at his hand. His finger hurt like hell.

"It's all right," said Lanie. "It's only cut."

"You bastard," said Graham, flexing his fingers.

"How did you learn of my employment at New World Financial?"

"I talked with one of your fraternity brothers."

"And what did you do with that information?"

"I flew to New York City and found out that the man who runs New World Financial—Jefferson Monroe—is the same man I knew as Mr. Smith. Or I should say he *was* the same man."

"What do you mean?"

Good, thought Graham. He didn't know. He hoped the news would set them free. "Just as I was about to talk to Monroe, he was gunned down on the streets of New York City."

"How do you know that?"

"Because I was standing next to him when it happened."

Jaeger started pacing around the room. Instead of being demoralized, the news seemed to energize him. "So the Gray Man came out of his bunker."

The Gray Man. It was a term Europeans often used to refer to intelligence agents.

"Who is the Gray Man?" asked Graham.

Jaeger shook his head, offering only a taunting smile.

"He's the one who pulls your strings, isn't he?"

"Ours is a symbiotic relationship. I have always liked that word. Symbiotic. He does his job, and I do mine. We complement one another."

"Your Gray Man is not a very good shot. Instead of hitting me, he shot down his own man."

"No. What he did was leave you for me."

Graham heard his death sentence announced. Their death sentence. Jaeger was going to kill both of them. Their only hope was sitting in a drawer in the kitchen. Graham had to free his hands, and somehow get to the gun. He looked around the room, desperate to see anything that might help. The point of Jaeger's sword was keeping him pinned close to the mat. Jaeger's sword . . .

"I challenge you to a duel," said Graham.

Jaeger laughed. "You jest."

"Why? Your fraternity brother said you were quite the swordsman. As I understand it, you only lost once."

"I never lost. Never."

"But the man who gave you your scar—"

"Was kicked out of the corps *cum infamia.* He struck me well after the end of the round, and by doing so he disgraced himself."

"Your fraternity brother said he was stabbed to death by skinheads."

"Most believe that."

"You killed him, didn't you?"

"We finished our match, yes."

"Match? Is that what you call stabbing someone in the back?"

Graham never saw the sword move. But suddenly it was under his chin, pressing up into his neck. "It happened as I said. He died with a sword in his hand."

"Honor was served," Graham said, his Adam's apple rubbing against the edge of the sword.

"Honor was served."

"I would like the same opportunity."

"What do you know about fencing?"

The sword came away, slightly, from Graham's neck. "My father was a foreign service officer. He served in consular posts abroad. I was educated overseas. Most of the schools had fencing programs. I have some experience with the foil."

"You played with buttons."

A button is the safety tip on the end of the practice sword. What Jaeger said was true enough.

"I know how to handle a sword. I can understand though, if you're afraid."

Jaeger smiled. "Am I supposed to take offense at that? Should I respond to your insult by doing something so rash as to jeopardize my position?"

"You should show me that you're the swordsman they say you are."

"First you insult, then you flatter. What will you appeal to next?"

"Your honor," Graham said. "You have been challenged."

"Sind Sie satisfaktionsfähig?"

Graham worked out a translation: Are you capable, or even entitled, to give satisfaction? "Haven't I proved myself a worthy opponent already?" said Graham.

"Still," Jaeger said, "when all is said and done, you're merely a paparazzo."

"And you're merely a hired killer." Graham repeated the man's challenge back to him: *"Sind Sie satisfaktionsfahig?"*

Jaeger laughed. "When you challenge someone to a duel you're supposed to prove that you're equals. I fear you don't present much of a contest."

"I want to duel, and you want to hide behind some fencing pedigree. So much for history and tradition. I saw all those pictures hanging in the banquet hall at your university, and all those brave words that accompanied them. Your little dueling society even has its own saying, doesn't it?"

Proudly, Jaeger recited: "*Durch Kampf zum Sieg, durch Nach zum Licht.* Through battle to victory, through night toward light."

The light at the end of the tunnel, thought Graham. "Do you accept my challenge?"

"Putting a sword in your hand would be foolish."

Graham felt his stomach drop. Their last hope was being kicked away.

"Foolish," Jaeger added, "for you. I can offer you a much easier death. Dying by the sword will likely be painful, and slow."

"It is the way I choose."

Jaeger's smile was rapturous. "Then your challenge is accepted."

"When are you going to untie me?" Graham asked.

"When the house is secured," Jaeger said.

He moved the hibachi table next to the door, barricading it. No one could easily enter or, more importantly, exit. Lanie and Graham watched him preparing the battlefield. She was already fighting a battle herself, struggling to keep her eyes open.

Graham said, "I am going to need time to stretch, you know."

"We will not start until you say you are ready."

"How about next year?"

Jaeger surveyed the empty living room. The space wasn't overly large, but fencing was always limited to confined areas. He'd learned his early craft on the *piste*, the strip on which fencers fought, an area two meters wide and fourteen meters long. The room was longer than that, and wider. Jaeger would have preferred an even smaller area. In the *Mensur*, you did your fighting a sword's length away from your opponent. You stood your ground with your *Schläger*, three feet from your opponent, with only rotational movements of the arm allowed. With arm and blade you guarded and attacked. Yes, the small space would be just fine.

To be safe, Jaeger decided to secure the other bedrooms. The windows would have to be barricaded. If the paparazzo thought he could run away this time, he was wrong.

When he left the room, Graham and Lanie looked at each other. Her eyes were determined slits. She wasn't going to fall asleep. She was going to be there for him.

"Indiana Jones," Graham whispered. Lanie nodded to show she understood. Movies were their own shorthand. The scene he referred to was the most memorable in that film. A fearsome, screaming swordsman suddenly appeared in front of Indiana Jones, and in a grand display of intimidation, the swordsman showed his deadly skill with the blade, cutting the air in frightening fashion. But instead of quaking in his boots, Jones looked almost disdainful, pulling out his gun and shooting the man.

Graham wanted to do the same thing.

Jaeger reentered the room. He presented the two samurai swords to Graham. "As the one challenged," Jaeger said, "I should have the choice of weapons, but I'll defer to you."

"I'll take them both."

"Choose, or I'll choose for you."

"I'll take the one closest to you."

Jaeger bowed, placing the sword on the tatami mat. Then he used the other sword to cut through Graham's hand restraints.

When Graham's hands were free he didn't pick up the sword. He didn't even want to hold it. Instead he started stretching his wrists, then his arms and shoulders. He pulled one knee up to his chest, lowered it, and did the same thing with the other. Then he moved toward a wall, braced against it, and stretched out his legs and hamstrings. Jaeger watched his every movement.

In his mind's eye, Graham visualized the location of the gun. During his visit Lanie had showed him where the loaded gun was. He visualized it in his mind. Near, very near. Hidden in a green tea container inside the chest. Graham took some deep breaths. They weren't for show. Neither were the exercises. He needed to make the most important sprint of his life. God, he was afraid.

Jaeger was maybe eight steps away. Graham had to travel about that same distance to the kitchen. He would have the element of surprise. If all went right, he would be in the kitchen before the German reacted.

Graham took off his shoes. No sense chancing a slip. He figured he could travel the distance in a little more than a second. Getting the gun in his hand and pointing it should take another second. Graham had to assume that Jaeger was armed. There was a bulge under his shirt that was probably a gun. By the time he got to the kitchen, Jaeger might already be firing at him. It was a good thing Lanie was off to the side. She would likely be safe from the gunfire.

There were so many things that could go wrong. But it was their best chance. Facing the German with a sword would certainly be suicide.

Go, Graham thought. Do it. But his feet remained rooted. He stretched some more. Jaeger's snake eyes stayed on him. Graham looked over to Lanie. She could see how scared he was. Her eyes tried to encourage him.

If he didn't run soon, Graham was sure he would collapse, but invisible bonds seemed to hold him. The first battle he had to fight was with himself. That was nothing new.

Graham looked toward the front door, and got Jaeger to look there as well. Then he made his break, racing to the kitchen. He never looked back, didn't know if he was being pursued or if a gun was being leveled on him. The long second it took him to get to the chest, the eight steps, seemed like an eternity. He skidded by the chest, grabbing it by the handle and in the same motion yanked out the drawer and pulled out the tea box. His heart almost stopped when he saw only the green tea, but then he spied the gun. He grabbed for it, whirled to his side, and found his target.

Jaeger was caught flat-footed. The German hadn't gone for his gun. He was still holding his sword.

"Drop the sword! Raise your hands in the air!"

"Or what?"

"Or I'll shoot you dead."

Jaeger held his sword defiantly. Then, with his free hand, he started to reach down.

He was going for his gun. Graham pulled the trigger. Then he pulled it a second time. He dry-fired a third and fourth time.

Jaeger pulled out a nine-millimeter clip from his pants pocket. He swung it between his fingers.

"Honor," he said, spitting the word. "You know nothing of honor." His face contorted in rage, and he touched his scar. "Saxe taught me well. In this modern world, honor does not exist."

Lanie started sobbing. While she had been sleeping, he must have found the gun. Instead of telling her, he had said nothing, playing them for dupes.

"You failed your final test," said Jaeger. He reached under his shirt and pulled out a gun. "You were not worthy of a duel. Now you die like a dog instead of a man."

"Your test was rigged," said Graham. "I offered you fair warning. I didn't pull the trigger before giving you a chance. That's more of a chance than you apparently planned to give me."

"You lie. All you had to do was pick up the sword."

"Had I done that, you would have shot me."

"Never."

"That's easy to say now, isn't it?"

Jaeger stared at him for a long moment before holstering his gun. Then he casually reached out with the tip of his sword, flipping the second sword into the air. It landed several feet from Graham's feet.

"Pick it up, if you dare."

Graham looked at the sword. How many years had it been since he'd played with a foil? That was the word for it—played. He had learned a little footwork and the basic moves, enough to know that he knew virtually nothing. Dedicated fencers were masters of second- and third-intention attacks. They were like chessmasters; they didn't even have to think about the basics.

Graham tried to visualize the fundamentals. Jaeger would be the aggressor, forcing him to parry. In his mind, he went through the nine forms of parrying. *Prime. Seconde. Tierce. Quarte. Quint. Sixte. Septime. Octave. Neuvieme.* In some the blade was up, in others down. Depending on where the attack came, the sword had to be positioned inside or outside. And the wrist had to be supinated for some parries, and pronated for others.

It was hopeless. He didn't remember any of it. The sword stayed on the floor.

"This is not a duel to see who will die of old age," said Jaeger.

Jaeger enjoyed having "conversations with blade." The Corps Normannia excelled in *Knattern*, the American equivalent of trash talking.

"Stop this!" screamed Lanie. "Stop this!"

He wasn't only fighting for himself, Graham realized. There was no choice.

Graham picked up the sword.

"Better late than never," said Jaeger.

The sword was a little over a yard long. It wasn't like the foils Graham had practiced with; the blade was shorter and heavier, thicker and more curved. He swung it in the air to get a feel for it. His arm already felt weighted down, and the finger that Jaeger had cut was stinging from all the sweat pouring off him. He wiped his hands on his pants, but that didn't help. A moment later he was dripping again.

"I need powder," Graham said.

"Have you wet yourself already?"

Jaeger enjoyed the mind games almost as much as the dueling. He motioned with his head toward the kitchen. "There's corn starch in one of those drawers. And just to save you the search, earlier I removed anything that could be used as a weapon."

Graham retreated to the kitchen and coated his trembling hands with corn starch. This was crazy. He was about to be impaled by steel. People didn't die like that these days. This was an age of mass destruction. Nuclear bombs. Biological weapons. Assault rifles. Automatic pistols. Death was impersonal, delivered from a distance.

From the other room, he heard Lanie pleading their case. "Please. Stop this madness. I'll make it worth your while."

"*Silentium*," said Jaeger.

"I'll double whatever you're getting. I don't care how much I have to pay."

"If you don't shut up, I will gag you."

Graham also coated his feet with the corn starch to prevent slipping. Then he poured some of the powder on the hilt of the sword. His hands and wrists were covered with the stuff, but he was afraid that he was sweating so much that it would soon be cornmeal. Graham thought of the Abbot. He wished he had been raised a Catholic, but his father had been indifferent about religion. It would have been nice if he could have confessed all his sins.

He was sorriest about Paris. That would never change.

Graham reentered the living room. Jaeger used his sword to point at his powdered shirt. "I think you missed a spot there."

"I like my shirts starched."

Jaeger smiled. "That's the spirit, Pilgrim. There's a right way to die, and a wrong way."

"Why don't you fall on your sword and show me?"

The German didn't even have a hair out of place. He looked relaxed, even comfortable. He raised his sword and saluted Graham.

Graham didn't answer his salute. That would signal the start of the duel. Instead, he took a last moment to consider his attack. His best chance, he decided, would be to throw his sword at Jaeger. It might hit him, or it might not, but either way the German would have to evade it. He could come in right behind his sword and tackle him low.

Jaeger got tired of waiting. "*En Garde,*" he said in a sarcastic voice. That was the salute of Hollywood screenwriters, not words uttered by any true fencer.

Graham's reply was to pull his swordarm back, but he never got the chance to throw his spear. In an eye blink Jaeger closed the gap between them and attacked, thrusting his sword at the left side of Graham's chest. Instinctively, Graham parried and then riposted. Their blades met again, and Jaeger delivered a cut-over, his sword passing around Graham's tip.

Stepping back, Jaeger announced, "*Rote plume.*"

Blood flowed along Graham's forearm.

Jaeger immediately pressed the attack again. Graham backpedaled. Any strategy he might have had was lost in his desperate attempt to keep Jaeger's blade away.

"*Mal-pare,*" Jaeger said, giving his sword-hand a moment's rest.

It was a fencing expression that announced the parry had failed to prevent a hit. The words were unnecessary though. Blood was flowing from a cut on Graham's shoulder.

Jaeger went on the attack again. It was all Graham could do to keep the sword in his hand. He backpedaled, all but running to get away, while Jaeger relentlessly closed. Jaeger used the room like an experienced boxer uses the ring, cutting him off at angles and forcing him to engage.

Graham neared where Lanie was sitting. Their desperate eyes met each other for an instant. Graham didn't want her near the flying swords, and tried to move away, but Jaeger blocked him in. Their blades met. Jaeger's advance was challenged on a second front, though. Lanie kicked hard at his calf, throwing him momentarily off-stride. He aborted his cut, stepping back. With the foible of his blade he slapped at Lanie's head, knocking her down.

"Bastard."

Graham jumped forward, pressing the attack. The sound of metal striking metal rang out in the room. Fury propelled Graham. He swung wildly, his body out of sync with his blade. Trained fencers are taught never to use their off hand or their feet. Going corps-à-corps, having any body to body contact, is illegal, and something automatically avoided by fencers, but that was the very thing Graham initiated. His rage brought him close. Where his blade was stopped by Jaeger's guard, his left hand wasn't. He struck out with hand and foot simultaneously, striking Jaeger's eye and doing his best to trip him, but instead of falling, Jaeger moved away using a backward cross, a *passe arriere*. As he glided by Graham, he reached out with his sword and made two quick cuts, scoring on the forehead and chest. Only because he was moving away was Graham spared deeper cuts, but they were still bad enough. Blood started coursing down his face, making it hard to see.

"You like my marker points?" asked Jaeger.

Graham managed to gasp, "I think they'd look better on you."

Fencers had once used ink points to show hits on their opponents. Graham's body was already a patchwork of red. The only mark on Jaeger was a puffy eye.

Graham was breathing hard. His lungs strained to take in enough air. There was a fresh, grainy scent to the air, activated by the pounding the rice tatami mats were taking.

He looked over at Lanie. She was just beginning to stir. "So much for honor," said Graham. "Did it make you feel proud striking a bound woman?"

"By interfering, she asked for her headache."

"What are you going to do next? Pick a fight with a blind child?"

"No. I have the prior engagement of killing you."

Jaeger advanced. Instead of retreating, Graham also strode forward. He wasn't about to run this time. That wasn't an option. Better to attack, to be the berserker.

Graham lunged, swung, and lunged again. Jaeger had an answer for his every stroke. And then the German countered. Coming out of *sixte*, he swung his blade across Graham's face, cutting open his cheeks and lips in an angled slash. His second cut came as a blur, but instinctively Graham lifted his left arm, a motion that saved his chest from being cut open from sternum to navel, but at the expense of his arm.

Jaeger stepped forward to finish the fight, but his shoe caught on the edge of one of the tatami mats. He quickly regained his balance, but it gave Graham enough time to stagger backward out of reach of Jaeger's sword.

The damage was already done, though. Graham's left arm had a deep cut in it, but even worse, it was broken. His face wasn't much better. The flesh was split open, and an alarming amount of blood was pouring out of the wound. The force of the cut had cleaved his lips and taken two teeth. Warm, salty blood flowed into his mouth and down his chin.

Jaeger surveyed the damage he'd wrought. His eyes were shiny, almost glowing, exultant from the blood sport. It was almost as if he were feeding off his butchery.

Graham could feel himself growing weaker by the second. He stood at an angle, unbalanced by his broken arm, listing to one side like a ship that's taken on too much water. Blood loss and shock were making him dizzy. So much blood was coming from his forehead and lips that he couldn't spit it out fast enough.

Through the blood, Graham could see Jaeger smiling.

Lanie was sitting up again, staring at him with horrified eyes. She was sobbing, her face as ravaged in its own way as his. Graham wished she hadn't awakened to see this. He turned away from her look of pity and focused on the blade. Lanie had told him the swords were made in Japan centuries before. Berserker hadn't worked, Graham thought.

Maybe kamikaze would. By sacrificing himself, Lanie would live.

Fleche, thought Graham. The word translated to arrow. In fencing, when you attempt a *fleche* you leap off your lead foot, attempt to make a hit, then pass your opponent at a run. In his days of playing with a foil, Graham's foot speed had made the maneuver a favorite of his.

He had to do it while he still could. There would be no second chance.

His deadened left arm was a worthless weight at his side. Graham took a step forward, and then another, trying to find the right balance. He had to breathe through his nose. There was too much blood in his mouth. His nose sounded like a teakettle at full steam.

Closer. Still closer. Jaeger was still smiling, watching the dead man shuffling along.

Now. Graham leaped forward, but even while he was in the air, he knew the hit-and-run wouldn't work. Jaeger had seen his *fleche* coming, and was prepared to parry and riposte. Instead of attacking, Graham jumped away.

Jaeger was smiling now. His prey was virtually helpless.

Blood filled Graham's mouth. He didn't spit or swallow. He couldn't stop the river.

But maybe he could ride it. He thought of his encounter with the Brothers. For what he had in mind he would have to get close, have to dance with death.

Jaeger came at him. Graham met his blade with his own, and stepped in even closer. Any sword-fighting discipline had long vanished. He was a fighter clearly on his last legs. Jaeger pulled his sword arm back for the final cut. The paparazzo's guard was wide open, the coup de grace a thrust away. But he had no defense for the mouthful of blood Graham spat into his eyes.

It struck him like a thrown bucket of blood, catching Jaeger open-eyed just as he was beginning his lunge. The red slap blinded him, throwing off his cut. For a second he lost control, his face awash in the blood of another man. There was so much blood for a single human. Blood he had spilt. He jumped back, wildly swinging his sword with his right arm as he furiously tried to wipe away the blood with his left.

Jaeger never saw the blade coming at him. The steel cut deep into his neck, severing both his vocal cords and jugular vein.

He didn't fall right away. He stood like one of those trees cut in half that somehow resist gravity. His gasps brought him no oxygen, and only accelerated the stream of blood. He finally dropped to the ground where his mouth opened and closed, as if he was trying to say something, but he had no voice to say his last words aloud.

It was almost time, Graham thought, to say his own last words, but all he could think of was that he had picked a damn silly way to die.

Fifty-one

You are not going to die," Lanie said. "Do you understand that? Because if you die, I will never forgive you. Never."

Graham couldn't have answered even if he wanted to. Lanie had all but mummified him to stop his bleeding.

He was drifting in and out of consciousness. If only Lanie would let him goddam sleep.

"We're only a couple of miles away from the hospital. Do you understand that? After all we've been through, you are not going to die on me."

Lanie looked at Graham. Too much time had passed, and too much of his blood had been spilt. She'd had to cut herself free, bind Graham's too many wounds, drive the car up to the house, and drag him into the vehicle. As fast as Lanie hurried, death moved even faster. Though she wrapped Graham in three layers of towels, he quickly bled through them all. The towels were now sodden masses of red. She was glad the darkness prevented her from seeing too closely.

It was her fault for not having a telephone at the property, her vanity for not wanting to be disturbed. Common sense should have dictated she have an emergency phone.

Lanie rode the accelerator. She was driving far too fast on a road with so many switchbacks, was barely holding on to the road, but nothing was going to slow her down. Her adrenaline had won out over the sleeping pills. Now she was wide awake.

"Kind of stupid of me to live in communities where you better not get sick after dark," she said. "You live in southern California, you don't really think about that."

Her headlights were on bright, but the darkness still seemed to be closing in on all sides.

"This is a role reversal, isn't it? Remember how you saved my life? I thought you were an angel. I really didn't want to die, and you wouldn't let me. You know how people who have near-death experiences say that it's like going through a tunnel, and that they see this beautiful light? We both had our tunnels. And now we've gotten through them. This is our time to live, not die."

She talked for both of them, her voice loud and commanding. She was going to give him her strength somehow.

"You are a pilgrim, Graham, whether you like it or not. But your pilgrimage isn't over. You have to be brave again. What you did tonight was the bravest thing I have ever seen. I don't know how you kept fighting, but you did. But you still have to fight a little longer.

"Do you hear me? You have to fight, Graham. Show me you are fighting. Show me."

Her words were fading in and out. Bad TV reception, thought Graham. And it was getting worse. All he wanted to do was sleep. There wasn't any more fight in him.

"Don't fucking quit on me," she said. "I didn't quit on you. Are you listening, Graham Wells? Give me a sign. Show me you're not a quitter. Show me."

Graham wanted to ignore her. Then he remembered something from a long time ago. Lanie's cursing the dying of the light. He put his mind to it. His body didn't want to respond. It was almost like nothing was connected anymore. But finally, trembling, he managed to raise his right hand and flip her off.

Lanie started laughing and crying at the same time. "That's right. I gave you the bird, didn't I? The thing is, even then I knew I really didn't want to die. It's just that I didn't see any options."

Graham had just about guessed it all. She couldn't own up to the accident, because that would have implicated Brett. Lanie was compromised in so many ways that it didn't seem like there was any way out. The accident; the Mossad; the affair. Guilt overwhelmed her. Alive, she was a bomb ready to be set off. They would find out she was a murderer, a spy, and an adulterer. And the vice president would be dragged down with her. Killing herself was the only answer. It would save Brett, and it would punish her sins. It was the logical sacrifice, she had decided, even though she so much wanted to live.

"Twice now you have saved my life, Graham Wells. That's a lot of good karma."

Three lives were lost in Paris, Graham wanted to say. But he couldn't talk. Even now he felt as if he were floating away.

"You hold on to life, Graham. You hear me? Hold on."

But he wasn't listening. He was out of body, beyond Lanie's words, anybody's words.

Fifty-two

He should have died.

You lose that much blood, the surgeon said, and you don't make it.

As it was, Graham barely did. They lost him three times on the operating table, and each time were able to bring him back.

He gained strength rapidly, though he wasn't conscious for most of the time to know that. His meds should have put an elephant into a deep slumber, but he kept waking up with a sense of urgency, only to be beaten down by the drugs.

Graham's eyes opened again, propelled by the same anxiety. It felt as if he were waking from a nightmare. He tried to sit up.

"Go to sleep," said Lanie, her tone like that of a mother offering reassurance to a spooked child. She hadn't left his side, had only taken catnaps on a cot the hospital had brought in for her.

"Mirror," Graham said.

The words actually sounded like "Ear-er," but this was the third time he had stirred in the last four hours, and Lanie was getting good at interpreting his sounds. Between his two missing teeth, and lips that hurt too much to move, Graham was doing his speaking from his throat.

"I don't think that's a good idea."

" 'Ease 'et it."

Please get it. Lanie dug out her compact mirror and held it up to Graham's face. It looked as if he had been through a war. In a way, both of them had.

"I'm no 'retty 'oy."

"No, you're not a pretty boy. But I don't like pretty boys."

"Good."

"While you were resting, a cosmetic surgeon came in. He thinks you can be made as good as new."

"I was 'oping 'or 'etter."

Lanie did the mental translation, and laughed. "So was I, actually."

" 'Uck 'ou."

"Sorry, I can't understand you."

"You're 'ull of 'hit."

"I still can't make out what you're saying."

What the hell, Graham thought. Lanie could choose not to understand what he said for the third time. "I 'ove 'ou."

Lanie leaned over, whispered, "I love you too," and as gently as she could, kissed the side of his lips.

Good medicine, thought Graham. The best.

"The surgeon said he can do the procedure when the swelling on your face goes down."

If you can't beat them, Graham thought, join them. There had been times when he had thought he was the last male in the L.A. area over the age of thirty not to have had plastic surgery.

" 'Ell 'im I need a 'ummy 'uck 'oo."

"You do not need a tummy tuck. I like your tummy just the way it is."

Lanie reached out and tried to find a part of his stomach that wasn't bandaged. As much as it hurt, Graham stretched his right hand out. She met him more than halfway. For a minute they held hands, then the fear that had kept awakening Graham came to the fore again.

"We 'ave 'o 'eave."

"What are you talking about? You're not going anywhere."

" 'A 'ray 'an."

At first Lanie thought he said, "A ray gun." Then she realized he was saying, "The Gray Man."

"We have security right outside our door," Lanie said. "They're keeping the paparazzi away. So far we've had photographers trying to pose as doctors, nurses, delivery people, and messengers. There is an army camped outside. Even if you were in a condition to be moved, we couldn't run that gauntlet."

Graham moved his lips. This was important. He didn't want to be a sitting target. "The Gray Man," he said, like a small child would have said "the bogeyman."

"You need medical attention."

"No."

His unease was contagious. Lanie's thoughts had been consumed by his medical condition. Now they both had to think about their safety.

"Maybe tomorrow you'll be well enough to move."

" 'Oday."

"Not today. I'll get more security. We'll be safe."

" '*Oday*."

"Didn't you hear what I said about all the paparazzi? They've got this place locked in."

" 'Arking 'ogs."

"What?"

Speaking clearly, though it hurt like hell, Graham said, "They're just barking dogs."

The catering truck did a brisk business. The vendor was a young woman. Her hair was tucked under a colorful bandana of tropical fruit, the Carmen Miranda look without the walking fruit bowl. The catering truck made several stops around the hospital, ending up in the delivery zone. No one took notice of the vendor wheeling in a large cart of her wares into the hospital. There was too much else going on. A helicopter was coming in for a landing, and two ambulances were hurriedly being readied for departure. The paparazzi knew that all the activity could be misdirection, but they were still prepared for the chase. No way was Lanie Byrne getting away without doing some explaining. Supposedly she and her boyfriend, who still hadn't been identified, had gotten into a donnybrook. Rumor was that she had stabbed him. It was the biggest stabbing story since Lana Turner's kid knifed Johnny Stompanato to death. Stompanato had been Turner's boyfriend and mobster Mickey Cohen's former bodyguard. Everyone was guessing who Lanie's victim was. There had been talk that it was John Cusack, but then he had turned up on location. Nicholas Cage was the current name of the hour. With cell phones, and scores of eyes ready to track it, even the whirlybird wouldn't be able to outrun the paparazzi.

The helicopter landed, but its rotor kept spinning. Its pilot was the sole occupant. The ambulance engines were also running, evidently prepared for a fast getaway.

Everyone expected a diversion. The chase was about to be on. But what no one anticipated was the arrival of all the sedans. They pulled up on all sides of the hospital. No vehicles, not even the ambulances, were going to leave without their permission. The cars were very plain, very American.

Government cars.

One of the sedans pulled up to the helicopter. A man in dark glasses got out and waved a badge at the pilot, motioning for him to cut the engine.

"Flight's canceled," he yelled.

No one took any notice of the vendor with the flamboyant fruit bandana as she wheeled her cart out to the catering truck. Two minutes prior to the arrival of all the sedans, the caterer and her cargo made their escape.

They drove to Isla Vista, cruising the constellation of motels near the UC Santa Barbara campus before making their choice. While Graham waited in the catering truck, Lanie paid cash for a room. The clerk didn't recognize Lanie with her fruit headdress.

"Without a credit card," the clerk said, "we will need a hundred-dollar refundable deposit as a guarantee for any incidental charges or expenses you might incur—"

Lanie pushed Ben Franklin forward to cut off the disclaimer and was handed two room keys.

Per their plan, Lanie dropped Graham off in front of their room, then took the catering truck and parked it almost a mile away from the motel. The walk back felt good. She had been cooped up for too long. Lanie returned to a room with closed curtains and a DO NOT DISTURB sign hanging from its door. She quietly entered the room. It took a moment for her eyes to adjust to the darkness. Graham was resting on the king-size bed. He wasn't moving, was so still that Lanie's heart raced. They should never have left the hospital. She hurried to his side, bent down, and saw that he was still breathing.

Thank God.

Graham opened his eyes. "Guess I dozed off."

"Keep sleeping."

He lifted the cover. "Join me."

Lanie got into the bed, nestled beside him, and almost instantly fell asleep. Four hours passed before Graham awoke again. Even with Lanie next to him, his heart was racing. He still couldn't shake his uneasiness. It didn't help that he felt like an invalid. He could hardly be counted on to provide any protection. Lanie felt him stir and raised her head. She knew he had to be in great pain.

"I'm going to call Dr. Burke and get him to prescribe you some pain medication."

"I don't think Dr. Burke would even prescribe an aspirin." Graham's speech was still slurred, but his words were clearer now.

Lanie had forgotten about her own suicide attempt. That seemed as if it had happened to another person a long, long time ago.

"I have some Advil in my purse," Lanie said.

She turned on a light, and after a short hunt found the pain medicine. His lips were so swollen it was difficult for him to swallow from the glass of water.

"I'm going to get you a straw. You must be hungry as well. There's a place nearby that sells smoothies."

"Do they also sell chocolate shakes?"

"You must be getting better."

"I doubt it. When you got in bed with me earlier the only thing I could think of was sleeping."

"That was then, this is now."

"I like the way you think."

He had a broken arm, and a host of cuts that were bandaged, stitched, and sutured. His lips looked like discolored sausages that wouldn't have passed muster at even the most dubious slaughterhouse. His head felt like it had been used as an anvil to a hammer.

None of that mattered. He was still instantly aroused.

"Does this hurt?" she asked, kissing one of his wounds.

"I'll need more than one kiss to be sure."

Lanie's gentle kisses traveled along his chest.

Graham murmured, "Don't stop, Florence Nightingale."

But she did, pausing long enough to take off her clothes.

He looked at her, sighed happily, and said, "I think my heart just stopped again."

"Then it's time to do CPR."

She did some gentle straddling to get atop him, then did her best to position herself without adding to his injuries.

"You sure this is CPR?" asked Graham.

"Are you complaining?"

"God no."

Lanie started moving up and down. The pleasure more than compensated for the pain.

"Porcupines," gasped Graham.

Her breath was short as well: "Porcupines?"

"When they make love, they have to do it very carefully."

• • •

This time he slept deeply, and when Graham awoke he didn't feel quite as panicked.

"How long was I out this time?"

"About three hours."

"It must be late."

"It is."

"Did you sleep again?"

"I'm ashamed to say that I did. But for the last hour or so I've been watching you."

"Which did you like better? My drooling or my snoring?"

"Too hard to choose."

"I shouldn't have slept so much."

"Why not?"

"We need to think through our situation. Figure out what to do. I should have made calls. I need to know what happened to Pierre Thierry. He was supposed to contact the Agency and tell them about his Citroën, the assassination attempt, and Hans Jaeger. In case I didn't make it, I wanted them to know they had a rogue agent."

"The Gray Man."

"I never said anything about you and Tennesson. And I never told Thierry I was in the accident in the tunnel. I made it sound like I was investigating their missing car."

"That's what has shackled us from the beginning," Lanie said.

"What?"

"Our secrets. They've paralyzed us from acting."

"Manslaughter and sexpionage," Graham said.

Sexpionage. The word made Lanie feel tawdry and cheap and stupid. "It wasn't that way," she said.

"But it would have been made to appear that way for both of us."

"Why didn't Thierry report his car as stolen?"

"Because by doing that, the biggest magnifying glass in the world would have turned on him, and he was sure his CIA connection would be exposed. Thierry was comfortable with being a retired diplomat in his own country. He didn't want to be known as a quisling."

"How did Thierry get a replacement car?"

"He called Walter Carey, the field agent who originally recruited him. A few days later, an identical Citroën reappeared in their garage. Thierry said it was a hush-hush operation. He said Carey took care of the problem unofficially. It's possible the CIA didn't know about it. Or maybe they did. It was just a fluke that I borrowed a car from owners who wanted their past to remain anonymous."

Lanie said, "Carey might be the Gray Man."

"Carey is dead."

She shook her head in frustration. "Another dead end. But there still has to be some kind of trail. You can't hide an operation like this."

"Can't you? Jaeger didn't think it was over. I doubt the Gray Man does either. That means our lives are still in jeopardy."

"I still don't understand why he did all of this."

"To gain the ultimate blackmail on the next president."

"We can't let that happen."

"No, we can't. We need to put a face to the Gray Man. It's possible I saw him, and didn't even know it."

"Where?"

"New York City. He might have been right next to me when he shot down Monroe. But why did he leave me alive? It doesn't make sense."

Graham sighed. He had to give up on that mystery for the moment. "Where did you park the catering truck?" he asked.

"About a mile away."

"Too close," Graham said.

"For the Gray Man?"

Graham shook his head and smiled. "The more immediate threat is the paparazzi. No one's better at discovering love nests."

"Is that what this is? A love nest?"

"It sure is."

"I better call Tina. She can drive the catering truck to Westwood or Santa Monica. That ought to throw the paparazzi off the trail."

Tina had driven in the catering truck and posed as the original vendor. She and Lanie had switched clothing at the hospital. Outside scrutiny had started and finished with the colorful bandana. No one noticed the cart was more weighted down coming out than going in.

Tina picked up Lanie's call on the first ring. She had been waiting to hear from her, and started talking immediately. From Lanie's expression, Graham could tell she didn't like what she was hearing.

As Lanie hung up the phone, Graham asked, "What?"

"We have to leave. Government agents swept down on the hospital just after we left. They questioned everybody and were upset at our absence."

"I'll call a cab. We'll rent a car."

"Where will we go?"

"We'll figure that out once we are on the road."

"Is it possible all those agents are working for the Gray Man? Could it be that large of a conspiracy?"

"I don't know."

The dispatcher told Graham the cab would be there in fifteen minutes. In obvious pain, Graham left the bed and made his way to the window. He cracked the curtain and looked around. There was no activity outside.

The time passed in silence. Every minute the tension built exponentially. Graham kept peering out from behind the curtain. He saw a few motel guests, or what looked like guests. Nothing else caught his attention. Finally, they heard the sound of a motor outside. Graham sneaked another look.

"The cab," he said.

They walked outside. As they approached the cab, Gray Men appeared on all sides. There were six of them, all wearing identical dark suits.

"Say nothing," Graham yelled to Lanie. "Get a lawyer."

He was being optimistic. It was possible the men were there to kill them, not arrest them.

Two cars pulled in behind the cab. Lanie resisted, but to no avail. She was bodily lifted in the air, a man on each side. Her yelling was abruptly silenced as she was stowed into one of the cars.

Though he was obviously incapacitated, Graham was still held while being frisked. One of the agents tapped on his cast. When he was satisfied Graham wasn't holding a weapon, he said, "This way."

Graham disappeared into the waiting car.

Fifty-three

What do you know about Graham Wells, Ms. Byrne?"

Her interrogator attempted a smile. Bad mistake. He wasn't good at it. The man had identified himself as James Finn. Lanie thought his name was appropriate. Shark fin, dorsal fin. He had that look, hungry and rapacious. Finn kept encouraging her to call him Jim. Lanie hadn't.

"He's a paparazzo."

"Sometimes people use their professions as a cover."

"Are you saying that's what Graham does?"

"I'm just asking how well you know him."

"I haven't known him long."

"Did he ever mention the name Jefferson Monroe to you?"

"I am not going to answer that question."

"Why not?"

"Because I don't want to. It's probably the kind of question a lawyer would advise me not to answer. In fact, I would like to talk to my lawyer now."

"We're not adversaries, Ms. Byrne. In fact, I think you are very talented. I enjoy your work very much. But people like Wells have a talent for taking advantage of people."

"How did he take advantage of me?"

"If you can tell us about all your dealings with him, we can be more forthcoming with our suspicions."

"I'd like a lawyer."

"That's your right, Ms. Byrne, but I think you should consider carefully before taking an adversarial position against us."

"You're not giving me a choice."

"On the contrary, we are extending an olive branch to you. It's Mr. Wells we are interested in. Cooperating with us is to your benefit."

"How so?"

"You scratch our back, we'll scratch yours."

"It's hard to imagine which would be more repugnant to me."

"I'm sorry to hear that, Ms. Byrne. I was hoping to offer you amnesty, but instead we might have to see you charged as an accessory to murder."

Lanie didn't react, didn't say anything. The shark moved closer, excited by blood.

"Do you know we found a body at your Ojai property?"

"Where is this going?" Lanie asked.

"That all depends on you." Finn paused, pretended to be listening to something. "Hear that?" he asked.

"No."

"It's the sound of a career flushing down a toilet. We leak news of the body to the press, and you go from diva to deviate. You take the O. J. Simpson elevator down, down, down."

"Do you practice this bad dialogue or does it come naturally?"

"Maybe you're too used to movie talk, Ms. Byrne. This is real. There's a big difference. Prison can give you a lot of leisure time to see that difference."

"Are you charging me with a crime?"

"That's not my charter, ma'am. That's police work. And you know what, something tells me the police still don't know about that body."

She heard the unsaid enticement: and they might never know. But for a price.

"Why are you so interested in Graham? He's been a victim in all of this. We both have."

"Some victims are innocent. Others ask to be a victim because of their activities. We have had Mr. Wells on our radar for quite a while. We believe he has worked closely with the Russian mob for some time."

Lanie laughed. "You've got to be kidding. He's a celebrity photographer."

"What better front to have? Wells traveled the world, and wherever he went, he met with the mob. We think he was a middleman between Jefferson Monroe and New World Financial to Ivan Proferov, a well-known Russian gangster. The three of them were seen meeting together on two different occasions."

"I don't believe that."

"It's documented. Your Mr. Wells is very, very dirty. During his time in the Baltic, he saw to the establishment of a drug pipeline. He was also an active participant in an elaborate money-laundering scheme. It was all perfect for him until there was a falling out among the thieves. Proferov was the first casualty."

"You're crazy."

"Am I? What do you really know about Graham Wells?"

That I love him, Lanie wanted to say. That he saved my life.

But the truth of the matter was that she knew very little about Graham.

Two of them took turns with Graham. At the onset of the interview, they had introduced themselves, but Graham didn't remember their names. They looked alike, both were white, with dark hair, impassive, even generic faces, and thin, bloodless lips. Neither man perspired. Not a single drop. It was almost as if they didn't have sweat glands. Their eyes were reptilian and hard; one set blue, the other set brown. That's how Graham thought of them, Blue and Brown.

And when you combined blue and brown you got gray. The Gray Men.

Blue said, "Your best chance is to make a deal with us."

"I'm trying to do that. You just don't want to hear that you have a rotten agent."

"But you don't seem to want to provide any details," said Brown.

That's because there were implications to anything Graham said. He couldn't talk about being blackmailed, because that would involve Lanie. And he had to skirt around Paris to save himself.

"Everything started in Paris," Graham said. "Like I told you, somebody took Thierry's Citroën. That was the car involved in the accident that took Le Croc's and Lady Godwin's lives. Thierry contacted his former CIA handler, and he came through with a substitute Citroën that looked the same."

Blue: "And how were you involved in all of this?"

"I heard the rumor about their Citroën, and was trying to track it down."

Even to Graham, his answer sounded lame. He tried a little harder: "On good authority, I know where the Citroën was dumped. I told Thierry to tell you that. I told him to have you check out the spot."

"We did," said Brown. "There was no car."

"You must have missed it."

Brown shook his head. "We checked *very* thoroughly."

"That's impossible."

"Why do you say that?" asked Brown.

Because I pushed the car over the cliff, Graham thought. But he didn't confess that. He couldn't.

"Thierry's a witness. He told you his car was missing."

"And then it turned up again."

"Someone substituted for it."

"They did a heck of a job then. The vehicle identification number matches. We're satisfied the Citroen is the original."

How could that be? Graham wracked his mind for an explanation. Either there were others in the cabal, or the Gray Man had salvaged and removed the Citroën. All he would have needed were a few parts to make the substitution look like the original car.

The Gray Man had apparently gone to great lengths to make Graham look guilty. There had to be holes in his being set up, though. There had to be.

"How do you explain the attempts on my life?" Graham asked.

"We were hoping you would explain them," said Blue. "How well do you know Hans Jaeger?"

"I didn't even know his name until I tracked it down in Berlin. He hired Bernd to kill me in Paris. Pierre Thierry told your people that, didn't he? And you did interview Bernd, right?"

"Bernd's disappeared," said Blue.

"We're afraid he might be dead," said Brown. "Bodies seem to follow wherever you go. You killed Jaeger, didn't you?"

Graham didn't know whether they were fishing or whether they knew.

"Why do you think that?"

"Because we found his body," said Blue. "It appears the two of you had a bit of a falling out."

"Take a look at me. I had no choice."

"Why did you go to New York?" asked Brown.

"I was following Hans Jaeger's trail and trying to see where it led. That's how I stumbled onto the New World Financial connection."

Both Brown and Blue had thick folders in front of them. Each took turns opening their folder and surreptitiously reading from various papers in them. They looked like men holding royal flushes.

"New World Financial," said Brown. "Yes, that does interest us."

"As does Jefferson Monroe," said Blue. "The New York City police have a composite sketch of Monroe's murderer. A dozen people saw the man who killed him. Does this face look familiar to you?"

From his folder, Blue brought out the sketch. Graham eagerly leaned forward. He thought he would be looking at the Gray Man. Instead, he saw a drawing that looked amazingly like himself.

Too late, Graham realized why the Gray Man hadn't killed him. He had been too busy setting him up.

"I was there when Monroe died," Graham said, "but I didn't shoot him."

Blue said, "Were you afraid he was going to bring you down? Or did you do the hit for the mob?"

"The mob?"

Brown tapped the thick folder. "It's all here, Wells. Your meetings. Who you saw and when. Your activities."

"I snap pictures."

Brown said, "You've worked for the Russian mob for years."

"That's crazy."

"Part of our job is watching the flow of drugs and weapons. You were caught in our web."

"Someone's been feeding you misinformation."

Graham desperately tried to think. The web had been carefully constructed. The first plan had been for Jaeger to kill him. That meant this was the default plan. How long had the Gray Man been building a case against him? Probably from the first. He would have hedged his bet. This was his insurance, his contingency plan.

"When your field agents submit a report," said Graham, "I imagine there's a protocol that shows time and date."

"We're asking you the questions," said Blue.

"Someone in your agency has made a convincing case against me. They placed the fiction neatly with the facts. I imagine they were tracking me through credit card expenditures or maybe real surveillance. I was in places where innocence could easily be shrouded in guilt. I need to know something about your protocol."

Brown relented. "Reports are submitted in timely fashion. They are logged in."

"And can those reports be subsequently changed?"

Brown shook his head. "Not without our knowing."

Graham asked, "When did I first turn up in one of these reports?"

Blue and Brown opened their folders, examined the paperwork, but said nothing.

"You know I can clam up right now," said Graham. "I don't have to say another word to you. You can give me a date at least."

"You came to our attention in 1998," said Blue.

Graham thought for a moment. The Gray Man would have wanted to tie everything neatly together.

"Probably August 28, 1998," said Graham. "Is that right?"

The two agents didn't answer. They didn't even blink. But Graham knew he had a bingo.

The Gray Man would have known there were some witnesses to Graham's arrival and stay in Paris. Fact and fiction. Graham suspected the Gray Man was in Paris then. He would have helped out with the Citroen. That's how he had gotten on everything so quickly.

"I need to know what I was doing on August 28," said Graham, "and I need to know the times I was under surveillance."

The agents didn't answer.

"I want to prove to you that I am innocent," said Graham. "You can give me that much at least."

This time it was Blue who relented. "You were seen joining a suspect we had under surveillance in the very early morning. Some of your conversation was overheard."

"What time did this happen?"

"You arrived very late, at just after one in the morning, and stayed for approximately half an hour."

"What lounge? Where?"

"The Côte d'Or. It's on the East Bank."

There it was, thought Graham. The Gray Man had wrapped him up neatly. It was time he couldn't possibly account for. And what kind of alibi was it to say that he was busy killing two of the most beloved people in the world at that time? The Gray Man had known his Achilles' heel. He had probably believed that Graham could never own up to what he had done in Paris that night. And even if he tried, there was no evidence to support his assertion. No witnesses.

"Before I continue," said Graham, "I need to know that both of you were not involved in the surveillance that placed me in Paris."

"Why do you want to know that?" asked Brown.

"Because this time you have a very smart Aldrich Ames in your midst.

He's incredibly thorough. He's covered his ass, and to do that he's blackmailed, and murdered, and done God knows what. So I need to know that neither one of you is that man."

"We had no involvement in Paris," said Blue.

"What if I can prove that the August 28 meeting I was supposed to be attending is a lie?" said Graham. "What if I can show beyond a shadow of a doubt that I wasn't in that lounge at that time?"

"We're listening," said Blue.

Graham shook his head. "You have to be more than listening. Someone's put a straitjacket around me, but there is one flaw. As far as I know, it might be the only flaw in my being set up. And if I'm going to yank on that loose end I'm going to need your Agency's help to unravel the rest of the lies. That might take a lot of work, because this man's clever, and smart, and I need to know you'll be willing to turn over all the rocks to get one of your own."

"Give us something to start turning them," said Brown, "and we will."

"I need some more assurances first. I need someone high up in the Agency in on this, the Directorate of Intelligence preferably. And I want the chain of evidence to be documented from start to finish."

"Anything else you want?" said Blue, not hiding his sarcasm.

"We'll start with that," said Graham. "And some aspirin."

He hurt all over. His body seemed to be reliving the sword fight all over again. But Graham knew he was about to feel even worse.

Fifty-four

Looking back, it made sense.

Monroe had pushed him on the point, and offered him an exorbitant amount of money.

But Graham hadn't bitten at his blood money. Something about the way Monroe did his probing had made him distrustful. It wasn't anything Graham could put a finger on, but just a feeling. Still, he had been tempted to cash in, of course. But a part of him, the part that felt he was responsible for the accident, couldn't do that. No one would ever mistake Graham for a saint, but that was one instance where he didn't want to profit from what he had done.

On his pilgrimage, the film had been in his pockets every inch of the five-hundred-mile journey. There were days the rolls of film weighed him down like he was carrying millstones. Every time he emptied his pockets it was a reminder of what he had done. Not that he needed the reminder. He couldn't escape the tunnel.

Graham felt like Coleridge's Ancient Mariner, the film the albatross around his neck. He wanted to get rid of it, but couldn't. It bound him. Time and again he vowed to destroy it, to lose it forever, but it had a power over him. There were times he stared at the rolls for hours on end. That was what his life had come down to. Graham never developed the film, afraid to open Pandora's box.

When he traveled through Kosovo, the film stayed in his pack. It was marked differently than the other rolls he carried. With that part of the world going crazy, with ethnic and religious hatred on all sides, Graham had been prepared to die. His only fear was that his rolls of film would be posthumously developed, but he deserved that.

Only death didn't come.

When Graham returned to America, he was finally able to put the film aside. It had burdened him for long enough. He deposited the rolls in a safe-deposit box. At least he didn't have to look at them. And for years they just sat.

Waiting.

After all this time, he wondered at the condition of the film. It was possible the pictures wouldn't even come out. Sometimes old film was temperamental. And all of it had been a shoot and run on a dark night. Some of the film had been shot without a flash, and some with. The shots could be overexposed or underexposed. And even with autofocus, there was no guarantee he had gotten a good bead on the speeding Peugeot. Everything could be a blur.

Graham didn't voice his uncertainty. He watched closely as the pictures were being developed. He wasn't the only one: the CIA was watching with him.

The images from the first roll became clearer. There was Anne Godwin looking at him, every inch a lady.

Graham was doing his best not to react. He was glad Brown and Blue and the assistant DI weren't looking at him. All their attention was on the photos.

He held his breath while the second roll of film was developed. The first shot was blurred beyond recognition. The second wasn't much better. It was going to be a bust, Graham thought. The Gray Man had won.

But then everything became clear.

The pictures of the Peugeot and its occupants approaching the tunnel were seen in all too vivid detail.

Graham blinked away his tears. The spooks weren't going to see him break down. Later, when he was alone, he would. He spoke carefully, concentrating on the words. He wasn't going to let his voice break, not now, and not in front of them. As each shot became clearer, he went through the sequence, remembering the moments up until the crash. The motor drive had captured a full roll of images.

He didn't need the pictures to remind him of that night in the Tunnel of Death. For years, he had been living that night. In his mind's eye, Graham remembered everything. But the pictures were amazingly clear for the conditions under which they had been taken.

Graham gave the CIA his proof of innocence, and his proof of guilt, all in one package.

Fifty-five

When Blackwell learned of Jaeger's death, he considered taking leave of the game. Money wasn't a problem. Monroe had set up several offshore accounts for him. And Blackwell had identities and papers cached in safe-deposit boxes around the globe. He was confident that he could disappear without a trace, but that wasn't something he wanted to do. His prize would be denied him.

Blackwell had neither the personality nor the stomach for politics. He didn't like chicken dinners and he didn't like suffering fools. But he had the ambition of politicians, the drive to hold power. Now, he just needed to be patient a little longer. His plan still appeared to be viable. As far as he knew, no one had connected the dots between Lanie Byrne and the vice president, let alone the death of the bicyclist, and that wasn't something that the actress or politician would ever disclose. It was the paparazzo the Agency was interested in, and the death of Monroe. That was how Blackwell had arranged it.

Monroe had been living on borrowed time for years. No matter how much you laundered money, you could never quite get the stain of the dirt off your hands. The FBI was finally realizing just how pervasive Russian insiders were at Western banks and securities firms. To penetrate the U.S. financial system, the Russian mob had placed moles inside financial institutions, much like the KGB had placed moles inside foreign intelligence. One of those purported moles might have helped to launder as much as ten billion dollars at the Bank of New York. Finance, more than spies or armies, ruled today's world. To combat the new threat, the FBI was now conducting sting operations. Unbeknownst to Monroe, Blackwell had been documenting his partner's guilt for some time. Blackwell always knew Monroe would have to be sacrificed; it was just a matter of when. Blackwell had arranged for a field agent to take pictures of one of Monroe's meetings with Ivan the Terrible not long before he ordered Jaeger to kill the Russian. Monroe had also been the perfect tie-in with the paparazzo. There were pictures of the two of them together on the oil rig. Travel records would show how their paths had crossed. Guilt by association.

Blackwell had known to cut bait when Proferov became a potential liability. The triumvirate of Monroe, Jaeger, and Blackwell had been a good partnership: money, muscle, and brains. But Blackwell always wanted more. Plundering Russia was like robbing a corpse. He wanted the combination to the world's vault, and the power that went with it.

The vice president and the actress had fallen into his lap during Blackwell's surveillance of a Russian mobster who owned a remote Maryland estate. To save man-hours, a camera trap had been set up to record all passing cars on the seldom traveled road. Tennesson and the actress, arriving in separate cars, had made the mistake of having an assignation at a property a half mile down the road from the mobster's house. It wasn't information that Blackwell could immediately use, but he knew ultimately it could be cultivated into something much more. The affair itself wouldn't be enough of a bargaining chip. Clinton and his ilk had proved that having an affair was no longer political suicide. But the potential was there.

Just days after that revelation, while Blackwell was still mulling possibilities on how he could use his information, the paparazzo and the Citroën had fallen into his lap. Carey had called in a favor, asking Blackwell to get a duplicate Citroën in a hush-hush job that no one was to know about. Carey had said they would be doing the Agency a favor. It was possible Carey was covering up some extracurricular activities of his own, or maybe he was just being extremely loyal to both Thierry and his employer. It wasn't an op the Agency could condone or even know about.

The need for secrecy in handling the Citroën served Blackwell's purposes. The plan began to formulate in Blackwell's mind. By knowing about the accident, he knew that he owned the paparazzo. Over time, he worked out the details. The Brothers, posing as fake Mossad agents, had suckered the actress into thinking she had a duty and a cause. And the paparazzo and his muckraking had helped bring the politician and the actress even closer together. Their lust wasn't enough to serve Blackwell's purposes. What they needed was the ultimate bonding experience: covering up some terrible crime. The paparazzo's own hit-and-run inspired the bicyclist scheme. He banked on the actress and politician running from what they had done. Once they did so, there would be no going back. Blackwell figured the sharing of that secret would put the next president in his hip pocket.

Blackwell had enjoyed all the long-term planning. It really was a simple scheme. Do it any other way, and he would have needed a platoon to get through the Secret Service and get to the vice president. All he had to do was bring Tennesson to him. Lust was a powerful tool. Nothing else could have gotten to Tennesson but that. Stars have that aphrodisiac quality that politicians don't seem to be able to ignore. Ask Kennedy about Monroe, or Kerry about Winger.

Being a puppetmaster was eminently satisfying, and the actual expenses of the operation were minimal. Besides, the potential payoff of being the ultimate insider had promised to be extraordinary. A thousand things could have gone wrong. The opposition party could have presented Tennesson with a greater challenge. The ardor between the man who would be king and the Hollywood queen could have cooled. The actress could have refused to bite at the Mossad bait. Pilgrim could have called their bluff about exposing his involvement in the Paris accident. And when Lanie and Tennesson believed they had hit the bicyclist, they could have owned up to their accident.

Blackwell had gambled on human nature, betting on lust and fear. Everything worked beyond his wildest dreams. The hit-and-run went perfectly, giving Blackwell more than a bargaining chip; he had his Pennsylvania Avenue passport.

It was a terrible fluke that Pilgrim stumbled on the actress while she was committing suicide. Just to be safe, the Brothers were still monitoring her. Her suicide would have been perfect. It was almost incomprehensible that the two Hollywood people Blackwell was manipulating, and keeping far apart, should have come together at such an unpropitious time.

They stood in the way of his Oval Office.

Years of work and planning had come off beautifully. Only after the fact was everything threatened. It was a good thing Blackwell believed in preparing for every contingency.

The paparazzo should have died a half-dozen times, but he had been unbelievably lucky. Luck had a way of changing, though. It was a shame Jaeger was dead. He had taken care of the dirty work, distancing Blackwell from any involvement. But for the right price, Blackwell knew there were mercenaries who would take on the assignment of killing the paparazzo with no questions asked. It would be a mercy killing really. The way Blackwell had arranged things, the paparazzo would end up rotting in prison. Maybe he should just let the paparazzo live. He was a loose end, but not truly consequential. Pilgrim would just be another prisoner protesting his innocence. That would hardly make him unique. His death might be investigated; alive, he would be ignored.

Blackwell's musing was interrupted when three men entered his small office unannounced. Unbidden, he remembered the saying that trouble comes in threes. Their eyes were watchful, their faces a blank. No smiles, no greetings. For the first time in a very long while Blackwell felt some uncertainty.

He knew one of the men: Drake. He was the assistant fucking DI, a self-important prick who had been promoted à la Peter Principle because he was one of the boys.

"Gentlemen," Blackwell said.

Drake took the lead. All business, he said, "Graham Wells."

If they thought a name was going to bother Blackwell, they were wrong. "The name sounds familiar."

"It should."

Blackwell appeared to search his memory a little more. "The photographer?"

"The same. You said he joined Jefferson Monroe and Ivan Proferov during their Paris meeting in 1998."

The meeting had taken place. There were pictures showing Monroe and Proferov talking. The only fiction was the paparazzo being there.

"Now I remember," said Blackwell.

"And this occurred on August twenty-eighth at around one in the morning?"

"If that's the date I noted in the report, yes."

"How did you ID the photographer?"

"At the time, I heard Monroe introduce him to Proferov. I believe that's in the report. In subsequent days I corroborated his identity."

Blackwell actually had been at the table next to Monroe and Ivan the Terrible. Monroe, acting as his beard, had been under orders to ignore him. Monroe thought Blackwell was there for his protection. And Proferov, of course, had never known his identity. Another agent had been stationed outside. In his report, the second agent verified Blackwell's proximity to what was going on. Arrange the corroborating evidence, and you could get away with anything.

"And because of that," said Drake, "you put Wells on a low-level watch?"

"Some monitoring seemed to be in order."

"But when I first said his name you seemed to have trouble recalling it?"

Blackwell attempted a tone of levity: "So many bad guys, so little time."

"Wells claims he was never at that Paris meeting."

"Should we be surprised?"

"You didn't file your full report until almost a week after that meeting took place."

Carey had called with the story about Thierry's missing Citroën, and his fear that it was the mystery car struck by Le Croc. That kept Blackwell busy for several days.

"I took copious notes. It took me a few days to put them together."

He hoped helping Carey keep everything quiet would serve his own purposes. But unknown to Carey, Blackwell conducted his own investigation. The paparazzo had been indiscreet enough to sign in with the concierge at the Thierrys' apartment. Jaeger tracked his movements out of Paris and arranged for a substitute Citroën. He even figured out where the paparazzo had dumped the original car and done a salvage operation. They hadn't needed the car, but had needed certain items from it. Salvaging the car's vehicle identification number—*la plaque d'immatriculation*—and a few substituted parts enabled them to make a perfect counterfeit. With a nationwide car hunt going on, they hadn't wanted to chance a phony or stolen *plaque d'immatriculation*. The French VIN numbers are specific, numerically identifying area and district. Obtaining the original had been the finishing touch. Afterward, Jaeger had seen to the permanent disposal of the Citroën, dumping the car several miles further offshore where no one would ever find it.

"Are you sure about the times for that meeting?" asked Drake.

Why was he asking about the time? Blackwell shrugged. "They might have been a few minutes off each way. No more."

"Wells says he was working that night."

"He was," said Blackwell. "Working out a scheme with Monroe and Proferov."

"He says he was taking pictures of that soccer star and Lady Godiva."

Blackwell had wondered whether the paparazzo would admit his involvement in the accident. Not that it would help his situation any. By making that claim, he looked like a drowning man grasping for straws.

"He's being clever," Blackwell said. "What better way to try and account for his time than by associating himself with a notorious incident? It's no secret that Europe's paparazzi flocked to the scene of the accident like flies to shit."

Fishing expedition, thought Blackwell. The three men might have their suspicions. No doubt Pilgrim was being vehement in his denials. But none of that mattered. He had thought of everything.

"Wells says he was driving the car that was hit by Le Croc's Peugeot."

So, when put between a rock and a hard place, the paparazzo had revealed his deep, dark secret. But it was too little, too late. Blackwell laughed. "That's impossible, of course. But you have to give him points for creativity."

"He's very adamant."

"Of course he is. No one ever found the mystery driver or mystery car. Wells knows that."

"The accident," said Drake, "occurred at 1:25 A.M."

"The same time Wells was sitting down with Ivan the Terrible and Monroe. No one could be in two places at the same time."

"No," said Drake. "They couldn't, could they?"

He dropped the pictures on Blackwell's desk. Blackwell picked them up and started flipping through them. His chest tightened at what he saw. He had planned so carefully, and been so close to what he wanted, so very close. Everything had been thought out. The paparazzo had sworn these photos didn't exist.

"Any comment?" asked Drake.

The bastard was so smug. He probably thought that Blackwell would start pleading with him. Groveling. Or try bargaining on bent knees.

"They're obviously phonies," said Blackwell, "and I can prove it."

He reached for a desk drawer. Drake's muscle was on him in a second.

"I'm getting a pencil out to show you that these are phonies," Blackwell said indignantly. "Or you can get one out for me."

One of the men opened the drawer, making sure no weapon was inside. The only writing implement was a pencil. He handed it to Blackwell. The muscle stood to either side of him.

"Now you can see in this picture—" said Blackwell, leaning over it with the pencil.

It wasn't one of the clearer pictures, but it would serve his purpose. The

Peugeot was racing by the Citroën, and the lens only caught it in passing. At that point, the tunnel was closing in. In the picture, it looked black and foreboding. Dark. Very dark.

Blackwell bit hard on the eraser, and then swallowed. He never thought poison would be necessary, but being the careful man he was, he prepared for everything. The pill was embedded within the eraser itself. The poison was quite fatal. In a few minutes he would be dead, and there was nothing they could do about it. He would be the master of his own destiny. He would fall on his own sword.

Drake was shouting, asking what he had done, but Blackwell ignored him. All of his attention was directed at the picture, his eyes riveted on the approaching black tunnel.

Fifty-six

Graham heard the turn of the key and looked at his watch. It was quarter of midnight. Lanie had spent another long day on the set.

So far they had done the impossible, keeping their relationship from the world. Graham knew that couldn't last. Lanie, ever the romantic, said it didn't matter if everyone knew. She didn't want to hear how potentially dangerous it could be if their relationship was exposed. Their secrets, Lanie wanted to believe, were safely buried. The Agency had cleaned up in Ojai, disposing of Hans Jaeger's body while at the same time managing to pin Jefferson Monroe's murder on the missing dead man. As for Blackwell's death, it hadn't extended much beyond the Agency, where it was referred to as a "regrettable suicide." To help others suffering from depression, the same depression that supposedly afflicted Blackwell, the Agency started a counseling outreach program.

More than ever, Graham thought the government and the movie industry operated very similarly.

Still, Graham knew that whitewashes didn't stand up to much rubbing. Neither of them could afford to have their secrets exposed.

She smiled at seeing him standing there waiting for her. Lanie had been on the set for sixteen hours, but still looked beautiful. She tried to hide her tiredness from him, just as he was hiding his stiffness from her. Both had their roles.

"I brought you chicken soup," she said.

In Graham's months of convalescing, Lanie had played nurse. She rarely came empty-handed, bringing liniment, epsom salts, ice cream, and what she called "Jewish penicillin"—chicken soup. Graham wasn't visited by Lanie Byrne, but by Elaine Bernsdorf, which was even better. It had been a wonderful time, a blissful fantasy of snatched moments.

Lanie set the soup on the table. She liked to watch him eat. Graham had no appetite, but he feigned enthusiasm. He was halfway through the bowl when Lanie noticed the packed bags.

"What are those?" she asked.

"I've taken an assignment."

"You're not well enough," she said, then asked, "Where? For how long?"

He tried to be nonchalant. "It's actually a series of assignments. My passport's going to get a workout. I'll be covering the Stones tour through Asia. They're calling it *Rolling Again*, but editorial is calling it *Geriatric Sex*. Then I'll be nosing around Australia on the set where Johnny Depp and Jennifer Lopez are supposed to be trying to outdo each other's temper tantrums."

Condemning silence followed his announcement.

"You know I have to work," Graham finally said.

"Not out of the country."

"We've gone over this before," Graham said. "We travel in different worlds. We're kidding ourselves to think otherwise."

Harrison Ford had offered the same rationale to Kelly McGillis in *Witness*. It was how his character had walked away from love. Graham thought of Bogie in *Casablanca*. Sometimes for the greater good you had to sacrifice love. It was easier for him to think of the movies than his own life.

Lanie still wasn't saying anything. Graham decided to go one step further. He would play Gable's Rhett Butler. Frankly, Scarlett, I don't give a damn.

"We had our on-set romance," Graham said. "We were caught up in something bigger than both of us. But the production has shut down now. There are no more lights, camera, action. The fireworks, the passion are gone. You know what happens to those kinds of romances after the final wrap."

In a small voice she said, "It doesn't have to be that way."

He didn't argue, but neither did he make any move to unpack.

She stayed the night. Both kept to their side of the bed as if a divider had been put up like in *It Happened One Night*. Neither of them slept. Lanie had an early call in the morning, and so did he.

Their good-bye was awkward. "You'll call?" she said.

Graham lied, "I'll call."

Like all stars, Lanie had at least four different telephone numbers to her house. The most private of those lines rang only in her bedroom. That phone's rings were reserved for her family and closest friends.

It was still dark outside. Graham walked Lanie to her Prius. As she settled into the driver's seat, he handed her a packet.

"What's this?" she asked.

"Some pictures of you."

They couldn't be in a picture together, so this was as close as they could ever be. His hand, by extension, on hers. Graham had snapped the photos during her many visits. One showed her with a hot chocolate mustache. There was another where she was blowing bubbles. Graham's favorite was her nestled in his bed with a hundred stuffed animals he had bought just for her.

Lanie didn't open the oversized envelope, didn't pause to look at the pictures.

"Commemorative photos of my time in Rome, Irving?" she asked.

Graham accepted her *Roman Holiday* reference. In Audrey Hepburn's imperious voice, but tinged with sarcasm, she said, "Thank you so very much."

He watched her disappear from his sight.

Graham stayed away from L.A. for six months. Eventually he returned, as he always did. Work kept him busy, and he was glad of that.

The invitation came unbidden in the mail. There was no note with it, no elaboration, and no return address.

It was the hottest ticket in town, but until almost the last minute Graham wasn't sure he was even going to use it. Finally, he brushed the lint off his tuxedo, ran an iron over, it and headed for the Academy Awards.

His outward wounds were long healed now. You had to look closely to even see the scars.

Graham was in the middle of the auditorium. The seats up front were taken by those nominated for major awards, and those stars with very visible faces.

Catherine Zeta-Jones and Michael Douglas, both resplendent, were now center stage reading off the names of those nominated for best actress. Lanie was one of the five names. Seated next to her was Derek Palmer, Hollywood's latest wunderkind director. What had started as a professional relationship was now a personal one. On the monitor, Graham could see the two of them holding hands.

Zeta-Jones said, "And the Oscar goes to—"

"Lanie Byrne," said Douglas.

Kissing. Music. Applause. Hugging and congratulations all around. And then there was Lanie, ordained queen of the year. With the eyes of the world on her, she looked remarkably composed. Lanie smiled at Oscar, then turned to the audience and said, "In the words of Tiny Tim, 'God bless us every one!' "

It had a Sally Fields "You really like me" kind of innocence and went over well. After the applause, Lanie thanked all the other nominees, then remembered a laundry list of names attached to her film and work.

The obligatory spots done, Lanie raised her eyes, looking past the cameras and lights and stars, seeking out one particular face and then finding it. Graham tensed. She must have known where he would be sitting. Her eyes were on him.

"This role will always be special to me," she said. "I was attracted to the character because despite all the obstacles in her life, despite the darkness, with some help she was able to find a light at the end of her tunnel."

Lanie shifted her eyes from Graham to take in the audience, and then returned to Graham alone. There were tears in her eyes now.

"I hope, in some small way, that I have helped others to find that light."

She wiped away her tears, then offered a smile to the world. "Thank you," Lanie said. "I shall cherish this night in my memory as long as I live."

Graham knew she was cribbing from *Roman Holiday*, and that her code was meant only for him.

Like Gregory Peck's Joe Gregory character, he watched the woman he adored disappear with the fanfare that was her lot. This was how it had to be, even if neither one of them liked it.

And like Peck, it was time to make his own sad retreat. Graham rose from his seat and started walking toward the exit. It was time for him to lose the tux.

Once outside the auditorium, he took a deep breath. Graham had arrived by cab, one of the few people not driven by limo. A long walk would do him good.

He was a few blocks away from all the activity when he raised his head to take in the night sky. A streak of light caught his eye, the celestial fireworks of a shooting star. Graham had always been drawn to shooting stars.

Warmed by the night's flare, Graham kept walking.